The single mums move on

Also by Janet Hoggarth

The Single Mums' Mansion

The single mums move on

Janet Hoggarth

HEAD
of ZEUS

An Aria Book

First published in the UK in 2019 by Head of Zeus Ltd

975312468

A catalogue record for this book is available from
the British Library.

ISBN (PBO): 9781838930615
ISBN (E): 9781788545693

Typeset by Silicon Chips

Printed and bound in Great Britain by
CPI Group (UK) Ltd, Croydon CRO 4YY

Head of Zeus Ltd
First Floor East
5–8 Hardwick Street
London ECIR 4RG

WWW.HEADOFZEUS.COM

For everyone in the Mews.

Thank you for being a real-life inspiration! You all rock. And for my husband, Neil, who's always my inspiration.

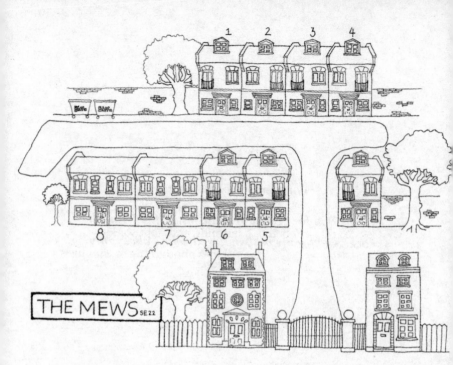

Map key

1 – Jo Lawson

2 – Samantha Crosby

3 – Norman Francis

4 – Nick Whitehead

5 – Francesca Hainsworth

6 – Debbie Stewart

7 – Elinor Ritherdon and Ali Jackson

8 – Carl Campbell

Main Cast List

Carl Campbell   Charming and handsome alcoholic photographer who lives next door to Ali

Lila Chan   *X Factor* winner and Ali's co-host of Clothes My Daughter Steals

Samantha Crosby   Flamboyant talent agent who lives on the opposite side of the Mews to Ali. She has two grown-up sons, Billy and Scott

Norman Francis   'Nosy Norman' who lives in between Samantha and Nick

Freya Gately   Jim's teenage daughter from his marriage to his second wife, Diane

Hattie Gately   Jim's third wife and the woman he left Ali for

Jim Gately   Ali's unconscionable ex-fiancé and father of Grace

Francesca Hainsworth	A Beardy Weirdy shaman, who lives on the corner plot of the Mews. She's in a 'relationship' with Ian
Ariel and Tia Hainsworth-Oliver	Francesca and Ian's daughters (sixteen and thirteen)
Charlie Heywood-Taylor	Debbie and Matthew's fourteen-year-old son
Isabelle Heywood-Taylor	Studious sixteen-year-old daughter to Debbie and Matthew
Alison (Ali) Jackson	Fashion stylist and single mum to Grace
Anne Jackson	Alison's sixty-nine-year-old mum
Grace Jackson-Gately	Five-year-old daughter to Ali and Jim; she has a very close bond with her mum
Jo Lawson	Self-appointed leader of the Mews, Jo lives opposite Ali and next door to Samantha
David O'Donnell	British TV stalwart and co-host of *Good Morning with David and Mina* on Channel Five. David is married to Trisha Templeton

Ian Oliver	Quiet, unassuming partner to Francesca, who owns half of Lordship Lane
Mina Prajapati	David O'Donnell's co-host on *Good Morning with David and Mina*
Elinor Ritherdon	Ali's next-door neighbour, a divorcee in her late sixties. Her daughter, Karen, lives nearby with her children, Princess and Tinkerbell
Ursula Simpson	Ali's oldest university friend and fellow party girl
Jacqui Snowden	An original member of the Single Mums' Mansion with Ali and Amanda. Jacqui emigrated to Australia to live with her kids, Joe and Neve, and new partner, Mark
Debbie Stewart	Immunology professor and single mum, lives in between Francesca and Elinor
Trisha Templeton	David O'Donnell's wife, a former Miss Great Britain, LGBT supporter and *Loose Women* panellist

Linda Whitehead	Nick's gregarious mum who visits him once a week
Nick Whitehead	Lives in the Mews and is known as 'The Spy' because he keeps himself completely to himself
Amanda Wilkie	Ali's former landlady and fellow member of the Single Mums' Mansion. Amanda still lives in the 'mansion' with her three children, Isla, Meg and Sonny, but is now happily remarried to Chris
Ifan Wynne-Jones	Ali's boyfriend before she moves to the Mews

Prologue

The East Dulwich Forum

26 July 2014
Re: Loud House Party near Terry's Tool Hire
Posted by: Fiwith2dogs 10.58 p.m.
Can anyone else hear the hideous party coming from behind Terry's Tool Hire? WTF is it? Someone's singing fucking reggae on a PA system at eleven at night. People need to sleep.

Re: Loud House Party near Terry's Tool Hire
Posted by: Neighbour12 11.05 p.m.
It's those annoying people in the Mews behind the tool hire place. Call the noise police. Shut those idiots down. They're always celebrating for no reason. Number seven is usually to blame.

27 July 2014
Re: Loud House Party near Terry's Tool Hire
Posted by: Linzicatlady64 12.04 a.m.
It's still going and I can hear it down by the Plough. I've called the noise police. Cannot believe people are so selfish.

Re: Loud House Party near Terry's Tool Hire
Posted by: Fiwith2dogs 12.11 a.m.
As much as I want those fuckers to get in trouble, I don't think you can hear it from the Plough. That's too far. You're obviously caught in the crossfire of another party.

Re: Loud House Party near Terry's Tool Hire
Posted by: Frankymews66 11.05 a.m.
Hello everyone. Very sorry if you were disturbed by the annual Mews summer party. We did tell everyone in the immediate area, invited all the neighbours and we switched off the PA system at eleven thirty, all in all not causing outrageous noise pollution. When the noise police arrived they were totally happy with the sound level coming from an iPod dock at midnight. Also, if you don't live in the Mews, how would you even know what number was hosting the music? If you can't stand the heat, Neighbour12 get out from behind your kitchen curtains. Everyone always welcome to join in!

Re: Loud House Party near Terry's Tool Hire
Posted by: Janemakescakes 11.15 a.m.

My baby was up screaming all night because of the noise, whatevs to you switching the PA off, we could still hear singalongs to shitting Oasis (torture) and lots of shouting into the small hours. What makes you people above the law?

Re: Loud House Party near Terry's Tool Hire
Posted by: Frankymews66 11.32 a.m.

Very sorry your baby was up all night, but probably would have been up all night anyway. Babies usually sleep through most things. Hope you have a better night tonight. Light and love x

Re: Loud House Party near Terry's Tool Hire
Posted by: Oldskoolraver 11.46 a.m.

Janemakescakes, you were probably just jealous you weren't at the party and stuck at home with a baby!

Re: Loud House Party near Terry's Tool Hire
Posted by: Janemakescakes 12.03 p.m.

Fuck you, Oldskoolraver.

Re: Loud House Party near Terry's Tool Hire
Posted by: Fiwith2dogs 12.34 p.m.

Joining in with a load of selfish knob-heads is the last thing I want to do. Next time I hear anything, I'm calling the police. Be warned.

Re: Loud House Party near Terry's Tool Hire
Posted by: Oldskoolraver 12.55 p.m.
I bet the Mews are quaking in their party shoes, Fiwith2dogs. Ignore the haters, Mews people. Party on!

I

I Do

Here comes the bride, sixty inches wide… Ali, you bloody heifer, why did you eat so much at Christmas? I silently fumed. My embonpoint was bursting out of my prom-style bridesmaid's dress, causing mild upper thorax asphyxiation and creating a fleshy shelf upon which I could probably rest a round of drinks. An irksome label was irritating my back; it hadn't been there when I'd tried the dress on in Coast months ago. I was like a dog chasing its tail, unable to reach the label without shedding the entire outfit. I couldn't face wrestling my boobs back into the dress so I left it as it was.

Jacqui, in a better-fitting version of my dress, her hair a stunning blond Farrah Fawcett bouffant, zipped a jittery Amanda into her striking grey chiffon ball gown.

'Five minutes, girls,' I warned Amanda's daughters, Isla and Meg.

They nodded, dressed in their identical dusky-pink John Lewis bridesmaids' dresses, delicate fresh gypsophila flower crowns adorning both their heads like angelic halos. Sonny, Amanda's little boy, was the ring-bearer, waiting with Chris at the town hall in a mini-me dark grey suit, a picture-perfect box-fresh family. Amanda's dad, suited and booted, sat on the over-stuffed blue velvet armchair by the door, looking like he was recounting his speech in his head. I felt a sharp pain below my ribs; Dad was never going to make a speech or walk me down the aisle in the vintage cream lace dress I'd always imagined myself in, even if I actually got that far. My latest boyfriend, Ifan, had spouted all sorts of romantic shit when we'd first met a year ago in Kebab and Stab after Jacqui's leaving drinks. He'd recited Dylan Thomas to me in bed and said he couldn't wait for me to have his babies, but as soon as he moved in three months later, real life tightened the drawstring on the blissful honeymoon period.

'He's so handsome!' Jacqui had swooned after I'd sent her a picture. 'You finally got the rock-star boy you always wanted.'

Ifan worked in an achingly trendy men's clothes shop in Covent Garden and had aspirations of becoming a model after posing for a few moody Instagram photo shoots for the store. He was certainly pretty enough and young enough (eight years my junior at thirty-three) and an improvement on all the hideous men I'd encountered in my recent dating past. We had spent the first week together tucked up in bed incessantly shagging – he was a veritable Clit Eastwood – until I was struck down with killer cystitis, weeing razor blades every time I went to the loo. I had to sneak him out under cover of darkness before my five-year-old daughter, Grace, surfaced. She slept in my bed so Ifan and I had appropriated the spare room as our shagging palace, a broom cupboard with a narrow single bed armed with a sagging mattress rammed against one wall like a coffin awaiting a corpse. I had earmarked it for Grace when we moved in, but the damp was now so tenacious that her clothes in the wardrobe had started growing mould on them, and I couldn't afford anywhere else, even with housing benefit. I wanted to be near my friends, Amanda and Ursula, but flats in East Dulwich were so out of my league.

The housing situation hadn't always been this dire. A few years ago I'd had it all – the roomy Victorian semi near Amanda with the ubiquitous stripped wooden floors and a free-standing Habitat kitchen (something of great beauty in the noughties). Added to that, I'd had a mad chocolate Labrador called Max, a stepdaughter, and a fiancé who also happened to be my agent. I kept having to pinch myself when I finally fell pregnant – all my life goals were real and happening in vivid Technicolor. Until my now ex-fiancé, Jim, had left me holding a newborn baby and sold our perfect house from under my feet to move in with Hattie (now his wife). Completely heartbroken and homeless with baby Grace, I had ended up moving in with Amanda for a few years while Grace metamorphosed from a baby into a strong-willed toddler. During our time in the house we affectionately called the Single Mums' Mansion, we became a patchwork family, along with Jacqui, another single mum. We spent Christmases together, hosted crazy parties, snogged unreliable men and helped each other through such an emotionally corrosive time that we formed an unbreakable bond. These women were like my family.

On the other hand, it gradually dawned on me that living in Amanda's attic with Grace, as if we were a couple of students, wasn't conducive to finding a much-wanted long-term partner. Grace and I needed our own space once she'd reached three, and we had to let Amanda move on with her life after she'd met Chris. Realising this had been a huge blow, but I knew it made sense. Leaving the safety net of the Single Mums' Mansion to forge my new life had felt like losing a limb. In the first few weeks away from the house, I'd continually questioned my sanity on the matter. I desperately missed the cosy warmth of the attic and the nightly catch-ups in the kitchen over a glass of red. I'd found myself crying at the sink when washing up, and Grace had wailed for the entire first week: 'Mummy, I want go home. I miss 'Manda.' My heart broke for her – the Single Mums' Mansion had been the only home she had ever known and Amanda was her other mummy. But every time anxiety swamped me, I heard Mini Amanda give me a pep talk inside my head: *This is your life, own it, live it, accept it. What will be will be…*

Mum had moved round the corner in Penge for a few months once her house in Spain had sold. Just having her there acted as a buffer against the low-level grey fug I couldn't shake off since leaving Amanda's. I'd been so excited about spending more time with Mum after she'd lived abroad for years, and Grace now had a granny she could see all the time. Dan and Alex, my brothers, were both married and had hectic family lives, and with Dad dying so suddenly four years ago it had felt all the more important that Mum lived near me.

However, after only six months it had been obvious that she was unhappy. I'd thought it was just because she didn't like Penge. I didn't blame her for that: every time I said 'Penge' out loud the word 'minge' reverberated in my head. I had suggested we club together to find a place in East Dulwich, but she'd been adamant. 'I've missed my chance at London, love. It's too busy, too impersonal. You and Grace are here and I love that, you know I do, but I can't live your life. I have to live my own.'

Mum headed for the south coast to be near Uncle Graham. I'd balled my eyes out as I'd driven off, leaving her in the cute little cottage in the centre of Whitstable, but I could see she was thrilled. 'Don't worry, Mummy, we can always visit. Granny Annie said so,' Grace wisely told me from the back seat. 'Don't be sad.' But it wouldn't be the same. I'd loved having that local family connection even if it had been only for a short while. It had made me feel cosseted, just like my time in the Single Mums' Mansion. Grace and I were alone once more…

Left to my own devices my life started to go completely off the rails with no grown-ups to rein me in. I'd lost count of the number of times I would say on a Sunday night after a particularly wonky weekend: 'Monday is the start of a whole new me!', but it must have been quite a few because Jacqui had threatened to get it printed on a T-shirt. By Thursday I would be climbing the walls and, in the weeks that Grace was off to her dad's, the bar-hopping treadmill would restart, more often than not dragging along terminally single Ursula, one of my uni mates, Jacqui, or Amanda. Not even the lure of my latest discovery, Radio Four, could keep the ants in my pants at bay. But my love of it did seem to mark my inevitable slide into middle age, especially when combined with a sudden interest in garden centres (I didn't have a garden) and a new appreciation for the benefits of flossing one's teeth in the knowledge that preserving your own set was essential with time ticking.

On the flip side of the coin, I was fighting being an actual functioning adult with every single atom of my being. For example, one morning after a one-night stand fuelled by Bolivian marching powder, I had found the draining board swept of dishes, what could only be smeared arse cheek prints on the steel worktop, and the green washing-up liquid overturned, dripping down the kitchen cabinets. This wasn't how I had planned to be approaching forty-two: as a single mum, living in a Dickensian flat, with a dead mouse in the hoover bag, indulging in a multitude of meaningless but fun one-night stands.

Meanwhile, Jacqui had met Mark, a psychology lecturer, when she was visiting her sister in Australia the Christmas after I moved out of the commune. She engaged in an all-out war with Simon, her ex-husband, about emigrating with their children, Neve and Joe, a year later (she had dual citizenship). But she won him round eventually with a deal to bring them over twice a year for a few weeks at a time. 'Yeah, I don't get why he's so fucking angry about it – he only sees them twice a month anyway because now he has two more kids, he hasn't got time for them. I told him this way he'd spend more quality time with them than his half-baked attempts at being a dad every other weekend.'

I had been devastated when she'd dropped the bomb – she had been my steadfast wing woman out on the Strip (our affectionate nickname for Lordship Lane), when our misadventures had seen us behaving like teenagers in the Adventure Bar, hooking up with the most unsuitable men, snogging behind the fruit machines in Kebab and Stab while awaiting chips for the journey home.

'In the words of Arnie: "I'll be back,"' she reassured me as I grizzled into my red wine. 'I'm renting my house out and if it's empty when it's time to come home for the kids' custody visits, we'll stay there. If not, I'll rent somewhere local. The kids will be with Simon most of the time, and Mark might come over too, depending on work. He's never been to the UK. We can all hang out.'

To top it all off, Chris proposed to Amanda just before Jacqui abandoned us, making me wonder if my time in the Single Mums' Mansion had only been a dream. I was so happy for Amanda – she totally deserved happiness second time round – but it had just served to highlight how far I was from finding that lasting relationship, until I met Ifan. Since we'd been together, the mould, the distance from my friends, and Penge itself had steadily grown on me, much like the spores in Grace's wardrobe. Bad Ali had finally been firmly stashed back in her box.

But now, my spidey senses were tingling. For two nights in a row between Christmas and the wedding, Ifan had failed to come home from a boys' night out. His phone was 'switched off' the entire time, sparking well-acquainted dread in me.

'Where were you?' I'd beseeched him when he'd nonchalantly resurfaced the day before we had to leave for the wedding, like he'd just popped to the shops for some milk instead of vanishing into a textless void.

'Nowhere. At the old flat. I told you I was going there. Things were mad at the shop because of the sales so I crashed with Niko both nights.'

'You never told me!' I'd screeched, hysteria bubbling dangerously below the surface. 'I would have remembered.'

'You were on the phone to Amanda talking about some wedding stuff when I told you – you nodded.'

'You're lying! I would've said something.'

'I'm not lying, babe. How could you say that?' He winked at me, his puppy-dog eyes coupled with his lilting Welsh accent making it impossible for me to get genuinely cross with him. 'We live together – I'm hardly going to sabotage all this, am I?' He waved his hand round the dingy living room like it was Versailles.

'I suppose not.' I really wanted to believe him. He was so good with Grace – well apart from when she had a tantrum; then he would storm off. But to be fair, *I* find her annoying when she's behaving like that. When it was good it was lovely to finally feel like a real family, and maybe one day, when he had a *proper* job we would have a baby of our own... 'Next time can you just make sure I'm listening before you think you've told me something?'

'Yes, anything for you, babe. You know that.'

'I hate everyone looking at me,' Amanda said tremulously, holding on to her dad's arm as we waited for the music to start in the antechamber of Rye Town Hall. 'What if I cry?'

'You're supposed to cry at weddings!' Jacqui said, rolling her eyes. 'No one's going to tell you off!'

'Stop catastrophising,' I said gently. 'Just enjoy it. It's your moment!'

However, when the time came to walk down the aisle, I hadn't heeded my own advice. As soon as the impressively ornate doors opened and the town crier rang his bell to announce us, I spotted Ifan standing next to Jacqui's Mark, his hand proprietorially on Grace's shoulder, eagerly waiting. The first thought that burned in the back of my mind was: *I can't marry a shop assistant.* I swiftly berated myself for being such a snob, but in reality, he didn't earn enough money to support us if we had a child.

He mouthed 'I love you' as I passed him and the predictable waterworks switched on. What did I even want? Why did weddings *always* emphasise all the glaring faults in my own life? *Cue tender violin music playing a dulcet tune and a close-up of my face as I realise yet again, I am the bridesmaid and not the bride. Cut away to Ifan, looking longingly at me.* STOP IT! I had been editing and imagining my inner movie since I was eight, when I first saw *Nine to Five* and realised I wanted to be a combination of Jane Fonda, Lily Tomlin and Dolly Parton when I grew up. Other leading ladies I'd cast in my internal film over the years included various girl crushes of the moment: Molly Ringwald during the John Hughes era; Julia Roberts when *Pretty Woman* and *Mystic Pizza* were released; Claire Danes when she starred in *My So-Called Life*; but my failsafe overriding choice would always be Madonna in *Desperately Seeking Susan*.

By the time the ceremony was over and we'd all posed for photos on the steps of the town hall, I had pulled myself together. Later that evening in the grand ballroom, still decked out in Christmas regalia for New Year's Eve the following day, Ifan disappeared from his seat at the top table during Amanda's dad's emotional speech in which he thanked all of us for standing by her in her hour of need. Later, I found Ifan escaping, halfway up the hotel's windy stairs to our room.

'Where're you going?'

'To bed.'

'Why? The party's just about to start.'

'I don't belong here.'

'Yes you do, you're with me.'

'No one will ever say those amazing things about me if we get married. Everyone here is so decent. I should go.'

'Stop being dramatic! Come on, let's go and dance. I want to see Amanda cut the cake and throw her bouquet.' He looked uncertain, like he was about to say something and then thought better of it.

'OK. Sorry. Can men get periods? I think I've got mine.' I play-punched him on the arm as we headed back to the ballroom and the disco, his sweaty hand in mine.

'Can you meet for coffee?' Amanda asked after she'd returned from her Sri Lankan honeymoon two weeks later, uncharacteristically ringing me instead of texting.

'I'm at work. I can do it Wednesday or Thursday.'

'Can you do this evening?' I was sure I could detect a cagey undercurrent in her voice.

'Is everything OK?'

'Yes, no everything is fine. Can you do later on?'

'I can meet you when Grace is in bed and Ifan is home. Where?'

'My house, if that's OK.'

'Sure, I'll see you there as soon as I can escape.'

All day at work, in between chasing mischievous toddlers round the studio, forcing new outfits on them for the catalogue shoot I was styling, I kept trying to guess what was so important it couldn't wait. Then it dawned on me: Amanda must be pregnant! She wanted to tell me face to face. Oh, how exciting. I couldn't wait to see her. I'd buy a bottle of fizz. Technically she could only have one glass, if she wasn't feeling sick, but Chris and I could polish it off. How was she going to cope with four kids, though?

By the time I arrived at Amanda's it was eight o'clock.

'Hello! You look so well. Glowing! How was the honeymoon? The pictures looked amazing on Facebook.' I leaned in to hug her in the hallway and she grasped me tightly, her face set in a rigid mask of concern. I glanced past her and noticed Ursula sitting at the central island in the kitchen, sipping a glass of red in her slick city work clothes, her wavy brown hair scraped off her face into a sleek topknot. Chris was nowhere to be seen.

'Come through and sit down,' Amanda said in a kind voice, the one she reserved for serving someone a dose of uncomfortable home truths.

'Oh, fucking hell, what's happened? Who's died?' I asked as I followed her down the hallway and into the homely kitchen at the back of the house.

Ursula stood up from the bar stool, taller than normal on account of her bitch heels. She also looked grave, but gave me a smile.

'It's not Jacqui, is it? Has something happened to her?' I clutched my throat, my hand shaking while Amanda stopped next to Ursula.

'No one's died. Fuck, this is so hard, so I'm just going to say it.' Amanda took a deep breath. 'Ifan has been caught on camera having a threesome with Sandeep and Mary from the newsagent round the corner from me.'

2

I Don't

'Fuck off! They're married. That would never happen!'

'Apparently they're massive swingers,' Ursula piped up regretfully, handing me a glass of red wine. I took it, my hand shaking so violently I had to temporarily put it back onto the wooden worktop.

'How do you even know this?' I spat out, the walls of the kitchen expanding and then rapidly contracting. I felt the force of my breath whacked out of me as familiar crimson rage gripped me tightly round the chest. 'I bet it isn't even true!' I was pacing now, both legs juddering like loose live wires sparking uncontrollably, making stillness a near impossibility.

'Ifan's other girlfriend posted the clip on a revenge porn site and someone saw it,' Amanda said quietly, the gravitas of the words visibly weighing her down.

'Other girlfriend? Who saw it? Did *you* see it?'

Amanda nodded.

'What the fuck were *you* doing looking at a revenge porn site?'

'I wasn't. One of Chris's friends happened to catch it. I daren't ask how or why, but they recognised Ifan from the wedding.'

'Have you got the clip?'

'You don't need to look at it. I can tell you it's Ifan.'

'I want to see it.'

'Ali, it will just make you feel worse,' Ursula tried to reason with me, but I was beyond that.

'How the fuck can I feel any worse? You've just told me Ifan has been unfaithful *and* that he actually has another girlfriend. Who is she?'

'That's the thing, we don't know,' Amanda admitted. 'She posted on this website. Shani something or other.' I shook my head – it felt like it was crammed with buzzing bees.

'I don't know who that is. She could be fake. Or from before I met him.'

'The footage was filmed a few months back. I think the date said November the ninth, which was when we were out for my hen do.'

'Fucker! He didn't come back until Tuesday after the hen do,' I roared.

'Has he gone AWOL before?' Ursula asked suspiciously. I winced, knowing what they'd say about the truth.

'Yes, but he always had an explanation.'

'Ali! You should have told us. How many times did he go missing?' Amanda cross-examined me.

'Half a dozen or so.'

'You've only been together just over a year,' Ursula protested. 'What excuses did he use?'

'He had to work late at the shop with Niko to do a stocktake after work a few times so they crashed at the flat. Other times he bumped into someone from home and they went on a bender.'

'Isn't this what Jim used to do before you gave birth to Grace?' Amanda eyeballed me. 'He used to go AWOL too.'

'Yes, but it was always after a row. I haven't had a proper row with Ifan, yet.'

'Ali, what the fuck? He's been treating you like a doormat and you're just covering for him. Has he been sponging off you too?'

'I've lent him money, yes, but he's promised to pay it back. He's trying to break into modelling.'

'You have a child and rely on benefits to help you out. He shouldn't be taking anything or expect anything!'

Amanda wore her crazy face; she'd abandoned her zen softly-softly approach.

'Can I see the video?'

Amanda glanced at Ursula and she nodded at her.

'Fine, if it gives you closure.' She handed me her phone with the footage already open. It was very blurry but then, when the lens focused, I could make out Ifan half naked on a flowery Cath Kidston duvet with a bare-chested man dressed in tight black leather chaps looming over him. The chaps were unflattering, pushing his gut up into a muffin top. It certainly looked like Sandeep, and in any other situation it would have been hysterically funny, the thought of him trying to squeeze into unforgiving black leather. Mild-mannered Sandeep, who always asked if you wanted one of the chocolate bars on special offer. And to think I had missed seeing him when I'd moved out of Amanda's! Mary must have been filming. Holy shit, there she was standing in front of a large canvas of the New York skyline. It looked exactly like one from Ikea, in fact the whole bedroom was kitted out with Ikea knick-knacks – some of them were in my home! She was in full leather bondage gear with a stick in her mouth, or was it a gag? I turned the volume up so I could hear. Who was filming then? Suddenly I heard a familiar voice: Niko, he was the cameraman. Sandeep started tantalisingly to peel down Ifan's underpants and I couldn't watch any more, my stomach swilled with what felt like battery acid, and I hastily thrust the phone at Amanda.

'I'm so sorry,' Amanda whispered. 'I couldn't not tell you.'

'It was like some fucking shit porn film from the seventies.'

'Was that Niko I could hear?' Ursula asked tentatively. She and Niko had shagged once when they were very drunk. Not to be repeated: apparently *his* sexual transgression was golden showers...

'Yes, the fucker. I always thought it was weird how much time they spent together. And Ifan was completely obsessed with anal sex.'

'That doesn't mean he's gay,' Ursula said reasonably. 'Lots of straight men are obsessed with it. The forbidden fruit and all that.'

'What are you going to do?' Amanda asked me; as always she expected there to be an exit plan just when I wanted to curl up into a ball and pretend none of this was happening.

'Throw him out. Oh God, why now? I fucking hate January, I hate being on my own, especially in winter.' Before I knew it I was howling my eyes out, my nose stinging from the deluge, and Amanda and Ursula were hugging me.

'You deserve so much better, you really do,' Ursula soothed me. 'You are too good for him.'

'Yes,' Amanda agreed. 'I think he has massive self-loathing, which is why he's so vain. I've seen him posing in the pub windows. He hasn't got anything else apart from his looks. He's never going to make it as a model now. He's too old. Don't they all have to have been spotted by the time they're eighteen?'

'Yes, but older models are trending now,' Ursula replied while I continued to snot into my hands. Amanda shoved a torn-off piece of kitchen towel at me. 'Look at David Gandy, he's old.'

'Hardly! He's the same age as Chris. *We're* old!'

'Speak for yourself!' Ursula cackled.

'I'm old,' I sobbed pathetically. 'I'll never find anyone now. I can't face going back out there. It was so shit last time.'

'Then don't go out there,' Ursula said firmly. 'You've got to bin Twat Face yet. Why are you talking about meeting someone else when you're still in the shit? One thing at a time!'

'I hate him! How can he do this to me?'

No one said anything. Fundamentally I knew what they were thinking: that I'd let this happen by being a pushover. Amanda was such a hard nut that no one would ever walk over her again. Chris was lovely and was besotted with her, but she was in charge and completely emotionally self-sufficient. And Ursula expected perfection from every man she ever met, most of whom were dumped for sniffing too much or breathing too loudly. She managed a massive job in recruitment in the city and didn't need anyone. She had a fabulous life travelling and dating only on her terms.

'Right, we're going now, you and me.' Amanda clapped her hands together as if she was rounding up her gaggle of children. 'You coming?' she asked Ursula.

'No, I have to head off. I've got a meeting to prep for.'

'What?' I cried, wiping my streaming nose on the sodden kitchen towel, looking from Ursula to Amanda. 'Where're you taking me?'

'To your flat. We're chucking out that cock womble.'

'Cock womble!' I spluttered, almost, but not quite, forgetting that I was aggrieved.

'Do you like it?'

I nodded enthusiastically.

'I've been waiting for an opportunity to use it. This feels like the right occasion.'

When we entered my flat, Amanda hung back in the poky kitchen situated by the front door. Ifan's shabby bike rested up against the assortment of coats dangling down from the rack in the gloomy entrance hall. His bulky orange cycling rucksack took up the rest of the space, so I had to step over it to walk into the open-plan living room. The urge to kick the bike until it was reduced to a pile of nuts and bolts was so unbearable I had to dig my nails into the palms of my hands until my knuckles turned white. Ifan was stretched out on the incongruous hot-pink fleur-de-lis sofa that was more suited to the Victorian house from my life with Jim.

He was watching some totally banal *CSI* crap I would never bother with, sipping one of the beers that *I* had bought for him.

'Hi, babe. How was Amanda?' He didn't even look up.

'Who's Shani?' His head swung round like it was on well-oiled castors.

'What?'

'You heard me. Shani. Apparently she's your *girlfriend*...' He opened and closed his mouth several times, presumably rushing through excuses to pick the perfect one.

'I haven't seen Shani for years. She was the one I was with just before you.'

'Is that the best you can come up with?'

'Babe, I promise, she's no one. We broke up ages ago.'

'Was she the one you were with when you should have been with me at Christmas? Or were you *with* Niko?'

'You *know* I was with Niko!' He looked relieved, probably because he was telling the truth.

'With Niko as in fucking Niko up the bum?'

'Are you mental? I'm not gay.'

'Explain this then!' And I shoved Amanda's phone in his face with the video already blasting out what could only be described as sex sounds and the occasional crack of a whip against bare flesh. My insides had melted into a queasy mess, the glass of wine stinging my throat as it threatened to reappear. Ifan's face drained of colour until only his lips were showing signs of life.

'Babe—'

'Don't fucking babe me, you total twat. Get your stuff and leave Grace and me alone. I don't ever want to see you again.'

'No, I can explain.'

'Really? Get your stuff!' And before I knew what I was doing, I'd launched myself at him and begun slapping him round the head, tearing at his hair, trying to yank it out.

'Stop it, Ali!' Amanda yelled, and she grabbed me by the shoulders and dragged me off him. He was covering his face like a child, cowering against the back of the sofa.

'What the fuck? You've got the cavalry here too?' Ifan cried when he dropped his hands.

'Yes she has, and you should be fucking grateful or she would have ripped your head off.'

'Look, Amanda, that video was years ago. Before I met Ali.'

'No it wasn't. Chris found the date in the original and it was in November. This Shani person posted it while we were on honeymoon. You've obviously been stringing Ali along and this poor Shani, when all the while you've been shagging whoever you like. Men included.'

'You knew I wanted a threesome!' he accused me, ignoring Amanda. The gloves were obviously off now there was no chance of redemption. 'This wouldn't have happened if you'd agreed!'

'Get out! Get your crap and leave. I hate you!'

He stood up, towering over me and Amanda, barely contained rage festering behind his eyes. I was so glad she was there because he suddenly felt menacing. He stormed off to the bedroom and proceeded to crash about and Grace stumbled into the living room minutes later, rubbing her eyes, her face all puffy from sleep.

'Mummy, what's the shouting?'

'Nothing, Grace. Here, lie down on the sofa.' She slumped down and lay her head on a cushion and I pulled the furry throw over her. Amanda sat down next to her and stroked her head. Ten minutes later Ifan thundered past us into the hallway and started ramming things in his rucksack.

'I'll get the rest of my stuff tomorrow.'

'No you won't,' Amanda said coolly. 'You'll give Ali her key now and she will bag your shit up and leave it in the hallway outside.'

'What if someone nicks it?'

'No one is going to want your crap, believe me.' Something about the way Amanda looked at him made him back down and open the door. He threw me the keys and I caught them one-handed, then he shoved his bike out through the door. I couldn't believe it was just ending like this; it was so sudden. I rushed to the door to watch him go and an image of Sandeep sliding his pants down assaulted me.

'You fucking cock womble!' I yelled so hard my throat almost split. The thumping started on the ceiling from Mr Watson upstairs. 'You can fuck off too,' I mumbled, defeated.

'Well done,' Amanda said, and gave me a massive hug. 'That must have been so hard.'

'I can't believe it. I was in a relationship this morning and now it's over.'

'He was so below you. It'll take time to get over it, but you've had so much worse happen to you that was way shitter than this.'

'Yes, but I had you then, and you were going through the same thing. Now I'm on my own.'

'You're never on your own. Come on, let's get Grace back into bed.'

I picked her up off the sofa and carried her through the doorway. The room looked like it had been rudely ransacked by psycho-grannies at a car boot sale: drawers spewing their contents and clothes strewn everywhere. I would sort it tomorrow. Grace buried herself under the duvet and I sat on the edge of the bed. This was an unexpected turn in the plot. As I leaned down to kiss Grace good night she stirred.

'Mummy, what's a cock womble?'

3

Reality Bites

The following week on my way to the French Café, I ran, head down, past Sandeep and Mary's shop, Kahn's News. Violent feelings seesawed between wanting to hurl a Molotov cocktail furiously through their window; to pinning them both to the floor under my knobbly knees while Amanda tarred and feathered them. Even in my revenge plot fantasy, Amanda remained as annoyingly Switzerland as ever. 'They didn't know he was your boyfriend,' she would reason with me outside the shop as I gripped an old pillow, a tub of PVA, a pair of scissors and a petrol bomb, dithering between the two methods. 'If you want revenge, move on with your life. It's the best revenge ever.' But not as instantly gratifying...

Kent Libraries,
Registration and Archives
www.kent.gov.uk/libraries
Tel: 03000 41 31 31

Borrowed Items 19/03/2020 12:28
XXXXXXX0023

Item Title	Due Date
* The holiday	09/04/2020
* Behind closed doors	09/04/2020
* Secrets of a happy marriage	09/04/2020
* The single mums move on	09/04/2020
Luckiest girl alive	06/04/2020

Amount Outstanding: £1.00

* Indicates items borrowed today
Thank you for using self service

The return of the post-break-up palpitations and clamped-shut stomach was most unwelcome. The only silver lining was that I could barely eat, which was a saviour after a gluttonous Christmas and working on photo shoots where a constant conveyor belt of tempting pastries and delicious cakes were always on offer. I'd found myself unwittingly humming the *Black Beauty* theme tune under my breath on a continual loop in an attempt to mitigate tension. It was my dependable musical mantra from my childhood that usually worked in any given situation: calming Grace down after a fall, soothing a raging hangover or just giving general succour to a busy head about to implode. However, today it was up against a tide of grief too strong to assuage.

How had I let yet another man just walk all over me? It wasn't like I'd suffered a traumatic childhood, or enjoyed people abusing me in some masochistic way, but it was a pattern I had noticed emerging over my love life's sprawling back catalogue. Every man I had ever loved had either been some kind of addict with a planet-sized ego or had needed rescuing. I missed Ifan so much, despite the fact he was an absolute turd, and even a whole week later all I wanted to do was text him. I had to physically sit on my hands as anxiety whooshed around my rumbling guts and tightened its grasp on my racing heart. I pushed open the door of the French Café and spotted Amanda sitting at the back by the TV fake fire. She waved me over.

'Are you OK?' she asked, sliding a laminated menu across the table towards me.

'No, I feel horrendous.' And I promptly burst into tears.

'I thought you would. It's starting to sink in now.' She patted my hand as I blindly surveyed the menu, not really wanting anything other than to stop feeling like this.

'I can't believe I'm on my own again. And I don't even know how I'll ever meet anyone new – you're married and Jacqui's not even on the same continent any more. All my wing women are in retirement.' I blew my nose on a paper napkin. I knew Ursula was still available for fun and frolics, but she wasn't a mum, and she also didn't mind being single.

'Hey, why do you need to meet anyone? You've just broken up with a douchebag. Having some time alone would be the best thing now. Gather your thoughts and find out who *you* are. Stop listening to Radio One like Ifan – you need to switch back to Radio Four and be you again; embrace it!'

I laughed weakly. She was right. Instead of the usual nonsensical post-break-up ritual of sleeping in Ifan's abandoned T-shirt, I had continued to tune in to Radio One to lessen the loss, even though I hated all the drivelling DJs.

'You need to feel the pain, not cover it up with another shit relationship or you will end up trying to mould that man into who you want him to be all over again.'

'Oh God, I did do that! The amount of times I wished Ifan had a better job or more money or more drive and ambition. He just didn't. I fancied his physical appearance but was always waiting for him to change. I think I wanted him to be more dynamic, like Jim.'

'We can't change people; we can only change ourselves. Honour all your feelings and let them pass through you or they will just try to face you down another time twice as badly and you'll be back to the beginning.'

'I hate the pain! It hurts. I'm not good at change or being on my own. I want to be married and live in a family.'

'I know, but think of the pain as the proving process, like if you were making sourdough. We all love sourdough bread!' And she waved over to the counter where delicious-looking crusty loaves were stacked up on top of each other, and glass cake stands groaned under the weight of sumptuous chocolate creations and pink-iced fancies. 'If you don't let sourdough prove three times, it stays flat and won't transform into something yummy. By speeding up proving or not paying attention, or leaving out a stage, you can damage the end result. Each stage of your grief is a prove and it takes time and effort on your part – it isn't a passive process. Once you actively work through the range of emotions, you will come out the other side a better version of yourself. You will have self-awareness and understanding, make better choices, be calmer, possibly be able to have some alone time without the constant need to fill it. Just see what happens. It's all positive – you don't want to be an under-proved flat loaf with no air bubbles, do you? We all need the bubbles: they're what make us yummy.'

'Why do you always make me cry with your Beardy Weirdy analogies?'

'But that's good. It means you're making bubbles. Acknowledge them and let them float off, like bubbles do!'

'I wish I lived nearer you. I hate my flat. It's too far and too small and damp, and Grace still hasn't got her own room.' I knew I was being a whinge bag but I honestly couldn't stop; my pity party was in full swing.

'Well, you can do something about that, can't you? Ask the universe for a better flat that you can afford, nearer me. Write it down and burn it. Don't set fire to the flat, though.'

The next day when Grace was at school, I decided to visit East Dulwich and pop into the Beardy Weirdy shop for some Rescue Remedy and anything else to improve my perennially shit life. Walking down Lordship Lane always made me feel so much brighter than looking at the dreary pound shops in un-gentrified Penge. I loved the individual traders and cute coffee places, bars, pubs and cafés in East Dulwich, where there wasn't a bargain bin of Hob Brite to be seen. I felt like I belonged here within the buzz.

As I approached my favourite shop, Mrs Robinson, it triggered a guarded memory from my life with Jim. When we had first looked round East Dulwich all those years ago, just as Jim's divorce had come through, we'd been so excited at the prospect of buying our first home together. We'd bought ourselves a present in Mrs Robinson, a large rustic blue salad bowl, a symbol of all the lovely meals and potential parties we would host as a couple once we'd found a house. I remembered feeling so happy in the queue to pay that I'd had tears in my eyes; we had the whole world ahead of us. It was everything I had ever wanted wrapped up in a beautiful neighbourhood filled with families and young people.

I yearned for that happiness again, that budding excitement at the beginning of a shared life together. Choosing things for a new house, painting walls, arguing in IKEA over which rug suited the living room, deciding whether we should get a dog, cooking huge Sunday lunches for lots of guests, our door always open. My own longing for it was like a physical weight in my chest, pressing my heart into my belly amid the hopelessness that it was now so far out of reach.

I stopped in front of Mrs Robinson's aspirational window display and gazed past the distressed leather bucket-seat armchair and shiny chrome standard lamp, my eyes settling on a young couple. The man was bouncing up and down and when he turned to the side I could see he had a baby in one of those slings, trying to soothe it. His partner was picking up cushions and showing them to him, and he shook his head at each choice. Then he nodded at an ironic print of a pug's head in a gilt frame and her face lit up. They kissed. I felt a sharp pain stab me in the throat as tears engulfed me. They were living the life *I* was supposed to have. I abruptly turned away and walked off, banishing any more memories that tried to surface. What had I been thinking, letting Jim in my head again. It was in the past. I had been going forward, until Ifan's antics. This was *why* I never allowed myself to wander too far down memory lane…

Once I was in the health food shop, I browsed the heaving shelves, searching for my miracle cure among the myriad bottles, reading the microscopic essays about their transformative properties. I looked up from one extortionate bottle of essence spray that promised to rejuvenate my life and curb my stupid twat ways and caught the eye of a lady who looked vaguely familiar. She smiled and I returned the greeting, trying to place her. She came over.

'You're Ali, a friend of Jacqui's, aren't you? You used to sometimes go to her yoga class on a Friday. I'm Francesca.' She had a really kind face, quite beautiful, with startling emerald-green eyes. Her vibrant wavy red hair was pushed off her face with an electric-pink headband.

'Oh, yes, I remember now.'

She had an air of openness about her, like you could divulge your life story in under a minute and she would somehow understand you down to the marrow in your bones.

'How are you?'

'Not great, to be honest. I just split up with my boyfriend.' I could hear my voice wobble and I silently summoned *Black Beauty*…

'Oh, you poor thing. I could kind of tell something was up. Your aura's dark *and* heavy.'

From anyone else this would have made me run for my life, apart from maybe Amanda, who was queen of Beardy Weirdy.

'Oh, sorry, I didn't mean to freak you out, it's just very obvious.'

'No, it's fine. My aura does feel dark and heavy. I'm here trying to buy something to help me move forward, but I'm a bit lost.'

'Well, that essence will help; so will some of these flower remedies. Have you thought about chakra cleansing? That can work wonders.' Her calm delivery made me want to sit in her house and ask her to fix my leaky life like an emotional episode of *DIY SOS*.

'I'd love that. Can you do it?'

'Yes, I'm a shaman. I practise at home, round the corner from Jacqui's old house in the Mews.'

'Wow, you live there? It always sounds so exciting.' The Mews was infamous in East Dulwich. There were so many rumours posted all over the East Dulwich Forum about the residents, the wild parties, the neighbourhood watch complaints and the supposedly D-list celebs that had been spotted zipping in and out of the electric gates.

'Oh, well, hardly. It's just a gated cul-de-sac – not glamorous at all!'

'It sounds perfect. I'd love to live somewhere less isolated. I hate my flat in Penge. That's part of the grungy aura problem: I wish I lived in East Dulwich again. I miss being here.'

Francesca tilted her head to one side and studied my face carefully, like she was trying to work me out. Or maybe she was actually performing a Jedi mind-reading trick, though you never had to do that with me with my heart constantly pinned chirpily to my sleeve.

'I think I might be able to help you with that one.' She smiled kindly and patted my arm reassuringly. 'Do you believe in fate?'

4

Norman

Norman peered out of his kitchen window, pulling his red silk dressing gown around him – not really a garment for a cold day, but he wore it anyway. Someone was moving into Tina's old house two doors down opposite, in between Elinor and Carl. Two women so far; maybe they were lesbians? He was sure he had seen the taller blonde lady looking round it a while back, and he swore she had brought a little girl with her. He sipped his coffee and sighed. More new people. He'd preferred it when it had just been him, Francesca and Jo those first three months fourteen years ago, before everyone else had arrived in dribs and drabs.

A gated community was probably not the best place when you preferred living on your own, but he'd promised Lucas he would use the life insurance money to buy it. Lucas had liked it when he'd shown him the developer's details, and the pot of money covered it completely. It was better than a flat in Brixton, where he would have had to deal with other people's noises from below and above. He could also sit in the garden when he felt like it, feel the warmth of the sun on his skin and have a holiday from himself. Norman would never have to worry about moving again, dealing with nasty landlords, or crazy young people who blasted music out at all hours. *Well, that's what he'd thought.* He had hoped the slightly higher house prices would mean sensible people, professionals, would move in, or maybe young families who would be so exhausted from constant care-giving that they'd all be asleep by eight at night. He hadn't bargained on moving into a neighbourhood where everyone was in and out of each other's houses like in years gone by, and partied even when there was nothing to celebrate.

Norman attended some of the parties, observed, had a couple of glasses of wine and then returned home. He thought he kept himself to himself, but he knew what they said about him: *Nosy Norman, the kvetch.* Except he wasn't nosy, he just looked, noticed, and carried on with his life.

At first when he'd overheard a few of them talking about him, their voices catching on the breeze, reaching him in his back garden, he'd been stung. He wanted to tell them that wasn't who he was, that they were being unfair, he was just being a good neighbour, but something stopped him. Deep down, he was scared of revealing too much of himself, letting anyone in again. He'd had enough of losing people he loved – his poor heart probably wouldn't be able to take it again – so, like a porcupine raising its quills, he used prickly words to keep everyone at bay. Occasionally he might suggest something to someone, like maybe they shouldn't park their car with the wheels on his share of the drive. And could people please remember that bin day means you have to wheel your own bin to the edge of the pavement the night before, not forget so that two more weeks of detritus spills out onto the ground and blows around the Mews like tumbleweed. And please stop parking across people's drives when you have a space that is yours in front of your house. It's not meant to be for pot plants and garden furniture, it's for a car.

Norman turned away from the rain-splattered window and walked up the stairs to the airing cupboard to retrieve a clean towel for his morning bath. As he opened the door, he steeled himself for the stench that had been lingering now for a good year. Sometimes it was worse than others, and sometimes it disappeared completely. Today, it was most definitely there, the strongest it had been since the month before. He had noticed it was cyclical, and he had mentioned it to Nick, his standoffish neighbour. He reached into the warmth and pulled out a fluffy black towel, like one from a spa embossed with his initials, a Christmas gift from Lucas many years before.

Norman knew what the smell was, but he could hardly go around pointing the finger and accusing neighbours of criminal activity. Nick hadn't the appearance of a convincing criminal either. He was slightly dishevelled when he wasn't in a suit for work, and looked like he wouldn't say boo to a goose. He also kept his head down, which Norman liked, never played loud music, didn't join in with the Mews, and went away twice a year, once in the summer and once in the winter, usually February time. All in all, he was a good neighbour, but then the smell had started. Norman looked online about making formal complaints, getting things in writing, putting the fear of God into people, and to his horror, it said in all the chat rooms, don't complain. Apparently it all gets chalked up somewhere and when you come to selling your property, all disputes are made public and potential buyers have to be made aware of any feuds with neighbours. He felt trapped – not that he was going to move; they would be taking him out of here in a box – but he liked to have the option *just in case*.

Several times he had tried to invite himself into Nick's house during the Christmas season, uncharacteristically bringing round a card and a bottle of wine, but Nick resolutely held him on the doorstep, thanked him for the unnecessary gift and wished him a happy holiday. Norman had started spotting an older lady there overnight once a week, whom he assumed (hoped) was Nick's mum, rather than Nick having a predilection for kinky granny sex. Norman shivered. The thought of that carrying on next door...

Norman lay in the bath, the mirror steamed up above his head. Even though he wasn't a party animal, he would go to Jo's this evening. She had hurriedly arranged it last week once they all knew about the new person moving in. Norman thought it was Jo's way of showing she was the leader of the Mews ecosystem. Every time a new neighbour moved in, Jo threw a party, like a test, to see if they would come for a drink, to say hello, to sniff them over, like one of her ratty little dogs.

There wasn't a massive turnover of new neighbours – these days the Mews was pretty solid – but he remembered when Nick moved in, he had poked his head round the door at one of Jo's dos, stayed for one drink, then buggered off. And he'd been like that ever since.

Norman wondered what the new woman, or women, would be like. Her little girl looked sweet. His breath caught in his throat every time he thought of little ones, the twist of a knife in his gut. Lucas's face swam before his eyes, ravaged by his impending departure. 'Don't mourn me, don't mourn what you chose, life is shit and then you die. So roll in the shit, make it count, don't hide, be a part of something. Promise me that.' But Norman sometimes wondered whether he was meant to be part of something. Living here was like his half-hearted attempt at fulfilling his promise. He was part of something yet, at the same time, he wasn't. The grief had robbed him of the things he loved and so he'd gradually let them go. He was someone else now; someone he didn't always recognise. Someone he didn't always like.

He got out of the bath and wrapped himself in the towel. The bloody towel smelled of *the smell*. He was going to have to say something again...

5

The Mews

'Good old cosmic ordering,' Amanda had laughed when I'd originally told her about the shaman in the health food shop. 'Who owns it?'

'A private landlord, friends with everyone in the Mews. He prefers to rent it to someone they like and trust, hence the low rent.'

'So you'll be OK with money for a bit?'

'That's the idea. Alice owes me so many pay cheques that I had to put the deposit on a card, but I can clear it as soon as she coughs up.' Alice was my agent and also by *huge* coincidence, Jim's wife, Hattie's, best friend. Fact was certainly stranger than fiction.

'Oh, wow, it's like a proper house only cut in half!' Amanda cried in surprise when we eventually stumbled inside the communal front door on moving day, her decrepit Volvo parked on the driveway rammed to the roof with boxes and bin bags. Chris was following behind the Man and the Van in my Golf.

'Thanks, now I know why they're called half-houses.' I rolled my eyes. It was essentially a wider-than-average terrace house with the shared front door slap bang in the middle, a joint hallway and then separate inside front doors leading to the two halves of the overall building.

'It's so much bigger than your flat,' Amanda marvelled once we were inside my new front door. 'I like the stairs leading up from the living room and the open-plan kitchen at the back. It's so light and airy. And you finally have a little garden you can walk straight into.'

I was ecstatic about having the Holy Grail of kitchen appliances: a dishwasher. Upstairs housed the master bedroom linked to a little ensuite, plus a white tiled family bathroom and Grace's marginally smaller bedroom. The landlord had redecorated it all from top to bottom in a neutral light grey and had even laid down new wooden flooring.

My interior styling definitely erred on the side of clutter; I didn't understand minimalism. I loved being surrounded by memories, pictures, candles, obscure ornaments I'd picked up on my travels and all my books. The collection of things made me feel safe, their familiarity a constant presence in my life. I liked curating everything together to add meaning to different rooms, making them feel snug and lived in, adding splashes of vivid colour with cushions and throws and framed posters. I was champing at the bit to transform this blank canvas into Grace's and my new home, something that the flat in Minge had never felt like.

'People rarely leave the Mews,' I said once we started emptying the car. 'Most of the residents have been here since it was built fourteen years ago. If someone does sell, the houses get snapped up like the free samples during Clinique Bonus time. There's the flats above Terry's Tool Hire and the tile place too – they're all part of the development. Apparently my landlord owns half of them.'

The magnificent main wrought-iron gate, reminiscent of Southfork Ranch from *Dallas*, was set back from Underhill Road, with less impressive pedestrian entrances either side. Straddling the triptych of gates stood two imposing redbrick Victorian mansions. I'd walked and driven past it a million times and always wondered what lay at the end of the long stretch of curved tarmac between the sentry post mansions. Now I knew. The rounded drive split into a two-pronged fork once you reached Francesca's house on the left corner plot. She owned a whole beige-bricked town house within a set of two stretching down to two further blocks of half-houses. Mine was in the centre with neighbours on either side. I had already met one when I came initially to view the house, an endearing posh lady called Elinor, in her late sixties. I had yet to meet the one on my immediate right, who was a photographer.

The car park for the flats above Terry's Tool Hire was at the end of our row behind a low box hedge. Opposite me was another stretch of four town houses, winding past the fork in the road to a tiny cul-de-sac where a stand-alone larger house stood backing onto the gardens of one of the stately mansions on Underhill Road. There was a secret coded gate down the side of the flats that led onto Lordship Lane and a string of handy shops. There was no traffic, so kids could safely play out in the street and every property had identical black mock-Victorian front doors and a bricked driveway on which to park a car. Most people had arranged pots or plants by their doors, and some palm and olive trees were dotted in front of other houses. The street had an uncanny stillness about it, rather how I imagined the *EastEnders* set looked without lights, camera, action.

April wasn't long off, but it felt more like January, the wind slicing through my chunky cream cable-knit jumper and skinny jeans as we cleared out the car. I looked up as I pulled the main door to and noticed a blind twitch in the house opposite. Someone was checking me out.

'What if the Mews is actually like *The Stepford Wives*? That's why no one leaves and why only friends of friends can live here.' Amanda arched her eyebrows at me, a smirk dancing round her mouth.

'Shut up! It isn't. The few people I have met have been really nice.' But I couldn't say it hadn't crossed my mind. It was so different from when I moved into the flat in Minge. I only ever met Mr Watson, who had lived above me, because he complained about every single noise I ever made: 'Your voice is so penetrating, Alison!'

'Helloooooo!' Francesca called through the open door later on as Chris and Nigel, the man who had come with the van, shifted my pink sofa to the back of the living room up against the breakfast bar to make way for all the other stuff. In the movie of my life, Nigel would be called Jonnie and he would be fit as fuck and flirt outrageously with me, and after everyone had left, we would have wild animalistic sex up against the freshly painted living-room wall. In reality he was about thirty-five, six foot five and super skinny in a *Where's Wally?* kind of way. Just the thought of my entire weight on him would no doubt snap his sapling legs in half.

'Come in!' Amanda was in the kitchen making tea for everyone after emptying ten boxes to find some mugs.

'I've brought you this, and Elinor's here, too.'

'Hello,' Elinor called softly from behind Francesca. 'We're just dropping off a welcome pack and then we'll leave you to it.' Francesca was wearing a red cotton kaftan with navy blanket-stitch edging over black jeans and massive gold hoop earrings. She looked like an archetypal Beardy Weirdy. Elinor, in contrast, was in a demure cream sweater and cargo pants with navy court shoes, and her blonde-grey hair was immaculately coiffured into a halo around her head. She looked so well turned out for a lady of her age and she reminded me of my own mum.

'Amanda's just making tea, if you want one?'

'No, you're busy, but have these with your tea,' Francesca said, and handed me two Cadbury's Celebrations tins. 'It's not chocolate, we made one each. Open them when we've gone. Just to let you know also, we're having drinks at Jo's opposite you later on, if you want to come.'

'Oh, wow, thanks so much. I might, depending on how much I get done here. What time?'

'From about seven. It might be a good way to meet everyone. Good luck with the unpacking!'

After they left I took the tins out to the kitchen.

'Open them!' Amanda insisted eagerly. Chris wandered in to inspect while Nigel hefted a final few boxes inside. I put both tins down on the kitchen breakfast bar and prised the lids off. Inside one was what looked and smelled like a delectably moist banana loaf cake and in the other were some golden, sticky-looking flapjacks. I reached in to grab one.

'What if it's made of breast milk or something weird?' Chris said cautiously. 'Are you sure you trust them?'

'Oh my God!' Amanda laughed. 'You've obviously never made a flapjack in your life.'

'No, but I saw something on Reddit about this couple who moved into a village in the middle of nowhere and their neighbours gave them a rice pudding as a welcome gift and told them after they'd eaten it that it was made from the wife's breast milk.'

'Chris! You're just trying to put me off. There won't be breast milk in a flapjack.'

'But there might be in the cake… That woman is a shaman. You've no idea what's in there. You might start hallucinating and turn into your spirit animal.'

'I'm having one!' Amanda said, snatched a flapjack from the tin and started eating it. 'Oh God, yuk!' She spat it out into her hand.

'What's wrong with it?' I cried, an image of a whirring breast pump flitting across my mind.

'Nothing, it's fine! Just thought I would wind you up!'

When everyone had left, I lay down on Grace's bed after I had made it up with her pink stripy duvet, the pile of fluffy cushions acting like a headboard. I hoped she would be happy, and that together we could make a fresh start. I needed to stop feeling like I was living the wrong life. I missed her and wanted a cuddle, suddenly feeling alone in the house, not yet knowing what our future here was going to be like, me and her against the world. She always knew when I was putting on a brave face and would ask, 'Do you need a hug, Mummy?'

'Please let this be a happy home,' I asked the house, and squeezed one of Grace's teddies to my chest. 'We need to be OK. I can't move again.'

At half-past eight that evening, surrounded by boxes, *Black Beauty* humming in the background, I fiddled with the TV remote. Chris had set everything up for me as well as building my and Grace's beds. I could hear doors banging and people chatting in the street outside. I switched the lights off before peering out of the window. There were thick cream curtains already hanging up in the house and I laughed at myself, twitching them like a prim nosy neighbour. I spotted two people smoking outside Jo's house, if it was her house. I didn't know who she was and I wasn't sure I was in the mood to go to the drinks, but every time the door opened, cheesy pop music blared out, and it sounded like they were having fun. I was exhausted and really wanted to go to bed. Just then my phone pinged; it was Ifan.

I turned up at your flat and you've moved. They wouldn't give me your forwarding address. I really need to talk. Xx

Right, that was it, I had to go out or I knew I would text him. *Fucking twat!* I ignored the traitorous fleeting flame of hope that ignited at the thought of us being together again, and for once I listened to Mini Amanda in my ear and deleted his text and number. This was a new start, a new me, and it wasn't even Monday. No more being a doormat. I jumped up from the sofa and headed into the kitchen to seek out the wine Amanda had given me as a moving-in present. Before I could change my mind, I bolted out of the house, strode purposefully across the road and banged loudly on the door, my heart beating in time with my humming. The door swung open and a short stocky woman of indeterminate age with long black hair stood there smiling like the Cheshire Cat. Like Francesca, she was wearing a kaftan but hers was canary yellow with red poppies embroidered round the V-shaped neckline. She looked like something out of a Beatles documentary with her centre parting and John Lennon glasses. I glanced down at her feet and almost laughed out loud at her leopard-print Crocs with brown fake-fur trim. I'd obviously missed the memo about the fancy dress.

'Ah, welcome! You must be our new neighbour, Alison,' she growled in a *Carry On* film manner while lasciviously eyeing me up and down, setting off my gaydar. 'Come this way, everyone's *dying* to meet you!'

I followed her into the back of the house where a whole crowd was gathered, disco lights flashed and the Spice Girls blasted out of some massive speakers on the floor next to a life-size model gorilla wearing a white trilby. One wall was covered with a monochrome pattern of pole-dancing girls and the other walls were splattered with gilt-framed art works of various naked women. Had I gatecrashed the Moulin Rouge? If this was just 'drinks', I was interested to know what lengths of madness a proper party stretched to. The rumours on the East Dulwich Forum weren't exaggerated after all...

'Everyone, this is Alison! Alison, this is everyone!'

I woke face down in bed, my lips stuck together with dried spit. Pulling them apart was like ripping off a two-day-old plaster. I had no idea where I was but a pneumatic drill was pounding in my temples. *What had happened?* I turned to face the ceiling, still clueless about my surroundings. Then I remembered I'd just moved; no wonder I was confused... though I didn't recognise any of the black lacquered bedroom furniture, or the purple satin duvet cover. I peeped to my right and almost had a heart attack. Also face down on the bed was Jo, still in her garish kaftan, her hair all over the place, one Croc on, one Croc off. Oh, Cunty Mcfuckflaps. Bad Ali must have escaped from her box...

6

Welcome to the Jungle

I was too scared to move in case Sleeping Beauty woke up – I could hear her softly snoring. I swiftly hatched an escape plan to creep out before anyone saw me and to dive into my own house undetected. Unfortunately, before I could move, something licked my foot and I started to scream... Jo forcefully jumped up sideways and fell awkwardly off the bed, her kaftan riding up, exposing her pasty bare bum as she landed in a heap on the floor.

'What the fuck was that?' she yelled. I remembered now she had a very deep voice. She pulled herself up to standing, which wasn't that much higher than the bed because she was so short, and flicked her hair out of her face, revealing rosacea-spattered cheeks and bee-stung lips. I bit my own lips, searching for any kind of residual snogging evidence but surely I would have remembered an illicit lesbian encounter?

'A thing licked my foot.'

'Oh, that'll be Bert.'

I turned round and sat up on the edge of the bed to find a slug-grey pug dog squatting there, wagging its stumpy tail and making snuffling noises through its squashed nose. I hoisted up my foot and wondered where my shoes were. The door nudged itself open and two more creatures casually waddled in, another pug-like thing and a portly brown sausage dog the size of a generous leather clutch bag. They began barking at Bert, who joined in the animated chorus.

'Boys, stop!' Jo bellowed. Surprisingly they obeyed. 'They're hungry. Come on, let's go downstairs.'

'Where are my shoes?' I asked.

'You took them off when we did the limbo.' A hazy cringe-worthy flashback taunted me. 'They'll be around somewhere unless one of the boys has eaten them. Let's go.' Jo had a certain drill sergeant manner that made you automatically step in line.

Her kitchen was at the front of the house overlooking the street and every surface was carpeted with empty bottles, lipstick-smeared glasses, scrunched-up crisp packets and half-eaten pizzas still in their grease-stained takeaway boxes, the crusts curling up to meet the congealed pepperoni topping. The evening swam back to me from the recesses of my memory and I recalled the pizza delivery boy being enticed inside for a beer. He had looked terrified. I half-heartedly began clearing up.

'Stop that! I'll do it later. Sit down. I'm just going to feed the boys.' Two tabby cats wound themselves round my legs, making me jump. This place was like a zoo. Jo pulled out a sack of food from a cupboard and shovelled kibble into five bowls on the floor up against the neon-orange back wall where a preposterously bombastic giant canvas of her face in the style of Andy Warhol hung. The dogs started fighting over who got there first and the cats hung back, their tails tickling my arm as I sat at the small round kitchen table. The air smelled of nauseating pet food and stale beer as Jo started pouring the remaining contents of open drinks cans down the plughole.

'What would you like for breakfast?' she asked, scratching her head and squinting at me.

'Oh, don't worry about me. I'll eat at home.' How could she stand the smell?

'Don't be silly. All your stuff's in boxes. I'll make you something. Scrambled eggs? Bacon? I'll get some coffee on the go.'

'Can I just have a glass of water, and maybe some eggs, please? I can help.'

'Noooo! Sit down. You're a guest. What time did you say your little girl was being dropped off?'

'At five.'

'Well, we've got all day then!' And she winked at me, setting my cheeks alight. I wanted to jump up and run, and she burst out laughing. 'I'm messing with you! Did you think we had sex or something?'

'I, er, no, of course not.'

'Your face was a picture, though. I wouldn't take advantage of you passed out. I prefer my partners to be conscious and willing. I'm attached, anyway, not that it's ever stopped me before!' She cackled away to herself and I wondered who on earth would be brave enough to go out with her.

'Why was I in your bed then?' I asked dubiously, knowing I wouldn't have climbed in voluntarily, even in desperate circumstances.

'Francesca and I carried you up there after you tried the shisha pipe. You went all funny and asked if you could lie down. My lodgers are in all the other rooms so I couldn't put you in one of their beds.'

'You have lodgers?'

'Yes, they're all students – you know the type, vampires. I hardly ever see them. They're still asleep recovering. So who's Ifan?'

'How do you know about him?' I asked suspiciously.

'You were calling him a cunt when we carried you up the stairs.'

'He's my ex-boyfriend and the reason I came out last night.' I told Jo about the text, hoping to hammer it home that some lesbian loving wasn't on the cards.

'I trust you're going to ignore him? What a tit. Do you have any idea what he wants to talk to you about?' I shook my head. 'Well, you're safe in the Mews. No one can get in unless they know the code.'

'Hello, you up?' Francesca called through the door, which must have been left open.

'In the kitchen.'

'God, I feel rough. Oh, hello! How are *you* feeling?' She laughed in a knowing manner, which set my teeth on edge.

'I'm OK. My head is sore but I'll live. I have to unpack everything today before Grace gets back.'

'Do you want me to rally the troops? I can get a team together and we can blitz the place for you.'

'No, I'm fine. Look, I think I am going to go. I do need to get on. I'm really sorry about crashing in your bed. Thank you for looking after me.'

'At least you got to meet everyone. Well, apart from Nick the Spy. He never comes to anything.' Francesca helped herself to the only clean mug in the cupboard and started making tea.

'I don't remember everyone's names. Is he really a spy?'

'*We* think he is. He just about says hello, miserable northern bugger,' Jo said, briskly whisking eggs in a glass bowl by the hob. 'He's lived here for three years and has never come to anything apart from some Christmas drinks when he first moved in. We see an older lady every now and then get in or out of his car, but no one else ever visits. He's a real loner. Geeky-looking, too. Old busy-body Norman frequently tries to muscle his way into Nick's house, says there's a funny smell, but Nick always shuts the door in his face.'

'Maybe he just wants some privacy,' I offered up, spotting one of my red ballet pumps on the floor by the fridge, covered in slobber.

'Well, he moved to the wrong place if that's what he wanted!' Jo roared, and Francesca joined in. I could feel a sweat break out on my top lip and I wanted to lie down in the dark. I abruptly stood up, knocking one of the cats out of the way.

'I'm sorry, I really must go. Thanks so much for having me. I'll just take this shoe, and if you see the other one, let me know!'

'So what happened at the party?' Jacqui asked on Monday when she Skyped me to see how the move had gone. I'd propped my laptop up on the breakfast bar and given her a virtual tour of downstairs but sadly the Wi-Fi signal couldn't stretch to a show-and-tell upstairs. I had managed to unpack pretty much everything and the place already felt like home. Something about it felt very different from the other flat. Maybe because it was an actual house with a front door and a garden, or maybe it was because on Sunday afternoon, Elinor had knocked on my inside front door.

'Have you recovered?' she'd asked, hovering in our shared hallway like a concerned mum.

'Yes, I'm fine, just a bit embarrassed. Tea and flapjacks helped. Thanks for those! Do you want to come in?'

'No, dear, I'm just making sure you're OK. I know these parties can take some getting used to, but everyone has a heart of gold and no one judges. Well, *we* don't. I can't say I speak for Nosy Norman.' She giggled. 'When I moved here fourteen years ago after my divorce, this place saved me. People all have their own dramas, but nothing is ever too much trouble for the rest of us, so if you need something, do let us know. I look forward to meeting Grace properly. Maybe Princess and Tinkerbell can be her friends.'

I vainly pressed down giggles, holding my core rigid. *Princess and Tinkerbell?* They must be her granddaughters.

'I know,' she said, reading my mind. 'Ridiculous names. Karen, my daughter, let them choose their own names once they were old enough. I'll tell you another time. Just glad you're OK...'

'So you passed out at the party and ended up in bed with the village lesbian?' Jacqui laughed. 'Who else did you meet?'

'I can't remember names, apart from Carl, my other next-door neighbour. He's a photographer. I don't remember much after the shisha pipe.'

'Jesus. So you made an impression then?'

'Yeah, I think Jo fancied me, which is awkward, and I think Francesca thinks I shagged her.'

'It's not like you to cause any drama, is it?'

I pulled a funny face at her.

'So you like it? How's Grace?'

'She wouldn't sleep in her bed last night but she was OK this morning going to school. I was expecting some kind of resistance. First impressions are good, though, I think. It reminds me of the road I grew up in with my parents back in the eighties or living in halls at university. The goldfish-bowl lifestyle will take some getting used to but you know me, I hate being on my own, so I will slot right in.'

My phone pinged with a text from an unknown number and butterflies flitted around my guts at the mere thought of it being Ifan. I hated that he still had a hold over me.

'What's up?' Jacqui asked, my face evidently betraying me. She was drinking wine while I was sipping a cup of herbal tea. The time difference always made catching up tricky – we had to be so organised.

'Ifan keeps texting me. I've deleted his number.'

'Block him then. He won't be able to get through at all.' I conceded it was the sensible option, but somehow

I couldn't bear to do it. It felt too final. And yes, YES, I *knew* it was over, and he'd been a total dick, and I was better off without him, yadda yadda, yadda, but try telling that to my heart. My phone pinged again. I was itching to check, but I knew I couldn't as Jacqui would notice.

'Just read it! I know you want to. I won't tell Amanda!'

I laughed. We both knew what a militant hard nut Amanda was for stuff like this.

Please ring me. I need to talk to you ASAP.

Then:

If you don't ring me I'm going to throw myself under a bus.

'He's threatening to kill himself if I don't ring him.' I shook my head in disbelief. He was always so histrionic. The sneaky flame of hope flickered once more. Maybe he was really truly sorry and would never ever EVER treat anyone like that again. Maybe he was going to grovel, tell me he had landed a major contract with Models 1 and was ready to make a serious commitment to us. *Maybe* he had turned over a new leaf and realised he couldn't live without me.

'Let him!'

'That's so mean.'

'Not really. Of course he isn't going to kill himself. He's just saying that to get your attention. People who say they're going to do it never do. The quiet ones who just go off and do it are the ones to watch out for.'

My phone started ringing.

'Don't answer it.'

'But what if he's got something to tell me, something important?'

'Like the fact he's really married with three children and lives in St Albans at the weekends?'

The ringing stopped, only to resume a second later. I answered.

'Hello? Ali?'

'What do you want!' I hissed. 'I told you to stay away.'

'I am staying away.'

Jacqui pursed her lips in the frame of the laptop screen. I turned away so she couldn't see me. It felt too rude to just walk off.

'Why did you threaten to throw yourself under a bus?'

'To make you answer the phone.'

Fucker.

'Look, I'm really sorry to do this to you, but I have to tell you something.' My stomach tied itself into a calcified knot, hope timidly flying a flag above it. 'I have chlamydia and I think you should get yourself tested.'

7

First Big Drama

'Oh my God, what a total wanker!' Jacqui cried when I burst into tears after flinging my phone on the sofa in total disgust. 'Stay calm, it isn't as hideous as you think.'

'What do you mean, it isn't as hideous? It's gross! I have a disgusting disease, all because he couldn't keep his Welsh cock in his Calvins.'

'Come on, it's way more common than you think. It's just that no one talks about it.'

'No it isn't. I don't know anyone who's had anything, ever!'

Jacqui remained emphatically silent, picked up her wine and started sipping it in a lady-like manner, her little finger jutting out like she was taking afternoon tea.

'Jacqui, have *you* had it?'

She raised her eyebrows at me while she swallowed and slowly nodded.

'Oh, dear Lord, really? When? Why didn't you tell us?'

She sighed, blowing her lips out. 'Because I felt embarrassed. It was during the Single Mums' Mansion madness when we went out all the time and had hideous one-night stands.'

'Oh God, yes, well, my mad years are still going on. Shit – what happened?'

'I had antibiotics and was fine. You will be too. You'll have to get tested for everything, though, just in case. Ifan was off having threesomes so you have no idea what went on.'

'I wonder if he's told Mary and Sandeep to get tested.' Rancorous thoughts of poetic justice flashed across my mind; then I remembered we were all in the same infected boat.

'Who knows? Maybe you'll see them at the clinic.'

'No way! I'm not going there.'

'Shut up. Yes you are. It's all anonymous.' I looked at Jacqui's wholesome face framed in my screen like one of Harry Potter's moving photographs with her perfect blond ponytail, the picture of vitality. I couldn't ever imagine her in a seedy clap clinic weeing into a test tube. Yoga teachers weren't supposed to be like that, were they? 'Just go! It'll be over sooner than you think. They send your results in the post a week later. Or you can order tests online that send you back results with a prescription. Just do it!'

Ten days later, I heard Elinor slip the post under my front door as I walked down the stairs. I knew what it was the minute I saw it poking out amongst the flimsy flyers from Lidl and Morrisons, advertising glistening Easter roasts, giant Cadbury chocolate eggs and bargain booze for that family get-together. I ripped it open and there it was: I had tested positive for chlamydia. Cunty McFucksticks. I didn't want to go to the doctor because only psychics seemed able to make GP appointments these days – you have to know precisely when you're going to be ill a month before you are since the hypochondriacs have it all sewn up and ring the second the phones go live at eight a.m. However, the real reason was I felt so ashamed and I couldn't face telling the doctor. I wished I could ask Jacqui what to do but she was asleep. Instead I typed in my question on the all-knowing oracle that was Google and, after filling out an extensive form on Superdrug's website, my antibiotics arrived in the post a few days later. What was so preposterous was I had no symptoms and could have gone on for the rest of my life not knowing I was infected. So for that, I *should* have been grateful Twat Face phoned me at all. But of course, this is me – spitting rage still coursed through me alongside the antibiotics. I prayed for Ifan to rot in hell while his knob gradually turned gangrenous and caused him endless agonising pain. No one got the clap in the movie of their life.

A few days later I kissed Ursula goodbye outside the East Dulwich Tavern on Good Friday evening, delighted at my restraint in having only one bottle of wine. We'd been celebrating the end of my course of antibiotics. I walked up to the bus stop, passing The Bishop, which was still busy, windows steamed up and the hypnotic throb of a tuneless bass leaking out into the chilly air every time the bouncer opened the door.

I spotted him instantly. He was sitting next to a girl on the benches outside where the smokers congregated and I could see he was holding her hand. As if in slow motion I watched him bring her hand up to his lips and he nibbled her knuckles gently. She looked to be in her twenties with a heart-shaped face and that gamine look that I knew floated his boat. Ifan was grandstanding his best seduction techniques, the same ones he'd used on me that night we first met. Blind fury erupted in a seismic explosion behind my eyes, sending out sparks throughout my entire body, making it jerk involuntarily. I had to stop walking in order to take a breath. Not even the *Black Beauty* soundtrack playing in my head could have saved me as Bad Ali burst forth out of her box.

He was still living his life like nothing had happened. I walked over to the bench, clenching and unclenching my hands into vengeful fists, a frenetic desire to wound pumping through my veins. Mini Amanda sang urgently in my ear: *Walk on by.*

'I'd be careful if I were you. Ifan has chlamydia. He gave it to me – I've just finished my antibiotics, but who knows if he took any. He also likes threesomes with men *and* women.' My voice crackled, thickly woven with adrenalin, the words tripping over each other.

'What? Fuck off, you nutter!' Ifan cried angrily.

The girl's stricken eyes widened in alarm as she stared at me.

'I'm not the nutter,' I growled. 'You ruined my life, lied, cheated, and now you'll do it all over again. Stay away from him, he's nasty and he's dirty.'

'You're a fucking psycho!' he yelled.

The bouncer poked his shaved dome out from the pub doorway; it was time to leave. Lordship Lane was open ground, rendering me vulnerable like an antelope cruising the African plain. I stepped stealthily into a side road, hiding in a dark alleyway between the pub and a house. Just as I did, Ifan whipped past the end of the road, frantically looking left and right. I was shaking now and had to clamp my jaws together to stop my teeth from rattling in my skull. He walked past a few minutes later, half venturing towards my bolthole, then gave up and presumably returned to the pub.

I remained in the shadows until my breathing had stabilised and the shakes had abated. When I ventured out into the street, I clapped eyes on a familiar bike locked up to the nearest lamppost. The yellow light cascaded down onto its battered seat, also revealing the half perished rubber on the right handlebar. Without thinking, I marched over, double checked, then thumbed the well-known numbers into order: 5677, and the lock split apart, releasing the bike into my thieving hands. I swung my leg over, lifted my bum onto the seat, my feet straining to reach the pavement. I pushed off and peddled along the backstreets towards my house.

When I neared the Mews main entrance, I decided to turn back towards Lordship Lane, by the row of shops, and abandon the bike there. I'd had thoughts of smashing it, but that felt too destructive, and it was better that somebody benefited from Ifan's misfortune.

The rage had evaporated by now; the cycle had exhausted it. All I was left with was overwhelming sadness. How had I got here, wreaking revenge when all I actually wanted was a loving relationship with someone wishing the same? Stealing the bike hadn't actually changed anything. I was well aware navel-gazing wasn't one of my strong points. Sometimes it set me apart from Amanda and Jacqui, who were great believers in all that introspection stuff. I would nod along when they went all zen and talked about letting things go and accepting the feelings as they came up, but I was different. I struggled to find quiet time peaceful. 'Keep busy' was my constant motto, deflect, distract, the complete opposite of what Amanda would do. 'Sit in the pain,' she always said. 'Just be with it because you will learn from it.' All I had learned from this was that I now felt like a twat, Ifan was still an arsehole, and that as well as being angry, I had also been insanely jealous at the sight of him kissing someone else. I knew it made no sense, but nothing about this did. Maybe the acceptance I needed was that I would never be like Amanda, able to be at one with all that shit. Even now, I felt I could still murder Jim on occasion if I really thought about it, which I tried so hard not to. Maybe my 'progress' with this break-up would be that in a year's time I wouldn't want to punch Ifan if we bumped into each other.

I dumped the bike on the corner by a tapas restaurant and walked up towards the dodgy fish-and-chip shop and the twenty-four-hour store that stocked everything you could possibly need during a zombie apocalypse or a party. Wine of the week was a constant highlight, usually something Romanian that doubled up as limescale remover. I spotted Francesca walking out of the convenience store with a bottle of said red wine and she waved.

'So, you've been in hiding since you moved in,' she commented as a way of greeting. I fell in with her stride as we idled up through the dark alleyway down the side of Terry's Tool Hire to the Mews' secret gate. *How long until Ifan discovered my theft?*

'Yes. I've had a shit couple of weeks, to be honest, and didn't feel like being sociable.'

'You're coming to my Easter Sunday lunch with Grace, though, aren't you?'

I nodded as I tapped in the code. We pushed through the gate and both of us could hear frantic banging and shouting.

'Shit, that sounds like Betsy,' Francesca said. 'Come on.' She began to run past the Biffa bins and towards my house, where a young woman was hammering on our joint front door.

'Elinor! Elinor!'

'Betsy, what is it?' Francesca shouted, reaching her just before I did.

'Something's wrong with Carl. He's having a fit.'

'Call an ambulance!' Francesca ordered me. 'Now!' She rushed into the house next door where light flooded out onto the drive from the shared hallway.

I rang 999 and asked for an ambulance but had no idea what I was telling them.

'It's a man in his forties. He's had some kind of fit and is very unwell.'

'Is he conscious?' I ran in through the door to find Carl lying on his back in the middle of the dimly lit living room with Francesca talking to him in a low voice. He seemed completely disorientated and very twitchy. His usually black skin was a worrying grey colour.

'He is but he's very confused.' I gave the address. 'The ambulance is on its way. I'm going to wait by the gate and open it.'

'Can you knock on Jo's door when you go past? Elinor must be fast asleep with her earplugs in. You can't wake her once she's gone. Always good when you're having parties, not so good in emergencies.'

I rang Jo's doorbell four times before she opened it.

'Hello, decided I'm the one for you after all?' she smiled easily in her blue and red stripy pyjama bottoms and pink T-shirt.

'Carl has had some kind of seizure; I'm just going to wait by the gate to let the ambulance in.'

'Oh fuck. OK. Is he breathing, awake?' She dived into her hallway and pulled out what must have been her dog-walking coat. It was as unsavoury as Amanda's ancient parka, and had the added attraction of a string of poop bags hanging out of one of the pockets. She pulled the door to as she rammed her feet into her beloved furry Crocs.

'He must have tried to stop drinking again. When's he going to learn? You can't go cold turkey.' By the time I got to the gate I could hear the sirens from Lordship Lane. I pressed my fob key and the gates slowly swung open as the ambulance cut the siren, turning into the drive.

I jogged behind the flashing lights as the ambulance cruised up to Carl's house. Bloody hell, trust me to be living next door to an alcoholic. When I'd met him at Jo's party he had seemed fine, but then I had been pissed and passed out. Christ, even Hunter S. Thompson would have seemed sober to me that night.

When I reached the house, the paramedics were urgently striding inside. There was lots of shouting and I heard one of them order Carl not to hit. I wanted to walk away: this was nothing to do with me. *He's your neighbour*, Mini Amanda hissed in my ear. *How can you think that?*

'What's going on?' a rich baritone voice asked. I turned round and an older gentleman in black thick-framed specs was standing behind me wrapped up in a red silk robe, his cropped Afro hair white at the temples. Right now, my grotty mouldy flat in Minge seemed preferable to this circus. At least I only had to contend with Mr Watson the Grinch.

'Carl has had a seizure.'

'Oh, not another one. He's obviously stopped drinking after a binge.'

'I have no idea. I've only just moved in.'

'I'm Norman. The lights woke me up.' Oh, so this was *Nosy* Norman...

'Hello, I'm Alison.'

'I know. You passed out at the party and stayed the night with Jo.' He looked at me intently like he was trying to gauge my reaction to the laying down of the gossip gauntlet. I couldn't be arsed. After the initial hit of adrenalin had abandoned my body, a wave of exhaustion swamped me, most probably fuelled by the bottle of wine I'd drunk earlier.

A flurry of activity jolted me out of my stupor as paramedics rushed back to the ambulance to fetch the stretcher and oxygen. Shortly after, Carl was carried out, a mask covering his face. I turned away so that I wouldn't catch his eye and be seen rubbernecking.

'I'll go with Betsy in the ambulance,' Jo offered to Francesca as they followed him out, Jo's arm round Betsy's tiny waist. 'I think we need a meeting to talk about an intervention.'

Betsy looked like she had been crying. She seemed so young, somewhere in her mid-twenties, too young to be dealing with this melodrama.

Francesca stopped next to me and we watched them climb in after Carl. I waited to see what the unspoken protocol was, if I would be judged on my clear desperation to escape as I yawned my head off.

'Just go to bed, Ali. We'll get you up to speed on Sunday.'

'Gosh, don't worry about it – it's none of my business. I hope he's OK.'

'Yeah, me too. I'll see you on Sunday.' She leaned over and gave me a kiss on the cheek. I caught a waft of patchouli oil. Norman just raised his eyebrows and nodded at me.

I shut the door in relief and flopped on the sofa, making sure the curtains were closed first. I'd loved living in the Single Mums' Mansion, but we never told each other what to do if we went off the deep end. Apart from when Amanda wouldn't let me key Jim's car, but that was different – I did it anyway! None of us had ever staged an intervention. Mind you, none of us was a raging alcoholic. But you can't force someone to stay sober. That has to be their choice, their decision, or it won't work… Bloody hell, maybe the Mews was *The Stepford Wives* after all.

8

Francesca

Francesca stared into space, her Yogi tea going cold on the kitchen work surface. One of those hybrid people carriers that were all the rage now pulled up further down outside. She leaned over the sink and craned her neck to peer through the window where she saw the car had stopped outside Elinor and Ali's house. A man jumped out of the driver's side, then walked round to slide the door open and Grace, Ali's daughter, climbed out clutching a rucksack. So this must be Ali's ex-husband, baby daddy, or whatever they called them these days. Francesca studied his face before he disappeared from sight and she could tell just from looking at him that he wasn't one of the good guys, but she thought she would check just to make sure.

Becoming still and unfocusing her eyes as the man grabbed another bag from the back of the car, Francesca zoned out of everyday vision, rather like gazing at one of those Magic Eye pictures popular in the nineties. She instantly picked up his residual anger as well as a sneaky secret he was hiding and something that was troubling him. Oh well, Ali wasn't with him any more, which was just as well...

Francesca had always had 'The Gift', as it became known later on in her life, and she'd learned to channel it properly once she began her own healing journey. She often speculated as to whether she'd inherited it from her birth mother. Mum had always been cagey about it, saying she had no idea, but Francesca could ask her if she ever decided to seek her out. She had followed the clues as soon as she'd turned eighteen but came up against the brick wall of a death certificate. With no one else in the chain – her real father had not been named – her story stopped there. Her mother had no more children, never married and had been listed as an office manager for the Hastings Fire Service. Even though Francesca loved her adoptive parents, the discovery had left her feeling rootless, with a burning need to search for some kind of meaning in life...

She turned from the window and surveyed the kitchen behind her. Every available counter was covered in food prep for the party. The chopping board was buried under a pile of sliced onions, which had triggered a fair few tears, and the stove housed the giant pot of chilli that was gently releasing intermittent bubbles from its steaming surface like molten lava. She just needed to finish making the Spanish omelette, the pasta salad and the rice. Her phone made a sound like a clown's horn, heralding a message.

Are you wearing any knickers?

She smiled and looked up before she texted back. She could hear Ian upstairs bringing down extra chairs for guests from one of the bedrooms.

Not today. Easy access.

Ironically, her knickers were actually uncomfortably wedged in her bum crack and she unpicked them through her leggings.

I think I might explode.

Don't do that, you'll make a mess.

'Have you made brownies?' Ariel asked. 'I told the others you were going to.'

'Yes, I made them last night. They're already on the table. And no, you can't have one yet. They're for later.'

You can clean me up.

'What about the French stick? Can I have a bit? I'm starving.'

I'm good at cleaning up dirty things.

'Yes, I got loads of them. Get a plate, though – the crumbs go everywhere. I would at least like to start off without the house looking like it's been ransacked.' Too late for that, she thought. The house always looked like it had been ransacked. Her phone honked again.

Good, today I feel very dirty.

Francesca laughed. She had way too much to do and she wasn't in the mood for sexting.

I'm busy, you'll have to finish yourself off. Speak soon x

'You in?' Jo called through the letterbox as Francesca decided to check on the bacon and leek quiche in the oven.

'Tia, let her in, will you?' she called through to her other daughter in the living room while Ariel was busy sawing off a chunk of bread, flakes of hard crust ricocheting in all directions from the bread board and landing mostly on the floor.

'All set, are we?' Jo thundered as she wandered into the kitchen. 'I just saw Alison's ex arrive. He looked like a right twat with his skinny jeans and polo-neck jumper. Why do you straight women always go for such unremarkable men who look like they would snap if you sat on them?'

Francesca turned round and widened her eyes at Jo, who, in relay, turned round to find Ian behind her with two fold-up chairs in each hand.

'Ah, Ian. How is the man of the house?' Jo pulled a face at Francesca.

'OK, Jo. How are you?' he said in a quiet voice that, even after twenty-odd years, Francesca sometimes still couldn't decipher.

'All good here.'

Ariel had disappeared up to her bedroom, taking her crusty bread with her, no doubt casting even more crumbs than Hansel and Gretel.

Ian pushed the back door with his foot and disappeared outside with the chairs.

'I like Alison. I think it's good she moved in next door to Carl. He needs someone like her.'

'You don't even know her,' Francesca said, used to Jo's snap decisions about people. 'She could be Keyser Söze, for all you know.'

'Nope, I can tell she's one of the good ones. She's been around the block. I'm going to see if she'll be a part of the AA tag team.'

'Give her a moment – she's only just moved in and she's got her own shit to deal with.'

'You spotted something? A grungy aura again?'

'Let her settle in and make some friends. It's hard being a single mum, and she's split with someone recently, which has left her vulnerable.'

'Well, this is the right place for her then!' Jo clapped her hands together. 'What can I have for breakfast?'

Just before people arrived, Ian tried to snake his arms around Francesca's waist while she was tossing the green salad, her back to him.

'Don't,' she hissed, flinching. If she'd been a hedgehog, her prickles would have whipped up a wind that ruffled his hair.

'I'm trying,' he said, dropping his arms limply.

'I don't want you to. I said to you before, there's no point.'

'Then what *are* we doing?'

She turned round, the salad servers in her hands, glistening from the oily dressing.

'You know what we're doing,' she said in a low voice so the girls wouldn't hear. 'I know why the caged bird sings.' Fuck my life, she thought, turning her attention back to the salad. How did I get here, fifty-two with nothing to my name?

Francesca had had big dreams when she'd arrived in London twenty-eight years ago. She'd just finished a summer season in Malaga, dancing and singing in the clubs with a brilliant bunch of girls. But it had been harder to get regular work like that in London, it had been so competitive. She'd come home because she'd broken up with Adrian, her first proper boyfriend. She'd wanted further qualifications after escaping to sea when she was eighteen in pursuit of something she hadn't been able to find. She'd been entertainment crew on a cruise liner, ten different Mediterranean ports in two weeks for three years. Oh, some of the antics she'd got up to. She was sure she had a book in her. She'd found her sea legs pretty quick; it was when she got back on land that everything felt wobbly.

After a secretarial course at South Thames College, Francesca found a job working at the *Stage*, the newspaper for the entertainment industry. It was the next best thing to actually dancing on the stage. She still felt a connection to that world. She'd loved the crazy hectic analogue mess of the place. She supposed now everything was online. She wondered when someone had last dictated their press release over the phone because the fax machine had broken down. Various other jobs had followed until she'd answered an advert for a PA at a local property company in East Dulwich, where she was now living, with Lizzie from the cruise liner. The money was a bit more than she was used to, and she could walk to work. When Ian had greeted her at the door of the cramped office above the bookmakers, she'd thought he was cute, and could instantly tell he fancied her. She didn't know what to do if he offered her the job. Well, she'd thought at the time, he may never act on it. We'll cross that bridge when we come to it...

'You can leave any time you like,' Ian said in the kitchen as she added more dressing to the salad. 'You know that.'

Francesca shook her head. It was a repeat of the same conversation they'd been having for the last year. She knew if she left it would most likely mean having to leave the girls too. They were her only living blood relatives, her real family, the loves of her life. She had been looking for them since she was eighteen. She wasn't about to give them up. She just needed a better plan.

Her phone honked.

Hey, I wish I was at the party later. I'd follow you into the bathroom and scrub you down.

She pressed delete. If only she could push a button in real life to erase all the crap.

9

Intervention

'Mummy, what's a sustitute?' Grace asked, unpacking her Barbies as Jim drove off, his mood decidedly dark.

'What do you mean, Gracey?'

'Well, Daddy and Hattie were shouting and she said she didn't want a baby sustitute.'

Time for me to act nonchalant and find out a little more...

'A *substitute* would be when you really want Ken to play with Beach Babylon Barbie, but you can only find Horse Riding Barbie, so you use her to take Ken's place. She's the substitute.' Grace looked at her Barbies and then at me.

'It's not the real thing then?'

I shook my head.

'Oh, so Hattie wants a *real* baby?'

'It would seem so.'

Grace nodded slowly. 'They shout a lot, Mummy.'

I stapled my lips together to prevent an evil smirk. Trouble in Paradise...

'Hello, I'm Debbie, I live next door to Francesca, and we met a few weeks ago at Jo's. This is Samantha.' I recognised them as the college professor going through a divorce and the TV agent – Francesca had given me a quick run-down on all the neighbours earlier. I was lingering by the food table, which was topped with so many culinary masterpieces I was worried I'd suffer buyer's regret and overload on the wrong things.

'Hi.'

'I believe you got caught up in the drama with Carl on Good Friday?' Debbie, the college professor, asked me in her soft Scottish accent. She was sipping a large glass of red wine and I admired her luxurious wavy shoulder-length blond hair.

Debbie's much coveted hair complemented her biker-chic outfit of skinny black jeans and crisp white shirt with a well-worn cropped black leather jacket. She appeared to be in her late forties and I inspected for signs of 'work'. It was unfortunately a bad habit I had picked up working in the fashion industry where ageing sometimes felt like a crime, and a nip and a tuck and a 'little helping hand' were all considered as normal as shaving your legs. I'd seen so many bad filler pillow faces, botched lifts and frozen shiny expressions that I could have made a horror film trailer to be shown in schools to prevent young girls asking for Botox as a sixteenth birthday present. So far I hadn't succumbed and was staving off the inevitable until the last possible moment. However, Debbie appeared unfilled and genuine.

'I didn't hear anything,' she added, I hoped not clocking my critical stare.

'I was away at my parents', so missed the entire thing,' Samantha joined in. 'I've seen it all before, though.' I was trying to work out her age too but it was tricky. She was one of those women who could have easily glided between late forties to late fifties. Her baby-smooth skin was most likely the result of winning the genetic lottery rather than Botox.

'Where is Carl now?' I asked. I hadn't seen him since Friday's ambulance had spirited him away.

'Jo said he was in hospital overnight, then he went to stay with his parents in Kent,' Debbie offered. 'It's such a shame, so sad. I guess we'll all have to keep an eye out now.'

'I have a client who needs some fashion advice,' Samantha said, abruptly changing tack. 'Are you around for a chat this week?'

'Wow, er, yes, of course. I'm free Friday...' Before she could answer, I felt someone blow in my ear – it was Jo standing on her tiptoes, dressed in another memorable ensemble of neon-pink T-shirt dotted with black flamingos and knee-length silver shorts. Instead of the Crocs, she was wearing black suede crepe shoes and pink towelling socks, like an extra from *Grease*.

'Wow, your, er, outfit is rather special,' I said, in awe of her nuttiness.

'Thanks, I aim to please. Can I steer you over here for a moment? We need to have a quick chat. Excuse us, ladies.' She guided me by the elbow and took me out to the back garden where a few more people I hadn't seen before were gathered further up the lawn. Francesca sat wrapped in a black poncho on a deck chair by a rusty lit brazier that was belting out some serious heat. Elinor sat next to her, a grey furry throw draped round her shoulders. Her granddaughters were playing with Grace in the living room, and Grace was in seventh heaven bossing them about.

'Carl returns tomorrow and I really want to talk to him about facing this and committing to AA. We've all been here before when he promises to stay clean and then binges, then he stops too suddenly, then has a seizure, some worse than others.'

'Can I just say something?' I asked, putting my hand up like I was at school. 'Why am I here? I don't know Carl.'

'You're his nearest neighbour.'

'I'm not, he has the two guys next door who share the hallway.'

'They keep themselves to themselves.'

I wondered if they had forcibly opted out of the Mews co-operative to keep themselves safe from scrutiny.

'OK, but I still don't see what this has to do with me. I have no idea what's going on.' And I genuinely didn't want to. My own life was enough of a car crash at that moment. I didn't feel I was in any place to help someone stay sober when my own relationship with alcohol was so shady.

'That's why we're having this chat, to fill you in,' Jo insisted, picking up her beer from the damp grass and draining it. 'I like you; you've been around the block. Carl needs people like you on his side.' In a normal version of my life, I would have just got up and walked away, but something indefinable was keeping me rooted to the spot. I felt obliged and I had no idea why.

'Just to get you up to speed, Carl is my best friend. I've known him since we were kids. His wife died four years ago – he's never really got over it. I know *I* still feel terrible about it so fuck knows how he feels. Well, I think we *all* know how he feels – horrific, which is why he drinks to block it out. Anyway, he lives here now after I managed to secure the house for him. I wanted him to be surrounded by good people. I thought it might help.'

The energy it took to live your own life was immense, but living and organising everyone else's like a sergeant major must be draining.

'So his drinking has slid downhill in the last year, work is drying up due to his addiction, his agency can't cover for him any more and pretty soon he's going to end up in the shitter.'

'Maybe he wants to,' I interjected. 'Sometimes that has to happen before you pick yourself up again.'

'We can't let him!' Jo barked like she was on the drill field.

'I think what Jo is trying to ask is, will you help?' Elinor asked me gently.

'I don't know what you want me to do. Hasn't he got a girlfriend? Can't she help?'

'Betsy?' Jo laughed hollowly. 'She's a child. If they haven't already broken up, they will soon, just like all the other ones. We need to sit him down and tell him we'll draw up a rota of who will go to AA meetings with him. He doesn't keep it up on his own.'

'You can't force someone to go,' I pointed out. I could feel my own capricious anxiety flare up at the thought of taking on someone else's life.

'We know that,' Francesca said. 'It will be more of a friendly suggestion, in a rota. He will probably keep drinking for a while because you can't stop suddenly when you drink like he does, so the advice is to carry on, but sooner or later the message has to get through.'

'I'll tell the others later. There's one most days so we should only have to go to one a week if we all chip in. We just all need to sit down with him tomorrow morning and let him know.'

I didn't want to get roped into an AA press gang. I just wanted to get on with my life with Grace. The mere thought of facing Carl and telling him what was going to happen made me break out in a cold sweat. What if he went crazy? I didn't say a word and decided to try not to get involved. But that could mean I might fall out with everyone after only just moving in. Argh, I hadn't signed up for this shit!

IO

Jo

Jo rubbed her eyes as she scrabbled around the kitchen drawer for the Nurofen. She'd had one too many beers, followed by red wine yesterday. Then she'd stayed late at Francesca's once most people had gone and started on the crème de menthe she'd found rammed at the back of Fran's odds-and-ends drinks cupboard in the living room. She never understood why people bought it – like drinking mouthwash. She laughed to herself and checked her phone. Carl had texted her. His mum was driving and they were five minutes away. That was two minutes ago.

Caro hadn't answered any of her texts yesterday. She had meant to come to the party but had texted at midday with some limp excuse about being double-booked. Jo blamed Caro for her stepping over the line with the crème de menthe. If she'd been there, Jo wouldn't have felt the need to stay out late and drown her sorrows. She'd ring her later and see if she was OK. Maybe take her out for dinner to that nice new Italian place in Dulwich Village. But knowing Caro, she would be busy, unless she needed her to put up a shelf. Were all relationships such hard work?

Jo heard the front door shut opposite at Elinor's. Ali was hurrying with Grace somewhere, leaving her car. Where was she off to? Jo had told her about the intervention. Ali glanced over her shoulder as she turned the corner at Fran's and Jo caught the furtive look on her face: she was escaping. Ooooh, Francesca had been right – it *was* too soon to get Ali on board with this. Francesca was usually spot-on with these things. She could read people; it was a real talent. She wondered if she had ever tried to read her. Not much to see. Maybe some sexy burlesque dancers and pug dogs doing the can-can inside her head.

Jo actually liked Ali. For one thing, she was right up her *Strasse* physically, but she was also fun, lively and had a great sense of style. To top it all, she could tell she was a team player, and Jo loved a team player, which was why she'd asked her to help with Carl. She'd like to see Carl settle down again, maybe have a family; she knew he was keen. She thought he might make more effort to stay sober if he had a reason, like a reliable girlfriend, not one of those models he kept chasing.

There was something about Ali that put Jo in mind of Janey, so she would bet that Carl already had a little crush on her. They would certainly make a handsome couple – imagine their baby! She'd keep an eye on them both and see if she could subtly push them together without their realising. She could drop a few hints to Carl, see how he felt once he'd been clean for a month.

Just as Jo pressed the plunger down on the coffee, Lorraine pulled up in her Datsun Sunny. She'd give them a minute then she'd pop over. She busied herself warming up the milk in the microwave, then poured everything into a mug, slipped on her furry Crocs and headed out. Lorraine opened the door.

'He's in here,' she said after she'd hugged Jo in the hallway. There was no chat of how Lorraine could tell this time it would definitely be the last. Jo knew they'd all been here too many times to expect anything. Carl was sitting on his sofa, looking like the twelve-year-old new boy he'd been on the first day of school in 1984. The day Jo had decided he was going to be her best friend. Jo had always collected people together, even at that age, but she had never managed to find someone she wanted as a partner in crime. Steve, her brother, had always tried too hard and, bless him, she'd let him think he was in that role, but he wasn't. The post had been vacant, until Carl. He'd possessed a certain magnetism that drew her in like a tractor beam. She loved him in a way that she knew wasn't sexual. It felt familial and always had. Their histories were so entwined that she couldn't imagine her life with him not in it. When the shit had hit the fan, something she never let herself think about, Carl had stepped up to the plate, taking on that brotherly role for real. She'd do anything to get him well.

'Oh, Carl, you gave us all a bloody fright.' Jo sat down next to him and gently touched his knee with hers.

'I'm sorry, Jo,' he said matter-of-factly. She could tell he'd said those words too many times now for them to have any meaning, so he kept it brief. 'Back to AA.'

'Ah, I'm glad to hear it. We'll all be here, you know that. In fact, a few of the others will be round in a minute to offer support.'

He looked at her then, unclenching his hands from his lap. 'Not the new girl?'

Jo inwardly sighed in relief: her instincts had been right. For a split second he looked like he did when he talked about his beloved Janey.

'No, Ali's not coming, don't worry.'

He nodded and relaxed his shoulders.

'Shall I get the kettle on?' Lorraine said brightly, changing the mood to one of efficiency. 'We'll need lots of mugs and I brought some chocolate Hobnobs and M&S cookies. Thought I'd splash out.' She chuckled to herself and clattered around in the kitchen, gathering everything she needed.

Jo smiled and sipped her coffee, suddenly transported back thirty years to one of the many times they'd waited for the rest of the gang to rock up and plan the next party. Lorraine had always been home and had handed out snacks and glasses of Soda Stream cola from her little kitchen, earwigging what they were getting up to.

There was a soft knock at the door, jolting Jo back to the present. No more parties for Carl for a while...

I I

Tinder

Hi, wondered if on the off chance Grace was free today. Was thinking of taking her to a breeder to look at puppies.

I'd ignored Jim's text when I was at Amanda's earlier, hiding from the intervention. However, traipsing back up the hill at lunchtime, Grace whinging because she wanted to stay with Meg and Isla, I checked it again. Fuck it, why not? I could have an afternoon to do some paperwork and not think about Ifan. But first I had to make it back into the Mews undetected. I walked round the long way and up through the secret gate, much to Grace's annoyance. Debbie was in front of her house tending to the terracotta pots and waved. I waved back, then noticed a car pull up outside Nick the Spy's house at the end of the block next to Nosy Norman in the cul-de-sac. A man jumped out and ran round to open the passenger door for an older lady, whom he helped out. I tried to get a better look at him, even though I was risking being discovered by Jo if I hung around on the doorstep. Just as I was about to turn away, he looked up and caught my eye. His thick-rimmed geek glasses were the first thing I noticed. His hair was hidden under a baseball cap and he wore a nineties throwback get-up: zipped-to-the-neck gunmetal-grey anorak and jeans. He could have been going to a rave. He didn't smile but I felt like I was receiving a once-over. I returned to fiddling with my key, trying to get it to turn silently so as not to alert Elinor. I swear I could feel eyes boring into the back of my head from Jo's kitchen window opposite.

As soon as we made it inside my doorbell rang almost immediately, making me jump. Fuck it, we'd been spotted. A creepy thought crossed my already paranoid mind: maybe Jo held a skeleton key for all the houses just in case of emergencies, and she was ringing to check before she used it. I poked my nose through the curtains to find Jim on the doorstep, and he waved when he noticed me.

'That was quick,' I said, looking around when I let him in.

'Well, these puppies are going to go like hot cakes if we don't make up our minds.'

'Isn't Hattie going with you?' I asked, stirring the pot.

'Er, no, she's busy. We'll surprise her!' Jim corralled Grace out of the door. 'See you later.'

A pin pricked my already withered inner balloon as the door shut behind them. I curled up on the sofa, wanting to stop feeling affected by everyone else carrying on with their lives. Seeing families in the park walking their hairy 'babies' (often facetiously called Judy or Dave) with their natty little neckerchiefs tugged at my own dashed dreams. I'd *been* one of those people. I'd walked round Dulwich Park with my burgeoning baby belly, Max lolloping across the grass to retrieve a slobbery stick, guessing he'd lick the new baby to death once she arrived. Max had since retired with Jim's mum in Southsea to chase seagulls. Now I had to watch as Grace got to pick her own puppy for her life with Jim, a life I knew very little about, and that bothered me more than I cared to admit.

I found it oddly upsetting that Grace met people I would never meet and spent time with her half-sister, Freya, who, after Jim left, had pretty much disappeared from my life overnight. I had adored Freya; she was my little shadow, coming everywhere with me when she stayed at ours. Our relationship had been rooted in friendship; I'd left the parenting up to Jim – I didn't want to be the wicked stepmother. I'd watched her grow from a gauche seven-year-old into a preteen girl who couldn't wait to meet her baby sister. Regretfully I never got to experience that part. At seventeen Freya was now approaching adulthood, and I had missed it all. I'd never witnessed her and Grace's day-to-day blossoming sibling friendship or showed her how to change a nappy or help Grace get dressed. At the time, I was buried so deep in grief that I hadn't immediately registered that a kind and earnest young girl with freckly cheeks had also left a huge gap in my life. It wasn't until I'd been on a catalogue shoot five months later that it hit me. I'd been styling a small twelve-year-old girl in an outfit Freya would have loved, and before I could stop myself, I said: 'You remind me so much of my stepdaughter. She'd love that skater-girl look.' As soon as the words had escaped, tears had started spouting and I'd had to run off to the toilet to sob silently in one of the cubicles.

Freya was my daughter's sister, but what was she to me any more? Technically nothing, and I rarely saw her apart from the odd drop-off where she would awkwardly smile and ask how I was. Jim scarcely volunteered any snippets about her, and Grace was very careful not to reveal much of what went on at Jim's house. Freya remained mostly a mystery no matter how many times I asked if she was OK.

At one time Freya had been like a daughter, a cheeky monkey who had loved After Eights and chicken ramen. She'd let me curl her hair and paint her nails and we'd watched *The Wizard of Oz* a zillion times snuggled up on this very sofa. On her tenth birthday I had called in many favours and hosted a sleepover for her with professional hair and make-up artists. She'd hugged me when everyone left the following morning. 'That was the best birthday ever, Ali. Thank you.' My eyes prickled from the memory. I knew I would forever love that little girl who had tightly held my hand when I'd sobbed at *The Railway Children* ('*Daddy, my Daddy!*'); who'd spent her pocket money on the perfect nail polish to match a dress Jim had bought me for my birthday; whom I'd overheard telling her best friend she couldn't wait for me to marry her dad. She'd made my heart sing countless times and now I just had to be content with finding her face reflected back at me whenever Grace smiled.

I'd rarely talked to Amanda about Freya or how I'd felt at the time. It had been too much to deal with on top of everything else so I'd buried it. I wondered if Freya was helping to choose the dog today. I also wondered, not for the first time, if things might be different one day...

I stared out of the window and into the Mews, hoping the intervention was well and truly over. I shouldn't have to hide from my neighbours on Easter Monday to avoid an unsavoury situation. The last few days with the antibiotics, my thievery, which I now regretted, and the whole puppy thing raking over old coals had left me feeling disconsolate. Yes, yes, Mini Amanda, I KNOW I should just honour the feelings, sit in my misery and work through it, but I don't want to. It's a bank holiday, people are supposed to have fun, not sit around looking into their pain and welcoming it with a cup of tea and a digestive. I could feel the walls closing in on me. Everyone was away or busy with boyfriends or husbands. I hadn't even spoken to a man for months (in the romantic sense), having actually heeded Amanda's advice about not diving back into the shark pool. Well, maybe it was about time things changed...

I slid my phone out of my back pocket and opened the App Store, attempting to forget all about work and feeling crap. I clicked on Tinder and downloaded it. I'd previously tried internet dating with Guardian Soulmates when Amanda and I had lived together but it had been an unmitigated disaster. The guy had walked into the bar with hunched shoulders and a pigeon chest, having lied about his age, his height and the fact that he'd developed a wattle chin in the ten years since his photo had been taken. Not wanting to be rude, and having had a skinful of Merlot, I had shagged him in my attic bedroom when he'd missed his return train to the Shires. I suffered the horrors all the next day and had tried to whittle away the shame by working on my flowery cross stitch Mum had sent me as a Christmas present, the idea being that the wholesome activity would absolve me of carnal guilt. It hadn't.

Tinder was something Ursula dipped into occasionally during dating dry spots but it was an alien concept to me. There was a plethora of other apps that promised to hook you up with a perfect match but, according to Ursula, Tinder was the best one if you were in your forties. 'All the divorced dads are on there looking for wild sex after being incarcerated in an institution for fifteen years!'

The main problem, according to *Woman's Hour* on Radio Four, was that they were all looking for twenty-eight-year-olds, while I was looking for a long-term love. However, right now, I just wanted a distraction. I wanted some fun, to flirt and to see if I still had 'it'.

Tapping into the mercurial world of Tinder, I set my distance preference to five miles and age range from thirty to fifty, and up popped a gaggle of profiles. Swipe left for the munters and right for the potential shags. I was keenly aware it was so appearance-based and ageist, but I settled down anyway with a cup of tea and Radio Four bumbling away in the background, there to alleviate the seediness. Swipe, swipe, swipe, swipe, swipe. Since when had every available man grown a skanky hipster beard and enjoyed brewing their own kombucha? Where were all the normal blokes? Oh, hang on – I burst out laughing – Nick the Spy was on there! I studied his face up close now – he was kind of cute if you fancied geeks. Without the cap his hair had a distinct ginger tinge, and he was only two years younger than me and worked for the CPS, a bona fide grown-up. Swipe left or right? Would he know if I had swept him into the bin or not? He might not even fancy me. I wasn't even sure I fancied him; it was just the proximity was so handy! I sensibly swiped left and waved bye-bye. Two swipes later I came across Ifan.

'You wanker!' I shouted at my phone. The profile picture (that I had taken) had Grace sinisterly cropped out of it. It was from Christmas in the hotel room at Amanda's wedding. 'You're sick!' How could he use that picture? But of course it was a good picture and he looked gorgeous in a suit, that was why. I wanted to hurl my phone at the wall, but shakily swiped left instead. In a rage now, I swiped left so many times (so many munters) that I almost missed blindingly handsome Rory. Rory was a vet, which meant he loved animals, and common sense would dictate he couldn't be a bastard. Swipe right. I carried on swiping but before long got bored and just as I stopped, a message popped up.

Hi, Ali, wondered if you were free at the weekend for a coffee?

Well at the risk of sounding too keen, I'm busy at the weekend, but I just happen to be free now.

★

'Hello!' a deep sexy voice said behind me an hour later amid the bedlam of the Blue Mountain Café. I spun round and came face to face with Rory the vet. He was well over six foot and was wearing a lovely navy pea coat to guard against the April chills. 'I saw you come in – I'm sitting by the door back there. Do you want to go somewhere quieter so we can talk properly? It's mental in here.' His eyes looked hopeful and a dimple punctured his stubbly left cheek. No visible wattle chin and his photo was up to date. He was adorable.

We retired to the new Greek place on Lordship Lane where he bought me a huge slab of orange polenta cake to go with my latte while he had a black coffee and a walnut muffin.

'So what did you do last night?' I asked, stirring my latte and picking at my cake. My tummy was churning with nerves but I didn't want him to have me down as a food dodger.

'I was on call at the animal sanctuary where I volunteer twice a month.' I swear a shining halo materialised around his head and angels began singing 'Close to You' by the Carpenters. *Why do birds suddenly appear...*

'Oh, how amazing,' I squeaked out, my cheeks flushing at the thought of him labouring over some fragile injured creature and nursing it back to health, then coming home and masterfully ripping my clothes off. 'Where's that?'

'In Norwood. We get so many poorly woodland animals. People come from miles around to drop off birds with broken wings and squirrels that have been hit by cars. What did you do last night?' He made eye contact and appeared genuinely interested in my reply.

'I went to my neighbour's Easter party with my little girl.' I cleverly reminded him of Grace, like a test to see if he balked. He didn't. We chatted for ages about his work, my work, the fact that I was a single mum, his love of animals, my cat allergy even though I had lived with Ginger, Amanda's cat. We breezed over past relationships – he had been single for two years, something I found hard to believe.

'So when are you next free at a weekend?' he asked me as I thought about how I would be plague-free in another week. I imagined him meeting Grace and showing her his veterinary surgery. Maybe she would want to be a vet one day like him? He could get her a chinchilla like Ursula's. She had been pleading with me for ages. She wanted to call it Vince.

'Two weeks,' I said, hoping he was going to say that was too long to wait and ask for a date sooner than that – maybe I could get Amanda to babysit.

'Well, I wondered if you'd want to come on a special date with me then?' he smiled expectantly.

'Well, it depends what it is.' I felt a jolt of excitement in my stomach as some kind of elaborate *Pretty Woman* fantasy played out in my head. Maybe he was going to jet me off to the opera in Rome for the weekend in his private plane. No, he was a vet, not Richard Gere! He was probably going to take me on a romantic dinner in town... In the movie flickering away in my head it would be somewhere like The Wolseley or Le Pont de la Tour with a view over the river, soft piano music tinkling in the background as a waiter popped the champagne cork...

'I thought you might want to come to a rave in the woods in Kent.' I could feel my face drop in disappointment but he blindly ploughed on, while I tried to rescue my fantasy. A rave, well, it might be like a cool festival with bell tents and a zen healing field. 'It's near where my parents live and we do it once a month. You'd have to bring a tent, and your own costume.' By this point I could hear Mini Amanda on my shoulder shouting: *Abort, abort, nutter alert, don't listen to any more of his shit; get up and leave!*

'Costume?'

'Yes! We all dress up as woodland animals. I'm a squirrel, but you can be anything you want. Not a tiger because tigers don't exist in the wild here. But you get the idea – it has to be indigenous. I think you'd look good as a deer.' The recently ingested polenta cake sank like a brick in a swimming pool. How had I managed it again? He wasn't an actual psychopath; he was just a fucking fruit loop with the face of a Greek God.

'A deer?' I whispered.

'Yes, with antlers. They'd suit your cheekbones and the fact you're so statuesque.' It was a backhanded compliment if ever I'd heard one. 'Once we've set up the decks and the camp, we all take acid and trip out. It's so cool.'

'Will you excuse me? I just need the loo.'

He nodded and picked up his coffee. Fortunately, the loos were halfway down the café towards the cake-laden counter. I put my head down and I pushed open the door, and cantered up the road past the bus stop like Bambi's doomed mother trying to escape the hunter. The universe was trying to tell me something. Amanda was right: I should just be on my own. I could hear her buzzing in my head: *One day you'll listen to me.*

12

Who the F*ck Is Alice?

Looking down at my phone, I tried not to swear. Why was Hattie ringing me? I let it go straight to voicemail. I didn't want to have a conversation with her in public. I knew about the puppy and didn't want to get dragged into a weird alternate universe where I had to sympathise about her lack of a baby. Grace was closely inspecting the ice cream freezer while I listened to her message.

'Hi, Ali, it's Hattie. I just wondered if you could ring me. It's urgent. Nothing to do with Grace or Jim, but I need to speak to you.'

Anxiety flared up like a grumbling appendix. I didn't want to ring her, but I couldn't not ring her if it was urgent. Should I wait until we got home? We were nearly finished at Sainsbury's, with just a few more items to find. I doggedly pushed the trolley towards the bread aisle, calling Grace away from the ice cream, but she reluctantly dragged her feet and pulled her spoiled brat face.

'I want ice cream,' she whinged in a devil-spawn baby voice.

'Not today, Grace. We still have some in the freezer.'

'But I want that chocolate one. You promised.'

'No I didn't! Don't make things up!'

'I'm not. You said I could.'

'I said you could choose some ice cream last week when you finish the one in the freezer.' Grace remembered everything I ever said, every swear word, what tone of voice I used and what it referred to. I was thinking of enrolling her as a police cadet. She would make an excellent detective.

'But I don't like that one.'

'There's nothing wrong with it. You liked it the last time you ate it.'

'Don't like it any more.'

'Tough.' I wasn't giving in today. Bad cop was on duty.

'That's not fair.' She was gearing up for an argument when my phone started ringing again. This time I answered it to avoid the scene.

'Ali?'

'Hattie. What can I do for you?' Grace stalked off towards the ice cream freezer. I turned my back on her; I could only deal with one impending crisis at a time.

'Have you heard from Alice? She said she was going to ring you.'

'Well, she hasn't. I spoke to her briefly last week but she's been avoiding me. She owes me thousands from jobs I did ages ago.'

'I'm afraid you won't ever see that money.' I almost dropped my phone and had to lean on the Mr Kipling display to steady myself, almost taking down the Bakewell Tarts and the Fondant Fancies.

'What? Hattie? Fucking fuck, has she done a runner?' It was every freelancer's nightmare – their agent running off with all their wages or going bankrupt owing bailiffs all your hard-earned cash.

'She's gone bankrupt. And yes, she's done a midnight flit. She rang me from a number I didn't recognise to say she'd be in touch once she got herself sorted. Her flat has already been repossessed.'

Stunned into silence, I scrabbled around for some words, any words.

'Are you there, Ali?'

I nodded.

'Ali?'

'Yes,' I whispered, tears now gushing from my eyes and fear draining my body of any heat. My teeth started chattering.

'Do you have income protection?'

'No,' I sobbed. 'I'm completely fucked.' A man walked past pushing his baby in a buggy and stared at me. I turned away and watched a thin-lipped Grace steamroller towards me with a tub of the expensive Belgian chocolate ice cream that worked out at three quid a spoonful.

'I don't know what to say,' Hattie muttered. 'I can't believe she's done this. You think you know someone...'

'How am I going to pay for anything? How are we going to afford to live?' I was hyperventilating now as I mentally tallied up my credit card bills, groaning from the weight of all the expenses I had racked up prepping for jobs, all the while waiting for Alice to cough up my wages.

'I'm sure you'll find a way,' Hattie said, sounding pained. 'Maybe Jim can help a bit or lend you some money.'

If I wasn't so floored I would have laughed contemptuously. Jim was so tight with me that any extra money he did need to shell out for Grace was handed over like he was doing me a huge favour, 'helping me out' by paying for his own child. I think Hattie was forgetting he'd turfed me out of our home when Grace was a newborn and expected us just to survive on the mean streets of East Dulwich.

'I won't hold my breath,' I managed to force out. 'I'm in Sainsbury's and I'm going to go. I'll see you later.' I cut her off before she could pity me further.

Grace looked at me defiantly and dropped the ice cream in the trolley. I stared at the mound of shopping

– the two emergency bottles of red wine, the posh crisps, the fancy medjool dates, the multi-pack of salmon, the organic eggs, all the fresh fruit that Grace would refuse to eat, and I walked away.

'Mummy, the trolley, I can't push it, it's too heavy.'

'I'm leaving it. We don't need any of that stuff.'

'Mummy! I want the ice cream!' she cried. I'd only ever smacked Grace once, when she was being a little monster and wouldn't stop screaming at bedtime over a disallowed chocolate bar the first week after we'd left Amanda's to live on our own. I'd crashed so low I'd been unable to rein in my rage so I'd smacked her bum in a fit of desperation, stopping her mid-scream. 'Why did you hit me, Mummy?' she'd asked, sounding more puzzled than hurt. I'd burst into tears and apologised, and she'd gone on and on about it for weeks. 'Will you hit me again, Mummy?' The worst was when she told someone at nursery that I had hit her and I was called in for a one-to-one with Sheila, her key worker, and shamefully admitted what had happened. I'd felt like Myra Hindley. Grace loved a drama and she loved to chat and tell people everything. I couldn't get away with anything.

I sharply turned round, about to shoot my mouth off, more tears ready to fall, when I spotted the man with the pushchair and the baby, eyeing us up. He was standing pretending to choose some wholesome organic rye bread for his wheat-intolerant perfect wife at home who never shouted or said 'dammit' (let alone 'fuck', 'cunt' or 'wanker').

'Grace, we have to leave,' I said as calmly as I could, the tears receding. 'I've got to do something and I need to speak to Amanda.'

'Can we take the ice cream? Meg likes ice cream.'

'No, but please put that back in the freezer.' She was about to kick off when she thought better of it. Maybe the fear of Amanda telling her off dissuaded her. She compliantly grabbed the ice cream and ran over to the freezer, then ran back to me. In the early days of our exodus from the Single Mums' Mansion, I would use Amanda as a regular threat to force Grace to eat her dinner or go to bed. 'If you don't eat all the pasta, I'm ringing Amanda.' But sadly, the amount of times I 'rang' was so ridiculous, that Grace soon cottoned on that Amanda wasn't there.

'Excuse me, are you just going to leave that here?' Mr Rye Bread said in a Judgy McJudgy tone, motioning to my trolley with his saintly loaf.

'Yes, what's it got to do with you?' I challenged him.

'Someone will have to put all that back before it goes off.'

'You can do it then, can't you? Now if you'll excuse me, I've had a shit storm of a morning and I need to leave. Enjoy shelf stacking.'

Ten minutes later I turned up at Amanda's door, knocking unannounced, praying she would be in and not hauling the kids out on some educational visit to a museum or something like she always seemed to do during the holidays. I was about to give up when the door flung open and Isla stood there wearing a full face of make-up, a pink silk nightie and back-combed hair.

'Is Mummy in?' I asked, anxiety clawing in my chest. I needed a glass of wine and it was only half-past ten.

'She's on her exercise bike. Come in.'

Grace ran in in front of me. 'Is Meg upstairs?' she asked Isla.

'Yes, come with me, we'll find her,' Isla said, taking her hand.

The familiarity of the house, the homely vibe, the mad yellow and brown flowery wallpaper that looked like the eighties had exploded in the hallway never failed to make me smile. But today all it made me want to do was sit on the bottom stair and cry for happier times. It was days like these that I wished I still lived here in among the creaky floorboards, the perpetual hanging washing like Aladdin's laundry in a panto, the sprawling kitchen with the central island that doubled up as Majestic Wines underneath the worktop, and the crazy haphazard purple living room that had been unconsciously modelled on Monica's apartment in *Friends*, Amanda's favourite TV show. I wandered into the kitchen at the back to find a beetroot-faced Amanda in the playroom, pedalling away like a demon, covered in sweat. She was reading a book and kept dabbing the pages with her towel. Only Amanda would read an actual book on an exercise bike. She looked up and momentarily appeared confused, then she smiled.

'I've only got two minutes to go,' she puffed, spit hitting her page. 'Make yourself a tea.' Ginger the cat was curled up on one of the round bamboo Habitat chairs. He barely acknowledged my arrival.

Sonny ambled in from the living room and stared at me.

'Hi, Sonny, what you doing?' He was holding a Lego creation that resembled some vehicle from *Star Wars*, maybe.

'Watching *Star Wars* and playing Lego.'

'Grace is upstairs.'

'Does she want to watch *Star Wars*?'

'I doubt it. She probably wants to play Barbies with Meg.'

He nodded and returned to the living room and I rooted around the cupboard above the kettle for a mug. Just as the kettle reached its steamy climax, Amanda staggered round the corner from the playroom, wiping her face and groaning.

'That was hideous. I thought I was going to die. The things we do so we can carry on eating cake.' She slid onto the floor opposite me and continued to sweat profusely. Just being here five minutes had already slowed the hamster wheel of panic whirring continuously in my belly. 'How are you? Can you get me a glass of water, please? I don't think I can stand up.' I grabbed one and filled it from the water jug and handed it to her.

'Pretty shit, to be honest,' I admitted, waiting for the tears to make a reappearance.

'Oh, no, what's happened? Has something gone wrong with the intervention at the Mews? Are they forcing you to go to AA as well?'

'Worse than all of that; I might need AA after today. Alice has gone bankrupt and run off with all my wages, or they've been sucked up into the black hole of her debt. Either way, I'm totally fucked.' My hands started shaking again and I abandoned making tea and collapsed on the floor next to Amanda.

'Oh my God,' she whispered in shock, 'that's appalling. How much did she owe you?'

'Nearly seven grand. My cards are almost maxed out; I have no savings. I've got a few jobs lined up but I don't know what else she was negotiating.'

'Probably nothing if she knew this was on its way. I doubt she was thinking ahead of next week. Maybe some of the clients haven't paid her yet. You should get on the phone and try to stop them. How did you find out?'

'Hattie rang and told me in Sainsbury's.'

'Chris and I can lend you some money to tide you over.'

'Thanks. I can't believe this. My life was supposed to turn around when I moved to the Mews, but it's actually just got worse.' I tried to breathe deeply, but my throat closed up. What if we ended up homeless again? I would have to go and live with Mum in Gimmerville by the seaside; she only had a small cottage. What if I had to make myself bankrupt because Alice had? What if I got blacklisted by clients? What if I never found work again? What if Jim took me to court to keep Grace permanently because I couldn't afford to live? What if—

'Ali! Ali! Take some deep breaths; you're panicking!' Amanda soothed, patting my back like I was choking. I could feel my lungs straining for air, sucking uselessly like a broken plastic straw.

'Close your eyes, and open your mouth wide, now unlock your stomach, let it go, stop tensing.' I did as I was told. My throat slowly relaxed. 'Start yoga breathing, like Jacqui taught us, in through the nose, Ujjayi breath.' Amanda joined in and we remained on the floor for a few minutes, both of us making a noise that sounded like the rushing of the sea into a cliff-side cave. My heart tagged along, linking in with my breath, decelerating.

'I'm just so sick of always having to scrape by, of always being in charge,' I said eventually. 'I'd like someone else to be in charge for a bit. I hate being a single parent.'

'I know you do, but being with someone just to not be on your own isn't a good idea either, is it? If you don't heal from Twat Face, you won't know who you are and probably end up with another total knob-head. You have enough to deal with right now. I think you should go home and ring all those jobs and see if you can rescue some wages. Leave Grace here and pick her up this afternoon, once you're sorted.'

'Are you sure?'

She nodded.

'Thanks so much. That's made me feel marginally better. Can I move back in if everything else fails?'

I sat in my living room for two hours, calling up all the jobs I had yet to receive money from, my heart beating wearily in my temples, seeds of a stress headache apprehensively trying to sprout. I could hear the desperation catching in the back of my throat every time I spoke. All the clients apart from two had already paid Alice – she had just been holding on to the cash, ready to take flight. However, there was some good news. Mothercare hadn't paid yet and neither had Next, and those were two big jobs paying almost half of what I was owed. So at least I had the rent covered and we could afford some food. Maybe I would go back to Sainsbury's and see if my trolley was still there...

I sat back on the sofa and idly scrolled through Instagram while taking two minutes off from the humiliation of revealing my misfortune. My thumb stopped on an 'inspirational' quote some fucking vapid guru person had posted. She always annoyed me with her zen thoughts about how we could all reach Nirvana by being the best versions of ourselves. I followed her because that was the social media game. If you wanted more followers, you had to follow popular people. However, in this one instance maybe I needed to hear what she had to say. Jocasta Smug Bitch Face (not her real name), who always seemed to be lying on an exotic beach lapping up the sun while drinking spirulina smoothies, said in GIANT letters across a soft pink background picture of a white dove: 'Don't focus on what went wrong, concentrate on finding a solution and the Universe will conspire to help you.' Codewords for: *Some minion didn't pack my Melissa Odabash white bikini, so instead of firing them I rang Gucci and got them to courier a gold one instead. Problem and solution sorted – thanks Universe.* I wanted to fling my phone at the wall, but she was right, there was no use questioning why I always seemed to pick up the sticky end of the lollipop. I knew what I had to do: I had to be my own agent until I found another one, and the best time to start was now. Half an hour later, as I made a cup of tea after securing another job with Marks and Spencer, the doorbell rang.

'Hiya!' Samantha chimed cheerily. 'Is this a bad time?'

No time was a good time today. 'Come in. It's fine.'

'Don't worry, I won't as I'm off out to a meeting, but I wanted to see if you were still around Friday. Lila is desperate to meet you and talk about a fashion vlog. I've tentatively booked a table at my club. I'll text you the address.'

'Oh, yes, I am free.'

'Brilliant. OK, come at eleven. Maybe this will be the start of a new venture? You never know, we could make some dosh! See you Friday, darling, toodle-oo.' And she sashayed off in a cloud of Chanel No. 5.

So Jocasta Smug Bitch Face was spot on. I wanted to kiss her.

13

Samantha

'Is it me, or are all the celebrities getting younger?' Samantha said aloud to the empty kitchen. She flicked through *Hello!* magazine while drinking her second milky coffee, feet encased in fluffy leopard-spot slippers she'd bought from Asda in last week's shop. It was already light outside, but she'd been up since dawn. She enjoyed getting up early, watching all the houses in the Mews gradually spring to life, lights flicking on, doors slamming as people left early for work or school. She caught Clive's eye in the photo on the window ledge, smiling at her from a Christmas party ten years ago. She sighed and reached over and touched his face, well, the dusty glass of the picture frame, tracing a line with her acrylic French-manicured nail down his ruddy cheek.

'Six years, Clive. It's gone quickly.' She'd never forget the look on Scott's face as he came downstairs after trying to wake Clive when he'd gone for a lie-down one Sunday afternoon. Finding your dad dead of a heart attack wasn't on anyone's bucket list.

Her phone made a chiming sound like a prayer bell. She picked it up, stretching her arm away from her so she could see who had texted her. Scott.

Morning Mum. Good luck at the meeting later. Hope you get it sorted. It's hot already here. Got a fresh load of tourists arriving later. No rest for the wicked. Love you xx

Love you, son. Don't get into any scrapes. Mixing business with pleasure doesn't usually work out! xx

Samantha laughed to herself; sometimes it felt like yesterday that the boys had been little, running under her feet while she juggled PTA commitments, working in town for William Morris, building the groundwork for her own business as a talent agent. She'd been in and around the scene now for thirty-seven years, starting in the typing pool after she'd dropped out of business college in Wimbledon. She knew back then she didn't want to work for anyone else. She'd watched her own father bow and scrape to other people and knew that wasn't for her. And people were so slow, they took so long to make decisions, to find the direct solution to things, creating problems for themselves. So much bullshit, procrastination, the old boys' network, the four-day week, no electricity, then boom, Margaret Thatcher came into power. Suddenly it wasn't an anomaly to be unmarried, pursuing a career, taking on the men, busting out of the typing pool. She'd voted for Maggie, even though she wasn't political, just because she was a woman, because she was sick of men being in charge.

'I didn't see you coming, did I?' she said to Clive. 'You took me by surprise.' She'd had her head down, nose to the grindstone, ploughing through the lower tiers, gathering her own clients, making her mark, assuming marriage may happen one day, but not yet. Clive had been an editor at a publisher, ten years older. He'd arranged a meeting with her latest find, some hotshot journalist who was writing an exposé of the music industry. He'd asked her out over the phone after the meeting, his voice shaking. They'd met at the Coach and Horses in Soho and left four hours later to catch the tube home, separately, kissing on the corner of Greek Street near her office. She'd worried someone might spot her, so she'd made him put his umbrella up even though it wasn't raining. He said later, he knew he wanted to marry her there and then.

She heard a door shut sharply, the letterbox swinging against its metal frame, clanging across the street. She pulled herself away from the past and, gazing out through the kitchen window, watched Alison buckling her little girl into the back booster seat of the Golf, setting off somewhere early. Their meeting wasn't until later on, but she expected Alison had to drop Grace now so she could make it on time. Alison reminded Samantha of herself – always busy, the main parent and breadwinner for herself and her daughter, just like Samantha had been all those years before. Clive's wages at the tiny publisher weren't enough to keep them all afloat for very long when Billy came along in 1986. She had been considered a geriatric mother at thirty-two in those days and wasn't allowed to give birth at King's; she'd had to go to a specialist birthing unit in Tooting. Bloody cheek! These days, women were having babies at an age that would be considered outrageous back then, often it seemed because they couldn't find a man suitable to mate with. How were you supposed to meet anyone when everyone was always checking out who else was available on dating apps. There was always someone with a tighter bottom, firmer boobs, a better job... It was no wonder anxiety was the new buzzword. With choice comes pain – Buddha knew exactly what he was talking about when he coined that phrase.

She'd told her boys to go out and have fun – after all, you only get one life and it was different for boys – they didn't have a ticking clock. She was glad she didn't have girls; she wasn't sure what kind of mummy she would have been for girls...

Samantha had had to let the Soho office go in the end. Rising rents saw to that, and then her carefully stockpiled nest egg had been halved by two bad investments just after Clive died. To top it off, Clive, who had been in charge of all the insurances, hadn't paid for the last two months on the life policy. The boys didn't know their parents were in financial difficulty; she'd kept it from them, as well as protecting them from Clive's failing memory. She'd found her husband wandering outside in the Mews at night a few times with just his pyjama bottoms on. Then there had been an incident when he'd had a panic attack in Sainsbury's car park and didn't know where he was. After he died, she found the house insurance had also fallen by the way side and she thanked God that nothing else had happened. Imagine if he'd left something in the oven and forgotten about it...

She filled the kettle for her third coffee of the morning, and fired up her laptop on the kitchen table. The coffee table in the living room usually sufficed as her desk most days, piled high with magazines and her unofficial in-tray spilling out of the Family Circle biscuit tin. However, she was feeling a bit stiff today, her back was giving her a bit of gyp, so she set up shop in here instead, the overhead light on. Twenty new emails, including one from David trying to arrange their monthly catch-up. She also had an invite to the *Strictly* tour, because Stephan, one of her clients, had appeared on the show last year.

She knew she was lucky. She went out a lot, constantly meeting people, always talking, schmoozing, being wined and dined, but with both boys away working, she sometimes felt lonely. It had been a godsend moving to the Mews a few years before Clive died. Here she had a ready-made support system in place, friends she could rely on, always someone to talk to if she felt the fear.

'Do you think you'll retire one day, Mum?' Billy had asked last year. 'You don't need to work any more. The house is all paid for.'

'One day soon, son. Just a few more years, then I'll be ready.' He had no idea that there had been no windfall or that the mortgage still ate into the small wage she paid herself. She knew she would never retire. Work had become her life, her clients like her children. Why else was her diary full until November when it was only April? She just needed one of them to land a massive on-going gig, and her fifteen per cent would smooth over some of the cracks.

'My girl, will you ever stop?' Clive had asked shortly before he died.

'When I'm dead,' she'd laughed. It didn't seem funny now.

14

Vlogging

The Arts Club in Dover Street was the embodiment of understated town house glamour and I was glad I had dressed smartly in tailored navy trousers and a red chiffon blouse with a black butterfly print. I needed the confidence that sometimes only stylish clothes could lend after my tumultuous week. My patent leather black and red brogues had been pilfered from a shoe catalogue shoot and they rounded off my look perfectly.

'Do you want to check your jacket?' the front-desk lady asked, harbouring faultless tattooed eyebrows beneath her sweeping Flock of Seagulls fringe and pillowy lip fillers. I declined. She led me up the thick carpeted stairs to the first floor where people were holding public meetings, accompanied by tea, fancy drinks and food platters. Some people were brazenly wanting to be seen while others were engrossed in important private conversations. The room was filled with a low-level buzz that was buffered by the plush carpets and heavy damask curtains. This was a nice little holiday from the anxiety conveyor belt that continued to hum along ever since Alice had absconded, and it allowed space for my brain to create one of my much-loved fantasies.

I imagined Hugh Grant waving at me as I wafted past, saying he would call me to arrange a meeting. I spot Meryl Streep and Colin Firth chatting animatedly, they stop mid-laugh and nod at me. I'm brimming with confidence, safe in the knowledge that I can work the entire room, that I am a dynamic clothes maven, assisting the stars with their wardrobe for black-tie events and photo calls, every designer in the fashion sphere at my beck and call. Goodbye Primark, New Look and Peacocks... Before I could wrap up my fantasy, eyebrow lady had delivered me to Samantha's table by one of the floor-to-ceiling windows overlooking the street below. Samantha stood up and air-kissed me. She was wearing a stylish black wrap dress that cut across her ample bosom making them look like one of Christo's fabric-wrapped artefacts: torpedoes, perhaps.

'Hello, darling. Thanks for coming. Who has got Grace for you?'

'Her dad. Where's Lila?' I had googled her profusely last night in an effort not to fall into any conversational black holes regarding her career, a practice I had learned when starting out styling *OK!* and *Hello!* magazine shoots fifteen years ago. I'll never forget a glamour model cutting me dead because I'd mistaken her for her nemesis (same plastic face, same blond extensions, same blindingly white teeth). Her management complained to Jim (who was my agent at the time) and I was blacklisted from working with her again. I couldn't afford that today. So I was now so well informed about Lila Chan's career and personal life that I could have completed an unblemished round on *Mastermind* all about her.

'She'll be here in about ten minutes. I wanted to brief you first.' I had to forcibly pull my eyes away from Samantha's chest. Her boobs were hypnotising me. How did she keep them so upright at her age, which I had now placed at perhaps mid-fifties? Had she had a boob job? I needed scaffolding to keep my own in place. I don't care what anyone says, big boobs are a hassle. Fine when you're young – annoying but manageable – but if you fall pregnant, they inflate so out of control that elephant hammocks aren't sturdy enough to contain them. When I'd finished breastfeeding Grace, they'd deflated like helium balloons and never really recovered. When I bend over now without a bra on, it's like two marbles swinging in the bottom of two crepey fleshy socks.

'What do you want to drink? I've got a bottle of white on ice, but you have whatever you fancy.'

'Tea is fine.'

Samantha served me from the white china teapot on the table, and I helped myself to an almond biscuit, not having had breakfast.

'So, Lila is the *Sun*'s youngest entertainment columnist. As you know, she started off in Three's a Crowd as a singer while she was at university and won *The X Factor* with them.' I remembered watching it with Jacqui. They were good but safe and never achieved the dizzy heights of One Direction after the predictably limp Christmas number one. They split up a year later, not seeing out their record contract with Syco. I bet they made no money, hence the *Sun* column, and now this vlogging lark. 'She's hoping the vlogging will lead to writing a fashion column for a magazine or getting into TV presenting. Fashion is her first love; *The X Factor* thing was just an accident really. The other two needed a third member and she volunteered, then it took off. The other members of Three's a Crowd have since returned to do a master's and work in PR so she's out on a limb, her star waning.'

Hadn't it already waned?

'I inherited her from a friend's agency, which was overcommitted,' Samantha went on, 'and because I do TV, books and most media, she's a better fit at my place. But all my other clients are more established, or older.'

'She studied fashion and journalism, didn't she? Did she actually finish her degree?'

'No, she didn't. She was on for a first too. She's a bright girl, but I'm not sure what she would be like vlogging. You've worked for so many different clients in the industry, and you said you were doing a lot with Instagram now.'

I nodded.

'I think she needs to come from a different angle rather than pushing other people's products.'

'All the vloggers I've seen are very young, with all the fashion aimed at that age group. It's a saturated market. Yes, she will have a head start because of her column in the *Sun*, but what's going to make her stand out?'

'Yes, that's what I thought too. There are women fashion vloggers and stylists for older women, and they tend to be more your age.'

'Is there a vlog with a younger and an older woman?' I suggested, tentatively. 'I don't remember seeing one. Like a double act kind of thing. Clothes my daughter steals, that kind of ethos.'

'No, I don't think so. Clothes my daughter steals – wow, that has a real ring to it.'

I beamed.

'Oh, here she is.'

Lila was tiny, a pocket rocket and so young, not yet Botoxed into oblivion. Her onyx-black hair was cut into a perfect shiny fringed bob that skimmed her jaw, framing her delicate features that I made a sweeping assumption were of Chinese origin. Her choice of clothes was interesting for someone who was involved in fashion – a Clash T-shirt and a pair of skinny black jeans with holes in the knees – my pet hate – and skanky trainers. Her incongruous perfect hair and make-up were at odds with her grunge get-up. If this was what she usually wore things would have to change.

'Hello, Lila, how are you?' Samantha stood up to air-kiss and I did the same. 'This is Alison, the lady I was telling you about.'

'Hello,' she said politely. 'Excuse my dreadful clothes. I stayed with my sister in Clapham last night and we got soaked running home after the pub. I had to borrow something of hers and this was all she had that wasn't in the wash.'

Samantha laughed and I joined in, relieved she wasn't a philistine like Amanda, who wore the same clothes for four days, even socks, and wore the same bra for a month without washing it. I knew she secretly stored biscuit crumbs in there for snacks.

'Alison has had a good idea about a vlog. Possibly teaming you with an older woman to do dual-age styling and fashion advice.'

Her perfectly symmetrical face puckered into a lopsided frown.

'I thought I was going to do something on my own,' she said, sounding disappointed but not petulant. I did actually warm to her; she seemed very unaffected.

'What did *you* have in mind?' I asked her, 'because the vlogging world is fit to bursting with girls doling out advice. What's your USP?' Wow, I even sounded like I knew what I was talking about, imposter syndrome still festering just below the surface.

'Well, I get invited to all the right parties, not the *Tatler*-style ones, but all the general opening of envelope things. I could report back on them. Dissect what people were wearing and maybe find cheaper versions for normal people to wear.'

'Yeah, that's a possibility. But it's very much determined by who's at a party and would anyone want to wear those clothes. Isn't it kinder not to dissect other women and choose nice clothes that two lots of women from completely different ends of the age spectrum could wear? Accessorise, adapt for different body shapes, that kind of thing.'

Lila didn't say anything for a few moments. I checked out Samantha and she nodded encouragingly at me.

'I suppose, yes.'

'It could be empowering. As well as you and the other presenter trying on clothes, we could find different women and do a makeover on them with the clothes from stores they would never think of looking at because of the age stigma. I know a few make-up artists who might do it for free for their CVs.'

'Yeah, OK. It sounds cool. What would we call it?'

I was used to spoon-feeding art directors stuck in a rut and this was no different.

'Well, off the top of my head, I came up with Clothes My Daughter Steals.'

Lila chewed it over, saying it to herself and rolling the words round her mouth with her tongue.

'I like it. What do you think, Samantha?'

'I think it's genius. We need to sit down and plan it out properly.' She winked at me. 'It's hard to monetise stuff, but after ten thousand followers it gets easier, so I think you just initially want the exposure. If it does well, it could lead to other things where you receive a decent income.'

'So when will we film it? How will it work, where will we do it?' Lila fired at us, obviously totally on board now. 'I'll be able to advertise it all over Instagram. I've got almost eighty thousand followers left over from *The X Factor*. That's how I got the columnist job, and the fact I can actually write my own copy. Samantha totally sorted it all out.' She smiled adoringly at Samantha, which was quite sweet.

'When are you free, Ali?' Samantha asked me.

'For consulting?'

'For filming. You're the other presenter!'

'No, I just came up with the concept. I can find you someone else, maybe. I know lots of stylists older than me who would be a better fit.'

'I like you, though,' Lila insisted. 'I want to do it with you. You know what you're talking about.'

'I hate TV, though. Especially live TV. It terrifies me!'

'It isn't live, silly,' Samantha said.

'Yeah, you can mess up as many times as you like,' Lila continued. 'So…?'

15

Clothes My Daughter Steals

'Do you ever think about meeting anyone else?' I asked, looking at all the pictures of Samantha's dead husband dotted around the living room. Samantha let out an enormous hoot, almost convulsing. We were rummaging through all the clothes I had managed to blag for the inaugural filming of the vlog.

'Oh, you young people. Can you imagine me on Tinder or any of those other horrible dating apps? No one my age goes on there. I would have to go on a Saga holiday and there's no bloody way I'm doing that. I like being on my own. I don't need to meet anyone else. I'm too busy, anyway. The few dates I have been on, the men have turned out to be so needy. I'm too independent for them.'

'How old *are* you?' I asked, well aware it was the rudest question ever, but I was still not convinced she was as old as she was implying.

'I'm sixty.'

'What? No way! You look great. Any age-defying top tips you can offer me?'

'Enjoy what you do, drink wine, be a bit naughty, marry for love, and don't take anything too seriously. And don't mess with your face. I've seen too many bad lip jobs and frozen expressions in this business; let life shine out.'

Samantha had shoved the coffee table to one side and set up the huge white roller screen over the unkempt floor-to-ceiling bookcase. It really worked at minimalising clutter! If only I could wipe out all the detritus in my life with a crisp white screen.

'Where did you get all this?' Lila asked, obviously impressed. 'And the lights?'

Samantha had set up two professional lights, one for illuminating the main area where we were going to 'present' and one to counteract the shadows.

'I've been around so long, sweetie, that I've collected things. The lights have been living in the shed for about five years, along with the screen. Now, have you brought the tripod, mic and camera?'

A full-length mirror on a movable stand was strategically placed to one side so we could gasp in horror or coo in delight at our transformations.

'Here's me thinking we're just going to shoot on an iPhone and hold the camera at arm's length,' I said, impressed with all the gear.

'No, love, we have to stand out from the crowd from the off. As you said, the internet is teeming with vlogs. We should just film you both chatting; I don't think we need a script.'

We farted around for about half an hour salivating over the clothes, practising what we would say about them, mixing and matching and trying on the same outfits, then tweaking. I kept forgetting that Lila had won *The X Factor*, performed at the London Palladium and had met Prince Harry, and all the rest of the star-studded triumphs she'd achieved in her short life. She was just a normal twenty-three-year-old woman who loved clothes and wanted to have a laugh trying something new.

'Shall we see what we're like on camera?' she asked, twirling around in a hot-red fifties prom dress from the Topshop vintage section. 'Are you going to eat your cinnamon swirl?'

'Yes. Hands off!' She had wolfed hers down in two crocodile bites, inhaling the buttery crumbs at the same time. 'I'm glad to see you're not on the paleo diet or any of those things. Most people I style are avoiding carbs or dairy, or only eat when it's a full moon. Madness!'

'God, no way. I'm from a large family and learned that you had to eat fast or you didn't eat at all! I love my food!'

Samantha laughed while she beavered away on her laptop and phone from the sofa on the other side of the room.

Lila set everything up, checked we were in shot and then pressed record.

'Welcome to Clothes My Daughter Steals,' she breezed as naturally as a duck bobbing on a pond. 'We're a fashion vlog with a difference...' Then she subtly gave me a cue.

'Ow! Don't kick me! Your hooves are sharp.'

'You're going to explain.'

'But you haven't said who you are yet.'

'Oh, right, yeah. I'm Lila Chan.'

'And I'm Ali Jackson. Would you normally steal your mum's clothes? No way? Is that because you wouldn't be seen dead in her threads, or because everything she wears came out of the Ark? Well, maybe it's about time to update everyone's outfits in your house with mix and matching for all age ranges...'

'How are you going to cut it all down to five minutes?' I asked, mystified, at the end of the shoot, the clothes heaped in piles at the side, shoes scattered like petals round the periphery of the 'set'.

'My boyfriend, Hayden, works in TV; he has edit suites on his laptop. I have ideas for graphics and everything. He's a total whizz and will help us out.'

'Thanks for that,' Samantha said after Lila had left. 'She's a lovely girl and I really think this will work well for both of you. I know at the moment you're not getting paid – she isn't either – but I'm hoping in time that will change.'

I pushed hesitantly on Elinor's half-open door at seven for my first ever weekly BBQ, a tradition in the Mews I had yet to sign up for. I hadn't seen everyone together since the Easter party when I'd opted out of Carl's AA press gang. To mitigate any potential awkwardness, the people pleaser in me had overcompensated by making a double batch of Marmite whirls and bringing a couple of expensive bottles of Merlot.

Now the nights were getting lighter I was filled with a longing for romantic summer dates, Pimm's and drinks in leafy beer gardens. I could hear loud chatting and low music drifting from Elinor's courtyard garden. She was in the kitchen unboxing sausages and some pre-prepped lamb kebabs.

'Ah, hello,' she said tensely. 'Thank God you're here.'

'Why, what's happened?'

'Jo has split up with her girlfriend and is horrendously drunk and no one else is here yet apart from Carl, and I think it's going to be too much for him to cope with.'

'Oh shit, should I go and grab Francesca?'

'No, she's on her way back from one of her Qi Gong classes. She's never here until eight thirty on a Wednesday.'

'Ah, here she is!' Jo cried as I emerged into the garden. 'The love of my life, the one and only Alison.' Carl rolled his eyes and mouthed 'sorry' at me. He was manning the BBQ and turning some golden chicken thighs with the tongs, the fat spitting on the grill.

'Hello, Jo. What's going on?'

Jo swung her glass of wine wildly in my direction like she was challenging me to a duel. She was unsurprisingly in yellow silk pyjamas and fluffy red googly-eyed slippers, her florid face a tell-tale sign that she had been drinking for a while.

'I'm a free agent again. Free to roam the market for pretty girlsh.' She was hammered.

'I know coming from me it's hypocritical, but don't let her have any more wine,' Carl hissed.

'Carl, shut your face! I can drink as mush as I want. I'm not the alcoholic here.'

I braced myself for some kind of retribution, but Carl calmly carried on checking the chicken, ignoring her.

'Hellooo,' Deborah appeared behind me, carrying a large glass of red wine, her son, Charlie, warily hanging back.

'Debs, I just bought a Rolls-Royce, on the internet. That'll show Caro I'm over her.'

'Jo, you didn't!'

'She did,' Carl said resignedly. 'It's like the time she bought the yacht after Penny.'

Who the fuck had money to just casually as you like buy a yacht and a Roller?

'Oh, Jo, what have you done?' Debbie said, shaking her head. 'You need to stop this. Do you want to go home for a lie-down?'

But before Jo could reply, she tripped on a tuft of grass that had audaciously squeezed itself through Elinor's paving slabs and face planted on the ground, blood splattering everywhere.

'My dose!' Jo squawked like Laurel or Hardy.

Carl jumped over and pulled her up. Her lip and nose were split and blood poured off her chin and down her once-yellow pyjamas.

Debbie took over, while Elinor grabbed tissues and cleared her up. It was bad, but Elinor managed to stem the bleeding.

'I'm taking you home to sleep it off,' Deborah said. 'Then it's A and E tomorrow for stitches. Better to go sober. Wasn't she supposed to take you to AA tomorrow, Carl?'

'Yeah, don't worry. I'll sort something out. I feel fine going on my own. Got to do it some time.'

'No, we all said we'd support you for the first month,' Elinor butted in, waving a matronly finger at him. 'When's the meeting?'

'Midday in the Barry Road church hall. It's fine. I can go on my own.'

'I'm out from eleven tomorrow,' Elinor said.

'I'll take you,' I nervously piped up, my mouth racing ahead of my brain.

'No, you don't have to,' Carl insisted.

'I don't mind. I'm not working.'

'That's decided then,' Elinor said. 'Ali will accompany you.'

16

Carl

Carl sat motionless on the floor of his living room with his eyes closed. He felt like he'd accidentally rubbed sand under the lids, his eyeballs twitching in their sockets, jittery and unsettled behind the shutters. He knew he was *supposed* to empty his head during his daily meditation, and observe the thoughts as they passed unattached through his consciousness on his way to mental clarity and zen wholeness. But he'd acquired an annoying earworm from the Radio Two breakfast show: 'Stop' by the Spice Girls. Quite a titular and pertinent message for his life so far. *Stop right now, thank you very much...*

He breathed in through his nose and out through his mouth, vainly trying to conjure up a gentle white light. *I need somebody with a human touch...*

'Fuck off, Ginger Spice!' That was enough of that for today. He needed to have a cigarette. He unfolded himself from the floor, his back resting heavily against the sofa. He couldn't sit cross-legged any more. Years of playing football back in the day had shot his hamstrings to bits and they were as rigid as a corpse. As for his knees, he could hear them creak like a rusty gate hinge. Everybody had joked once he'd hit forty that everything would go downhill and they weren't wrong. Betsy had tried to get him to do yoga with her, but he looked like he was crouching in the recovery position after a heart attack during downward dog.

He stood at the open back door that led out to his paving-slabbed patch of nondescript garden, mostly evergreen plants in moss-covered pots, the plastic tabs rammed into the soil long since rinsed of their information by the elements. He gave them a cursory water in the summer just when they thought their time had come. They (who were the pervasive 'they'?) said that if you could keep a plant alive, you could then graduate to a pet, and if that was still hanging on in there, maybe *think* about a baby. He studied the plants – they were OK. Few brown bits here and there, but alive. He wasn't keen on animals…

'Mummy! MUMMY! Where's my bag?'

Carl smiled. Grace had such a gruff voice and she could certainly project it well. He liked eavesdropping on her in the garden playing with her Barbies while he had a cigarette; she was very bossy. He'd realised that Ali had no idea he could hear a large chunk of their life filtering in through the party wall or out of an open window or door into the garden. He didn't want to say anything because he liked it. It was comforting listening to their daily hum, unselfconsciously going about their business.

He inhaled the smoke, the first cigarette of the day always his favourite. All the others that followed had a diminished effect because the hit wasn't as perceptible, just topping up the levels. He could apply anything to his recovery now – there were metaphors everywhere. He finished his fag and stubbed it on the wall, then ran it under the tap before throwing it in the bin. He always wet the end now. He'd had a nasty almost *Towering Inferno* experience when he'd been shit-faced in a girl's high-rise flat a few years back, put his fag end in the bin and slowly set light to the entire thing. It had caught on one of the girl's make-up wipes, which are almost fifty per cent alcohol. They woke choking in the morning with the bin smouldering, a fog of smoke blackening the bedroom. That had caused him to have one of his many lightbulb moments about his drinking. How he should 'cut back'. He shook his head. What a fuck-up. When he'd finally read chapter three in *The Big Book*: 'More About Alcoholism', rather than just carrying it around like some magic talisman against denial, he'd seen himself reflected back in a slew of situations over the last twenty-odd years. *That* had been the defining lightbulb moment, and having the seizure to end all seizures. He'd pissed himself during it, not that he remembered, but he was pretty sure it was his incontinence episode that had driven Betsy away, rather than his untethered drinking.

Carl snooped through the gauze curtains he'd put up to prevent everyone seeing in so easily. They worked like a two-way mirror – he could still see out but no one else could see in, something he revelled in – weren't all photographers nosy? Alison was marshalling Grace into the car for the school run, with the lost bag under her arm. When he'd first met her at Jo's party, he'd been with Betsy, but she'd managed to blindside him. She'd reminded him so much of Janey that he wasn't able to speak to her properly for about an hour, the quicksand of unexpected grief threatening to pull him under. She was sweetly pretty with her tufty blond crop and Slavic cheekbones. It had been more about the way she held herself, how she walked into the party not knowing anyone but deep down knew she would make friends because why wouldn't she. They'd had a stilted conversation in the kitchen about how he might be able to get her some work, which was a joke really because his work had been drying up like a slug dipped in salt. He was lucky that Jeff, his agent, hadn't dropped him.

It had been the subject of work that had lit the fuse for the bender that brought him to this meeting today, accompanied by Ali. He wasn't sure whether he was edgy because of the meeting – he already knew he was going to share because he was finally ready to be honest – or because Ali was coming. About ten times he'd walked to his front door to knock on hers and say he was fine going on his own, and then the fear gripped him round the throat and he'd bottled it. He knew he needed someone there today to bear witness because *this time it was different*. He was well aware that phrase was worn paper thin now, so actually having a fresh, unseasoned pair of ears might be helpful.

He watched Ali reverse into the road and pull away round the corner. His phone chimed on the breakfast bar in the kitchen where he'd left it charging. Jo and her morning chivvy.

Meeting today at 12. Good luck. Keep it up. I can come to one Friday if you want. x

Jo – she was a piece of work. He could talk about her for hours. As much as he loved her (and he did, like a sister), he also needed a break from her. Living opposite her was like being back in Kent in the eighties, with her and Steve round the corner on their estate, when they'd lived in each other's pockets. What you wanted when you were a teenager wasn't necessarily what you wanted when you were an adult, but he admitted it was what he needed. He didn't want to move out, he just wanted to ease back into his own life without the constant commentary from her. He knew the only way to do that was to stay sober, and today felt like he'd come to the end of a road. Time for the less-travelled path.

17

AA

'Hello, my name is Katrina and I'm an alcoholic.'

The camera panned around the room, finally resting on a shifty Hugh Grant hiding at the back, obviously feeling superior that his own drink problem was no way near as severe as everyone else's here. Just the odd gin binge...

'Hello, Katrina,' the room answered back to the middle-aged woman wearing jeans and a faded grey hoodie. I glanced round at the people sitting on the orange moulded plastic chairs that had been set out in a semi-circle on the perimeter of the church hall. There was no typical age, typical attire, no one looked like I'd imagined, but I didn't even know what I had imagined, if I were honest, hence conjuring up good old Hugh, a reliable stalwart in all my everyday fantasies. There were equal numbers of men and women, black skin, white skin, one Asian gentleman – I heard the cheesy hymn we used to sing in primary school ring out through my head: *He's got the whole world in his hands...* The only person that stuck out for me was a very young girl who appeared to be about eighteen, and that made me feel strange, wondering how long she had suffered as a child to end up here.

A youngish woman, maybe around thirty, sneaked in late and scooted into a seat opposite me, stashing her black briefcase under her seat. Kerry, the forty-something woman with shocking red lips running the group, was a vivacious bubbly chairperson who commanded respect but who also radiated kindness. I felt a fondness for her already.

'I've been coming to these rooms now for five years,' Katrina began softly. 'And I want to say to those of you who are new here, just keep coming. You might not think you're an alcoholic...' I shot a sly glance at Carl to my right. Did he think he was one? *He must do.* 'You might think none of us are like you, or that you didn't end up blacked out on a pavement face down in vomit so you must be OK. Alcoholism wears many masks, spits out a million different excuses, doesn't care about how rich you are or how poor, whether you drink wine because it's not as bad as neat vodka, whether you would never drink before breakfast. Just keep coming, keep listening, soon you will hear the same things. Don't look for the differences. God bless.'

'Thank you for that, Katrina,' Kerry said. 'I'd like to add that I was one of those people. I never thought I was an alcoholic. I think we've all been there. I didn't even drink that much. It creeps up on you.'

Fear collected in my belly. Did I drink too much? Was *I* an alcoholic? Yes, I had also never ever woken up face down in my own puke, but I did sometimes drink *way* too much, occasionally carrying on long beyond any sensible limit. I was overcome with a desperate urge to run from the room but remained rooted to my chair. I did actually want to hear what others had to say. I wondered if Carl would speak.

'Katrina pointed out about the similarities and she's correct. All of us are individuals, so our experience of what it is like to be an alcoholic will be intrinsically different. But start digging deeper and soon the parallels will reveal themselves. Themes, actions, thought processes, which is why we hold these meetings. Support for those who need it and no judgement.' She smiled beatifically and soon another member repeated the war cry and revealed a fragment of his own drinking journey. The stories were as varied as the people in the room. Some just numbed the pain but functioned in their lives, then realised it was no way to exist once they had lost everything. Others trail-blazed through a warzone of their childhood, arriving at adulthood as raging alcoholics. And some had no discernible motive to begin a drinking career at all other than that they could. The latter reason scared me the most.

'Hello, my name is Carl and I'm an alcoholic.'

'Hello, Carl.'

I was transfixed. Carl had barely spoken other than to express thanks for bringing him when we jumped on a bus down the hill. 'I appreciate you coming. I know I can go on my own, but embedding it with a support really does help me at the beginning.' We had sat for the rest of the journey in silence, *Black Beauty* accompanying me as I surreptitiously studied his face. He was classically good-looking in that tall, dark and handsome way that I usually zoned in on, but there was something about him that made me not fancy him. I skated through some possibilities: maybe it was knowing his wife had died and competing with her untouchable ghost was far worse than competing with a fully animated ex-wife; or perhaps it was because he was vulnerable right now and it would be morally wrong. Or it could have been that he was an addict and we all knew they were like catnip to me and I needed to avoid the drama. Another consideration was quite revolutionary – maybe I actually wanted to be on my own and all men were temporarily off the table. Thoughts and turbulent emotions about Ifan still regularly bombarded me: anger, sadness, wishing we were together, then a volcanic fury when I remembered my infection, and praying his cock would shrivel up to the size of a hamster's scrotum.

'I haven't shared here for a while,' Carl addressed the room. 'I fell off the wagon spectacularly again and ended up in hospital, trying to escape my bed and asking why I was in the liver ward with all these sick people.' Some people laughed faintly while Kerry pulled a concerned face and nodded empathetically. 'I think all the other times I shared I was just paying lip service, which I know happens and is all part of my journey. I've never been completely honest. I always said when my wife died it pushed me into drinking to block out my feelings, that I used it as a coping mechanism. But that's not true. It gave me an excuse to openly drink shitloads because I had a concrete reason to. People were a lot more tolerant of a grieving husband than of an out-and-out drunk.'

I sat very still, listening with every fibre of my being. I felt like I was the wrong person to be here. Jo should be witnessing Carl lay down the truth as his best friend. I didn't even know Carl.

'I have always drunk far too much, and when Janey and I met we went crazy, going out all the time, drinking, taking cocaine, Es, clubbing. But when we got married, she calmed down and stopped all the craziness. She wanted a baby, but we couldn't get pregnant. The doctor did loads of tests and it was me: I had lazy sperm, most with no tails, probably caused by years of partying, smoking and drug abuse. I promised to rein it in and get healthy for her. But I couldn't. I hid my drinking up to a point. If we went out I would get hammered and she would drink too, but not anywhere near like she used to; she knew when to stop. Every day I was getting up early in the morning and drinking vodka before going on a shoot. I stashed miniatures around the house where she would never find them, but I told myself it was all OK because I had completely knocked the drugs on the head. I loved her so much, but I loved booze more. Before we started a round of IVF, Janey found out she was pregnant. We were so happy, but I ruined it by going out and celebrating after work and getting so leathered I was in bed for two days. That was when she said she knew I had a drink problem, but she also knew giving me an ultimatum would never work. But what she *did* think would work would be the baby's arrival; that I would want to stop for *them*. She was beside herself, crying, saying she didn't want the father of her baby to be an alcoholic but she loved me and it was for better or worse, etc.'

My eyes stung. How could Carl sit there so calmly and cut his heart from his chest and offer everything out on show?

'So I said I would get help. I started coming to AA near where we lived in Barnes. I hated it. I wasn't like the other people there, I didn't live in a phone box, I hadn't lost everything. I didn't like the whole God part of the meetings, the Serenity Prayer, listening to other people's shit. My wife was pregnant and my business was booming, so what if I liked drinking? So I carried on boozing, but only at weekends, genuinely thinking I had it under control, and going to the meetings made me feel like I was being proactive. Janey seemed happier and then at the three-month scan, we found the baby had never developed further than six weeks. Janey had experienced a missed miscarriage. She was devastated. I stopped going to AA. I didn't need to – there was no baby. She was so enveloped in grief that she never even noticed. I easily slipped back to drinking heavily every day, but promised myself I would go back to AA once Janey was pregnant again. We tried as soon as we were able, but nothing happened. And this is the really hideous part: secretly I was glad. I wanted a baby, but I wanted to drink more. Then the worst day ever happened. Janey was on a work night out and a driver lost control of his car and ploughed into a crowd of people and killed her and another girl from work. He was drunk – the irony wasn't lost on me. I was broken and I'm not going into that. It's a whole separate story and I've shared it before to some of you here. I gave up drinking for six months, completely stopped. I took the drunk driver killing my wife as a warning shot across my bows. But I stopped drinking as some kind of punishment, not a positive step at all. When nothing changed, I felt worse. All the aftermath support of casseroles and friends stopping over petered out and I was left with drink. And that's where I began my story in AA here, with the untruth of Janey's death pushing me over the edge.'

Tears were streaming down my face. A man on my other side silently handed me a tissue. I thanked him and blew my nose loudly.

'Wow, well done, Carl,' Kerry said quietly. 'That must have been very hard to admit, but as you know, it's one more step forward on the journey to recovery.'

'Carl, I needed to hear that,' the woman in the business suit said. 'My own story of excuses is very similar. Thank you.' A few other people expressed similar feelings and then a few more shared. But I was done and I zoned out from the few who opened up before the meeting closed.

'Have you never said that out loud before?' I asked Carl as we walked back up the hill. It felt somewhat surreal, having a deep and meaningful with someone I barely knew day to day, but whose soul I'd had a fleeting glimpse into.

'No, not even to myself.'

'That was so moving, so raw. I was in bits. I don't know how you were so composed.'

'Because in a way it was like it all happened to someone else. I know it happened to me, and I now know I was an alcoholic before Janey died. I knew before I last fell off the wagon and I think I fell off because I wouldn't admit the truth, so once again, blotted it out.'

We carried on up the hill with just the sound of the traffic and distant sirens punctuating our companionable silence.

'Are you and Betsy still together?' I eventually asked as we reached the brow of the hill where the buses turned left.

'God, no!' he laughed. 'She freaked out after the ambulance situation.'

'I'm sorry to hear that.'

'Don't be. She was too young. We'd only been dating for a few months. It wasn't serious.'

'How long did you leave it until you started dating after Janey died?'

'Once I started drinking again and went downhill, so about six months after. I was desperately trying to fix the pain by fucking it away with models at work, girls I met at parties, and when that didn't work, I drank to excess. I barely functioned and that was when Jo stepped in. We'd been best friends at school. She told me I was going to die if I didn't sort myself out. I wanted to die, though. Janey had been the love of my life.'

'What did Janey do? How did you meet?'

'I met her at a club when I was out with Jo. She was a midwife, entirely disconnected from my fake world. She delivered babies and nurtured people. I thought she was amazing. She was so beautiful too – not like the models I worked with, more in a girl-next-door way, very natural. We just clicked and were engaged after six months. I just knew I wanted to be with her. I never looked at anyone else again until she died.'

'It must have felt pointless getting sober then, once Jo intervened.'

'Yes, it really did, but she made me see I still had a life. She knows all about this kind of shit. My parents were worried sick, my brother had a baby during the whole débâcle of Janey's death and I'd never met my nephew. So Jo took me to see him when he was about eight months old. I'd been on the piss solidly for two weeks and she threw me in the shower and drove me to Kent. When I saw this little baby boy who was related to me, something shifted. I realised I wanted to be a father at some point. So Jo helped. I sold my house in Barnes, where Janey and I had lived. By the time I moved out she had been dead over a year. And I bought this place to be near Jo and closer to Kent and my parents. And be part of the Mews. I'm no good on my own.'

'Me neither!' I laughed. 'So you kept falling off the wagon? Do you think this will be it now?'

'As in stay sober? In AA, you always say "one day at a time". For me, at the very beginning of my journey it was a minute at a time, then an hour, then a day.'

'How do you feel about meeting someone else now?'

'I think I need to be on my own, which is a first for me as I hate it and I never last more than a month. AA don't recommend embarking on a new relationship when you're doing your twelve steps. I have to get back on track, concentrate on my recovery and get on top of work.'

'I hate being on my own too. I broke up with my last boyfriend in January and it was a total nightmare.' No one else in the Mews knew what had really happened. Something about Carl made me want to spill my guts; I could tell he wouldn't gossip.

'No way!' Carl exploded into raucous laughter when I recounted my sob story, immediately slapping his hand over his mouth. 'I'm so sorry, it isn't funny at all. It was just when you mentioned the leather chaps.'

'I know!' I burst out laughing too. 'I mean, all I could think about when I saw him on the screen was I bet they're sticking to his leg hairs and how icky and painful that would feel.'

'What a dick,' he said once we'd calmed down. 'You're better off without him. Have you started dating again?'

I launched into my recent disastrous crowning glory with Rory the squirrel. Carl had to stop walking once we reached the row of shops and Terry's Tool Hire, he was laughing so much.

'Oh my God, that is honestly the best thing I have heard for ages.' He wiped his eyes. 'I really wish you had gone on the date just so we would know what his costume looked like!'

'Thanks very much! I'm glad my dating disaster is so amusing.'

'I'm sorry, it's just that it makes my life look less chaotic and mad.'

'Maybe we should start a support group for dating addicts. I've got a spotter's badge for nutters, and you also need to stay away from the ladies. Both of us need to get on track with work and shouldn't be allowed to even look at anyone until we're more sorted.'

'Sounds like a good idea to me. Will we have DA meetings with biscuits and watery tea?'

'And a secret handshake.'

'Like this?' And he bent down and threaded his arm under his leg and offered me his hand.

'That's not really secret, is it?' I said, grabbing it and shaking it so hard Carl almost fell over. 'Anyway, we've shaken on it now, we both have to remain single. It's an anti-love pact!'

18

The Spy

Samantha cracked open a chilled bottle of cava and poured it into twinkly crystal glasses arranged on a pretty Brazilian-style cocktail tray as we huddled round her laptop. Lila and her boyfriend had done a brilliant job transforming the rough footage. It was snappy and funny, fast and engaging with on-point graphics. Lila and I came across as if we had lived in each other's pockets for so long we'd collected fluff.

'You two are a bit of a double act,' Samantha enthused as she handed me my fizz. 'Well done for finding your inner presenter, Ali.'

'Cheers to you!' Jo said. 'Maybe this is the start of something new for you? Will you be modelling bikinis? We could film a whole episode from inside my Roller.' She winked cheekily at me. Her Rolls-Royce had suddenly appeared on her drive a week after her accident. It was a gleaming maroon slick-fest and we'd all piled in in turns while she drove us around the block for a spin, Abba blaring out of the speakers.

Apparently, according to Lila, between 3 and 4 p.m. on a Thursday was the most lucrative time to launch a new vlog. She had advertised it all over Instagram and had garnered thousands of likes. We now had to wait and see how many viewers would get sucked in and subscribe to the channel.

'You did look good in that dress,' Carl said, sipping his orange juice. 'You should get your legs out more.'

'Oi, perv! I do. I wear skinny jeans.'

'You know what I mean. Summer's coming, wax your pins and show them off.'

'Wax my pins – who says that? You're like a gay man trapped in a straight man's body.' He laughed.

'It's working in the business for twenty years. I've sucked up all the magazine speak by osmosis.'

'Wow, look!' Samantha cried at the end of our debut. 'The subscribers have stacked up!' We all craned our necks to get a better view. Samantha had refreshed the screen and it showed five hundred in ten minutes. 'It's amazing! That almost never happens.'

As I was leaving Samantha's with Grace and Carl, a bit giddy from fizz on an empty stomach, I noticed Nick the Spy's car pull up outside his house. He ran round to the passenger side and whipped open the door, helping the older lady out like the previous occasion, this time handing her a walking stick. He looked up and, emboldened by the cava, I waved at him and smiled. He jumped like I'd tazered him and the lady turned round so I waved at her too.

'Oh, you've just made the spy's day,' Carl hissed. 'Look at him. He's going bright red.'

The woman beamed openly at me; Nick slowly ushered her inside the house while shooting me some kind of strangulated grimace that I think he thought passed for a smile.

I was checking the subscription numbers once more after Grace was in bed (up to seven hundred and sixty. Come on, little vlog, you can do it!) when my outside doorbell startled me. I opened the door straight away without first checking and standing there was a complete stranger with a twitchy lip and geek glasses.

'Hiya,' he said in a vaguely northern accent that could have swung from anywhere up the M6 between Leeds and Manchester. 'I'm really sorry to disturb you, but I'm having a bit of bother.'

'Nick the Spy!' I cried, my brain performing its usual motor-mouth party trick.

'The spy?' he asked, nonplussed. 'I'm the guy at number three. My mum's fallen and I need some help getting her up again in case she's broken something.'

'God, how awful, can't you just call an ambulance?'

'No, I can't.' He squirmed uncomfortably.

'Let me knock for Elinor and then I'll come. My daughter's asleep upstairs.'

'OK. Thank you.'

'What on earth can Nick the Spy need?' Elinor asked, mystified.

My gut instinct told me not to mention his mum. 'I think he needs some furniture moving. New stuff. I won't be long.'

When I reached his front door, it was ajar.

'Hello?'

'Come in, we're in the kitchen.' The first thing I noticed was an expensive Jo Malone diffuser balanced on the hallway radiator cover, acting as an inept decoy for another very discernible smell. If someone had blindfolded me and spun me around outside then plonked me inside Nick's house, I would have known immediately that this was a man's pad. The kitchen had been revamped with shiny black cabinets and sparkly granite work surfaces. There were no utensil jars or pictures on the stark white walls. Nothing personal cluttered up the surfaces apart from a scented candle on the windowsill. In the words of Amanda: the space was energetically male.

The older lady was lying prostrate on the black and white tiled kitchen floor with her leg bent awkwardly. I didn't understand why Nick couldn't help her up.

'Oh, you poor thing, are you OK?' I bent down to hesitantly grab her arm. She was like a frail baby bird fallen from the safety of its nest.

'I'm fine, just a bit dizzy. Nick can't help me – he's just had a hernia operation and might bust his stitches.' She laughed softly and Barbara Windsor came to mind. Maybe it was her curly white hair and naughty eyes or possibly her gravelly voice, though the distinct northern accent was very un-Babs.

'Is your leg OK?' Nick uselessly hovered behind me as I helped his mum up to standing. 'Do you need your stick?'

'I'm fine. I don't need my stick… What's your name? Nick didn't say. I just asked him to call you over because you waved earlier. I'm Linda.'

'Alison, call me Ali. Can you put weight on the leg?' She tentatively tried and winced. 'How bad is the pain?' I thought once more about the ambulance, a common occurrence in the soap operatic Mews.

'It's not because I fell, it's just normal pain.'

'Thanks for helping,' Nick butted in. 'I'm sure we don't want to keep you any longer from your little girl.'

'Oh, you have a little girl?' his mum asked, sitting down at the circular white kitchen table and straightening up her black trousers. 'How old is she?'

'She's five going on thirty-five. She's called Grace. My neighbour is watching her for me.'

'What a lovely name. Nick, why don't you offer Ali a glass of wine or something?'

He glared at her and she glared back, a spikey unspoken communication whiplashing between them.

'Would you like a drink?' he asked woodenly, like an actor reading through his lines.

'I'm fine, thanks. I should get back. Are you sure your leg is OK to walk on?'

Linda stood up warily, holding on to the table, rested her weight from one foot to the other and then gave me a stilted twirl.

'Go on, stay for a drink. I don't get out much and Nick never has guests.'

Probably because he was an awkward bugger, I thought, but I liked Linda. She seemed like fun.

'OK, just one, then I'd better leave.'

'Red or white?' Nick asked, obviously unimpressed with his mum hijacking the situation.

'Red, please.'

'I'll have red too, please,' Linda chimed in.

'Mum, you really shouldn't.'

'One glass won't hurt.' He tutted and pressed one of the cupboard doors behind him and it slowly lifted horizontally, revealing two shelves of neatly ordered wine glasses and mugs grouped together by size and use. All the flutes were clustered on the right upper shelf, stable-mates with the everyday wine glasses, and the lower shelf housed the mugs and water glasses.

Nick placed two small glasses of red down on the table in front of us both.

'Are you not having one?' I asked.

'I have work tomorrow.'

'All work and no play makes Nick a dull boy,' Linda deadpanned, her aphorism obviously meant to gently sting. He rolled his eyes. I felt like I had started a box set two discs in, jumping the explanatory opening.

'Fine.' He got himself a glass and poured a measly slosh of wine in it and sat opposite us. His lip twitched and he drummed his fingers on the table a few times so I had to turn my attention to Linda to quell my own uneasiness.

'So, Ali, what do you do?'

I launched into my stylist spiel and ended with the vlog.

'Well, we have to watch it now you've said that.' Linda clapped her hands together excitedly. 'Nick, where's your laptop?'

'No, please, not when I'm here. It's embarrassing. Look when I've gone home, if you must.'

'I do love clothes and I used to love dressing up, but I don't get out to the shops any more, and online isn't the same as real browsing.'

'How come?'

'Oh, various things, mostly because I have MS.'

'Multiple sclerosis?' I asked uncertainly.

'Yes. I haven't been able to drive for a few years and get tired so easily.'

'Mum, I thought you weren't going to talk about it,' Nick said brusquely.

'Oh, Nick, it's not a secret.'

He sipped his wine silently.

'I'm sorry to hear that,' I said, genuinely sad for her. 'Does it affect you badly?'

'I'm in constant pain and have bad muscle spasms, which is why I fell over earlier. My vision can deteriorate too when I have a prolonged attack. It's boring and I've had it for years, but old age and the menopause have made it worse.' She sighed and picked up her wine.

'So you don't go out at all?'

'I do occasionally. My daughter, Lesley, Nick, and John, my husband, take me. However, the most convenient way to get around now is in a wheelchair, and that's so bulky in clothes shops and none of them are interested in fashion like I am...'

'Are there drugs you can take? Is there a cure?'

Nick subtly stiffened in my peripheral vision.

'No cure – it's degenerative. But people can live with it for decades successfully as I have, and some people eventually die from it. There are certain things that can give pain relief but they're—'

'Mum!' Nick snapped.

'I'm sorry, Ali, Nick doesn't like to be reminded about it all the time.'

'I should probably go.' I necked my wine, eager to escape whatever was simmering under the surface here.

He must be a fucking spy – he was so weird and insular, his house so devoid of any personal touches as if to keep his identity a secret. Then I remembered the dating profile. Would a spy go on Tinder? Wouldn't it be a security breach? Unless he just shagged and left like James Bond, but looking at him in his geeky specs I couldn't conjure up a love rat or a dynamic killing machine.

'It was lovely to meet you, Ali,' Linda said warmly. 'I'll look your blog thingy up online.'

Nick stood up abruptly and pushed his chair out behind him.

'I'll see you out.' He made it sound like I was going to filch something. As I walked into the hall, a very faint smell wafted up my nostrils. I couldn't tell what it was now with the Jo Malone diffuser almost masking it. Maybe my nose had desensitised since being in the house, like when you unconsciously douse yourself in perfume and everyone else is coughing up a lung from inhaling your fumes.

'Thanks so much for helping out. I'm sorry about my mum going on.'

'I don't mind, it's fine.' I stood on the threshold, one foot on the step, one on his pristine doormat. Maybe he would be less weird if he actually talked to people? 'You know there are Mews barbecues most weeks, don't you?'

'Maybe. I can't remember.'

'You should come to one. Samantha's hosting next week's from six.' He stared at me blankly.

'I'll see.'

'OK, no worries, bye.'

Before he'd even shut his door, Norman's door flung open.

'Hey,' he hissed at me from the front step. 'How come you were in there?'

Norman was in a dressing gown again.

'His mum fell over and needed help.'

'I've lived next door to him for three years and he's never ever asked me in there. I've invited him countless times here.'

'Maybe he's shy?'

'No, he's odd. Did you notice the funny pong? I can smell it on my upstairs landing sometimes. It must come from his side because it's not me!'

'No, Norman, there was no smell and everything was normal. Good night.'

19

Nick

Nick walked back into the kitchen after he'd shut the door on Ali, picked up her glass from the table and placed it carefully in the sink. Through the window he watched her walk back to her house and let herself in, lit by the streetlight outside the college professor's house. He couldn't remember her name.

'She was a nice girl,' his mum said in an overly casual way that meant something else entirely.

'Hmm,' he replied non-committally. He squeezed some washing-up liquid on the sponge and ran it round the rim of the glass, eradicating the lipstick smudge, then inside to clean out the red wine residue. He then rinsed off all bubbles and placed it upside down on the draining rack.

'How long have you lived here now?'

'Three years.'

'And you don't know anyone.'

'Ali's new – she's only just moved in.'

'I'm not talking about her; all the others she's friends with. If she's just moved in, how come she's already going round for drinks to people's houses and getting involved?'

'Mum, you know *why* I don't get involved with the neighbours.' He'd sat back down now and thought about having another glass of wine, but voted against it. He couldn't risk it in case he had to drive in an emergency.

'Nick, even before all this, you hadn't talked to them.'

He shrugged. He didn't like talking to people if he didn't have to. He had to talk all day at work, lead teams, direct people; when he got home he just wanted to *not* talk. His mum used to make life-long friends just waiting at a bus stop when she was younger. As much as he hated to admit it, he was more like his dad. His sister was somewhere in between the two extremes.

'Mum, I'm not like you, I like my space.'

She eyed him from above her wine glass. 'Do you go on dates?'

He rolled his eyes. *Here we go…*

'Not that it's any of your business, but I do go out, yes.'

'I just want you to be happy.' His mum was one of those people who thought you could only be happy if you were married or in a relationship. His dad drove her round the bend a lot of the time but, at the end of the day, Nick knew she would be lost without him. It was almost like she had to have him there to complain about or life wasn't happening. Maybe it was watching their lopsided marriage, the fact that his mum was so reliant on her husband even before she had major relapses, that made him less inclined to get to that point with women.

Nick's friends up north were mostly married or with someone, or getting divorced. He was the only one who had never found 'The One'. He didn't believe in 'The One'. He was too logical for that kind of thinking. For him it was most likely all down to timing. He'd had girlfriends in the past, in his twenties, and he'd actually been in love with one of them, but getting married wasn't on the set of cards he'd dealt himself. Shelley had got sick of waiting and said she wasn't wasting her time on someone who wasn't committed to the same things she wanted. He'd been twenty-nine. How was he supposed to know if that was 'it' at twenty-nine? He knew how to manage his career, but he couldn't work out if he wanted something everyone else around him was throwing themselves into.

'Just because I'm single doesn't mean I'm about to kill myself because I don't have another half to share my wonderful life with.'

His mum made a huffy noise and sipped her wine.

'You're forty, Nick,' she replied eventually. 'Don't you want to have a family?'

'What's brought all this on?' he asked in a strained voice. He was used to the occasional dig or interrogation and he indulged her, but this felt like a graver level of probing.

'Nothing.' She looked out of the window. 'I just worry I'll never get to meet anyone you'll marry because you're leaving it so late.'

'Mum, I might never get married and you'll just have to accept it. It's not on my dance card.' She smiled weakly at him. 'Anyway, you might not like them if I did meet someone.'

'I would if they were like that nice Alison.'

'Mum!' He started laughing. She was like a dog with a bone.

'Well, I'm allowed. I'm your mother and I worry, that's all.'

'Don't. I'm the one who should be worrying. Bloody Nosy Norman tried to interrogate Ali when she left.'

'About the smell?'

'Yep.'

'What are you going to do?'

'Nothing I can do except deny it all.'

*

After his mum had retired to bed, Nick stretched out on the sofa with the news for company, not really absorbing events. He must have dozed off because he woke two hours later with some comedy panel show blaring out at him. Fuck it, he was wide awake now and he had a massive meeting in the morning that had potential to creep into lunchtime, eating up his planning session, which meant he would have to stay late again. He'd wanted to get a proper night's sleep.

What he never told his mum was that he *was* seeing someone at work. He texted her from his room.

You awake?

Yes, what you doing?

Can't sleep.

Do you want me to help?

That would be nice…

His phone rang immediately.

'Hello, do you want me to go upstairs? I can put something lacy on…'

After phone sex, Nick always felt a bit dirty, like he had somehow done something inherently wrong;

he possessed enough self-awareness to know he was a walking male cliché. He always made valiant attempts to initiate a conversation afterwards, but Kelly wasn't interested. He obviously preferred seeing Kelly in the flesh, but Kelly was also busy, so they met up after work if they had time, or on the odd weekend when she arranged a catch-up with a 'friend'. She lived in north London with her husband, who was a lawyer, and had two kids – he couldn't even remember their ages but he knew they were old enough to go to school, but not old enough to be left on their own. The north–south London divide was almost as much of an obstacle as the fact Kelly was essentially unavailable. People would make jokes about needing a passport to come all the way over to East Dulwich, and Nick found Crouch End to be the back of beyond. He liked Kelly, though. This arrangement had worked now for six months without it getting out of control or needy on either side, but he could tell it was running out of steam, becoming harder to find the time. He could hear it in her voice, like he was another tick on her to-do list. She was a paralegal in another part of the building so he didn't have much to do with her. Being Director of Digital Transformation for the CPS meant he never came into contact with her or any of her team.

This was the longest Nick had come to having a 'regular' connection with someone since Shelley, even if it was about to draw to a close. He wondered which one of them would pull the plug first. He had previously dated women on and off, had his Tinder and Bumble accounts as backup, but work was paramount. He had some friends in the area he saw for football and beers, but he shied away from the Mews. He hadn't felt the need to buddy up with anyone. He liked living here because it was gated, he would get more money should he want to rent out one of the other three bedrooms, and he could park outside knowing his Audi wasn't going to get bashed by some joyrider or white van when he was at work.

He'd spotted Ali on Tinder in the last month, but she'd since vanished. He wondered whether she was now with that tall black guy she lived next door to. They looked very cosy every time he spotted them together. She was Nick's usual type – tall, blonde, athletic-looking, with something very sweet about her eyes. She definitely had a presence. When his mum had fallen, she was the only person he could instantly think of that he felt comfortable asking for help. He didn't know why; he'd only seen a close-up photo of her on his phone, and he knew Jo, the small officious one at the end, would have stepped in just as admirably. But he had to be careful who he invited in now Norman was continually sniffing around, prying, desperate to prove something. Why it bothered Norman he had no idea. It wasn't like the smell of drains or dead rats (they released a deadly stench and attracted flies too).

Nick closed his eyes and tried to sleep, but all he could see once the darkness enclosed him was Ali's face, smiling, being kind to his mum, making her laugh.

20

It Takes a Village

'I'm not going to be around in two weeks' time to have Grace,' Jim said shiftily when I picked her up after work. His eyes kept darting away to some indeterminate space above my left shoulder. I waited on his front garden's bricked path for Grace to gather her things.

'Really? How long are you away for?' I felt my shoulders sag as I reluctantly leaped into the future, flicking through my mental diary, checking what potential fuck-ups it would throw my way.

'For ten days. Mum's not well and I said I'd go down and stay, work from hers. She's got to have an op.' His right eye twitched feverishly, catapulting me into a flashback, a night where I recalled throwing a full mug of steaming tea at Jim's head from across the kitchen, missing him by a hair's breadth. The mug had exploded against the white wall, just below the oversized clock. Jim's eye had twitched that night too as he had impatiently tried to explain his late arrival (midnight) for dinner with my parents. Grace had only been a week away from landing. He had been drunk and spewing a poisonous stream of venom in my face.

I had work in two weeks' time. Two jobs, one of them an overnighter in the Midlands for Next. No one could have Grace. Hattie was at work, Mum was on a holiday those two weeks, some sightseeing tour for gimmers in Italy, and Amanda had two different school runs already. The maw of debt opened wide and threatened to chew me up again; I was going to have to turn the jobs down.

'I can have Grace for extra time once I'm back.'

I sighed. That didn't appease my runaway heartbeat. 'Grace, hurry up, Mummy's waiting.'

I pulled up outside my house, still inwardly fretting, wishing for a time in the future when I wouldn't waste so much energy fighting against the fire-pit of fear constantly stoked in my belly. It was so isolating. I didn't hear Elinor the first time she called out.

'Ali! I said, are you OK?' She was watering her budding pots of geraniums outside the front door.

'Sorry, I'm miles away. How are you?'

'I'm very well. Something's up with you, I can tell.'

Out of nowhere a lump forced itself up my throat, choking off my words, making my eyes leak. *Black Beauty* began but it was too late.

'Oh, no, what's happened? Grace, do you want to come in to mine? Tinkerbell and Princess are in there watching a film.' Grace nodded shyly and slipped past Elinor, through our shared front door and into her house. The panic of the last few weeks, Alice's disappearance and now the thought of having to let those jobs go crashed down around my ears. I was usually so good at spinning plates.

'Jim's going away for ten days during a busy time for me at work and I haven't got childcare. But it's not just that...' The entire story came tumbling out in disjointed bursts as Elinor patted my back with one hand and gripped her watering can with the other. 'I feel like I never quite make it. When I get money, something happens to spirit it away again. I'm forever chasing my tail.'

'Ah, you poor thing. I know exactly how you feel.'

'You do?'

Elinor placed the watering can down on the drive just as Jo, Debbie and Francesca emerged from Debbie's next door.

'Yes! I spent my early years as a working mum when not many were doing it in the eighties. Phil was playing away from home the entire time I was senior buyer at Debenhams and had to travel to Asia on buying missions. He would tootle off to his fancy-pants lady of the moment and I would be left the night before a flight with three kids and no one to have them for me. It was a bloody nightmare.'

'Oh, Elinor, why did you stay with him?'

'Because I was scared of being on my own. It was different then. But as time went on, I realised I was on my own anyway, and left him. He couldn't see our marriage had died a death from a thousand sluts.' She laughed flatly to herself. 'He fought it tooth and nail, which is why it took so long and I was only free of him when I was fifty. The children don't have much contact with him now. They were old enough then to see what a bastard he really was and not this man who showered them with money; he was really papering over the cracks of his absentee parenting. That's why Karen let her kids choose their own names – he admitted when he was drunk that he'd named *her* after one of his fancy women.'

'What?'

'I know! What a shit. She didn't want the girls to feel anything negative about their own names, so as soon as they were able she changed them by deed poll.'

'Well, they're, er… interesting. They'll make good TV presenters.'

She shook her head laughing. 'Princess and Tinkerbell? Don't try and be nice. Maybe one day they'll change them to something normal, but maybe not. Anyway, they're lovely girls.'

'Ladies, mothers' meeting, is it?' Jo cawed, sporting a pair of eye-bleeding-orange leggings, a démodé fluffy blue jumper and red flip-flops. Classic Jo.

'Yes,' Elinor replied. I realised my cheeks were still wet with tears and hastily wiped them, but Francesca had eagle eyes.

'What's up, Ali? Are you OK?'

'I am now Elinor welcomed me into the sisterhood of single working mothers. I'd no idea she had worked in fashion too!' Women had been juggling life since the dawn of time and we always managed it. *Hold the baby while I chisel this arrowhead out of a shard of flint, there's a good man, and I just need to send your mum a birthday card.* The mental load was real.

'Do you need some help?' Debbie asked kindly. 'Tell us what's happening and we might be able to come up with a solution. I know how emotionally draining being a single mum can be. If you ever need help with Grace, we'll rally round. It's not a bumper sticker – it's the truth. We all mean it, don't we, ladies?' All four of them nodded earnestly as I regurgitated my sorry tale of woe... 'Now, what are the exact dates and we'll come up with a plan?'

A single tear ran down my cheek and dropped off my chin.

'What's the matter now?' Jo cried, throwing her arms up in the air and then grasping my hands.

'Nothing, you're all just so lovely. Honestly, they're happy tears. You have no idea how worried I've been about it all. I guess I bury stuff sometimes.'

'Well, there's no point burying loads of shit under the carpet, is there?' Jo said pragmatically, giving me a hug, her head only reaching my shoulder. 'It only makes it harder to hoover.'

And just like that, the fear blew itself out, headed off at the pass by the welcoming conviviality of the Mews.

21

The Airing Cupboard

'Ah, hello,' Nick said, his eyes darting away over my head. As usual he looked like he was off to a nineties rave; he was just missing some white gloves.

'I wondered if your mum would like to try on some of these clothes. I got a load from Marks and Spencer and some other shops. I can leave them here; I'm not trying to intrude or anything. I'm off out in a bit anyway.'

I hadn't stopped thinking about Linda since I'd met her. There was something about her that I'd identified with. I thought it was sad that she didn't feel she could go shopping any more and I had to agree with her: online wasn't the same. As a stylist, I need to feel the material, see how it hangs, check for pocket details (everyone loves pockets!) and you can generally get an idea of how it will look. Though there are always the on-hanger corpses.

You know the ones – looks like someone had used it to wipe a skanky toilet floor, then on it goes, ta-dah, somehow it's transformed into some exquisite sheath of fabulousness that makes you look like a total goddess. I call it the Cinderella moment: *from rags to bitches.*

Linda deserved to have some fun and she needed to try on some clothes that would make her feel and look marvellous. So many people think fashion is vacuous and style over substance, but I see a different side. I've done countless makeovers in women's mags for ladies who have suffered hardships, have forgotten to take care of themselves and lost that integral part that loves finding joy in the small things. Just the gesture of telling that woman to try a different set of clothes from her utilitarian uniform can make a huge difference to someone's day. It's not frivolous, it's self-care and it changes people's frame of mind, makes them remember who they were before the proverbial shit hit the fan.

'Is that Ali?' Linda called from inside the house.

'Yes,' Nick shouted gruffly.

'Invite her in. I've got some wine here.' Nick stood back and dramatically swept his hand like a doorman in a fancy hotel. I found her in the kitchen sitting at the table, a bottle of red wine in the centre and two glasses.

'Did you know I was coming?' I laughed. 'I spotted you arrive earlier when I was curtain twitching!'

'I hoped you would. I asked Nick if he would invite you anyway, but I think you can tell what he said about that.' She giggled and I joined in. Nick must have felt like his balls were in a vice. 'I watched your vlog – it was so fun. Did the last one star the woman from over the road?'

'Yes, we asked Francesca and her two daughters to take part. We really do need people to make over rather than just us.'

'I think you and that Lila girl from *The X Factor* were so good together.'

'Thank you! I have some clothes here I thought you might like to try on.'

'Really? For me?' I suddenly hoped I hadn't done the wrong thing, assuming she would want to try them on. Her chin wobbled slightly.

'Yes, I saw them when I was out scouting clothes for the vlog. I thought they might suit you. You had said how much you liked fashion.'

'Oh, you dear. That's so kind.' I brought the bags round so she could rifle through. Nick came in and leaned against the cooker. 'Here, have some wine.' She picked up the bottle but her hand was wobbling. Nick dived over and took it from her, pouring wine into the two glasses. 'Nick, for the love of God, have a glass!' she chastised. 'It's Saturday!'

'Mum, you should probably just have one glass too.' He gave her a coded look and she rolled her eyes as he poured himself a small measure. The doorbell rang loudly, making me jolt my drink. I was terrified of ring-staining the surgical kitchen and wiped the glass with my sleeve, unable to spot a cloth anywhere.

I could hear some chatting and then a raised voice. Linda stood up and made a move to go to the front door, but the effort of just standing was too much, forcing the colour to drain from her cheeks.

'Linda, why don't I go instead?'

'Would you, dear? I think Nick is getting hassle again from that gentleman next door.'

'Nosy Norman?'

'Ah, yes,' she giggled. 'You've come across him too?'

I nodded.

'He can't keep his beak out of things, can he?'

'Everything OK, Nick?' I said as I hovered behind him in the hallway. Norman was standing on the step looking particularly aggrieved in what could only be described as lounge wear – navy silk PJs.

'Yes, just some neighbourly banter,' he replied.

'I disagree,' Norman said petulantly. 'I'm sick of the stink in the upstairs of my house. It's got worse this week and all my towels in the airing cupboard are smelling now too. Don't say you can't smell anything in there, Alison.'

I quietly breathed in through my nose.

'All I can smell is the Jo Malone diffuser, Norman,' I said innocently. 'Maybe something is rotting under your floorboards or a dead mouse is decomposing in your airing cupboard. Amanda and I always used to have dead mice under the floorboards when they ate the rat poison. The smell lingers for weeks.' He looked at me like I was mad. 'Do you want me to come and check for you?'

'If it's a mouse it's been dying for a year.'

'It could be an infestation,' Nick joined in. 'I might have mice too, in that case. I can check in my airing cupboard and look for evidence. They could be sneaking between the two houses because that's where the party wall is thinnest.'

'I want to come and inspect your upstairs.'

'There's nothing up there. I can't smell anything, Ali can't smell anything, you are the one with the bad smell, not me. Why don't we help you find out what it is in *your* house?'

Nick's frank reasonableness wiped the floor with Norman's concern.

'Fine! Come round then.' He flounced off the step and walked round to his front door.

'Mum, we're just going next door.'

We walked into the dimly lit hallway to find an imposing floor-to-ceiling gilt-framed poster of *La Cage aux Folles* leading the way up the stairs.

'I love that poster,' I said. It was stunning – a dancer swathed in a bright red feather dress wrapped herself down one side.

'Thank you,' he said tersely. 'I worked on that show.'

'No way! Where?' I was impressed.

'I did a tour in rep, years ago, all round the country.'

'Are you an actor?' I grilled him. Nick remained silent.

'No. Come on, it's worse just here on the landing.'

When we reached the door to the airing cupboard Norman turned to look at us.

'I can't smell anything,' Nick admitted.

'Me neither.' I really couldn't, but then that could be because my nose was so accustomed to the stronger smell next door. I didn't know what to say even if I could smell something.

Norman huffed and pulled open the door. We peered inside at the yellow water tank and piles of towels neatly stacked above it on wooden slatted shelves. I breathed in the musty smell of hot brass pipes and unmistakably pungent weed. Cunty McFucksticks.

'Now?' he demanded.

'There's a definite smell of something, but I'm not sure what,' I said after a moment of working out my reply.

'It smells of weed,' Norman boldly stated. 'Don't go telling me it's something else. I've been around the block enough to know what it is, and it's coming from your house.'

'But I don't smoke weed,' Nick said, aghast.

'I've poked as far as I can all around the tank and can't find anything. It must be coming from your house.'

'Look, I can assure you it isn't. I work for the Crown Prosecution Service, I cannot have anything to do with drugs or I would be sacked,' Nick reasoned. Maybe I was imagining the smell at his house after all. But I wasn't imagining this. The smell wasn't overpowering but it was unquestionably there.

'So I'm supposed to just put up with it?' Norman glared at us.

'But it's in *your* house, and it's in *this* cupboard, nowhere else – how is it affecting you?' Nick asked him. 'Apart from the towels smelling, is your life ruined by it? You've been trying to invite yourself in to *my* house now for a year because of *your* smell. Hopefully you'll leave me alone now.'

Norman opened and closed his mouth, Nick's cogent argument shutting him down.

'Growing drugs is illegal,' Norman said darkly.

'Bye, Norman. I hope you have a great rest of the evening.'

'Just keep the airing cupboard shut if you're worried,' I said, feeling slightly sorry for him, but also uneasy because I could tell this wasn't over. I followed Nick down the stairs and back into his house.

'Was he on about the smell again?' Linda asked once we were in the kitchen.

Nick nodded.

'You should just tell him the truth.'

'Mum, I can't, and you know that. He's like the bloody Mews Gazette.'

'I'm not stupid, Nick, so I'm just going to go as this feels massively awkward now. Whatever you're up to, I don't want to know.' I made to leave the house.

'Nick grows marijuana in his greenhouse at the bottom of the garden, but dries it in the airing cupboard.' Linda's hand was shaking. 'He does it for me. It helps with the constant pain and spasms.'

'Mum!' Nick's stricken face burned red.

'You're not Pablo Escobar?' I asked him light-heartedly.

'No, am I fuck.'

Linda's face pinched at the use of the F word, but it was fine that her son grew illegal drugs that could get him thrown in jail.

'Why all the secrecy, apart from the fact you could end up in prison?'

'If I tell Norman, he'll tell everyone else and I just can't have anyone knowing. Apart from that, Norman might shop me out of spite for lying to him.'

'I don't think Norman would be that bitter, especially as it's for your mum.'

'No matter, I can't have the information out there. My job would be on the line.' Linda sipped her wine slowly. I could tell Nick wanted to talk, so I sat down next to her and picked up my wine.

'When Mum was having a particularly bad attack last year after a few years in remission, Dad and I looked into alternative therapies. I'd always known about cannabis; there are derivatives of it around but doctors won't prescribe it. We're hoping one day it might be legal, but at the moment, this is the simplest way to get hold of it. And we absolutely have to keep it secret, because Dad is completely against it.'

'How come? Apart from it being illegal.'

Nick sighed and sat at the table, draining his small glass of wine.

'My husband, John, is a retired deputy commissioner in the police. He is avidly anti-drugs, having seen the violence committed in their name. He is very black-and-white about it and if he knew about this he would hit the roof.'

'OK. So how does the operation work?'

'John thinks that Nick takes me to an MS support group, staying the night here for ease, then Nick drops me on the way to work in the morning. Nick usually puts the dried flower buds in an omelette for me. Oh, you should have seen the first time we tried it, he got the dose wrong and I was babbling nonsense and was awake for hours seeing things. I felt like such a rebel. I had to stay an extra night.' She giggled at the memory. 'But because of the smell and the greenhouse, we've stopped John from coming here for a year. We're running out of excuses, to be honest.'

'Can't your sister help out? Or a friend? Store the stuff when he's due to come round?'

'No way. My sister is a barrister and super straight. The fewer people who know about this, the better. It's too big an ask for someone else to step in and help.'

'I could have the dried flowers for you in an emergency, if you wanted. But my garden has no room to hide the plants.'

'That's so kind of you,' Nick said, smiling properly so his eyes twinkled. 'I couldn't impose on you, though.'

'Do you take it too?' I asked, unable to imagine him letting go and having fun. I know I would have to lock the cupboard and give the key to an adult in case Bad Ali started adding it to everything I cooked on a daily basis, so probably it would be best I didn't store it for him at all.

'No way! I have to stay *compos mentis* in case Mum feels funny.' I didn't believe that someone with a huge stash in their airing cupboard wasn't going to try it another time.

'Where did you buy the plants?'

'On the Dark Web. You can get anything there.'

'Why don't you just buy the drugs on there?'

'Because I couldn't have a trail leading to me, even if it was on the Dark Web. It all felt so seedy. I thought a one-off purchase would be fine and then I would grow it myself. I had to learn all sorts. How to cross-pollinate and all that. I reckon I could now teach people how to grow their own drugs so they never have to go to a dealer again.'

'So how come your family are all from the North but live down here?'

'We followed the kids to London when I started to go downhill. John had retired years ago and so it didn't matter where we lived. We live in Bromley and Nick's sister lives in Crystal Palace with her husband and two kids, so it's easy for us to see them both.'

'I think that's lovely. I wish my mum was near me.'

'You won't say anything, will you?' Nick asked me cagily.

'Of course not. Your secret's safe with me.'

'You'll still pop by, won't you?' Linda asked me in a worried tone. 'I don't see many people other than immediate family. When I start feeling stronger it might be nice to join something.'

'Would you not go to a proper support group?' I asked her.

'Nooooo, I went once, years ago, and everyone was acting like they were on Death Row. I want to feel alive, not on borrowed time.'

'We're *all* on borrowed time,' I said, and smiled, patting her hand.

22

Debbie

Debbie swished her tea bag, the boiling water bleeding brown against the white. She squashed the bag on the side of the mug, completely staining the water, then added some soya milk. People who added milk first should be rounded up and shot, or sent on a tea-making awareness course, at the very least. There was nothing worse than milky tea in Debbie's book.

Through the window she saw the sky was patchy with clouds, allowing for some sporadic sun to break through. Debbie needed sunbeams today – she was finally celebrating cutting the cord from He Who Shall Not Be Named (Matthew), the man formerly known as her husband. Of course the children weren't as happy as she was with the arrangement. They didn't like living a week with him and then one with her, carrying school books and clothes between homes like Bedouins. She wasn't allowed in his new house so had to drop them round the corner, even if they had lots to carry. She'd noticed Ali and her ex earlier execute a peaceful handover. Well, there was no shouting like the first time she'd tried to drop the kids at Matthew's front door. She knew that they would probably never reach those civilised dizzy heights of normality. She could bet her future happiness on the fact that in twenty years from now, he would still be a bubbling cauldron of bitterness because she'd been the one to call it a day. His ego couldn't take the bruises.

When they'd met at Liverpool University in the mid-eighties, Debbie had been all-consumed by Matthew's idealistic notions about changing the world, working as an A and E doctor, helping people in crisis. His easy charm and altruism had sucked her in and before she knew it, she was deeply in love with him. They married before they hit thirty, but while her career developed successfully in immunology, he appeared to show signs of what could only be described as jealousy. It worsened after Charlie was born. It appeared Matthew couldn't handle that she was both a wonderful mother *and* a professor in her field, eclipsing what he saw as his own glittering trajectory. It was a side of him she'd never experienced and she naturally assumed it was stress-related. Stress played a part but it also seemed to be *Debbie*-related…

She'd tried everything – books, couples counselling, anger management, anything to save the marriage – because she hoped the man she'd fallen in love with would return. He'd try things for a bit, then dismiss them as New Age shit. Matthew saved people's lives daily, but couldn't see he was killing his relationship. She sighed – no one should have to be less to appease anyone else's sense of self. It was amazing how time had dealt her the ability to fully untie her heart from his. When she'd been madly in love with him she couldn't imagine not feeling that way. Now it was the complete opposite. So much wasted promise…

'Why can't we just stay here all the time?' Charlie asked once the custody agreement had been thrashed out between five pointless two-hundred-and-fifty-pound lawyers' letters. She couldn't be in the same room as Matthew after years of his controlling unreasonable behaviour. Even now, his underhand machinations twisted things so that she felt as if she was going crazy and he was the sane one, her heart galloping like a bolting horse. He'd even tried to shoehorn an outrageous clause into their divorce whereby if she met anyone else within a year, she had to pay back her share of the house. Deluded. As if she was going to meet anyone, she'd thought at the time. *The last thing I want is another man in my life.*

'I'm sorry it has to be like this,' Debbie had replied guiltily to Charlie. She omitted to say his father would bleed her of any more money and patience, trying to claim a stake in the remaining years of their children's childhoods if she hadn't settled it this way. Of course the children were old enough to say what they wanted now, but when the divorce had started, three years ago, they hadn't been. Isabelle resolutely wanted to please both of them, so she just went along with it, but Charlie, who had always preferred his mum, finding his father's stern manner and regular unhinged outbursts too much to handle, resisted to the last.

'It's not fair,' he had objected. Debbie wasn't a fan of the final conclusion either, wishing the children could stay with her for the majority of the time, but she could see that there might be some advantages, especially now.

It was Jo who'd found the lump, or rather voiced concern regarding what she'd thought was an undetected anomaly. Debbie may have known it was there but was choosing to prioritise her list of worries that week, especially as her divorce was about to be signed off, amid a desperate eleventh-hour addendum (even more extreme than the previous one). Debbie was still trying not to think about the lump a few weeks later, especially today, though she had gone to the doctor. She'd had lumps before and they'd always been benign cysts. She had particularly lumpy breasts, according to the specialist who saw her last time. Why would this one be any different? She could think of several reasons why it *could* be different, the main one being the breasts cover the heart chakra and somewhere during her marriage, her heart had given up, rolled over and died. It was quite an upheaval to go through a divorce and the body throws up all sorts of signals and warning signs that something may not be going to plan. She'd lost so much weight that even Jo had said she was looking a bit like a supermodel from the nineties. 'Heroin chic doesn't turn me on, darling,' she'd said in bed the other morning when the kids were at Matthew's. 'Are you eating? I'm worried about you.'

But she was eating when she remembered. Most days felt like she was wading through waist-high mud, but wasn't that what a divorce was supposed to make you feel like? It wasn't supposed to be a party; she'd expected difficulties and pain when she'd at last mustered up years' worth of courage to say the monumental words out loud. It also didn't help that her mum had finally been allocated a place in a care home miles away in Birmingham near her brother (at least they had got her out of Glasgow). She had to help empty her mum's flat the next weekend. Her to-do list was already escaping off the page.

Anyway, she would know on Tuesday. The mammogram was at eleven and Jo and Samantha were coming with her. She'd had several before so she wasn't nervous; she had the party to prep for. Guests were arriving at two to raise a glass to her new chapter and she had made a chocolate roulade with fresh cherries, whipped cream and brandy, her special roast vegetable salad with fresh basil, tomato and feta tart, and various other bits and bobs. People were also bringing dishes and Ali was making her special Marmite whirls – she could never make enough of them: they always vanished in the first five minutes. Jo was popping back over to help set up and collect all the glasses and fizz from Majestic Wine. Today was going to be about new beginnings, fresh starts, freedom. No, she wasn't worried about the mammogram.

23

Francesca's Secret

'So, hang on,' Jacqui said, her voice cracking as if the excitement was proving just so much she might self-combust. 'Let me get this straight, you found out there's a secret lesbian relationship going on up there, someone might have breast cancer and someone else is having an affair? Are you sure this isn't *EastEnders*? Is someone about to be kidnapped or dramatically find out their older sister is actually their mum?'

'Exactly! It *is* like a soap opera!' Amanda cried, shaking her head in disbelief at the latest Mewsflash. 'I wonder if that place is built on a ley line? It might explain all the drama triangles that seem to constantly spring up.'

It was Tuesday morning and the kids were all back at school after the late May Bank Holiday. Jacqui was busy drinking wine on the screen on Amanda's laptop and Amanda and I were chastely sipping coffee at the butcher's block island in her kitchen.

'Obviously I am still the new girl so the information overload was a lot to take in. I think they were supposed to drip-feed me stuff; instead it was a baptism of fire.'

'And?' Amanda asked. 'Spill the beans.'

'Well, Debbie's divorce party was fun, Nick the Spy actually came for an hour with his mum! She wore one of the outfits I'd given her – she looked adorable.'

'Oh, how cute!' Jacqui said. 'Did you snog anyone, man, woman, spy?'

'No! It wasn't that kind of party. Grace fell asleep upstairs in Isabelle's bed and I asked if I could stay in Charlie's room rather than drag her kicking and screaming home. Debbie's kids had stayed at their dad's. She had felt rubbing the divorce in their faces wasn't the work of a good parent.'

The girls nodded as I let them in on the weekend's events...

The sun had woken me by slowly boiling my eyeballs like eggs in their sockets. I'd forgotten to close the curtains last night and I'd foolishly slept with my lenses in so my eyes were like milky cataracts. I blinked twenty times until I could jiggle them with my finger. I was still wearing my yellow dress and I'd passed out on top of Charlie's Yoda duvet. *Drunk, you were.*

I wobbled down the stairs to find Grace in the living room watching TV, and Francesca in the kitchen initiating the clear-up. Debbie was sitting at the kitchen table; she smiled at me, but the sentiment didn't reach her eyes. She looked as rough as I felt.

'Do you want coffee?' Francesca asked me.

'Yes. I can make it. I'll help in a sec; I just need to find my feet. Coffee will sort me out. Where's all the stuff?'

'I'll get it,' Debbie said in a quiet voice and stood, only to immediately fold in on herself. I dived forward and caught her before she hit the deck. She was out cold. Francesca dropped the bin bag and grabbed her round the waist. She was surprisingly light: I guess stress had worked its way inside and whittled away at her body. Amanda had looked like a cadaver when Sam left her. The heartbreak diet was drastic; one I was only too familiar with myself.

'Here, on the chair, head between your legs,' Francesca soothed Debbie as she surfaced, her face a startling impression of ripe brie. 'Deep breaths. Can you get Jo, Ali?'

I nodded and headed in the direction of the front door.

'No, she's upstairs, in Debbie's room.'

I hastily changed direction and took the stairs two at a time, slipping on the top step: bastard trendy hessian carpet, it was like skinning yourself on gravel. I pushed open the main bedroom door and found a supine Jo passed out on the bed, the blue stripy duvet scrunched in a heap on the floor. She was completely naked, and on closer inspection, was entirely bald in her fanny region. I tried not to look, but it was kind of magnetising. I snapped my eyes away.

'Jo! Wake up!' She groaned. 'Debbie's fainted.' The magic words forced her to sit bolt upright.

'Where is she?' She scooted over to the edge of the bed where I was standing, reached over towards me – I ducked, just avoiding being boffed by one of her tits – and grabbed the white towelling dressing gown off the back of the door.

'In the kitchen.' She barged past me down the stairs, her face red and blotchy. I took a more considered approach, knowing the carpet was evil.

I entered the kitchen to find Debbie sobbing into Jo's arms and Francesca rubbing her back. I felt like an intruder and didn't know what to say for the best.

'I'm sorry you're feeling so shit, Debs. Divorce is awful. Maybe now it's final you'll start to move on.' It was a bit of a lame offering.

'It's not the divorce,' she cried, looking at me, 'though that doesn't help. I have a mammogram tomorrow and I've been pretending I was OK about it but I'm not...'

'Shit. Fuck, that's awful.' The blood drained from my own head as the spins took hold. 'You have a lump?'

She nodded.

'It might not be what you think.'

'Aye, but I think this time it is. After everything that's happened, it would just be the icing on the mouldy cake.'

'You don't know that,' Jo said, wiping Debbie's face with her hand. Debbie nodded slowly.

'Is there anything I can do?' I asked.

'Help me clear up, then we'll scoot,' Francesca said. 'Jo, take her back to bed. She needs to rest. She has to save her strength for tomorrow.'

After blitzing the house and garden with Francesca, we let ourselves out. Freya had asked if she could take Grace to the park with the new dog and I was only too glad to let her while we cleaned, instead of her being glued to the TV. The little dog was cute and quite a handful. Freya had had all her hair cut off since I'd briefly seen her four months ago. She looked so grown up and I had to bite my tongue not to mention the fact she looked so like her dad. 'Text me when you're on the way back.'

'What are you doing now?' Francesca asked me in the street.

'I don't know. I feel kind of flat. Things like that make you want to go out and live like it's your last day on earth instead of feeling profligately hungover.'

'Do you want to pop in for more coffee? Or something stronger?' She winked at me.

We lounged in Francesca's back garden on two deck chairs, half-heartedly sipping Yogi tea. It tasted like feet. Her girls were out with friends for the day and her partner was nowhere to be seen.

'I can't remember your husband's name,' I said apologetically, 'or what he does for a living.'

'Oh, Ian, we're not married.'

'What does Oh Ian do?'

She laughed. 'Annoys the crap out of me mostly, but he's in property. Owns half of Lordship Lane.'

'Wow, Mr Big.'

'Not really,' she said, sounding distinctly unimpressed. 'He has massive mortgages on a lot of them. He's always juggling money. I can't keep up. He's off meeting a potential new tenant now, which is good – gives me the house to myself. Me and Ian aren't really together any more.'

'Oh, gosh, I'm so sorry.'

'Don't be. It's been coming for a while. It's my decision and because it's my decision, I'm trapped.'

'How come? Surely you can just leave or he can?'

'I have no money, not enough to buy him out and stay in the house.'

'He's threatening to chuck you out?' I cried, incensed, fury suddenly igniting in my belly, fuelled by my own similar experience.

'No, not at all. Ian isn't a bastard, but even he won't gift me a house all of my own.'

'So what is he suggesting?'

'He said he'll buy me out of the house, and he will

continue to live here, but I have to leave. Everything is in his name so he could give me nothing, seeing as we aren't married. But as I said, he isn't a wanker, I just don't love him.'

'Did you ever love him?'

She sighed. 'Fuck being zen and this Yogi tea, I need a drink if I'm having this conversation. You joining me?'

Five minutes later Francesca had popped open a bottle of cava.

'Hair of the dog! The universe will shine down on us now and hold us while we tend to our hangovers.'

'Really?'

'No, but it sounds good. I can give you a hangover crystal to absorb last night's excess...'

'Yes, please.'

She pulled out a long clear pointy crystal wand from a hidden pocket in her baggy yoga trousers.

'Hold it on your sacral chakra, on your tummy. Put it next to your skin. Ask that it absorbs all the toxins. It will leave some room for some new ones!' The crystal was cool against my belly.

'So, Ian – I did love him once – we've been together twenty-four years and the first eight were lovely, but he always said he wasn't into getting married, probably because of the whole money thing, sharing his business with me should we ever split up. I originally hoped he would change his mind, but when the girls were toddlers he suffered depression and cut himself off from me. His mum died, then one arm of his business folded and he fell out with his business partner, and I was left to bring up the girls pretty much on my own. He wasn't present for a lot of their early childhood, absent in mind and body. As for sex, well, that never happened. He hasn't physically touched me for over seven years.'

'What? Not even accidentally?'

'No. So when I asked if we could sell the house and stop living the charade now the girls are teenagers, he broke down, begged me to stay, said he would marry me. I thought about it, but all the ignoring has shut me down. I tried so many times to get him to come to counselling, relationship guidance, healers – any straw you threw my way, I grasped it! He refused. So I went myself, and that's how I got into being a shaman. But unfortunately while I was on a healing journey of my own, he was trapped in aspic and the chasm feels too big to fill now. I have a whole life ahead of me.'

'It must be so awkward. Isn't it better to be somewhere else if you don't love him?'

'Technically, yes, it is, but despite everything the Mews is where I have been the happiest and most settled. I travelled around so much when I was younger, running away, really, looking for something that wasn't there. So when we finally moved here and had the girls, it felt solid, a real anchor after years of feeling displaced. I gave up work and threw myself into family and home life in the Mews. I'm not sure I can leave it...'

'Can you afford to live round the corner to soften the blow?'

'Have you seen property prices?' she cried, shaking her head. 'I can't afford anywhere with my income where the girls can live too, and I'm not leaving them either. I'd have to move miles away and go back to being a PA. It would feel like taking a step backwards when I want to be going forwards.'

'Do the girls know?'

'Of course, they don't want us to split up, but they're old enough now to work out I'm not happy.'

'Aren't you desperate for sex, for human contact?'

'Yes, so badly I think it has rendered me un-dateable because I *am* so desperate. I'm at the stage where sitting on the washing machine during the spin cycle is the highlight of my day.'

I burst out laughing. 'But can you date? How would that work?'

'I can't; if Ian found out he would make my life hell. The girls would hate me. They've already made noises about how mortifying it would be if I got myself a toy boy.'

'So you're telling me you're in limbo? Not even looking?'

She sipped her wine and arched her eyebrows in a way that begged for an inquisition.

'Ah.'

'Ah what?'

'You *are* looking.'

'Maybe.'

'Is there anyone?'

She looked like she was weighing up whether to divulge the details.

'Teyo, my Qi Gong teacher,' she eventually whispered, like the bamboo was going to shop her in.

'You're shagging him?'

'No, I'm not *that* much of a middle-aged cliché.'

'So what *are* you doing?'

'Sexting.'

'Have you even kissed?'

She shook her head.

'Why not?'

'I don't know. It isn't like that, it's just all over text, for some reason. He texts me all the time, night and day, and we do see each other, but only during class. The last time I was properly single in the dating game, I was twenty-eight. Things are so different now. I don't know what's normal any more. I actually think I've forgotten what it's like to have a man's touch make your insides melt. Jo has also been lecturing me on how Teyo is leading me on, but I can't help it – the heart wants what it wants, and I want to fuck his brains out!'

I spat my wine onto the grass in surprise.

'What are you going to do?' I asked eventually.

'I guess I'll get more batteries for my vibrator and stick to Plan B.'

'Which is?'

'Fix everyone else's lives and maybe some of it will rub off on me and some divine inspiration will visit in the night and tell me what to do.'

'Oh, Francesca, that's so shit. You're so good at helping others. It's your job.'

'I know; the irony is killing me. And the number-one rule of healing is heal yourself first before you heal others. I dole out advice to people, see things for other people, hold space for other people, but I can't do it for myself.'

'But you deserve a happy-ever-after.'

'Not everyone gets one, though, do they? This isn't a film; it's real life. The best we can do is have our happy-ever-after in the moment we are in right now. And right now, I'm happy sitting here with you, baring my secrets.'

I felt a tear sting the corner of my eye: her words touched me. But she was wrong about one thing – my life *was* a film and Miley Cyrus (as me) was going to gloriously stride her way into the sunset, singing 'The Climb' with the world at her feet and a queue of Greek gods waiting to kiss her hallowed toes.

'Do you want to see my wish box?' Francesca asked, changing the subject.

24

A Tale of Two Dresses

A chaotic white Ikea desk stacked with spiritual magazines and clear plastic boxes of crystals piled up like mystical Jenga leaned up against one wall in Francesca's office opposite the single bed, which was covered in a patchwork quilt and mirrored scatter cushions. The cream walls had several posters tacked up of the reflexology meridian points on the feet, and all the different bodies we possess: spiritual body, emotional body, physical body – Beardy Weirdy stuff.

'It's under here.' She got down on her tummy, lifted up the edge of the quilt from the floor and disappeared halfway under the bed.

'Do you need some help?'

'I've got it,' she said in a muffled voice, commando-crawling backwards. She dragged out a long black plastic box the size of a very large suitcase. It was tied tightly with two secure leather belts that had combination locks attached to them. No fucker was getting in there. She fiddled with the locks until they snapped open.

'Why the secrecy?' I asked.

She looked at me pointedly, lifted the lid off the box and lay it on top of the bed. A sea of white froth, sequins and sparkle spread out before me. She took the dress out of the box, revealing a different one underneath.

'Oh, right. Are these your dresses?'

'Yes, they're proper wedding dresses. This one is my current favourite, but the other one is a close second and I'll be able to wear it if I ever lose a stone.'

She pinned it up against her body so I could get an idea of what it would look like.

'Why don't you put it on?' I asked, the cava obviously taking charge of the situation.

'I will if you put the other one on.'

Giggling, we stripped off to our underwear. I had never tried on a wedding dress in my life. I had styled wedding dress shoots for *Brides* magazine, and helped Amanda choose her second-time-round dress, but even when I got engaged to Jim I never ventured forth into the wedding gown arena. I must have known it was never going to work out.

I zipped Francesca into her dress, which was a sexy fish-tail sequined affair with a tulle tail embossed with tiny crystals.

'You look like a beautiful mermaid!'

My white prom dress had a beaded bodice and a wide tulle skirt that reached my calves. A layer of silk covered the skirt and it was edged with white ribbon. It was classic fifties starlet; I felt magically moonstruck.

'I've got shoes too!' Francesca said excitedly. She pulled two pairs of white strappy sandals out of the box, both of them encrusted with intricate diamanté detail. 'Cinderella, you shall get married.'

I couldn't twirl as there wasn't enough room with both of us clogging up the office with flouncy glitter and sparkles, our dresses making crackling sounds.

'What else is in the box?' I asked, eyeing colourful notebooks, house brochures, random women's magazines, and a white A1 piece of card partially obscured at the bottom. Francesca bent down and pulled out the card. It was plastered in photos of yoga studios, holistic treatment clinics, fancy massage beds, a white dove, a couple of brides and several handsome men from catalogue shoots. Aspirational words were carefully written in gold pen around some of the pictures: *manifest, dreams come true, live in the now, I am grateful, trust...*

'Wow,' I whispered in awe. 'Are you cosmic ordering?'

'Yes, it's my vision board. All the things I want to come to me are on here.' I realised we had already drunk a whole bottle of fizz, my hangover temporarily receding into the wings.

'Don't you feel shit that you have to hide your dreams under your bed? I assume Ian has no idea about your dresses.'

'It's how I stay sane.'

'But you'll never meet anyone while you're with Ian.'

'Good old Joseph Heller and his *Catch Twenty-Two*.'

'Or *Hobson's Choice*,' I said, recalling a programme I'd heard on Radio Four last week. 'You either leave and suffer the consequences or you don't.'

The front door suddenly jangled shut, the letterbox cover clanging, alerting us to the fact that someone was in the house.

'Shit,' Francesca hissed. 'It must be Ian. We have to take these off.' Her zip had snagged on the material, catching on a sequin, chewing it up. It was jammed half on half off without any way of getting it past her sizeable boobs.

'Fran? You in?' Ian called up the stairs.

'Fuck, fuck, fuck,' Francesca hissed. 'I can't let him see me in this. He'll go mental.'

'He might not. I'll think of something. We need him to help us get this off you. Two people will have to pull the material away from the zip while I undo it.'

'Fran?' he called again from the bottom of the stairs. I heard the creak of footsteps.

'Shit, OK, get rid of the box,' Francesca panicked, and I rammed the lid back on and slipped the box back into its hiding place.

'We're in here,' she called out in an overly bright voice. 'I'm a bit stuck.' The door slowly opened and Ian's face reflected back his shock.

'Bloody hell, is this fancy dress or did I not get the memo?' he managed to force out between clenched teeth.

'I can explain,' I said hesitantly. 'They're mine from a shoot I'm prepping for *Brides* magazine. We thought it would be funny to try them on, only now we're stuck...'

'What happened?' Jacqui asked, riveted by the tale of two dresses.

'He told Francesca she looked beautiful. It was actually quite sweet. I felt sorry for him because she was grossed out by the attention.'

'The thing is, you don't know what their relationship is like from the inside. You only have Francesca's take on things.'

'Oh, bloody Amanda!' Jacqui laughed. 'Always playing devil's advocate! You should train to be a high court judge!'

'I'm just trying to see both sides. Of course I feel bad for her, hiding her wishes in a box under her bed is like an LGBT person remaining in the closet...'

'Anyway, will you let us know how Debbie gets on at the hospital?' Jacqui asked before we got on with our day and she finished hers.

★

Jo's Rolls-Royce was parked on her drive when I returned home. Her door swung open as I reached my house and I whipped round to catch her beckoning me over from behind the door.

'It's cancer,' she said solemnly as I reached the front step.

'Oh God, I'm so sorry. Where's Debbie now?'

'She's at home. She wanted me to tell you because she can't. She's in shock. The kids come back from school this afternoon and she has to tell them. I don't know if it's a good idea when she's feeling so dreadful. I've tried suggesting to her not to do it today, wait until she's got her head around it. They don't know she was at the hospital and they don't know she's been feeling ill.'

'They'll know something's wrong, though. Isabelle will definitely know: girls always do. Charlie is probably in his own little world, like most boys.'

'Maybe. I just wish I could go over there and help, but the kids don't know about us. We were going to tell them after the divorce party if her results were clear, but it's all gone tits up, excuse the pun. I have to stay out of the way.'

'What happens next?'

'She's got to have a lumpectomy, then chemo, then radiotherapy. But the waiting list is enormous and she's worried it could turn into a grade three or four and spread to her lymph nodes before the operation if she has to wait a few months.'

'Can't she go private? I know I would beg, borrow and steal the cash if that was the case.'

'I've suggested that, but she's dragging her feet. We'll see what happens. Anyway, Samantha has disappeared back home too – some kind of emergency over at hers now. The world's gone mad!'

Not the world, I thought, just the Mews.

A text dinged just as I was cooking Grace's fishfingers after school. It was Samantha.

Can we rearrange the filming this week? I have other plans and can't use the house for the vlog.

Bugger. I had all the clothes piled up in the corner of my bedroom. We had some luxurious outfits from Stella McCartney, which was an enormous coup. Lila had put in a word because Stella had supplied some dresses for her final on *The X Factor*. It was all part of her plan to up the subscribers by throwing in a bit of aspirational fashion rather than concentrating solely on high street. We were working towards monetising our work and as far as I was concerned that was a good thing; my debt was the ever-present elephant in the room.

Any idea when we can shoot? I have some outfits on borrowed time.

Will let you know. Something important has happened.
I'll talk to Lila and let her know. xx

Slouching on the sofa at ten that night, I scrolled through Instagram, dishing out likes with the benevolence of Mother Teresa, the news on in the background.

'David O'Donnell is still in hiding today after being outed by the *Daily Mail*,' the news anchor informed.

'Oh, fuck me, not another paedophile scandal,' I muttered to myself, and turned up the volume to catch the rest of the report.

'Mr O'Donnell, former game-show host, original ITV breakfast television presenter and co-host on *Good Morning with David and Mina*, has reportedly gone to ground after the *Daily Mail* published an article claiming that he is a transvestite. Mr O'Donnell has been off air from presenting *Good Morning with David and Mina* on Channel Five since the scandal broke two days ago. Stephen Jones, the outside broadcast correspondent, has been filling in for him. Trisha Templeton, his wife, *Loose Women* panellist and a former Miss Great Britain, has tweeted "could people please give us some privacy and allow us to collect their thoughts during this difficult time".' The screen flicked to scenes of a pack of baying paparazzi outside a tall white Georgian town house somewhere in London, surrounding the gate so no one could get in or out. 'A spokesperson for *Good Morning with David and Mina* has said that Mr O'Donnell will return to the show as soon as possible.'

'Fucking *Daily Mail*. Who cares if he's a transvestite?' I switched the TV off and could hear a lot of banging car doors and low voices outside. Naturally I poked my head between the curtains after I switched the lights off. A flurry of activity was happening outside Samantha's house. I could make out Samantha silhouetted in the doorway, and a man and woman grabbing bags from the boot of a Porsche and hurrying inside. The man's head was bent low into his chest, but his companion turned round cautiously before also dipping her head down. It was impossible not to work out who she was. Her glorious mane of blond hair and iconic height made her stand out a mile, even in dusky evening light. Trisha Templeton.

25

Jo

Jo didn't know what to do with herself. She paced round the kitchen, a familiar sensation raging in her chest, forcing her back where she didn't want to be, shaking Steve's lifeless body, a waxy sheen on his face already letting slip he'd gone. The repressed memory always unravelled her from the inside out.

'I must be able to do something,' she mumbled. She finally settled on the task of feeding the menagerie of pets. Her lodgers were all at college so the house felt less hectic, not something she relished. The animals were always here and always needed a cuddle, or a walk, or food. She pulled the two giant sacks of kibble out of the cupboard and spooned the food into the various bowls. The cats were already in the kitchen, sitting on the table, viewing her with impassive eyes; cats and their conditional cupboard love. The dogs came waddling in as soon as they heard the cupboard open. 'Pavlov's dogs,' she chuckled affectionately.

She sent another text to Debbie.

If you need anything, please let me know. I can go to the shops, get you guys a takeaway, you name it.

Debbie didn't reply. Jo gazed out of the window to see if she could spot the kids coming back from school. Jo would have liked her own kids. She always thought she would one day, but time was ticking now. She was past forty and she'd ideally like to bring them up in a relationship rather than as a single mum. She'd obviously pay a surrogate; she wasn't having all that nonsense of pregnancy, no drinking for nine months or vomiting night and day. Someone else could do all that shit. She'd almost made enough money to retire now and could offer a good life to a young family. Daring property deals in the nineties supporting her property development business in the early noughties meant she could pick and choose when to work. Working in property, traditionally considered a very male-dominated industry, had never fazed her. In fact, the challenge egged her on to succeed where so many had failed.

Jo didn't like failing, or being told what to do, or being on her own. The longest she had been single was about three months, and even then, she was constantly going on dates, the thrill of the chase like a chemical high, *always* with straight women. To be fair, they were invariably up for a change of scene. She knew she could never persuade Ali, so she'd let that one go, but Debbie had been ripe for it. She sighed and her shoulders sagged when she thought of Debbie.

The one thing all these women had in common was some bastard bloke treating them really badly, so in swooped Jo on a charm offensive and before they knew what had hit them, they had fallen for her. All of them subtly needed fixing too, but Jo didn't register any of that. She just felt drawn to them like a moth to a flickering flame, dancing in their fading light until another spark caught her eye, needed her and the dance began again...

Jo didn't understand why she managed to plough through relationships at a rate of knots. Fran had mentioned maybe not trying to constantly control every aspect, trying to live in the moment, but Jo liked things how she liked them. What was wrong with that? She wasn't purposely vindictive, abusive or sneaky, though she had been known to carelessly overlap before and wasn't averse to running two people round the block at the same time. Francesca would always shake her head and tell her she was terrible in an indulgent way, like you do to a favourite naughty child. It would seem people rarely said no to Jo.

Jo was used to managing everyone, including her

parents, whom she adored. She'd bought them a lovely little retirement home near Bromley – just the right distance away. So she was struggling to work out why Debbie was ignoring her in her hour of need. When they'd got together after Jo's trip to A and E, they'd made plans to go away for a holiday, tell the children about their relationship so they could get used to the idea that their mum was possibly a lesbian. Jo liked the idea of the ready-made family, though the children were a lot older than her preferred ideal. She loved little kids – cute button noses, chubby knees, squeaky voices – but Charlie and Isabelle appealed because they were beautifully brought up. They had lovely manners, and Jo approved of that. She knew it would take time for them to accept her, but she thought they would eventually; children were adaptable, weren't they?

She ran upstairs to her office and switched on her laptop. She googled oncologists in London, scribbled down numbers of clinics, checked out their websites, the facilities, their mission statements and started making calls.

'Hello, yes, could you tell me how soon I could book someone in for a consultation in regards to a lumpectomy? Yes, she's already been seen by the NHS, it's a ductal carcinoma in situ in her left breast... a DCIS, yes. Friday at ten? Fabulous. Yes, that's fine, I can do a bank transfer. What's your name, my darling? Well, thank you so much, Tessa. We'll see you then.'

Jo finished the call and sat back on her office chair. Money talked and if she could help, she would. She didn't see the point of not acting on something, getting the ball rolling. Why procrastinate? Bish bash bosh, tick that box, get a result, move on. It worked for most things. She had that sorted, but she didn't want to tell Debbie in a text. She'd wait until the kids were at school tomorrow and go round, surprise her. Yes, that was the best plan. She breathed a sigh of relief. The memories had been successfully encased in their lead box.

26

PR SOS

I need to talk to you urgently. Can I come to your house
with Lila for a meeting?

Samantha's text popped up like a slice of toast at six
the following morning. I was already awake, having
been subjected to an unsettling raunchy dream involving
Carl, a pair of handcuffs and chocolate body paint from
back in its late nineties' heyday. I shook off the remnants
of the dream and texted back a yes. I decided to get
up and win against the day by attempting yoga in the
living room before Grace woke at seven but I couldn't
escape the image of Carl licking chocolate goo off my
naked thighs with his nimble tongue. Was this how
desperate I was, having fantasies about my next-door
neighbour, who wouldn't fancy me in a million years

because I wasn't a skinny twenty-something model? Even in Savasana, lying in relaxation at the end of the practice, my head lolling to one side, Carl's beautiful face loomed into my third eye and the kiss he delivered had me coveting a sly quickie with Rampant Rabbit. There was no Om going on.

Later on, I handed out coffees and a poor selection of biscuits for our meeting, perched at the breakfast bar.

'So, I know I said I needed to cancel the filming this Friday. Well, I've changed my mind. It's back on.' Samantha picked up a custard cream and inspected it before nibbling the end.

'How come?' Lila asked.

I remained silent, in possession of an uncertain inkling.

'OK, this is highly confidential and I am going to have to get you to sign these NDAs before we can go any further.'

'What on earth?' Lila blurted out. 'We've got an A-list celebrity on the vlog using your connections? It won't be just Ali and me arsing around in Stella McCartney?'

I was a non-disclosure agreement virgin. Z-listers never used them and glamour models wanted all the press they could get. Samantha slapped her Louis Vuitton handbag on the counter and leafed through it, retrieving an A4 manila envelope. She slipped out two binding agreements and handed one to each of us.

'OMG!' Lila cried. 'No way!'

I scanned the top of the document to find the name I had expected: David O'Donnell.

'He wants to come out publicly in a sympathetic environment. He has final say, and we are to air it the night before he returns to the show with Mina. Mina will be there too. Everyone's on board.'

'Oh, I love her!' I cried. Mina Prajapati was a presenter who had solidly worked her way up through the ranks of Saturday morning kids' TV that post-clubbing kidults would customarily watch in a catatonic comedown. She had forged a successful break-away career into adult presenting in her thirties and now she was my age, with three kids, she was co-hosting her own show. She was no dolly bird, or arm candy for David; she was feisty, very funny, and she said it how it was in her strong Bradford accent.

'Is it being filmed by *Good Morning with David and Mina*?' I asked.

'No, you two are doing it. Mina is going to interview David before you girls help him transform, along with his daughter. I just need a few identical outfits. The production team and Channel Five are all behind it.'

'I can't take it in,' Lila said, clearly in shock. 'How did this come about?'

'David is godfather to my two boys. I used to be his agent when I worked at William Morris. He wanted to stay there when I set up on my own because Trisha was already there, but we remained very close. We meet for lunch once a month.'

'So he asked you to do this for him?' Lila quizzed, shaking her head at the enormity of it all.

'No, I suggested it. He and Trisha are staying with me until things die down. No one knows they're here. The press can't find out because we would all be under siege – their home is surrounded by press, waiting for them to leave. Thankfully, they have a back entrance through to a neighbour's and escaped last night.'

'So they came to you for advice or to hide?' Lila continued her interrogation.

'Just to hide. But we stayed up all last night going round in circles. David is mortified. He feels justified in keeping his cross-dressing a secret because there is still so much stigma attached to it, especially if you have never alluded to it before. It's different for Eddie Izzard because it's synonymous with who he is, but David is so far in the closet he's in Narnia. He's always managed to keep his identity secret when he goes out dressed as Viola.'

'Did his family always know?' I asked, fascinated.

'Not always. He came out to them about ten years ago. Trisha is a legend and so supportive. She has always known – they go shopping together; it's very cute.'

'Did any of his friends know? Did *you* know?' I asked.

'Yes. I did know. I've known David for thirty-five years – I introduced him to Trisha after his first wife died. I knew she would be the best companion for him because she is so kind, and also totally non-judgemental. She came from a very tough mining background that hardly anyone ever escaped.'

'Didn't she support the miners during the strike in the eighties?' I said, my foggy brain grasping at a hazy image of a very youthful Trisha marching with a placard, her Miss Great Britain crown on her head.

'Yes, she did. She was also a huge supporter of gay and lesbian rights back in the day when no one was. She's fab. I think that's why she's so popular still – the gay community love her and when the gay community love you, your star always shines!'

'So is this a bit of PR SOS?' Lila asked, dipping a plain digestive into her coffee.

'I actually think this will be the making of David and *Good Morning with David and Mina*. The show has been going only a year, and it lags a long way behind *This Morning* in the ratings. It was kind of the big hope for Channel Five after previous shows failed to make a dent. Mina is obviously a big draw, and David has always been popular with the older viewers, but maybe now this is a chance to reach out to a different audience. People love an underdog and they love redemption. Not that he's done anything wrong, but the way the *Mail* have portrayed him, you would believe he's been caught as a practising paedophile.'

'Isn't he scared of a backlash?' I asked. 'I mean, there will be equal numbers of haters. All the Britain First dickheads and UKIP supporters.'

'There will be anyway, Ali. He's been outed. What's important is to not take any of it on board, show you don't care and carry on as normal. When people make protests like that, it's usually because it's ignited something inside about their own lives.'

'Shouldn't we do it somewhere more glamorous then, if so much is riding on it? How will everyone fit in the house?' I suggested. 'Doesn't he want to do this on TV instead?'

'No – platforms like YouTube are the future of broadcasting instant content like this. He doesn't want to be live, and TV takes so long to record. We can be in and out, and Lila can edit in a day. Lila, your boyfriend will also have to sign an NDA.'

My head was spinning out of control. I was mentally tallying up where I could go to source women's clothes and shoes that would fit a man – I needed to measure him.

'I think we need to stick to the original premise of the vlog, in a neutral house, nothing fancy, and it's all about the clothes and how they make you feel – the audience will relate to that so much more than in some swanky hotel. Why don't you both come over to mine now?' Samantha said calmly. 'David and Trisha obviously have to stay inside; you know what Nosy Norman's like!'

Ten minutes later, we nervously entered the living room where they were both sitting down on the sofa, nursing cups of tea. They jumped up, instantly revealing their height disparity. Even in her ballet pumps and simple green tea dress, Trisha was a good three inches taller than David; she must have been over six foot. He wasn't tiny, and was taller than me, it was just that Trisha's Amazonian height was breathtaking. In real life, she was leonine, her impressive mane of hair enriching her majestic aura. Make-up free and subtly tanned, her fifty-something face appeared well tended.

'Hello,' she greeted us in her sing-song Welsh accent. She offered out her hand for us to take turns in shaking. 'I'm Trisha, and this is David.' I wanted to laugh – did the Queen ever offer her hand and reveal the ineffable secret that she was indeed the Queen? David reached over and shook our hands too.

'Hello,' we said in unison. He appeared older in the flesh, probably because studio make-up does its job well. If Trisha had had work done, it was subtle because she wasn't line-free, just naturally blessed with cheekbones that the rest of her face could confidently hang off without collapsing into the Pillsbury Doughboy.

'Would you like a cuppa?' David asked in his Irish brogue. 'I just boiled the kettle.'

'Yes, that would be lovely,' I answered as Lila declined. David made a move towards the kitchen when Samantha intervened.

'Dave! I'll make the tea. You've got to be measured and discuss outfits. Stop trying to escape!'

'So, I know you both understand what has happened,' Trisha opened with.

Just before Lila and I joined them, we had googled it all and got up to speed online with what utter bollocks the tabloids were reporting. Some of the headlines were ridiculous and plain nasty.

'We're not staying at Sam's because we have anything to hide or are ashamed of David in any way, it's purely because we were trapped inside our house with people constantly focusing lenses on our every move. We couldn't think straight in there.'

'It must be awful and so invasive,' I sympathised. 'When is David back on the show?'

'Monday, so really this all needs to happen now.'

'How soon can you turn the vlog around?' David asked softly, sitting back down so we all followed suit.

'Well, if we shoot Friday, me and Hayden can just stay up all night and edit it, get it to you Saturday. You can make changes, approve it, whatever you do, and then we're ready to launch Sunday evening.'

I was desperate to ask personal questions, like had David always worn ladies' clothes? How on earth did he walk in heels and could he teach me? And finally, did he wear the dreaded Spanx? He seemed rather subdued compared to his screen persona of jovial gentleman in a jumper softly probing guests on the studio sofa while Mina dived in with a more direct approach. Could there be a chance of him appearing as Viola on his own show?

'What kind of clothes are you looking to wear on Friday?' I opened with, hoping it was the right thing to say, scared I was going to ask the wrong questions or inadvertently say something offensive.

David glanced at Trisha before answering, his lip twitching while he clenched and unclenched his hands.

'Come on, love, these girls aren't going to bite.' Trisha smiled encouragingly at him.

'I want to wear something classic.' He endearingly flushed pink, finally letting his guard down. 'I know you haven't got much time and can't reveal who this is all for to shops or designers, so I know we'll just have to go with what you can find.'

'You could mention you've signed an NDA; that might put petrol in the fashion PRs' engines,' Trisha butted in with.

'That's a good idea,' Lila agreed. 'Who are your favourite designers and shops?'

'Designers hardly ever make the clothes big enough. Chain stores are better. I tend to go to Next, which is amazing for casuals, and M&S for more formal stuff. I can usually fit into a size twelve to fourteen; my shoulders get in the way, you see, and I have size ten feet, so you might not be able to find anything decent. I can always get Caroline to bring my own shoe collection from home.'

'I have the same problem,' Trisha lamented. 'I have to get my clothes made or from Max Mara because they always seem to be too small elsewhere.'

'I have to wear things that disguise my muffin top,' I admitted, sucking it in. 'I've never been able to get rid of it since I had my daughter, Grace, no matter how many cakes I don't eat.'

'You look wonderful, my dear,' David said kindly. 'At least you don't have bricklayer's shoulders. Have you tried Spanx?'

I almost choked. 'I hate Spanx,' I revealed, then suddenly realised that David probably loved Spanx, 'but I know they have their place. I always seem to find the fat gets redistributed somewhere else, usually round my neck.'

'I know what you mean,' he said, laughing, relaxing his shoulders, which didn't look like they could hod carry at all. How surreal was this? A conversation with David O'Donnell on the best underwear to disguise back fat.

'You're the lucky one here,' David said, nodding at Lila. 'You can just walk into any store knowing the clothes will automatically fit you.'

'I disagree!' Lila blustered. 'I'm so small that sometimes nothing fits lengthways, and I have no boobs and a wide back so I look like a boy. I often have to buy kids' clothes, which are cheap, but Barbie can take a hike.'

'No one is ever happy, are they?' I chuckled. 'Now, let's measure you, David, and then we can discuss clothing. I'm assuming you will have your own underwear and necessary enhancements.'

'Oh, of course. Breast forms and decent underwear are the staple of any cross-dressing wardrobe,' Samantha said, reappearing with tea for me and her. 'Ooh, you should see Dave's boobs – he has different sizes for different moods. Even a Dolly Parton pair.' The ease with which she was able to tease him revealed the depth of their friendship.

'Do you?' I asked, surprised, finding it hard to envisage him with a prominent chest.

'No! Sam's being naughty.'

When I'd jotted everything down in my notebook, including their daughter, Caroline's, height and size she'd texted through, we discussed the vlog, what direction we all saw it going, Caroline's role and the end result.

'Will you be needing a make-up artist?' Lila asked. 'We can find someone if you do.'

'No, Trisha always does my make-up. She's a genius! I can do it myself, but for this I'd prefer if she did it.'

He smiled lovingly at her and she winked at him. They were adorable.

'Carl has agreed to take behind-the-scenes pictures and to hand over everything to Dave,' Samantha revealed. 'I spoke to him while I was making tea. We can auction off the pictures for charity to the highest-bidding magazine. I reckon *OK!* or *Hello!* will battle it out.'

'I can't thank you enough, girls,' Trisha gushed as we got up to leave. 'This means a lot to both of us. If we can pay you – if not in cash, in kind – it would mean the world.' It was on the tip of my tongue to shout 'YES, PLEASE' because it would save me from the proverbial gutter of debt.

'No, no one pays us for coming on the vlog,' Lila jumped in before I could say a thing. 'If word got out that you paid us, it would look dreadful on your behalf. It needs to be a favour, people helping each other out. Believe me, this will probably propel Clothes My Daughter Steals into the vlog stratosphere, so we should really thank you!'

27

Viola

Samantha's downstairs was teeming with people on Friday morning. Carl niftily darted about with several cameras strapped across his body, silently clicking reportage-style photos. I hadn't been able to look directly at him because I could still imagine him smearing chocolate on me as if I was a nude canvas that he was painting an intricate picture on with his tongue.

'Are you OK?' he asked after I walked off numerous times in order to keep my blushing under control. *It was just a dream, it didn't happen!* I chanted mantra-like in my head in time to *Black Beauty*.

'Fine. Nothing to worry about.'

'I wasn't worried really, but are *you* worrying about something?' He tried to catch my eye in a game of cat and mouse, but I steadfastly refused to play, keeping him in my periphery.

'Nope, all good. Do you want tea?' He stared at me and shook his head in bewilderment.

'Is there something going on with you and the cute photographer?' Lila hissed at one point when we were clearing the living room of all movable furniture into the garden.

'No! What made you say that?'

'You could cut the atmosphere with a knife. Just shag him and get it over with!'

I couldn't think of a snappy retort, so had to suffice with a paltry huffing noise and a limp: 'As if.'

Lana, the series producer of *Good Morning with David and Mina*, was scrutinising everything very closely, but was under strict orders not to interfere.

'It's not scripted,' I'd informed her nervously. 'We wing it mostly, with a bit of an idea where we're going.'

'Oh, I'll be fine,' David assured us. 'Like treading the boards without an earpiece. Ad-libbing was always my forte.'

A power-dressed Mina Prajapati was stationed at the kitchen table with a jug of coffee and some prepacked M&S melon cubes. She had been asked to arrive at six in the morning to avoid being spotted by Norman, who wasn't trusted not to spill the beans.

'Hello, ladies,' she'd said when we arrived at 7 a.m. 'Well done for doing this; we'll show those fuck-pigs at the *Mail* a thing or two about inclusion!' Mina was instantly elevated to the canon, my brand new BFF spirit animal.

On Sunday evening, Lila, Hayden, me, Samantha, Carl, Elinor, Jo and Francesca crowded round Samantha's laptop – a miniature diorama on the kitchen counter – hearts in our mouths. I had texted my crowd, pressing upon them that they wouldn't want to miss it live. I'd knocked on Nick's door to let him know Linda might want to see it, but he was out, so I slipped a note through his letterbox, telling him to watch it.

Grace was staying with Jim, absolving me of any parental responsibility, and David and Trisha had safely returned home. The ring of journalists had dispersed after catching no sight of them for days. Another scandal had obviously distracted them. Lila had taken to social media, as was the plan, posting a couple of Carl's photos of the back of David's head, his chosen wig in place, a dressing gown wrapped round the rest of him. She'd hashtagged the shit out of it, alluding to a big celebrity name. I had also appropriated a few of Carl's photos, teasing my followers with tantalising snippets of the clothes ready to be worn. In addition, I'd picked a sneaky close-up of Trisha's hand painting fuchsia pink lipstick onto David's lips, his surrounding skin heavily pancaked to disguise the recent brush with a razor. You honestly couldn't tell who it was.

Lila sat with Hayden at the kitchen table on a separate laptop and, at five to eight, she uploaded it to our channel.

'There it is!' Samantha cried bang on time at 8 p.m. She clicked play. The usual graphics rolled, then Lila's cherubic face filled the frame, her fringe skimming the tops of her heavily made-up cat eyes.

'We've got a special edition of Clothes My Daughter Steals today. We'll be part of a transformation like no other. But rather than me doing the introductions, I'll hand over to someone with a bit more experience and inside knowledge on our special guest.' The camera cut to Mina, reminiscent of Val Doonican, sitting on one of the kitchen stools from my house. All that was missing from the tableau was a guitar and a Christmas jumper. We'd tried two armchairs for the interview but they were too bulky and took up all the space. David and Mina had given standing a go, but both of them said they felt more comfortable perched on the stools.

'Oh my God!' Francesca cried as soon as she saw Mina. 'You didn't! I wondered what all the toing and froing was on Friday with the stools.' Jo shushed her so we could hear what she was saying.

'I'm Mina Prajapati and I'd like to welcome David O'Donnell onto Clothes My Daughter Steals. Sorry we haven't got a sofa, Dave.' David appeared from the wings and sat down next to her, wearing his trademark navy slacks and cream casual shirt. Everyone else started screaming in the kitchen.

'Shush, you lot! We need to listen!' Samantha warned them. 'Scream at the end.'

'Hello, Mina. Thanks for being here.' She leaned over and squeezed his hand in a touching show of unity. The room made a collective 'Ahhh' sound.

'Now, you've had a bit of a tough week and I think you want to tell the viewers of Clothes My Daughter Steals a bit about what's been going on for you. How has it been?'

'Well, Mina. It's not been the best, I'll admit, and I never thought I would be on the internet discussing cross-dressing, but the time has come to stop hiding in the closet, as it were.'

'So how long *have* you been cross-dressing?' Had Mina always known?

'As far back as I can remember, really. I always used to sneak into my mum's wardrobe and try on her nighties. She caught me once when I was about ten and the guilt that it stirred up was enough to shame me from doing it again for years. However, when I went to drama school in Manchester we were always dressing up, so I kind of got away with it in plays and skits. I used to go to specialist clubs once I moved down to London. I did get beaten up a few times, which was humiliating and frightening, but I never let it stop me. When I got my big break hosting *Take a Chance* and then was part of the line-up on *Good Morning Britain*, the first ever breakfast show on ITV, I wasn't sure I could be so open about it. My agent at the time put feelers out, and came back with the verdict that it would be career suicide. Everyone who cross-dressed in the public eye – apart from Eddie Izzard and Grayson Perry, who both manage to celebrate their cross-dressing – was gay and I wasn't, which some people probably wouldn't understand. I didn't feel like I fitted in anywhere apart from the clubs, where I continued to go in secret.'

'Did anyone guess, or know? How were your family?'

'Trisha has always known. She has been my rock from the very beginning, but then she is a special kind of lady. My first wife didn't know, and sadly she died before I could ever tell her. Both the kids have known for a while now and they accept it. They buy me make-up for birthdays and Christmases. They're lovely.' He smiled off camera to where I knew Caroline had been standing.

'So what do you hope to achieve today by shining a light onto your world and introducing us to Viola?'

'I want to shed some of the inaccuracies attached to people within the TV community. Wanting to wear clothes of the opposite sex doesn't automatically mean you're gay, or have a mental illness. A large majority of us are straight men with families who want to remain in their families, but the part of us that needs to wear women's clothes is as important as the part that is a partner, a son, a husband, a brother, a father or a work colleague. Just because we cross-dress, doesn't take away those other parts of us, but we have to suppress it to fit in to make other people feel secure. Imagine taking away Christmas Eve from a child – that's what it feels like to me when I put on women's clothes and dress as Viola. It's integral to my happiness and I know it is to other men too. No one died – I was just caught by a journalist wearing an evening dress from Debenhams, hurting no one and expressing myself. Surely there are more important stories that need reporting in the world.'

'Eloquently put, David. I think that has definitely answered a few questions for our viewers. Now what's going to happen next on Clothes My Daughter Steals? Have we got someone else joining you?'

'Yes, my beautiful daughter, Caroline. She works as a TV producer and has kindly agreed to step in today. Jessica is away on holiday so can't join in, but I believe she will be watching from Thailand!'

'Well, I shall hand you over to the very capable hands of Ali and Lila, who are going to orchestrate the transformation, along with some help from your wife, Trisha. I think we're all excited to meet Viola!'

The video cut to Trisha making up David's face and talking about how she approaches it differently from when she does her own make-up. His hair was scraped back in a hairnet and Hayden cleverly time-lapsed the footage so that David was made up in no time.

'Viola has several wigs,' David explained in a voice that was now somehow genuinely softer and more feminine without appearing affected. It had been totally mind-blowing to see it all happen in front of us, but watching it on screen, I noticed a different, more detailed account of before and after. 'This blond one is my favourite. It reminds me of Farrah Fawcett, whom I used to adore. But I also have red ones and two chestnut ones. I don't really suit black hair – it makes me look like a vampire.'

'And what make-up brands are your favourites?' I asked on screen. 'Do you need to use foundation that has a heavier coverage?'

'I find I need sweat-proof foundation, especially in the summer. And yes, it needs to have decent coverage. Rimmel London do a great sweat-proof one and I tend to use that a lot. I love Mac lipsticks. Mac is probably my go to for most stuff. Trisha and I shop for it together because people naturally always think it's for her.'

'What's your number-one make-up tip?'

'Well, if you can't see your highlighter from the moon, you haven't got enough on!'

'Brilliant – I will take that on board!'

We talked about underwear, fake hip and butt padding, the benefits of foam breast forms for the summer versus silicone ones for the winter. Then we were ready to get dressed.

'So, Caroline, would you ever borrow any of Viola's clothes?' Lila asked as we all stood in front of the clothes rack.

'God, no way!' she laughed, making Viola giggle. 'She goes for mega glamour a lot of the time,' Caroline admitted in her plain Zara three-quarter-length blue trousers, ballet pumps and floaty cream peasant blouse. She looked lovely, a perfect hybrid of David and Trisha. She was also blonde and tall, though not quite reaching Trisha's telescopic height. 'I am more practical because, working in TV, there's a lot of time being squashed into edit suites and running around. I need to be comfortable.'

'But we're going for glamour today!' Lila cried. 'Let's leave work behind!'

We shimmied Viola into a Zara straight green full-length, one-shouldered gown with ruffles down the right-hand side.

'Does it make me look hippy?' she kept asking, twirling this way and that in front of one of the full-length mirrors. I had hauled my mirror over from my bedroom for this shoot, what with it being super special.

'How about I team it with a stylish silver belt to cinch in the waist a bit?' I offered. Caroline wasn't keen on the dress and tried it on without the belt. She looked stunning but it bumped up her age – she could only have been in her early twenties. We tried massive gold hoop earrings on her from my stylist bag and twisted her hair up into a topknot. Pairing the dress with strappy jewelled leather flip-flops from my own Aladdin's cave shoe bag and some dangling beads suddenly lent it more of a boho feel – her height made it work.

'Ah, yes, I like it! I would wear this out now it doesn't make me feel so glamorous granny.'

'Oi, you, watch what you're saying,' Viola laughed in her towering black sling-backs (apparently easier to walk in than stilettos). 'I'm not ready to be a glamorous granny just yet!' On set you could hear everyone burst out laughing in the background, astutely kept in the edit by Hayden.

'This is amazing,' Jo whispered as we watched speeded up footage of them both trying on jumpsuits from Topshop for the Christmas season, Viola swapping wigs, Trisha touching up both their faces with make-up brushes, with me and Lila constantly suggesting alternative accessories or looks to go with the outfit Viola had chosen to make it relevant for Caroline.

'I think it's going to propel David into some kind of iconic spokesperson status. Talking for my people, obviously!' Jo winked. 'As they say, there's no such thing as bad publicity.'

'It feels like we're watching you all get ready for a party at your house and we're flies on the wall,' Elinor said in my ear. 'It's so well done.'

We had achieved what we had set out to do. What no one witnessed was the mountain of discarded clothes off camera, and Sam running up and down stairs to find shoes that might fit Caroline from her own wardrobe when none of the preferred ones fitted. Or Viola's wig getting stuck inside a jumpsuit and a breast form flying across the room when she almost tripped in some red wedges while Trisha was doing up her bra.

'OK, girls, this is the last outfit and you're not allowed to look in the mirror. It's Stella McCartney and I think you're both going to like it.' I brought in the baby-blue halter-neck chiffon dresses with microscopic crystals sewn into the overskirt. On Viola I upped the ante by adding fake diamond drop earrings and bracelets, and teamed the ensemble with vertiginous silver glitter stilettos Caroline had brought over from Viola's own wardrobe. Trisha braided Caroline's hair so she looked like Helen of Troy. Caroline preferred to go barefoot because the dress came up a little short.

'You look like a star,' Viola said to Caroline quietly, her voice catching in her throat. 'Like someone from one of the fairy tales I used to read you at bedtime. You have a halo round your head.' Lila and I crept to the side so they could twirl admiringly together in front of the mirrors, the straight skirts creating a dramatic swishing noise like the sound of a stage curtain opening as they swung, the crystals dancing in the lights like mini disco balls.

'Ah, thanks, you really look radiant. The colour brings out the blue in your eyes and it's transformed you. You're Viola, but a mega upgrade.' They hugged,

Viola's bracelets snagging the back of Caroline's dress, so I had to nip over and untangle them.

'Thank you for being here with me today,' Viola said, facing Caroline and grasping her hands so they were both side-profiled on camera. 'It means so much, I don't think I will ever be able to put into words what it feels like to be here, accepted by everyone in the room as me, feeling a million dollars.' She turned towards everyone and smiled, tears brimming in her eyes. 'I feel so happy.' Tears spilled over now and Caroline bit her lip, desperately trying to stem her own tide. 'I love you, Trisha.' That was it, I was gone, my throat hurt from my own pathetic attempt to squash sobs back down into my belly. I looked sideways at Lila and she was also weeping. I gently pushed Trisha forward to go and hug them both. The family stood in the centre of the room, united by make-up, glitter and love, a perfect triptych of acceptance. The room spontaneously burst into rapturous applause.

'Oooh, you two,' Trisha chastised, pulling away. 'All my hard work will end up on the floor. You need to stop crying before I have to start again. Tissues!' And she waved her hand as Lila dived over to the make-up station and thrust a box into her hand.

The camera cut to me, Lila, Caroline, Trisha and Viola all facing forward, make-up all retouched.

'Lila and I would like to wish Viola all the luck and love for the future,' I said.

Viola curtseyed and smiled demurely.

'Thank you for having me. We've all had an amazing experience. You girls are consummate professionals. Stella – can I keep the dress?' A chuckle rippled round the room.

'So goodbye from us,' Lila continued. 'Spread the love, people. Anything is possible!'

'Can we scream now?' Francesca asked, her cheeks streaked with tears.

Samantha nodded and raucous shouting exploded, ricocheting off the cupboards, drowning out the short burst of nondescript title music.

28

The Aftermath

Last night I'd dreamed about Carl once more – we were married and deeply in love. I woke up at five thirty feeling ecstatic because for a millisecond I believed it. The cosy cocoon of finally achieving the Nirvana of actually not fucking it up was so all consuming. Reality crashing in forced me into about five minutes of genuine mourning for our perfect life that never was. Ridiculous!

We broke Twitter, Lila had texted at 5 a.m. while I had been married to Carl. It appeared she was awake too. I headed to the kitchen to make a cup of tea and shake off my blanket of inappropriate emotions. I switched on Radio Four and caught the beginning of the news.

It was already a beautiful summer's day and my dinky patio garden was bathed in crisp early morning sunlight, the wooden trough of cucumber plants showcased star bursts of canary yellow, and the fuchsia geraniums, added for colour and to diminish the likeness to a prison exercise yard, followed suit. I was about to take my tea outside to my postage stamp oasis when I caught something the newsreader was saying.

'Finally, last night, television presenter David O'Donnell officially confirmed he is a transvestite. Mr O'Donnell appeared on a YouTube channel called Clothes My Daughter Steals, hosted by Lila Chan, a former winner of *The X Factor*. Mina Prajapati, David's co-host on Channel Five's *Good Morning with David and Mina*, interviewed him about cross-dressing and the after-effects of being publicly exposed by the *Daily Mail*. In an emotional speech in which David thanked his wife and family for their continuing support, he introduced Viola, his female persona. Mr O'Donnell has been applauded on social media and in the press. The *Daily Mail* have yet to comment. Mr O'Donnell is donating all proceeds from the sale of behind-the-scenes photographs to the Terrence Higgins Trust.'

As the presenter went on to parliamentary news I texted Samantha and Lila, then sat in the garden to scroll through social media land before I had a shower. David's hashtag was trending on Twitter. I hated Twitter. Nothing was sequential and I never knew who was saying what to whom or where the tweet had originated from. It felt like trying to decipher a protracted treasure hunt where the end prize was a steaming dog turd. Instagram and Facebook felt more like comfortable old friends whereas Twitter was like that snooty twat at school that turned every tweet into a bitchy comment and then rolled their eyes and pronounced you thick when you had no idea what a semi-colon was used for (I'm still struggling with that one). I rarely posted on there and had a measly and unpopular one hundred and four followers at the last glance. Acrobatic cats had bigger followings than me. But this glorious morning I had suddenly gained over one thousand followers, including David O'Donnell, Trisha Templeton and Mina Prajapati. I searched vainly for Lila's tweet that tagged me in with the link to the vlog, scroll, scroll, scroll, and eventually worked out that it had been retweeted over three thousand times. It dawned on me I was a cog in the wheel of some grand plan; we were trending and surfing a wave.

Our YouTube channel had accrued a walloping fifteen thousand subscribers and I knew it would steadily rise as the story unfolded in real time today.

Samantha texted.

Are you free later? Do you want to come and watch David's return to the sofa?

'Do you think he will ever present the show dressed as Viola?' I asked as we waited for the adverts to finish.

Samantha's living room had returned to its natural state, the screen stored back in the shed, her coffee table piled high with paperwork and the sofa facing the TV once more.

'I don't know. I think it's a big risk, not one they might want to take. But I think presenting an article on cross-dressing would be brilliant: make-up tips, something David can personally contribute to. Viola isn't an act or a show that he wants to parade publicly. He's not ashamed, but he's kept her in the dark for so long that it might feel forced and that's something it can't be. It has to be natural, like the vlog was. That felt so genuine.'

I nodded in agreement. The familiar music fanfared out of the TV and we stopped talking. The camera panned across the studio and on to David and Mina smiling on the yellow sofa.

'Hello, and welcome to Monday morning. It's OK, you can start your week now, we're back!' Mina said genially.

'Yes, sorry for my sudden disappearance last week,' David said. 'Personal matters.'

'Personal matters that have affected our entire audience!' Mina spoke direct to camera. 'David kindly let us into a side of his life he has felt the need to keep hidden due to prejudice and fear of recrimination.'

'Oh, Mina, it wasn't as big as you're making out,' he said modestly. Coming from anybody else it could have been interpreted as a humblebrag, but knowing David, I felt it wasn't. He'd apparently not seen all the comments and thanks and virtual cheering out in the social media landscape.

'David, let me read out some of the tweets.' And Mina trawled through Twitter highlights. Obviously there were the haters, but the outpouring of positivity outweighed them. David smiled bashfully.

'If it has helped one person then it's worth it,' he said finally. 'Thank you, Clothes My Daughter Steals, for allowing me the platform.'

'Yes, I think we need to get Lila and Ali on the sofa with us to thank them properly!' Mina said firmly.

'I'll hold you to that,' Sam muttered. The show moved on to the schedule of events and Sam muted it, turning to me, holding her coffee cup. 'I'm getting a lot of enquiries already about Lila and, by default, you. I don't represent you, so you need to talk to your agent today and let her know what's been going on if she doesn't already know.'

'Ah, shit, I don't think I told you, I don't have an agent at the moment. It's a bit of a sad story.'

'What do you mean? Now is the time you'll need one the most.'

'I know; I just couldn't face searching for another one right now. Finding Alice was hard enough.'

'I think you'll find it will be different now. You heard Mina – she wants you on the sofa!'

'I hate live TV, though,' I whispered, shot through with instant fear, an old wound twinging like a rheumatic knee in winter.

'You'll be great, don't look so scared! But you need to sort an agent.' She gave me a hard-core Paddington Bear stare. 'I don't have a fashion stylist on my books at the moment...'

I remained silent, unsure how to react.

'I can tell you're not keen...'

Fresh fear licked at my toes, kicking off the 'What if...' game: What if we fell out? What if I said I couldn't do a job because of some made-up reason and all Sam would have to do is peer in my windows to find me hiding under the coffee table? I'd already had two agents fuck me over, one literally from behind, and one metaphorically. Letting it happen a third time would either be viewed as very unlucky or carelessly stupid on my part.

'It's not that I'm not keen; it's just that we're neighbours and friends. What if something went wrong?'

'Like what?' She took a sip of her coffee, keeping her unwavering hawk eyes trained on mine. 'We're already working on the vlog together.'

'Like what happened with Alice.' I let Samantha in on Alice's betrayal and midnight flit.

'Why on earth didn't you tell me? I know any decent agent will have the same response, but I would *never* do that! I have been working in this business for thirty-odd years. The last thing I would ever do is a runner with all my clients' earnings. I don't have a desire to spend my golden years in prison! This Alice sounds like she was flying by the seat of her pants and cooking her books. Totally unprofessional.'

'I know. I liked her, though. So many agents are full of bullshit and don't care; she did seem to care. Obviously it was all a massive lie.'

'Look, I can help you. I have Ben de Lisi and a few other smaller designers on my books and I have fingers in a lot of the pies of the fashion world. I know people. Your agent wouldn't have had the experience to broker TV deals, and I do.'

'TV deals? I don't want to work in TV.' More wobbly guts. I was happier goofing around on our vlog or on the other side of the camera, the power behind the throne...

'Yes, more TV deals! You and Lila are hot property at the moment. I honestly think we need to strike while the iron is hot. What do you say? TV would help clear your immediate debts.'

I was tempted. It had been so hard recently pimping myself out for work while trying to be present in the job I was doing, at the same time as looking after Grace, running a house and keeping on top of an endless list of chores.

'I can bash out a temporary contract, three months, and then you can opt in for real if you think it's OK. How about that?'

'OK. I'll do it.'

'Now, I've been thinking about the vlog. I think to make it a success we need to have human interest stories, like David's. The emotional back stories in those TV talent shows are very popular – everyone always wants those guys to triumph.'

'Wouldn't we have to advertise to get a breadth of people in? I've been thinking of someone who would love to do it. In fact I messaged her twice last week. I'm still waiting to hear.'

'Great! We need to keep up the momentum, but we have no time for vetting outside people right now. It's also a health and safety nightmare. Let's use our contacts. You OK with that? We also need a permanent make-up artist; do you know anyone who can dedicate regular unpaid time in return for exposure?'

'I'll ask around but it won't be easy. If a paid job comes in, that will always take priority. We need someone just for us, which is a lot to ask at the moment!'

Debbie's children were at school when Samantha and I visited a few days later. Jo was there but something was amiss.

'So – stupid question – but how are you feeling?' I asked Debbie. Even though she was still recovering from her lumpectomy, the haunted look had left her eyes and she had unfolded her arms and shoulders from unconsciously protecting her chest.

'Hopeful. This felt like the right decision – to pay for surgery. Waiting filled me with fear. I don't want the cancer to spread, and no one could assure me it wouldn't if I lingered on the waiting list. I wanged it on my card and closed my eyes!'

'She wouldn't let me pay!' Jo huffed from her seat next to Debbie's bed. Jo's outfit today would have won an award for best in class at Crufts – she'd tied her black hair in bunches resembling a Cavalier King Charles spaniel. At the same time the furry Crocs were honoured with an outing, adding that extra illusion of doggy paws, while the rest of her body was clothed in what could only be described as a beige *Ghostbusters* boiler suit with the ankles rolled up. I struggled to think where she found her inspiration, or indeed, her actual clothes.

'I didn't want you to pay,' Debbie said briskly. 'I can pay for my own life, thanks.' A permafrost settled on the room.

'So when is chemo?' Samantha asked, attempting to defrost the atmosphere.

'Hopefully in a few weeks.'

'What will happen to your hair?' I asked. 'It'll be OK, won't it?' Debbie's glossy waves framed her delicate face like a halo of light and were a big part of her attractiveness.

'No, they've told me it will probably fall out. But I've decided to shave it off before I start chemo and donate it to charity. It will make up for going bald. I can cope with it if I know the alternative is death.'

'Wow, you're an inspiration, Debs.' I was taken aback by her forthrightness. 'When you're feeling better, would you come on the vlog?'

'Yes, of course.'

'Well, I was wondering, I know this might sound controversial and perhaps insensitive,' Samantha geared up, 'but how would you feel sharing your hair loss journey on the vlog, and perhaps appearing during treatment? Show other cancer sufferers that life carries on, you can still be glamorous. Would Isabelle come on too? I know she's shy.'

Debbie looked thoughtful and I could see she was mulling the idea over.

'You know what, I think it would be a great idea. If it benefits someone else, then that's good, right?'

I nodded enthusiastically.

'Would you help me find a wig? Apparently you get the first one free, and after that, you have to pay.'

'We could do an outside broadcast!' I squeaked. 'Film you trying them on.'

'Maybe I could go radically different, pink or orange.'

'I don't think they do clown wigs,' Jo said quietly.

'No, they're more suited to *you*,' Debbie retorted snidely.

'I'm sure they offer wigs for all tastes,' Samantha refereed. 'Anyway, we just popped in. Let us know when you're ready to go wig shopping and we'll organise to be there.'

'What the fuck was that about?' I hissed as we stood outside Debbie's front door.

'Jo being Jo,' Samantha said matter-of-factly. 'Doing what she always does – trying to take over and Debbie is resisting. Just watch – it'll all fall apart now Debs isn't playing the game.'

'Really? It's a pattern?'

'Oh, yes, Jo *has* to be in charge. Surely you've worked that out. Anyway, let me know how you get on with locking down the next fashion victim. I'll get the contract over to you tomorrow.'

While we'd been talking, Nick's car had pulled up outside his house. I wondered what he was doing back from work in the day, but needs must and I knocked on his door. He opened it after a short wait and I noticed he looked particularly rough with dark circles under his eyes and even more of a pasty pallor than normal.

'Oh, gosh, are you OK?'

'Yeah, just knackered. Mum's been in hospital. Thanks for your notes. I haven't had time to respond.'

'Oh God, don't worry. What happened?'

'She slipped at home and broke her shoulder. She's in a lot of pain and of course, the MS makes everything worse.'

'How is she in herself?'

'She's OK, but obviously her weekly visits here have had to be curtailed, so she'll be trapped at home with Dad, which I think is going to drive her mental.'

'Is she able to travel at all once she comes out?'

'Yes, but Dad is being a real pain about it – "only if it's necessary"!'

'Would he think appearing on YouTube is necessary?' I asked, smirking.

Nick leaned against the door jamb and laughed sardonically. 'What do *you* think?'

My phone vibrated in my pocket and I pulled it out to check it wasn't about Grace. Carl. He'd sent me a picture of Homer Simpson hiding in the bushes like a stalker. I almost choked. I wanted to look round and see if he actually was lurking in some undergrowth, but I expected he was just curtain twitching from his house.

'Everything OK?' Nick asked.

'Yes, fine, Carl's just being an idiot,' I said fondly, not able to control the stupid grin from spreading across my face.

'I see.'

'Do you want my number?'

'Er, what for?' He looked a bit taken aback.

'So we can see if your mum wants to take part? Or you could give me her number and I can arrange.'

'Ah, yes. You have to get past my dad first.'

'I think I can manage him. I'm a parent-pleaser – it's one of my many talents.'

As I walked off, my phone pinged. It was Samantha.

Just had an offer from Spanx. They want to sponsor the vlog! We're on our way, baby!

29

Elinor

Elinor heard the front door slam and peered through the net curtains in her front room. Ali must be shooting the vlog today; she was carrying lots of glossy shopping bags over towards Samantha's house. Elinor would secretly love to be featured on the vlog but knew her daughter, Karen, would never ever parade herself in front of a camera and allow anything as shallow as a makeover. 'Mum, you're all just bowing down to the patriarchy's idea of what beauty and image is.' Elinor didn't blame Karen for saying that; anyone would be militant after having a father like Phil. He'd objectified women based on looks for his entire life.

Elinor had been what was known as a 'stunner' in the sixties and seventies, very reminiscent of Catherine Deneuve, and of course Phil had chased her until he'd eventually caught her. She was different from his usual ladies: independent, sassy, had her own blossoming career at Debenhams at a time when women didn't fly all over the world on buying trips, making use of expense accounts. They married when she was twenty-two; naturally Phil had expected her to squeeze out a few babies and become a stay-at-home mum. She didn't. She knew he hated it, but she didn't want to give up her hard-won rung on the career ladder.

Phil took up with his ladies again (had he ever *really* stopped?) and started commenting on Karen's appearance as she grew up. 'She's a bit chubby, isn't she?' he would say within earshot. 'She needs to grow her hair long, it looks better.' Meanwhile their sons, Jamie and Michael, never got reprimanded for clothes and hair choices. It was no wonder Karen had developed anorexia. She shrank to gain his approval, and he paid her compliments, telling her she looked beautiful, praising her rapidly disappearing frame. Phil realised too late that he had stepped over the line when Karen passed out at school and they found out she hadn't eaten for four days.

'I don't understand why she's like this,' he'd said to the head teacher, genuinely perplexed. 'I constantly tell her she looks lovely.'

Elinor wished she had left him earlier, and used to blame herself for Karen's illness. But it had been different then, and three children were a lot to cope with on your own and on top of work at a time when it wasn't the norm. So she turned a blind eye, slept in the spare room most weeks, and carried on carrying on. Things would always plateau when he finished his latest affair. Then he was all smiles and attentive, and Elinor would let her guard down slightly for the sake of the children, but it wouldn't be long before the absences began again.

Karen only recovered once she went away to university, no longer under such scrutiny. She'd taken it upon herself to get some help (she wouldn't talk about it) and when she returned home at Christmas, she looked so much better. She had also joined a women's group and challenged everything her father said. That Christmas, home had been a war zone and it wasn't long after that Elinor left Phil. Elinor since discovered from all the articles in the papers and online that Phil had been emotionally abusing her for years, gaslighting her about the other women, instilling feelings of worthlessness. That was why she clung to work like she did – she felt like she counted there.

A few years later the children told her Phil had got some thirty-year-old pregnant and was up to his ears in nappies again. She wondered if his other ladies were still on the scene... Meanwhile Elinor was living how she wanted to in the Mews, dinner parties galore, never short of someone to talk to and enough disposable income to travel when she fancied it. Karen lived in nearby Sydenham with her husband and daughters, so she saw them regularly, and the boys both lived in Surrey with their wives and families. She'd recently guessed Michael and Sarah were going through a rough patch but she'd kept quiet. On a few occasions she had noticed some familiar behaviour patterns emerging from her son that made her feel sick to her stomach.

'He's turning into Dad,' Karen had mentioned after a family birthday party. 'And what's so awful is that he can't see it. Someone should say something.'

'Someone' being Elinor, but how do you tackle your eldest child and tell them something they don't want to hear? She hoped they would work it out between them; it wasn't her place any more. He was a grown up.

She had got to the stage where she felt she'd done her bit for her offspring. Was it wrong for her to want to have her own time now without the constant worry about grown-up children? Maybe she was being rather optimistic. Her parents had died in a car crash when she was just seventeen and her childhood had abruptly ended. Growing up overnight had been terrifying. When each of her children had reached seventeen she had wondered how on earth she had coped at the time. They still seemed so young to her, not yet fully formed or capable of supporting themselves. They couldn't even vote. Yet she had been cast out into the world and had to make decisions about her future in a cramped lawyer's office in Croydon mired in a grief so all-consuming she'd felt numb. All she'd been able to think about had been the wretched row she'd had with her mum about the two inches she'd chopped off the length of her staid school skirt. It was their parting conversation as her mum climbed in the car to attend Conservative Club drinks with Father that evening. She never saw either of them again. Robert had identified the bodies.

Elinor had inherited her parents' money and house with her older brother. Split down the middle, it had been enough to sustain herself through a year at business college and buy a small top-floor flat in Putney two roads away from the river. In hindsight, the most likely reason she had married Phil was because she'd never really got used to being an orphan. She craved security. Funnily enough, she found living at the Mews gave her a similar feeling of safety in numbers. If only it had existed when her parents had died – she would have moved straight in and maybe escaped the need to fill her empty chest with a rotten marriage. Though she wouldn't swap anything for the children. They were the best thing to come out of all of this. Even if they still caused a few sleepless nights...

Elinor's phone beeped in the kitchen, snapping her back to matters in hand – an email had arrived. Wasn't technology wonderful, she always thought. To think that twenty years ago she'd been given her first mobile phone brick for work. She'd been convinced it wouldn't catch on; now she organised her life on one.

Dear Elinor

I'll see you at the Crown and Greyhound at 5.30.
Looking forward to meeting you.

Paul

The email was via a dating website, Guardian
Soulmates. Elinor had dated on and off now for a few
years. It had taken her a while to dredge up the courage
to join the site. Samantha had encouraged her, saying if
she signed up, she would too, but Elinor knew she still
hadn't done it. Elinor had begun to feel like she was
missing out by not having some male company in her
life. Just because Phil had been a total bastard it didn't
mean she was a man-hater. She'd worked alongside men
for years and she enjoyed their company, the way a lot
of them could be so phlegmatic about things and get on
with the job in hand without making a fuss. And she
missed sex. That was the one thing she could say about
Phil, he knew his way around the bedroom, which was
also why she'd probably stuck it out for as long as she
had – that and the children.

She'd had sex with people during and after her
divorce: a few men through work and one in Hong
Kong on a buying trip. That had been daring. He had
been a pilot with Cathay Pacific, probably married –
she didn't ask at the time – and they'd met in the hotel

bar. The sex had been amazing, a real eye-opener. They kept up a light-hearted postcard correspondence for a few years, until email was mainstream, and whenever he was in London, or if she was in Hong Kong with work, they would meet up. It ended once he mentioned his real life, something she had avoided, so she was knocked sideways when he said he was married and about to have his third child. Elinor took a long hard look at herself in the hotel bathroom mirror: she was as bad as one of Phil's ladies. She returned to the bedroom and broke it off with him. He had shrugged, and that's when she suspected he probably had a woman in every port. Not that she cared – she didn't need him – but she shied away from casual affairs after that and threw herself into building up her nest egg and preparing for early retirement.

This date today was the first for a while. The trouble with dating in her late sixties was the men were so institutionalised, they didn't know how to be on their own. She wasn't a babysitter. Anyway, this Paul sounded promising, and he looked handsome too, with a neat beard. She checked his profile again, just to make sure. Yes, he had sexy eyes. She tried to remember the last time she'd had sex – about five years ago. Maybe this date would end the famine.

30

A Star Is Born

I shuffled along the aisle in the slow-moving queue at the zombie apocalypse shop, eyeing the ever-changing display of merchandise. It was a busy evening in here; everyone had been caught short by the unexpected heatwave after a lengthy wet spell. I looked at what people were buying – rosé wine (or paint-stripper substitute), bags of charcoal and ice cream. I, on the other hand, was buying wine of the week (Portuguese red with used teabag on the nose), Rizlas, a lighter and cigarette filters all from behind the counter. I checked my phone to see how long we had before Nick got back: maybe an hour and a half. Long enough. I thought of Linda, still decked out in all her finery, sitting at the kitchen table waiting patiently.

'Don't move until I get back!' I'd instructed her. 'I will get in so much trouble if you injure yourself even more.' She'd saluted me with her good arm as I'd rushed out of the door.

We'd had a lot of fun earlier, filming her for Clothes My Daughter Steals. 'Or rather, I should say Clothes My Granddaughter Steals!' Lila had announced to camera after school a few hours ago. Nick's sister had refused to appear with her mum, but Lottie, her fifteen-year-old daughter, had been only too happy to step in...

Lottie was initially very quiet, obviously underwhelmed by the whole experience. I don't know what she was expecting, but from the face drop when she walked into the cluttered living room/studio with Nick and Linda, I could only imagine the inflated fairy tale she'd told herself. She was probably wondering where all the other people were, the free make-up, the racks of glamorous clothes and spangly shoes and the minions running around after her, offering bespoke Krispy Kreme donuts and frothy hot chocolate. The make-up artist I had begged to help us out had let me down at the last minute so we were left with mine and Lila's not-so-polished skills and depleted make-up bags, which were fine, but didn't bring that special touch to the proceedings.

'Please don't make me wear that,' Lottie begged at one point in front of the camera, after two other try-ons were kiboshed. 'If my friends see me in it, it'll be social suicide.' She was referring to an M&S pleated peach skirt, the same one as Linda was wearing.

I had created Linda's look using inspiration from forties glamour photos. We had managed to find a lovely black cashmere shrug cardie that draped perfectly over her sling and shoulders, working with a plain black top I'd instructed her to wear. I jazzed it up with costume jewellery and Lila had deftly tonged Linda's hair into flattering waves, the light bouncing off her head giving the illusion of volume. Linda managed to get her feet into some delicate sparkly black sling-backs, but was under instructions not to walk in them – we couldn't have a twisted ankle.

'I love it!' Linda had chimed, her voice turning girlish as she carefully swung around to admire herself in the mirror. 'I feel young, glamorous.'

'You look it, Nana!' Lottie smiled for the first time since she'd arrived.

'We promise not to kill your reputation,' Lila said solemnly to Lottie, who'd returned to biting her nails, looking suspiciously at her version of the same outfit.

'I'll look hideous,' was all she offered up as a further protest. 'You won't be able to make me look good.'

'Oh, I can't wait for you to have to eat your words, young lady!' Linda had laughed gleefully. 'There's nowt wrong with M&S!'

'Yes,' I agreed, 'challenge accepted!' Samantha hovered in the background, observing, making us the occasional cup of tea, and taking calls in the kitchen.

'I think that's it!' Lila cried cheerfully after we'd flitted round Lottie like mother hens brandishing the tools of transformation. 'What do you think, Nana?'

'Ooh, Lottie, you look a picture!' Lottie rolled her cynical teenage eyes and pouted her lips. I suddenly had a stab of doubt that I'd lost my touch, terrified she would hate it. I don't know why it mattered so much, but it did. I wanted it all to be perfect for Linda.

'Come and look in the mirror.' I chewed my lip as Lottie shuffled in front of the mirror set sideways on so the viewers could simultaneously scrutinise her reaction.

Lila had found the coolest fitted cropped black T-shirt with the faded cover of a Stones album printed on it, paired with a battered flying jacket that had a soft sheepskin lining (hot for today, but worked for the shoot), the offending skirt and, on Lottie's feet, stylish grey Ash buckle-up leather baseball boots. I had teased her hair into that just-got-out-of-bed tousled style with the curling tongs, terrified I was going to burn it, and given her smoky eyes and pale lips, the only look I could reliably do for myself. She looked absolutely stunning, quirky, and effortlessly chic, like she was supposed to be famous but you couldn't quite work out why.

As she stood silently in front of the mirror, my heart was pounding in my mouth.

'Well?' Linda asked eventually. No one moved. I could hear the humming of the fridge from the kitchen. We needed a bloody professional make-up artist – I hated the pressure of winging it when I didn't really know what I was doing.

'It's peng,' she squeaked. 'I look like one of the cool people!' Relief flooded through me as I gathered 'peng' was good. God, I felt ancient.

'Thanks for today,' Linda said after Nick had left the Mews to drop Lottie home. 'I needed to do that. It's made me feel twenty years younger in here,' and she tapped her head. 'Sadly not in body.' She winced.

'Is it your shoulder? Can I do anything?'

'It's everything. My hands are tingling so much, the one in the sling particularly badly, like burning.'

'Maybe Nick can make you a mowie wowie snack when he gets back?'

'Apparently I am banned in case I fall over.'

'But if you stay sitting down you'll be OK. Surely it's up to you? Why are you letting both the men in your life tell you what to do? It's your illness…'

'I guess because Nick has put himself out there growing all the marijuana for me. I feel so guilty.'

'Well, he isn't here, is he?' I said, looking round his kitchen meaningfully.

★

'Hello! I'm back. I have a visitor.'

Linda was still at the kitchen table with two wine glasses waiting to be filled next to the white saucer full of dried cannabis florets.

'Oh, hello!' Linda said, clearly surprised. 'Elinor, isn't it?'

'Yes. I'm so sorry for barging in. I hope I'm not ruining your cosy evening.'

'You're not,' I reassured her. 'Linda, we can trust Elinor.' I winked at Linda.

I'd bumped into Elinor outside our house as I steamed up the Mews back to Nick's, trying not to waste precious time. She hadn't seemed her usual self and I felt bad abandoning her, so invited her on one condition: 'You blab in a Mewsflash and I'll have to kill you.' She'd understood completely and had drawn an imaginary zip across her lips...

'Are you going out somewhere nice later?' Linda asked, eyeing up Elinor's professionally blow-dried hair, lovely pale blue silk shirt and skinny black trousers with beaded sandals.

I handed her a glass of wine, getting out a third glass from the cupboard and pouring some for Linda and me. She sat at the table as I pulled out my illicit purchases from the shop.

'I've already been on a date.' She picked up her glass and took a delicate sip.

'Oh, how exciting!' Linda cried. 'How did you meet him?'

'On Guardian Soulmates.' My wine went down the wrong way and I tried to choke it out of my lungs. Elinor slapped me ineffectively on the back. I had visions of Wattle Chin from Guardian Soulmates and his grateful drooping Deputy Dog face as I sat astride him, shit-faced in Amanda's attic all those years ago, giving him the pity shag of his life. It was hard to imagine Elinor falling at the same hurdle on date one.

'Sorry,' I spluttered. 'It just brought back terrible memories of a hideous Soulmates date of my own. Carry on.'

'Is this your first date for a while?' Linda enquired, clearly enthralled.

'Gosh, no! I have been dating on and off now for years.'

'Have you been keeping it a secret?' I asked, opening the Rizlas.

'No! The others know; I've just not met anyone I like yet. I haven't been on a date for about three months because no one has taken my fancy.'

'So, how was it?' I asked, pulling the white saucer towards me, picking up the dried cannabis that I had foraged from the airing cupboard earlier.

Elinor stared at me. 'Is this what I think it is?'

I nodded.

'I couldn't help notice the smell when I walked in and spotted it on the table. It's very distinctive, isn't it? Is it Nick's?'

'Technically, yes, he grew it,' Linda explained. 'But it is for me to help with my MS symptoms.'

'Oh gosh, I'm so sorry. That must be dreadful. You poor thing.' Elinor paused. 'I've read that it's also supposed to be amazing for arthritis. I suffer from that in my knees and fingers…'

'Yes, it helps relieve pain and it helps me relax,' Linda agreed. 'But I've never smoked it before. Because of the broken shoulder I've not been able to get over here, but Ali kindly arranged it all. Nick would have a fit if he knew we were about to make a roll-up.'

'Oh, I see. Why would he go mad if he's grown it?'

'I think because smoking it can be misconstrued as taking it recreationally, but also, he's terrified of me having another fall. He said all bets are off until this has healed.'

'But it's up to you, surely?' Elinor said.

'I agree,' I butted in. 'Hence a mowie wowie cigarette. Pure gear, no nicotine, so no nasties.'

I proceeded with constructing the rollie, while Linda explained to Elinor about her weekly 'medicinal' visits. I was impressed that I hadn't lost the knack after all these years. At uni, Ursula and I were crowned the spliff-rolling queens. I could do it one-handed while drinking a beer, gaining the respect of all the boys in our student house. I crumbled the dried flower heads into the flat doubled-up papers stuck together, the smell already pungent.

'I haven't had one of those for years,' Elinor admitted in her cultured accent as I sat back down.

'What?' I almost screeched. 'You've smoked weed?'

'Darling, I worked in the fashion industry for thirty years. I've also done cocaine and speed, but that was to keep my weight down and not for fun. That was just the cherry on top, also handy when you have to put on two washes and make dinner at the same time.' I stared at her, then burst out laughing.

'You worked in fashion?' Linda asked, more interested in that than Elinor's chemically enhanced past.

I twisted the end of the joint and popped it between my lips. I lit the tip and waited for it to burn before inhaling the contents. I wasn't used to smoking any more and winced as the smoke scorched the back of my throat. I took two tokes and handed it to Linda.

'Have you ever smoked fags?' I asked, blowing the smoke away from her face.

'Yes, a long time ago, but I gave up when the kids were little.'

'OK, only have a few drags because I don't know how you're going to react.' She dutifully obeyed, passing it to Elinor.

'Oh, I don't know if I should,' she blustered, waving the wafting smoke out of her eyes.

'Think of your arthritis!' I cajoled. 'Have a few puffs then tell us about your date.' I stood up and switched the cooker extractor fan on. My head felt like it was filled with hot air and I had to sit back down again pretty sharpish. I'd forgotten how strong pure grass joints were. Elinor inhaled the smoke, dabbing the ash in the saucer. The kitchen stank and I spotted the posh candle on the windowsill and got up to light it. The head rush was insane and I had to steady myself on the edge of the table.

'Are you OK?' Linda asked me. 'My head feels a bit funny – in a good way, though. I don't think I had better have any more.'

'See how you get on after ten minutes,' I said, wobbling over to the candle.

'Do you want this?' Elinor offered me the joint as I sat back down.

'Thanks. I can't believe I'm smoking weed with my posh next-door neighbour,' I laughed, taking two more drags. The joint was dwindling quite fast; I'd obviously not packed it tightly enough. The florets had still been a bit springy so it was hard to crush them small enough.

'I'm not posh, darling,' she said, sounding like Joanna Lumley in *Absolutely Fabulous*. 'I was born in Croydon.'

Giggles rippled out of us as we kept repeating 'I'm not posh!' in a cut-glass accent.

'Will we feel normal soon?' Linda asked. 'I think I might be a bit stoned. Oops.'

'It wears off quicker when you smoke it, so we should be OK by the time Nick gets home.' Who was I kidding? I watched time stretch out before me like an endless pair of tights with no indication of normality resuming in the next half-hour.

'I want to know about Elinor's date before we pass out,' Linda said, smiling.

'What date?' I suddenly found I couldn't remember what I had been saying moments, minutes, hours ago, and something mithered me at the base of my throat, that familiar panicky paranoid feeling. I tried to squash it down by sipping wine.

'The date I went on earlier this evening,' Elinor said patiently. 'Remember, I bumped into you outside.'

'Oh, yes, the date. I can't imagine you going on dates,' I foolishly gabbled. Talking now felt like dropping off a cliff at the end of each sentence. I should be taking notes to keep up to speed with what was leaving my mouth.

'Why? Because I'm older?' Elinor asked. 'I'm not dead yet. I'm only sixty-seven. I'd still like some romance while all my parts work!'

'Does Nick actually have any food here?' I asked, eyeing the barren kitchen. 'Is anyone else hungry?'

'Ravenous,' Linda deadpanned. 'Look in the breadbin. There might be something.' I toasted three stale bagels, slathering them with fake butter from the fridge and brought my offering back to the table. Linda whipped out her good hand and snatched one, still hot from the toaster, and greedily bit into it.

'It tastes so delishous!' she said, her words muffled by the buttery carb-fest. 'Elinor – the date.'

'What date?' she asked, looking genuinely startled, a bagel in her hand.

'The date you went on earlier,' I remembered, triumphant that I could salvage some information.

'Oh, yes, silly me,' she laughed. 'So, yes, well, I hadn't been on one for about three months... I was sick of everyone being so old-fashioned.'

'Like how?' I asked.

'A lot of the single men out there my age have recently lost their wives or are just divorced and can't be on their own. Most of them are completely incompetent. They're just desperate for someone to look after them.'

'But that would be me if John died,' Linda lamented. 'For all my moaning about how he fusses, I would be lost without him.'

'Is John your husband?' Elinor asked.

Linda nodded.

'Ah, OK. What was I saying?'

'The date!' Linda cried, laughing now. Nick's weed was strong.

'Ah, yes, well, he was good-looking in his photo, for a start, said he was sixty-eight, had a nice trimmed beard, liked outdoors, weekends away, being independent – he had been on his own for a while, so there were no red flags.'

'But...' I interjected.

'Yes, a huge but. Actually a huge beard: it walked into the room before he did.' Mid-chew I inhaled to laugh at the thought of a runaway beard peering round a corner and spat out a chunk of bagel across the kitchen. It ricocheted across the floor towards the sink.

'You're so classy, Ali,' Linda commented, and started giggling.

'He looked like bloody Captain Birdseye!' Elinor yelped, dramatically throwing her hands up in the air. 'He was all beard and no face, and do you know why?' We both shook our heads. 'Because he wasn't a day under eighty-five! He was wearing the beard as a blimmin' disguise, just these two eye-holes peering out from all the white fuzz.'

We dissolved into hysterics, as Elinor squinted and waggled her hands around her face, imitating the woolly camouflage.

'Would you like to try my fish fingers, me hearties?' she mugged in a West Country accent. Linda placed her good arm over her broken shoulder, holding it safely as she shook with mirth.

'Oh, you have to stop. I might do myself some more mischief.'

'Joking aside, I was so disappointed. It's left me feeling so despondent, like this is it, alone now until I die, never to have sex again...'

'I think the reason you find it hard is because you don't need anyone,' Linda deduced. 'You have everything here, in the Mews. You have companionship, a social life, your family visit, neighbours who help when something goes wrong – it's all on a plate. A man would have to fit into all that and be worth it for you to give it up or let him join in.'

'What's going on here?' Nick said suddenly from behind us. I hadn't heard the key in the door. 'Have you been smoking weed?' he snapped in an accusatory tone, clearly taking in all the evidence laid out before him. Ashtray: check; half-shredded cannabis stalk: check; charred remnants of a rollie: check; the pungent smell of a teenager's bedroom: check; three stoned and red-faced ladies: check, check, CHECK!

Mini Amanda's voice echoed in my ear: *Always start with the truth. You can't go wrong with that.*

'Yes,' I admitted shamefully, totally aware how this contravened his wishes.

'Mum! What did I say?' he cried, clearly exasperated. 'What if something had happened?'

'It did happen!' Linda replied. 'We had a bloody good time; my shoulder is less painful and I feel relaxed for the first time in a week. Ali was doing me a favour.'

'But you've invited an extra person!' he raged. 'Sorry, I can't remember your name,' he directed at Elinor, quietening his approach as he realised it's hard to rail against someone when you yourself are severely lacking in basic social niceties.

'Elinor, dear. Don't worry, I have trouble remembering it myself,' she smiled at him, and it kindled the evil fire of merriment burning my chest as I tensed to halt more giggles escaping.

'So yet one more person knows about all this!' He waved his hands in the air like he was batting away the drugs.

'Elinor isn't just a person!' Linda cried.

I exploded into raucous laughter, provoking Linda and Elinor's sniggers at the same time.

'What is she, then? A duck?' he huffed. That was like a red rag to a bull. Elinor struggled to breathe in between stifled giggles and Linda cradled her shoulder as she shook up and down.

'Oh, what's the fucking point? You're all wasted. I'm going to watch telly.' He stormed out of the kitchen and left us to it.

Once I'd calmed down, I went to find Nick in the living room where he was staring at the news. Even the living room was stark, and not in a contrived designer way but in an 'I am a clueless bloke' kind of way. The

L-shaped grey sofa was stylish, but there were no cushions and it looked as if it only served as a seating area upon which to watch dry documentaries about splitting the atom, and the ten o'clock news.

'Look, Nick, I'm sorry. Your mum hasn't done anything wrong. I suggested it to her. We didn't use tobacco, I bought filters, and she only had two puffs.'

'It doesn't matter about that; I could smell it outside in the road – Norman will be all over it. You invited Elinor round too. Now everyone will know and then the shit will hit the fan.'

'She won't say a word. Your mum had a nice evening and it helped her.'

He pulled his eyes from a war-torn landscape and gazed at me. I suddenly felt really self-conscious.

'Ali…'

'Yes?'

'Thank you for letting her come on the vlog. I know it meant the world to her.'

'That's OK, no worries. I'm really sorry.'

He nodded and returned to Syria as I backed out of the living room. He was a total enigma, impossible to read.

31

Hattie

It was still light when I left Nick's with Elinor, so I could clearly see the person crouching on our doorstep checking their phone, her head bent over scrolling aimlessly.

'Who's that?' Elinor hissed in my ear. 'She looks like a homeless person.'

'Hattie?' I called out across the Mews, hoping she was a figment of my stoned imagination, but her Pantone-grey clothes betrayed her. Her head snapped up and she glared at me Medusa-like. I could almost feel my blood turn to stone.

'Oooh, that's not good,' Elinor helpfully pointed out.

'What are you doing here?' I asked, my tongue thick in my mouth, furry and oversized now that dehydration had hit me hard. Dread thumped me like a sledgehammer, propelled by paranoia – she must have come bearing bad tidings about Alice.

'I know you've been having an affair with Jim,' Hattie growled, her face curled into the sort of scowl reserved for bare-knuckle fighting or bitch slapping.

'What?' Elinor and I ground to a halt outside our front door.

'I'll let us in,' Elinor said calmly. 'Let's not make a scene.'

Hattie budged out of the way and I hung back, convinced she was going to try to punch me the second Elinor turned her back. Why did I have to be banjaxed out of my head?

'I'll see you tomorrow,' Elinor said. 'Are you going to be OK?'

'I hope so.' I kissed her cheek in the hallway and slotted my key into the lock on the second attempt, praying Hattie didn't have a knife, or anything worse, with which to attack me. I was genuinely terrified to let her into my house.

'So, what's this all about?' I asked, finally facing her in the living room, the coffee table a feeble barricade between us. She stood at the bottom of the stairs, and defiantly stared me down until I snatched my eyes away, my heart trying to bolt out of my chest.

'I know you and Jim had a week away together recently.'

My head shook involuntarily.

'You did. He went to his mum's when she had that operation and I rang the hospital to send flowers and they said there was no one staying there of that name. I've gradually been piecing it together over the last month once the credit card bills came in, and found evidence on a card that he forgets I know about, a place down in Epsom, some spa hotel.'

'What the fuck has that got to do with me? I was working in Birmingham. You know how stressed I was about recouping all the money lost from Alice. I had no childcare and my neighbours had to step in. If you think I would be turning down jobs for a quick shag with Jim, you're mental.'

She temporarily looked like she believed me, then ploughed on with a double-jeopardy accusation.

'It supposedly didn't stop you last time.'

'Well, I could say the same to you, Hattie.' Handbags at dawn.

'I didn't know everything about you,' she said lamely. 'Only what Jim told me. He said you were over.'

I arched my eyebrows; I had just been the incumbent fiancée. We'd never had this chat, just a screaming tirade down the phone when I'd had a secret fling with Jim after Dad died four years ago while I was living with Amanda. Jim had had second thoughts about our split and I was broken in two with grief. He was missing Grace and fleetingly enticed me with false promises. I'd since realised he and Hattie were most likely navigating a rough patch, and knowing what I knew now, she was probably nagging him about a baby the way I had. Instead of working through it, he sought solace in my bed (or rather in the back of his car). He'd managed to convince her she was imagining it and had consequently asked her to marry him to distract her from pursuing the truth. Well, that was how I had interpreted it. No wonder she was on high alert.

Mini Amanda fired up in my ear without me even summoning her. *There's no point rehashing the past; it can't change anything and can only hurt. Stay in the present.*

The temptation to lash out with old allegations was so overpowering I had to tense my core to hold it in, my tongue weighted down with ancient vitriol. *Be a grown-up,* I told myself. *Don't be a cunt...*

'Look, Hattie, I swear on Grace's life that I did not have a week away with Jim. I can show you hotel receipts, the pictures from the shoot, my invoice. There's no way Jim and I think of each other like that any more, I can assure you.' I wondered who he *was* shagging, though. All the signs were there – he had been so cagey about his time away, even with me.

She sagged against the banisters. The facts had beaten the bravado out of her.

'Does he know you're here?'

'No. We just had a massive row, a real belter. He's at home with Grace and the dog.'

'Maybe you should go back.'

She sighed and shrugged.

'Would you like a drink first?' I surprised myself by suggesting, spotting an open bottle of red pushed up against the bread bin.

'Yes, please.'

'Cheers.' We ironically clinked glasses at the breakfast bar in an alternate universe.

'What really makes you think he's having a fling?' I had to concentrate very hard in order to keep hold of the conversation, the tail end of the weed still trying to overturn me.

'Well, it's cooled off now if he was, but before he went away there were late nights, not coming home on time, and when he did he was drunk and passed out on the sofa. He took his laptop to work with him and locked his phone in his office.'

I breathed in deeply through my nose and blew out loudly through my mouth, familiar territory feeding my hunch.

'You out of anyone know the signs.'

'Did it coincide with anything?'

It was Hattie's turn to blow out her breath. 'Kind of. We were arguing loads, still are... I didn't want a dog...'

I nodded, interpreting the code. 'What will you do?'

She ran her hands through her hair, almost tearing at it. 'I don't know. I can't go back there tonight. I can't face another row.' Her phone started ringing. She switched it to silent.

'You can stay in Grace's bed if you want.'

'Really? Are you sure?'

I nodded. Two refugees who'd survived Jim's ego. She wasn't going to stab me in my sleep now.

As I lay in bed, the weed dragging at my eyelids, I thought Jim must be mad to contemplate divorce again. Something didn't add up. He would have to pay out loads of cash, something he was allergic to. That week away might have been something else entirely...

The hammering woke me up. I blindly felt around for my phone; I must have left it downstairs.

'What are you doing here?' I panicked when I opened the door, a retreating Elinor mouthing 'sorry' over Jim's shoulder.

'I've been texting and ringing all morning. I have an emergency and can't have Grace.' It was nine in the morning. I let them in, at the last minute spotting Hattie's silver Converse at the bottom of the stairs. Fuckshitbollocks.

'Can I have some juice, Mummy?'

I nodded, the trainers flashing like a warning beacon in my periphery; I prayed detective Grace wouldn't spot them.

'What are Hattie's trainers doing there?' she said in a loud voice.

'They're mine,' I shot back.

'No they're not. You don't have any.'

Jim glanced down and then back at me. He looked like he hadn't slept.

'Hattie!' he yelled up the stairs. 'I know you're here.'

She appeared on the landing, slightly dishevelled, her barnet rivalling my shagger's clump for a bad-hair day award.

'Can we go home and talk, please?' he asked, a desperate edge to his voice.

'No, I think we've done all the talking we need to do.'

'Fuck's sake, Hattie. For the last time, I'm not shagging anyone, especially not Ali!'

'Jim, Grace!'

On cue Grace ran to my side and looked up at me, unsure about what was happening, her bottom lip trembling.

'You need to tell me what's going on then. The truth.' She started walking slowly down the stairs, her arms crossed. 'Not at home. Now, before you can think up an excuse.'

'Grace, let's go and see Elinor,' I said, taking her hand.

'Please stay,' Hattie asked.

'No, it's weird.'

'Please.'

After asking if Elinor could have Grace for half an hour, I returned home feeling slightly icky.

'So?' Hattie demanded of Jim, standing at the bottom of the stairs. He'd collapsed on the sofa, almost disappearing into the cushions, his face grey.

'Jim, are you OK?' I asked, hoping he wasn't about to have a heart attack.

'Yes.' He sounded beaten. 'I wasn't at Mum's. I was in hospital, then at the hotel recuperating for a week.'

'What?' we both shrieked like Harpies.

'What's wrong with you?' Hattie cried, striding over from the stairs to sit next to him. 'Why didn't you tell me?'

'I wanted it to be a surprise.' Now I wanted to laugh. The only surprise Jim could give her apart from a penis extension was a personality transplant, and as far as I could tell, it had been unsuccessful.

'I had my vasectomy reversed.'

'Holy fuck, your what?' Hattie screeched.

I was unable to utter anything. The word 'vasectomy' stole my breath, missing jigsaw pieces falling into place.

'I thought you knew,' he said disingenuously.

'How the fuck was I supposed to know about that? You never mentioned it.'

'I said I never wanted any more kids. I thought you would guess.'

'Hang on a minute. When did you have this vasectomy?' I butted in, feeling I had a right to ask questions, nascent anger waiting in the wings.

'A while back.'

'Obviously after Grace,' I pushed.

'Obviously.'

'So when, exactly? Before she was born?'

He squirmed. Lying was as natural as breathing to him, but having both of us there turning the thumbscrews must have loosened his conscience.

'After we got engaged.'

'I knew it. You disappeared for two days to visit your mum the minute the plane landed. I thought you were going to tell her we were engaged; you went to have the snip and wouldn't touch me for weeks!'

'Did you, Jim?' Hattie backed me up.

He hung his head. 'Yes.' I knew exactly why he'd confessed. Not out of any sense of duty but just to get him off the hook with Hattie. It was his way of showing her she deserved the truth, and a redemptive action of reversal.

I stormed into the kitchen and started slamming things around trying to make coffee, not offering it to anyone else.

'Can you leave now?' I stammered. 'I don't want to be a part of your circus any more. I don't know what I might do if you stay any longer. You're a piece of shit, Jim.'

He opened his mouth to protest, but common sense must have intervened.

'I've got a busy day today that Grace will just have to be a part of and I haven't time for a breakdown.' Debbie was going to shave her hair off and we were filming it at Samantha's with everyone.

'Come on, Hattie. Let's go.' Jim stood up, suddenly finding the strength to leave now he'd offloaded.

'Er, Jim, Ali's upset.'

'This isn't about her.'

'What!' I thundered, abandoning my attempts to open the fresh packet of coffee, my hands too jittery. The mood I was in it would explode everywhere, coating me in a fine crumb of Italian Every Day Blend. 'This is EVERYTHING to do with me. You had a vasectomy despite getting engaged, knowing I wanted a baby and falsely agreeing to it. But it was too late, I was already pregnant!' I laughed bitterly. 'Soon after, things went downhill. You *never* wanted Grace! Then you left me. It all makes fucking perfect sense now!'

'I did want Grace... in the end,' he blustered, the addendum negating the sentiment.

'If you don't want any more kids, why have you had this reversal?' Hattie asked tersely.

Tears had already started pooling behind my eyes and I angrily wiped them away. I refused to let him see me cry any more tears over him. But the heartbreak came crashing over me in a force-ten storm, thoughts, feelings and memories I hadn't revisited for a while washing up on my shore. I turned away from them and snatched the scissors from the utensil pot, snipping the coffee open. Ifan's face mingled in there somewhere too, pulling at my insides, reminding me what a fuckwit I was at relationships, always choosing the wrong ones.

'Because without it you would leave me eventually,' Jim said pathetically. 'I was freaking out, sneaking around, trying to organise it all in secret so you would never know, then hey presto, I was hoping you would get pregnant. Most reversals work within a year.'

'But you don't want a baby.'

'I do if you do.'

'You do if I leave, you mean. I don't want a baby like this, Jim.' I almost felt sorry for him, but remembered he was a cunt. I blew my nose on a piece of kitchen towel and turned round, blinking, making sure the tears were at bay.

'So I've gone through all that for nothing,' Jim complained.

'As I said, can you take this discussion home?' I slammed down the coffee pot, almost shattering it from the force, and started scooping in mounds of coffee, humming *Black Beauty* to myself. Fuckers.

'I'm so sorry, Ali,' Hattie started with the platitudes. 'We'll get out of your hair. I hope you're OK. We'll take Grace so you can work.' I could feel more tears threatening. I dug my nails into my palms. All I needed now was for Ifan to ring me and tell me he was getting married and had signed with Models 1 and that would just about push me into the abyss.

'I'm fine, just go, please.'

I followed them into the corridor and collected Grace so she could carry on her weekend with Jim, though she protested massively.

I shut the door on them and slid to sitting on the floor, my legs splayed out in front of me, my breathing ragged in my ears. The tears had dried up but all the long-standing anxious thoughts, feelings and memories fought for precedence in my head, swilling about, chasing my heart round my ribcage. It felt like my life was built on sand, that Grace's existence was in fact the very reason I had endured all that pain after she was born: being made homeless, Jim leaving, fighting legal battles to get my money out of the house, all because he hadn't wanted a baby, though he had played along that he did. And now he was going to have another child. My phone pinged with a text, jolting me from one crisis to another.

Have you seen this? See you later.

Carl had sent me a link to the East Dulwich forum.

4 July 2014
Re: Drug smells in the Mews
Posted by: Neighbour12 8.02 a.m.

Has anyone noticed a smell coming from the back gardens of the Mews on Underhill Road? Either they are smoking or growing it there. It was particularly strong last night early evening.

Re: Drug smells in the Mews
Posted by: Philmecrackin67 8.33 a.m.

I don't think you can say stuff like that on here – it's libel. Unless you have proof, call Crimestoppers on 0800 555111.

Re: Drug smells in the Mews
Posted by: PhatBiffa86 8.52 a.m.

Now you say it, I have noticed a smell, but I think it's the bins down the alleyway. Has anyone noticed how rubbish just gets left by the Two Brothers Fish Bar? I trod in a Pukka Pie yesterday…

Holy shit, do you think anyone will call Crimestoppers?

No! You can't report someone because there might have been a joint smoked round the corner from their house or the whole of London would be arrested.

*

My coffee had stewed by the time I poured it and, searching for milk, I found the fridge bare. I jumped in the car to zip to Sainsbury's but when I reached the mini roundabout by the graveyard, it died. I managed to steer it coughing and spluttering to the edge of the road.

'It needs so much doing to it, it's amazing it's lasted this long,' the AA man said an hour later, wiping his oily hands on a rag and slamming down the bonnet. 'You're lucky it didn't happen when you were on the motorway.'

'Is it worth fixing?'

'Depends if you've got a bottomless pot of cash. I would bite the bullet and get rid of it.' The poor AA man didn't know what to do when I started howling like a wounded animal. Thankfully no one was around when he dropped me home, his lights flashing as he disengaged my car from the tow chain. I let myself into the house and lay on the sofa and screamed into a cushion, bashing it with my fists and sobbing.

'My life is an endless fucking shit storm!' I wailed to the empty room. I don't know how long I lay there before the outside doorbell rang.

'What's the matter?' Carl asked, carrying two kitbags into the living room.

'Everything, my car, various other shit. I've had the worst day on record for years.'

'Are you going to be OK to do the shoot? Do you need a new car?' I nodded, fresh tears sliding over the moist snail trails on my cheeks.

'I'm impecunious, Carl!'

'Ah, don't say that about yourself. You're a lovely girl.'

'It means I'm broke. I heard it on Radio Four yesterday. How fucking apt. I have money to get by, but not for a new car. And without a car, my job is fucked. I'm fucked. Fuck's sake!' All the fucks...

He placed his kitbags down on the floor and hugged me. The minute he did, my stomach melted; his proximity was too much. I was scared to move even a millimetre in case he let go because for the first time in months I felt safe, even if it was for a few seconds. I hoped my feelings wouldn't seep into his skin via osmosis. He must know. My face was burning whilst being soaking wet. I was surprised steam wasn't wafting off it like a Turkish bath. The hardness of his muscles underneath his T-shirt pressing into my face was reassuring. As Carl stroked my hair a sigh escaped, giving me away.

'Are you OK now?' he asked, pulling away.

I looked right into his eyes and I swear, just for a second, he looked unsure, nervous. There were no jokes to hide behind. I nodded, and the mere movement of my head seemed to trigger some kind of electric current between us. I know I wasn't imagining it. He bit his lip.

'Cooee! Are you in there?' Elinor called through the half-open door from the shared hallway.

'Yes,' I croaked and stepped back from Carl, my legs clumsily banging into the chair. I glanced at him but he was busying himself with hoisting his bags up on his shoulder.

'Oh, fab, you're both here. Shall we pop over now? I wonder how Debbie's feeling about the shave.'

32

The Big Shave

'Are you ready?' I asked Debbie, her hair meticulously brushed and scraped into a glossy ponytail, tied securely with a brand-new hairband. Lila and I were standing in front of the camera with Debbie sitting on a kitchen chair in profile, clutching a clear zip-lock bag, the white backdrop behind her. Lila was brandishing a pair of professional hairdressing scissors. I crouched down on my haunches and took Debbie's hands. I'd left all my shit at the door. This was her moment and I was keenly aware that her bravery and forthcoming journey dwarfed my petty troubles.

'Yes. Let's do this!' I could see everyone else in my periphery standing behind the camera holding their collective breath: Charlie and Isabelle, her two kids; Elinor, Jo, Francesca, Samantha, and Carl just to the side of the tripod, gripping his camera, ready to capture the moment.

'How do you feel?'

'OK. This feels better than just letting my hair go to waste, falling out in clumps. I'm taking control and helping someone else at the same time.'

'Yes, Debbie is donating her hair to a children's hair loss charity where it will be made into a wig. We'll put the details up on the vlog later.'

'Don't people normally choose their wigs while they have their hair, so they can match it?' Lila asked.

'Normally, yes,' Debbie replied. 'But I don't want to match my hair, I want to go for something completely different, outrageous even, if the NHS wig stash allows it!'

'Good to go?' I asked.

Debbie nodded.

'Right, Lila, chop it off!'

Lila carefully picked up the hair in her left hand, lifting it away from Debbie's neck and cut through the base of the ponytail, holding it up like a trophy once she had freed it. Everyone cheered.

'You're sure about the shave?' I checked as she opened the bag and Lila placed the hair carefully inside like a specimen from a crime scene, sealing it up.

'Yes. Just do it, please.'

I felt wrong shaving off the remains of Debbie's hair. Her pale scalp gradually revealed itself and images flashed through my mind of concentration camps, prison films where new inmates are stripped of their dignity and their hair. I shivered. Debbie looked vulnerable, exposed like a newly hatched chick without any feathers, and as the hair dropped down her back and into her lap, I felt surprise tears close up my throat. I swallowed hard, forcing them back down. I wasn't allowed to cry if Debbie wasn't. Out of the corner of my eye, I saw Isabelle put her arm round Charlie to comfort him and suddenly questioned making this a public thing with her children watching. It wasn't a joke, it was Debbie's life, and it suddenly hit me how brave she really was letting people in to this very private moment of losing her hair.

Carl clicked away and as soon as I was finished I stood back, not knowing what to do with myself. Did I hug Debbie? What did I say? I wasn't sure I could even speak. Isabelle and Charlie wordlessly crossed from the other side of the room and hugged their mum as she remained seated, Charlie unable to hold himself together. Now I started to cry. Samantha ushered us all out and into the kitchen. A reluctant Jo, who obviously wanted to go and offer some kind of comfort, was practically dragged back to give the family some space.

'Oh shit, I left the camera running,' Lila gasped, wiping her eyes.

'Just leave it,' Samantha said. 'They need some time. To be honest, I had no idea how this was going to go. When Debs said the kids were coming I wasn't sure. But we can't shield kids from everything.' I looked at her and she winked at me, and I remembered now about her son, Scott, finding her husband dead from a heart attack.

'Did anyone see that post on the EDF?' Francesca hissed, purposely changing the subject. 'The one about the drug problem in the Mews?'

'What?' Samantha squeaked as Carl nodded along.

'Yes, someone was accusing one of us of growing weed or dealing it or something.'

Elinor looked at me, her eyes wide with alarm. I shook my head at her and she nodded almost imperceptibly.

'Wow, I wonder who it is. Maybe it's Norman and that's why he's so grumpy and nosy – he's deflecting from his own misdemeanours,' Samantha suggested.

'Yes, maybe,' I murmured.

'More likely to be Nick the Spy,' Jo said. 'You've been over there – seen any evidence?' she aimed at me.

'None whatsoever.'

'I can hear you all whispering in the kitchen!' Debbie shouted from the other room, interrupting the conversation. 'I'm going to start drinking all the champagne unless you stop me!'

'Do you think the kids noticed that Debbie and Jo are together?' I asked Carl as we walked home from Samantha's.

'Isabelle definitely has, or suspects something. Jo is desperate to be part of it all and it seeps out of her pores like a pheromone.'

I could stare indulgently at Carl through my sunglasses without him noticing. His profile was delineated by the sun's rays, casting his eyes into shadow above his strong cheekbones. Had I imagined our *frisson* earlier?

'I think she only wants Debbie because she's a project and a challenge as a straight woman,' I whispered outside my front door.

'Shall I come in so we can talk properly?' he asked, taking me by surprise.

'Sure, why not?'

'She does really like Debbie, and yes, she also revels in the challenge of winning over breeders, as she calls you all!' he said, once we were in the house, away from prying ears.

'But would she like Debbie if she wasn't going through some shit?'

Carl pensively cocked his head to one side from his perch at the breakfast bar where I had emptied the last packet of crisps into a bowl.

'I mean, what were all her other girlfriends like?'

'Well, more recently, Caro had escaped an abusive husband and Jo met her when she came to do a quote to put in a fireplace at her new house.'

'So Jo is a builder?'

'Slash property developer.'

'Caro is the reason she bought the Roller?'

'Yes. Caro decided that actually she preferred men after all and left Jo after she had put in the fireplace, built a new kitchen and sanded the floors.'

'Oh wow, mercenary! Has she ever been with anyone who didn't need "fixing"?'

'Actually, I don't think she has. Her heart is in the right place and she's seen some proper shit.'

'How so?'

He sighed and quickly crunched his mouthful of crisps.

'Oh, I'm sure she won't mind you knowing, Steve was *my* best friend too.'

'Who's Steve?'

'He was Jo's twin brother. Jo and I were best friends all through school and Steve automatically became part of our crew. She was always this powerhouse of energy, organising us, hosting the best parties, bossing everyone, looking after the underdogs. She was more fluid then. Girls and boys used to love her and she would pair up with either sex. It was revolutionary for the eighties, but she never got any flak for it because it was "just Jo". Steve, on the other hand, kind of dwindled in her shadow. He wasn't as clever as she was, wasn't as magnetic, didn't have the gift of the gab or the ability to talk himself out of tricky situations with teachers. Jo was almost like his voice and he flew in her slipstream, basking in her popularity. When we all began experimenting with drugs at fifteen, smoking weed and drinking vodka at parties, Steve found something he was good at. He became the fixer, sniffed out the places you could buy stuff from and soon became the Go-To Kid – that's what we called him. He liked the adoration it brought; he wasn't just Jo's quiet twin any more. But it soon became apparent that drugs didn't like him. He messed up his last year at school and had to retake it before he could go to sixth form. But he failed it again at seventeen. Soon he wasn't coming home and Jo had learned to drive and would go and drag him out of bad places where he was dealing weed, and later all the hard drugs, too.' Carl paused and shook his head sadly. 'You think something like that can't ever happen to a friend of yours, but it's so easy to slip very quickly to somewhere you didn't mean to go. Mine was a gradual decline and I'm pretty sure my addictive behaviour started with Steve at school, always chasing the next high, the next party, the next whatever, but I always felt one step removed from me having a problem because back then I really did keep it in check, and I never did heroin or crack. That was for proper smack-heads.'

Carl tugged at his thumbnail distractedly.

'Steve was addicted to everything. Jo's parents had no idea – Jo was shielding them from it, making sure she kept tabs on him, which was hard, pre-phone days. To cut a very long and painful story short, he died of an overdose at nineteen. I was in my first year at uni and

Jo came up to Manchester to tell me. It was shit. She felt dreadful, guilty, took on all the blame for not trying harder, not being there enough, not telling her parents. She managed not to have a breakdown through sheer willpower. But ever since then, she's been trying to save people. Me, her friends, her parents, and every woman she has ever dated has always had some kind of thing that needed fixing.'

'Poor Jo, that's too much to take on. It makes perfect sense and explains why she is like she is. She's very generously offered to take me to one of her geezers tomorrow to buy a cheap car.'

'Yeah, see – she just can't help getting involved in other people's stuff, helping them out. I think it's her way of making up for Steve's tragic death. I don't think she has ever come to terms with it, so *she*'s now the Go-To Kid but for entirely different reasons. I let her organise me. It's fucked up and probably a bit co-dependent, but it helps her too. But I think it's time it stopped... And as for Debs, you're right, if Debbie didn't have cancer and hadn't just been dragged through a horrific divorce, then no, Jo wouldn't have given her a cursory glance.'

'Does anyone else know about Steve?'

'I think Francesca knows, but that's it. Jo never talks about him.'

I shook my head sadly, trying to imagine the hideous pain if either Dan or Alex had died when I was still a teenager. I shivered.

'How is she still organising you, then, if you're back in AA and properly committed to the twelve steps?'

He didn't speak for a moment and I felt the leaden weight of the silence press down on my chest, forcing my breath to come out in shallow bursts.

'She just is, but she doesn't know everything.' He stood up abruptly. 'I just remembered; I have to fire off some emails for a job next week. Thanks for the crisps. I'll get the photos over to you tomorrow, is that OK?'

'Yeah, great, thanks.'

'Bye then!'

What the fuck happened there?

My phone pinged in my back pocket.

Have you seen the EDF? Has Elinor blabbed? Nick

'Hello, only me!' Samantha called through the door as I wandered out with the watering can to soak my pots of lavender on the drive a few evenings later. 'Nice car. I love a Merc. Rather big, isn't it?'

'I need the space for all the clothes I hike around for shoots.' I didn't really. My showboating tendencies had flared up when it came to choosing between the equally priced Beetle and the silver Mercedes estate in the dodgy showroom in Kent Jo had kindly driven me to in the Roller the day after the shave. All credit cards were now thoroughly maxed out and I was without options, standing on the port, waiting for my ship to come in.

'Nice. Well, you'll be pleased to know, Lana called. They want you on the sofa with David and Mina, with Debbie if she'll come. They're very interested in featuring her cancer journey.'

'What? Really?'

'Yes, really. And I'm hoping it means they'll consider offering you two a regular paid slot for makeovers. We need this to get our foot in the door. I've been in talks...'

I stared at her, my legs felt hollow, like someone had sucked the marrow out of my bones. This wasn't the ship I was looking for...

'Live TV?' I whispered, scared she was going to drag me by my ears and throw me to the lions. 'I hate it. I'm happy with the vlog and all the other work, but live TV?'

'Listen, you have a massive debt to recover. If you get this gig, your debts could be wiped out a lot sooner. And now you've added to the mounting debt with this car, I assume? It all needs to be paid for and TV pays well.'

'But I don't think I can do it.' Nerves already rinsed round my guts. What if I actually puked on the sofa? Or fainted and wet myself?

'They won't take just one of you. Lila is ready for this and you're a team.' She stared at me, a flinty glare in her eye. All the routine jollity had been brutally pushed aside and Samantha the Rottweiler agent was baring her teeth, snapping at my financial Achilles heel. 'I obviously can't *force* you to do anything, but you have to consider this if it comes up. You'll do the one-off live show?' Her voice dripped like treacle off a glinting hunting knife. I nodded, not used to this version of her. Trust me to mix business with pleasure yet again.

'Fabulous. Now, you're coming to the annual party meeting at mine later?' And with the flick of a switch, jolly Samantha was back in the room.

'Yes, I'll be there with Grace.'

'Ciao!' She swanned back to her house and my phone pinged. It was Jacqui.

Only five more sleeps and we'll be reunited. Single Parents Alone Together!

God, I bloody missed her. I couldn't wait for her summer visit to distract me from my life.

SPATS for ever. What time will you be in East Dulwich?

Wine o'clock...

33

Debbie

Debbie felt that she had exhausted all topics of conversation with Elinor other than What They Were Doing Here. Her head feverishly itched where her stubble was desperately trying to grow back before it eventually withered and fell out. She felt too hot and bothered to wear her new wig, her eyes were so scratchy, and she had drunk lots of water but it hadn't soothed her claggy mouth. Her arm was already throbbing where the cannula had been inserted though it had only been half an hour. Apparently she had weak veins.

'I'd better woman the fuck up,' she muttered under her breath.

'What did you say?' Elinor asked, drawing her eyes away from *Period Living* magazine.

'Oh, nothing. Just that there's no point thinking this is shite. I've got a long way to go yet and it's going to get a lot worse.'

'Are you feeling sick already?' Elinor asked, concerned, putting the magazine down on the side table next to the reclining chair where Debbie was stretched out like she was sunbathing instead of receiving chemotherapy.

'No. I don't think I'll feel properly poorly until a couple of treatments in. Just a few wee things really. I'm fine.' She smiled at Elinor to reassure her all was well. But it wasn't. She had a painful job to do this week and she wasn't looking forward to it. She'd originally thought that when she'd been officially diagnosed she would be subsumed by terrifying thoughts about cancer every waking moment and that regular concerns would recede into the background. Instead she had found herself feeling fairly normal as soon as the crippling shock had initially worn off, only to be suddenly caught unaware at times when she had been pootling about in Sainsbury's or about to walk into a lecture theatre at work. Overwhelming waves of fear and rage gripped her heart, making it race, anxiety catching its coat-tails. When this happened she felt paralysed and had to close her eyes and breathe through it until it eventually passed.

She'd never forget the children's faces when she'd sat them down and told them her news. Isabelle had reacted how she'd expected: calm and collected, a few tears. Charlie's face had crumpled, and he was unable to contain his emotions.

'My cancer is the most treatable one you can get,' she'd explained, holding him in her arms as he sobbed. 'I have the best outcome possible, and a huge chance of it never returning.' She didn't think Charlie believed her at first. The look on his face told her that he thought she was hiding the sinister truth.

'Will we have to go and live with Dad all the time?' he'd asked in a trembling voice, seeming much younger than his fourteen years.

'No! Nothing is going to change apart from further along you might have to help me a lot more than normal. I'm going to be very tired. You still have to keep your room tidy!' she'd joked.

She'd rung Matthew to let him know and for the first time in five years, he hadn't tried to get the last word in or accuse her of some petty fabricated misdemeanour.

'I'm really sorry to hear that, Debbie. You're in the best place. Andrew Berger is a top-class oncologist. If there's anything I can do, just say.' She had put the phone down, stunned. 'Maybe I should have got cancer sooner and I would have got a better settlement,' she mumbled to herself.

Ali and Lila had accompanied Debbie to choose a wig at the Macmillan suite at King's a few days after Ali had shaved Debbie's head. Lovely Petra, assigned to her, couldn't have been more helpful and had brought out a varied selection for her to try on. They'd had a real hoot gurning for the camera, wearing blond curls, vampy black curtains and a bright red bob. Debbie had settled for a long wavy strawberry-blond wig that really suited her. The experience had been so full of laughter that she had almost forgotten the reason she was there at all.

Debbie hadn't told Jo the exact date of her chemo until she'd definitely known she was busy taking her mum for her cataract appointment. 'Dad can take her on his own. It's fine. I want to be there with you,' Jo had persisted when Debbie reassured her Elinor was going to come.

'I'll be OK. Your mum needs you. And you know your dad shouldn't really be driving with his eyesight.'

'Why won't you let me help with anything?' Jo had asked her peevishly. 'All I want to do is help.'

Debbie had bitten her tongue because she felt so ungrateful. Jo had been cross when Debbie had visited the Macmillan support nurse without her. It was a service for the kids and her and she could hardly invite Jo along too. The children still didn't know about their relationship. Where had Jo been when Debbie just wanted to hang out and have a coffee, or go for a walk in the park, or watch a film? She dropped everything for the drama, but boring real life seemed below her...

Debbie glanced at Elinor, who had returned to reading her magazine, and smiled. She hadn't known what to expect, moving to the Mews after she'd filed for divorce. She had just been desperate to put some distance between her and Matthew once the house had sold. She had lots of friends in Dulwich Village, at work, in Glasgow, abroad; she didn't need any more. However, she had been surprised at how quickly she'd felt so accepted, so safe behind the Mews gates. Her neighbours had quickly felt like life-long friends, always a bonus in any circumstances, but especially now. Samantha had filled her freezer with homemade lasagnes and stews for her and the kids. Elinor had asked for all the chemo dates so she could attend the hospital with her. Ali had come and helped her pick another wig at Selfridges. This time the experience had been far from joyous. The shop assistant had been a hard-bitten harridan who hadn't a sympathetic bone in her body. Ali had complained and they had got a ten per cent discount off the red shoulder-length wig from the floor manager. A bit of a silver lining...

Debbie had been overwhelmed by everyone's support, especially with her own family being so far away and her mum incapacitated by dementia. Her world had shrunk in the last month. She hoped she wasn't about to blow it apart and make everything awkward for everyone else in the Mews...

34

The Summer Party

'Who's that really young guy dancing round Francesca?' Ursula asked, squinting into the sunlight.

'That's her Qi Gong teacher, Teyo. He's a bit of a twat.' To be fair I'd only met him for about a minute when he arrived but that had been enough for me to make my mind up. I didn't need my Mini Amanda to warn me about being judgemental, she was right here!

'Look at her partner's face. He looks like he's going to kill him,' Amanda said, full of concern.

'Her daughters are looking pretty fucked off too,' I said. 'I hope she doesn't do anything stupid. They totally know something is up.'

'And that's Norman, the grumpy one who's like a sniffer dog?' Jacqui was getting the lowdown on some of the residents.

I nodded.

'And that's Carl, the alcoholic photographer? Wow, he is fit as fuck, like Idris Elba.'

'Good job Mark isn't here!' I laughed, my crush a secret only I knew about.

'Oh, he would know I don't mean it!'

Grace was in her natural habitat. She loved parties, especially if Meg, Isla and Sonny were in attendance. They'd disappeared off and chased around the Mews, a mini kid-gang, creating their own fun. It was a shame Neve and Joe, Jacqui's kids, weren't here, but they were on holiday with their dad.

'Hello,' a voice said behind me as I bent under the pudding table in the shade outside Debbie's house to pull out some trays of cling-filmed brownies. I turned round once I was upright. It was one of Carl's friends. 'I recognise you but I can't think where from.'

'Maybe we met at one of the barbecues here? How do you know Carl?'

'Shared interests.'

'Photography?'

'Yes, that among others. Do you live here?'

'Yes, next to Carl, we're neighbours.'

He nodded like he actually already knew and was just asking for the sake of it.

'My name's Ali, by the way.'

'Jez.' He leaned in and kissed me on both cheeks with the slickness of someone who was sure of their own attractiveness.

'Jez! I got you a burger, mate,' Carl called from the giant gas BBQ stationed in front of Samantha's house. Apparently Jo was banned from BBQing because she was too impatient and one year poisoned people with undercooked sausages.

Carl ambled over with the burger slapped on a paper plate and offered it to Jez.

'I was just introducing myself to Ali.' I could see Amanda and Jacqui goggling from the deck chairs down at the bottom of the Mews where the hedge disguised the car park for the flats above Terry's Tool Hire. A little seating area had been set up with a hodgepodge of deck chairs donated by all the houses, like the ones laid out in front of wrought-iron bandstands in public parks. My best friends were basking in my obvious discomfort.

'Sorry, is he bothering you, Ali?' Carl asked, all smiles and arched eyebrows.

'No, he's being well-behaved.'

'That will be a first. Here, stuff that in your gob and leave the ladies alone.'

'Excuse me, can I borrow Ali for a second?' Elinor butted in, tapping my elbow to grab my attention. 'Sorry, boys…'

'What's going on?' I hissed as she ushered me away. 'That bloke was chatting me up!'

'Jez?'

I nodded.

'He's a one.'

'How do you know?'

'He's one of Carl's friends from AA. Bit of a ladies' man. Debbie's having a crisis; she won't leave her house. The children are asking where she is. I've said she's just cooling off.'

I followed Elinor over to Debbie's where the door was on the latch, as all the doors were in the road so people could use the downstairs toilets and move in and out easily.

'Debbie, are you OK?' Elinor called through the door. The coolness of the hallway was most welcome as it was baking outside and the fizz had gone to my head. I went into the kitchen first to grab a glass of water. I heard Elinor walk up the stairs. I hadn't seen Debbie since we'd chosen her Selfridges wig just before her first round of chemo.

I heard Elinor talking in the main bedroom and poked my head through the door. Debbie was lying on the bed, her head completely bare, a damp flannel over her eyes. She was wearing navy shorts and red vest top, the pallor of her limbs contrasting with the dark colours and the stripy blue and white duvet cover. Seeing her without her wig was still a breath-catching moment.

'I don't want to come down,' she said in a quiet voice. 'I feel so stupid.'

'You're not stupid,' Elinor replied. 'You're feeling terrible because of the chemo.'

'I've only had one round of chemo; it isn't enough to make me feel this dreadful yet, it's everything else. Chemo's a process I have to go through in order to get better. How am I going to get better from the Jo situation if I have to see her all the time?' Oh dear. I recognised that war cry. I sat down next to her and grabbed her hand. She pulled the flannel off her eyes.

'Oh, I didn't know you were here too.'

'Do you still have feelings for Jo?' I asked. Debbie had broken it off with Jo after chemo, something I wasn't entirely shocked about.

'I love her, but she terrifies me,' she cried, sitting up.

'She really liked you,' I started to explain, though really I knew I shouldn't.

'She had a funny way of showing it. She only wanted to see me when she could do something practical, or rescue me, and then shower me with attention afterwards. She has this way of making you feel special, and then dropping you when you show any kind of rebellion or independence. I didn't have a choice but to break it off.'

I couldn't disagree with her. I looked at Elinor and she shrugged.

'We know what she's like,' was all she said.

Other people's relationships were so complicated because even when another person inflicted pain, you had to weigh up your own reactions when you had a relationship with the perpetrator. Really, it was none of my business, but it felt like it was, and I know I was guilty of wading in and pointing my judgy wand at people at times. Jo was a walking dichotomy. I didn't want to join in slagging her off. I liked her enormously and she also did so much for other people, including me!

'You gave me the impression you didn't want to be with her,' I said tactfully.

'I did! I didn't want her pitying me, or trying to fix me. I wanted her to see past all the divorce drama, the cancer drama, and want to be with *me* the person, but she was treating me like a fucking victim. I think it was the drama that she was in love with. So I automatically withdrew and dealt with my own shite, but she didn't want me to. I don't get it. I know she'll be with someone else now; she can't be on her own...'

'Look, the children want to know what's up,' Elinor tried. 'Why don't you come down, just for a bit, see how you feel? Ignore Jo, all your friends are out there and want to see you. Samantha's stuck behind the barbecue trying to keep up with the demand.'

'Aye,' Debbie smiled weakly. 'We can't let Jo anywhere near there.' She slowly got up off the bed.

'Here, let me fluff you up a bit. Indulge me,' I said. 'What wig do you want?'

As I straightened Debbie's red hair in the hallway, just before we re-entered the Mews, I had to pose my own burning question.

'Can I just ask something?' I ventured, my curiosity getting the better of me. 'Were you bisexual before you got together with Jo?'

She didn't say anything, just pursed her lips.

'Shit, I'm sorry, that was way too personal and intrusive. Forget I asked.'

'No, it's fine. I'm thinking. I don't believe I was.'

'What's so special about Jo, then? Would you consider dating another woman?'

'No, I doubt it. It isn't about whether Jo is a woman or a man, it's about the person she is. She makes you feel safe, wines and dines you, pulls out all the stops, knows what you want before you do. But... the flip side is she wants everything on her terms. She wants to rescue you and if you're not up for it, then it's bye-bye.'

I nodded.

'She thinks she's being altruistic, but really it's about her... God, I wish I'd known that, having a relationship so close to home. What a mess!'

It was on the tip of my tongue to mention Steve, hoping Debbie would see through Jo's peccadillos. Maybe they could work it out... *Do NOT meddle!* Mini Amanda blasted in my ear. *Nothing good will come of it.*

I waved off Amanda and Chris at eleven – they had taken a strung-out Grace with them, who was desperate for a sleepover with Meg, but would also be in a coma by the time her head hit the pillow. Ursula left early to go on to another party with one of Carl's friends, and Jacqui staggered after Amanda. It had been an eventful shindig – the noise police had joined in, rolled their eyes, and informed us to keep it down and that actually we were within the parameters of normal levels for the time of night, but they had to investigate every complaint (and there had been a few).

Elinor and Samantha had been distracting Debbie and steering her away from Jo, who was getting progressively hammered, her cheeks stained puce. She'd started barking orders, an indecipherable stentorian diatribe, words crashing into each other. I sat her down in a deck chair and forced her to drink water, as she roared at me: 'Just shag him, you both want it!' Then she passed out.

Francesca had sent a shit-faced Teyo home in a taxi after he'd drunkenly tried to chat up one of the girls from the flats while the others from the Qi Gong class looked on, all of them obviously caught in his thrall like a doting Playboy Mansion harem. It didn't end there.

'Mum, how could you be so cringey?' Ariel, Francesca's eldest, blasted after Teyo's disgraced departure. 'Everyone could tell you fancied him. The shame – he's not even fit!' She'd stormed off with a group of mates she'd invited, escaping through the side gate, not returning until much later, clearly pissed.

'Are you OK?' I'd asked Francesca after she'd returned from putting Ariel to bed with a sick bucket next to her.

'Not really, but if you pass me some more wine it'll block it out until tomorrow when I'll deal with it!'

I think I saw, but wasn't entirely convinced, Francesca and Ian emerge from behind the Biffa bins at about midnight, rearranging their clothes. I *must* have imagined that...

'Where was the spy tonight?' Carl asked at two in the morning while we picked up the worst of the party debris. Most people had sloped off to bed half an hour ago.

'I think he was at a wedding.'

'I think he fancies you.'

'I really think he doesn't.'

'He does.'

'He doesn't.'

'He does.'

'Are we going to do this all night?' I eyed him and he laughed. I was surprisingly sober, but knew by the laws of science I couldn't be and that alcohol was most likely the main component of my blood. I'd managed to keep Bad Ali at bay; no blow jobs down the alleyway tonight; not from me, anyway.

'We can do something else.'

I stopped myself from bending over to gather up a couple more cans of lager from the floor. I'd been catapulted into a parallel universe where the real me was watching from behind a two-way mirror. I had been OK with Carl throughout the entire party because ever since Debbie had mentioned her regret over a home-grown romance, I took it as a sign from the universe. I'd kept up a mantra in my head: *He's just a friend, in the friend zone, just a friend.*

'I meant we can talk about something else.'

I picked up the cans and dumped them in the black bin bag he was holding.

'I'm knackered,' I replied. 'I'm going to bed.'

'We've just a few more cans on this patch, then we're done.'

'You do it.' I turned to head over to my front door. 'Great party. Night.'

'I was jealous.'

That was the moment – the key phrase, the 'let me get you into bed' moment, the money shot, the winning formula, the words that won the prize.

Watching from my two-way mirror, I banged on the glass, screaming at myself – 'Don't do it, walk off, ignore him!' But I couldn't hear. All I could think about was what he was saying.

'I felt sick when Jez was talking to you, every time he looked at you, when he asked about you.'

I opened my mouth to say something but just sighed in disbelief.

'I've said too much.'

'No, you haven't.'

I was facing him now and leaned over and kissed him before I could stop myself. Bad Ali had busted out. Carl dropped the bag to the floor. It made a jangling sound like the empty cans tied to a newly-wed couple's car. My fists tried so hard to smash through the glass, to grab myself round the waist and rugby-tackle my body to the ground, knocking in some much-needed sense. But I couldn't redirect the tornado. It had a life of its own.

The kiss was everything I had imagined. No clashing teeth, no lizard tongue, no drooling or, worse, licking (freaks!). It was gentle and sexy, then urgent with a decent amount of restraint. I pulled away, feeling dizzy, and as I did so, noticed Nick's front door shut behind him. *Had he seen us?* He must have: we were standing in the middle of the road snogging like blithe teenagers.

'I need to go,' I said. 'I think Nick just walked past us.'

'He'll be jealous.' Carl smiled dangerously and my insides melted, common sense already abandoned as it usually was by this stage of the proceedings. 'Can I come with you?'

Carl led me up the stairs to my bedroom, which now looked like a stranger's room – had I even bought those cushions? Who would choose so many clashing patterns? As for the carpet of knick-knacks cluttering up every surface... He lay me down on the bed, tantalisingly removing my clothes one garment at a time. The suspense was killing me. Once he was naked we rolled around for what felt like too long – I was ready to explode. His body was lithe and he carried no extra weight. I, on the other hand, wished I could employ Miley Cyrus as my body double just for this scene.

'I have some condoms in my drawer just there,' I said, pointing to the bedside cabinet. He ignored me and carried on teasing me. He was an expert at foreplay – he easily beat Ifan and Jim into submission – but was in real danger of ruining me for the main event. I let him kiss my neck until I could stand it no longer.

'Carl, we have to use one. I'm not doing it without.'

'I know,' he said, his face buried in my neck, his voice muffled. I was on the verge of tipping over the edge and reached for the condoms myself. 'I've never had... *successful* sober sex.'

I breathed out forcefully, my shoulders sinking heavily into the bed. I rested my arm across my tummy, leaving the condoms where they were for now, desperately hoping I could rescue the situation. After all, we both wanted this so badly; I was sure we could work it out...

'Never?' I found it hard to believe and stroked his cheek hopefully, longing to continue at a slower pace if necessary. 'Even when you were younger?' I ran my fingers down his side towards his perfectly toned stomach.

'Never.'

'Even with Janey?'

'Even with Janey.'

He rolled off me and lay back, staring at the ceiling. I knew then it was over. My desire had extinguished in that capricious way it does when faced with serious shit. This was too big a burden for me to take on.

'I thought it would be different with you.'

'Why?' Did I even want to *know* why?

'Because you're so different from the girls I normally go for.' He wouldn't look at me.

'What? Old and saggy and grateful?' I spat out, pulling my crumpled knickers from under the bed, and jabbing my feet furiously through the leg holes.

'No! Is that what you think of me? I thought we were friends.' I pulled my knickers up and shimmied them over my bum while lying down, my right tit getting trapped under my armpit.

'I don't know what to think, Carl,' I huffed. 'You're not explaining yourself very well.'

'You're normal.'

'Normal? As in, I'm not a model with perfect stats and the same age as my shoe size?'

'Oh my God, will you stop taking things the wrong way? No, I mean normal as in I can talk to you, like I could to Janey, about real things, not just work crap and fake stuff. You're genuine...'

'Oh.'

'And I fancy you.'

'Oh. OK. It doesn't look like you fancy me now.' I ogled his deflated manhood.

'Yeah, sorry about that.'

The old Oasis T-shirt I slept in was stuffed under my pillow and I reached and grabbed it, ramming it over my head. I couldn't have these conversations naked.

'I do really like you, but this *thing* is a problem.'

'I don't expect it's something you can talk about in AA?' I ventured.

'No, can you imagine? Hello, my name's Carl and I have never had proper sober sex and the thought of it makes my penis shrivel up inside my scrotum.'

I smiled, trying not to laugh. 'But you can beat off, though?'

'Yes, like a teenager, four times a day.'

'Carl! TMFI! When the fuck do you find the time?'

'Oh, there's always time. My favourite slot is when the pasta is boiling. Ten minutes is the ideal time to tease one out before dinner.'

'Jesus, remind me not to come round to yours for pasta and sauce. So your cock works then?'

'Yes. However, throw another person into the mix, it always… dies a death.'

We lay there in silence; I wasn't sure how to fill it.

My eyes started drooping and my succession of yawns caught Carl on the wrong foot and he started yawning too.

'I need to sleep,' I groaned. 'Sorry. Can we talk about this in the morning?'

'Do you want me to leave?'

I did. I know it was awful, it really was, but I wanted to be on my own.

'No, it's fine. Go to sleep.'

He leaned over and kissed me on the forehead and I curled over on my side of the bed, pulling my knees up into a foetal position. And that's where I lay for the rest of the night, wide awake despite feeling ridiculously wrung out. I tried not to move while berating my spineless willpower like Oliver Hardy to Stan Laurel: 'Well, here's another fine mess you've gotten me into.'

By the time daylight had started filtering through the gaps in the curtains, I knew I had to run away. I slid noiselessly out of the bed and slipped down the stairs to the kitchen. The clock above the back door said 4 a.m., but really it was 5 a.m. because I still hadn't changed it to British Summer Time from the clock change in

March before I'd moved. No point now: it was almost August; it would be Christmas soon...

I made a cup of tea, and sent Amanda a text.

Please can you text me when you get this? I need to escape to yours.

Then I realised I still had a key somewhere and I knew how to disable the badly fitted chain on the door by slipping my hand through the too-wide gap and unhooking it. I could let myself in and fall asleep in the spare room or on the sofa.

Forget the last text, don't be cross, it's an emergency. I'll let myself in and sleep in your office.

I scrawled a note on a scrap piece of paper and crept up the stairs. I was too scared to text Carl in case it woke him up. I left the note in the middle of the floor where he couldn't miss it.

I've gone to pick up Grace – Amanda texted and said she was asking for me. I'll see you later. Ali x

'So you liked him when his penis worked, and now it doesn't, you don't fancy him?' Jacqui surmised with the expertise of a hard-nosed lawyer instead of the gentle touch of a yoga teacher.

'Yes, you could say that, m'Lud.'

We were all huddled on the benches in Amanda's sprawling back garden, jumpers on to ward off the inconvenient chill. Typical British summer – as soon as the schools broke up, it decided to hang out its grisly weather instead of blazing sun. Amanda had pegged out her plastic bag collection on the washing line, dripping wet and snapping in the breeze. I swear some of those bags she lovingly rewashed and reused predated all her children.

'Is it just the penis situation or is something else in play here?' Amanda asked judiciously. 'Or was it because he was nice and you know how you're allergic to that?'

'No, it's something else.' I sighed. I felt so awful even telling them about Carl's issue with sober sex, but I had to talk to someone about it; anyone in the Mews was out of bounds.

'It's because he has so many issues – he's only just in recovery, only just begun to be honest about the depth of his addiction, and the icing on the cake is the sober sex thing. I don't think he needs a girlfriend; I think he needs a therapist. I couldn't even be in the same bed as him afterwards because the fear of being sucked into the black hole was overwhelming. It was actually a fun, sexy distraction from Ifan when it was all Ross and Rachel. I can't take on someone like this when my own life feels such a multi-storey car park of disasters. Jim's revelations have made me realise my whole relationship with him was built on a bed of lies. I know it ended on one, but somewhere in the middle I thought maybe it was genuine love with the same goals for Grace.'

Amanda shrugged. 'I don't think it's helpful to linger too long over it. It happened in the past. Hattie is the one dealing with him now.'

'Yes, but it feels like she was The One. She was worth having the reversal for, worth a baby.'

'I disagree!' Jacqui piped up. 'It's all about timing, not about who's more deserving or more loved or The Bleeding One! If I hear one more fucking person bang on about The One, I'll shove a crystal up their arse during downward dog.'

I started laughing.

'Jacqui's right. The only reason Jim has had the reversal is because he's approaching fifty and in a blind panic that Hattie's going to leave him. He can't afford another divorce. He most probably feels no different about her than he did about you. He's just in a different place now. He was right really when he said it's nothing to do with you, it's about him. Same with all the other men who have ever fucked you over. It's their shit.'

'So coming back to Carl and his cock, if it had worked you would have shagged him, wouldn't you?' Jacqui said emphatically. She lit a fag and inhaled deeply, blowing the smoke up in the air, away from us.

'Yes. I'm fucking shallow. I did fancy him rotten, but it doesn't work and I think it saved me from Bad Ali.'

'Has he texted you?' Jacqui quizzed.

I shook my head.

'He must know why you really disappeared. I would know.'

'What if he starts drinking again? It will all be my fault.'

'It won't!' Amanda cried. 'He has to be able to live soberly within the addiction – alcohol was his coping mechanism for everything before, now he's just left with himself. Someone taking up drinking again is their own decision, regardless of how serious the prompt is. I think you should talk to him about it, though. Don't be that person who just ghosts him. Treat people how you want to be treated.'

'I know! I just don't know how to go about it. It's so shittingly awkward.'

'If *you* think it's awkward, imagine how he finds it,' Jacqui scoffed. 'He's the one with the problem, and you're supposed to be his friend, and you physically made the first move, even if he was all talk and no trousers. You have to take responsibility too.'

'I hate it when you're both right,' I grumped, kicking a leaf on the patio from the bench. 'I HATE difficult conversations!'

'The perks of being a grown-up,' Amanda said sarcastically.

'I HATE—'

'Yes, we know, you HATE BEING A GROWN-UP!' Jacqui finished for me, flicking her ash on the floor. 'That's why they invented wine.'

35

Neighbourhood Watch

Can we talk?

I'd sent the text an hour ago and still had no reply. I assumed Carl was in next door. His car was there; I could almost feel his presence radiating through the walls. I *knew* the grown-up thing to do was to knock on his door, but I was busy tidying the chaotic cupboard underneath the stairs. It was vital work and someone had to do it. So many plastic bags rammed inside other plastic bags left over from the move months ago – I was turning into Amanda, thinking I could save the world, one plastic bag at a time. I heard a defiant ping and I pulled my head out from underneath the stairs.

We can but not on text. Shall I come round? Do you have Grace?

She's in bed. Come round.

OK.

Cunty McFucksticks. I stuffed all the crap back into the cupboard exactly how I had found it and slammed the door just as he knocked gently on the window. I had put off sending the text all day, hoping he would go to bed early. I couldn't sleep even though I was desperately tired. I had tried, but my head was racing, trapped in a loop of guilt and fear. Guilt that I had made him drink again and fear that Jo would come after me with a pitchfork.

'Hello,' he said.

I couldn't look directly at him. 'Come in. Do you want a cup of tea?'

'If you're having one I will.'

'OK.' Anything to prolong the fact I had to have this conversation.

'What have you been doing today?' he asked in a brittle manner while I waited by the kettle as it bubbled away.

'Oh, I stayed at Amanda's till after lunch then came back here and pottered.'

'It took you that long to text me?' Here we go: no procrastinating small talk.

'Carl, look—' The kettle clicked off, the steam misting up my glasses.

'I know you left so early because you couldn't be in the bed. If I was you, I would do the same…'

'Carl, I feel so—'

'Embarrassed?' I shook my head. 'I do, I feel… shit. Like a failure…' I started to protest, but he held up his hand to stop me. 'Just look at me, will you?' I did. It was excruciating. How could something so ordinary as eye contact make you wish you had been struck down by temporary blindness. I felt myself squirming and had to stiffly splay my hands to stop them involuntarily wriggling.

'I think this is all too much. Can we forget it ever happened?'

What a loaded question. If I jumped down his throat shouting 'Yes!' like I wanted to, I was worried I would hurt his feelings. What would Mini Amanda say?

'If that's what you want, Carl.' Oooh, nice return.

'My sponsor keeps banging on about not getting involved in a relationship until I've been full-on sober for a decent amount of time. It's only been three months.'

'Well, yes, it worried me, if I'm honest. I forget you're in recovery because you're doing so well. It feels like you're coping. Like you'll never drink again.'

'I can't say that, though. It's still one day at a time.'

'Did *this* make you want to have a binge?' I knew I would probably reach for the wine if my vagina suddenly decided to pull up the drawbridge.

'Weirdly, no, it would be counter-intuitive. Not that obstacles have ever stopped me before – it would be the first excuse to dive back in! It's different this time. I actually want to stay sober. I think temporarily being on the pink cloud is helping at the moment.'

'Pink cloud?'

I placed his tea down next to him at the breakfast bar and lifted mine to my lips, blowing on the scalding surface.

'People say you're on a pink cloud if you feel euphoric early in recovery after admitting you're an alcoholic, like suddenly everything is instantly fixed, you're better, you can't believe you didn't sort yourself out earlier to free yourself from addiction.'

'So what happens then?'

'You start skipping meetings, think you can handle your sobriety, you don't need help or counselling, you're basically cocky and overconfident in your ability to stay sober. The pink cloud doesn't last, and more often than not leads into relapse once the cloud evaporates and real life as it was before crashes in.'

'Oh Jesus, Carl, you sound like an AA leaflet. But you're going to the meetings, aren't you?'

'Yes, twice a day sometimes if I've missed one because of work. I am very aware of the pink cloud and its consequences. I know what'll happen if complacency slips in. The devil in my ear could start up again. And I don't want to listen, I want to embrace this feeling but still be committed to remaining sober and facing problems sober. And that means dealing with this... sober.'

'What will you do then? About the... about your... situation?' I felt my cheeks burn.

'My erectile dysfunction?' he said through gritted teeth.

'Yes. That. Have you ever had this conversation with anyone else after it's happened?'

He shook his head. 'Every time I've done a runner as soon as I can and hope I never see them again.' He bit his lip.

'Every? How many were there?'

'Ten.'

'Fuck me, Carl! Also, what about our pact?'

'I know, sorry. I can still do the handshake.' He bent down and threaded his hand under his leg, making me laugh.

'If you knew it was going to happen and keeps happening, why were you flogging a dead horse, excuse the pun.'

'Like I said, I thought it would be different with you. I thought I wouldn't get the fear because we're mates. Jo also said you fancied me.'

'She's such a meddling nosy parker! Was this all her idea? Some fucking sex experiment to cure you?' I was raging now. 'She shouted at me at the party to shag someone. She must have meant you!'

'No! She has no idea about it. I've not told anyone! Jo always thinks she knows what's best for people, you know that. I think she had some romantic idea of us getting together. She worries about me being on my own, most likely because she can't be.'

'Maybe you need to be.' I could almost see Mini Amanda waving an accusatory finger at me, mouthing the words: *Would you listen to yourself!*

Carl nodded.

'So what will you do?'

'Never pester you again.'

'No, about this?'

'Go to the doctor. I think it's about time I faced it. It's so...' He trailed off and picked up his tea, blowing on it first before he took a sip.

'Yeah, I know... I bet they tell you it's very common.'

'I'm sure it is. I googled it along with addiction and it's everywhere. Still, doesn't stop it being humiliating.' We stood at the breakfast bar, both of us silently sipping tea; light had faded fast in the kitchen, the cloud cover making the evening feel like it was drawing in much quicker. It was almost dark outside. Before I could say anything else on the subject, there was a knock on the internal door.

'Ali, hello, I think you'd better come. Something's happened,' Elinor said, her face pinched with concern when I opened the door.

'Go, I'll stay with Grace,' Carl offered.

I followed Elinor out into the Mews and noticed Francesca and Samantha in front of Nick's house, illuminated by the streetlight. Nick looked like he was having a head-to-head with Nosy Norman.

'You were trespassing on my property.'

'Only because I know you're growing illegal drugs. You're a criminal.'

Nick opened his mouth as if he was going to speak and then just sighed heavily instead.

'Norman, you can't go around accusing people of things you have no idea about,' Francesca chastised him. 'It's slander.'

'Can we talk about this inside?' Nick said in resignation. 'I don't want to do this in public.'

'No, because you'll worm your way out of it, move all the plants somewhere else.'

'I don't know what you think this is going to achieve,' Nick said. 'Are you going to call the police on me?'

'So you *are* growing marijuana?' Samantha asked incredulously. 'That thread on the EDF was right.'

'That thread was probably Norman,' Francesca added in Nick's defence. Norman didn't deny it.

'I want you to destroy the plants and stop drying it in your airing cupboard. I don't want any part of your dodgy dealing. God knows why you need to grow enough to sink a ship unless you're a dealer. And we don't want the likes of that happening round here. The whole point of the Mews is that it's safe. We don't want drug addicts, buying your wares, and eyeing up our houses for likely break-ins.'

'Oh, for fuck's sake, Norman! He isn't a dealer,' I cried angrily. 'No one is going to come in and steal your dressing gown collection.'

'Ali!' Nick warned me.

'Nick, just tell him.'

'NO! He trespassed into my garden and tried to break into my greenhouse.'

'Yeah, Norman, you don't have a leg to stand on,' Samantha agreed. 'If you want to report a crime you have to go about it the right way. Not turn all vigilante.'

'But Nick isn't committing a crime,' I insisted. 'No one can do anything without a search warrant.'

'That's actually true,' Nick said, nodding.

'I saw what was in there; why you keep it locked. I *will* report it to the police,' Norman said darkly.

'You actually have no idea,' Nick said, and stormed back into his house.

I gave Norman a Paddington Bear stare. 'Norman, that was an underhand thing to do,' I said crossly.

'I am at the end of my tether with that smell. I know what it is, and both of you pretended you couldn't smell it. That's gaslighting! I feel crazy because it's there and yet no one will corroborate it.'

'Why don't we go and test it out now then?' Samantha said reasonably. 'Prove once and for all that there is a smell.'

I knew what I would be doing if I were Nick... Samantha and Francesca followed Norman to his front door, Elinor and I remained outside.

'Do you think he's moving it?' she asked, reading my mind.

'Yep.' And predictably the landing light went on upstairs.

'I think Nick should tell him the truth. Norman isn't a completely heartless sod, though I know he can act it sometimes in residents' meetings. The amount of times he complains about parking, the communal gardening, bin day... He wants only one car per household too and you have to pay to park the second car. How does *that* even affect him?'

'I just think he's a lonely old man who wants to take the world down with him.' This was such a stupid situation that could be resolved if everyone stopped being so dramatic. 'I'm going to talk to Nick.'

'I'll stay here, wait for the others. Too many cooks...'

I nodded, strode over to his door and rapped the brass knocker. He ignored it so I pushed open the letterbox and bent my head down to it.

'Nick, it's Ali. Open the door, I want to ask you something.' I heard approaching footsteps and the door swung open. He stood there glaring at me and wordlessly raised his eyebrows in a 'come on then let's hear it' way. 'Why don't you just tell Norman about your mum and all this will end?'

'Because he's being a twat.'

So are you, I wanted to say, but didn't. For someone who was usually so reserved, he was acting like a stroppy teenager.

'How did you notice him by the greenhouse?'

'I saw his torch bobbing around down there and grabbed him, marched him out through the front of the house.'

'He's obviously reached desperation point for him to climb a fence! God knows what goes on in his head. We did gaslight him, after all.'

'He shouldn't have broken into my garden,' Nick said sulkily. 'None of this is really a big deal. It's just a fucking smell and it's none of his business. People live next door to noisy neighbours, messy neighbours, annoying for whatever reason neighbours, but you don't barge into their houses and try to take things to prove they're annoying.'

'Just tell him.'

'What if he calls the police anyway, just to spite me? I *knew* I should never have let anyone in on this.' He avoided my eyes.

'*Anyone*, as in *me*? I've had nothing to do with Norman acting like this. He was all fired up way before I found out about your little operation.'

'But you invited Elinor round and smoked a fucking joint; the smell escaped into the air when you switched the extractor fan on. It was the joint that broke the camel's back, as far as Norman was concerned. Rubbing his face in it.'

'I was trying to help your mum; she was in pain.'

'Don't tell me about my mum! I know you were just having a jolly with your mates from the Mews, thought it would be fun to get stoned. I'm surprised you didn't invite your boyfriend over.'

I shook my head angrily. 'He isn't my boyfriend.' I walked off before I said anything I couldn't take back.

'I'm going home,' I said to Elinor as I stormed past her. 'He can sort this mess out himself.' I heard Nick's door slam just as Norman's door opened behind me so I turned round; his face was set in a mardy mask of disgruntlement. Samantha and Francesca shrugged at us as they left his house, and Samantha mouthed 'No smell' at me. Right, fuck it. I was sick of sitting on the fence pretending I was in Switzerland with Amanda. It wasn't fair on Norman, and Nick was being a dick. Mini Amanda kicked off: *It's none of your business, Ali! The Mews has claimed you as its next curtain twitcher!* I pushed her to one side and carried on.

'Norman, can I have a word?' I asked.

'Why? So you can come and say I told you so? The smell's magically disappeared, I can't think how...' He pressed his lips in an ironic grimace.

'No, I want to explain something to you. Can I come in?' He shrugged at me and stepped aside so I could fit through the door. I hovered in the gloomy hallway, waiting to see if I would be invited further into his house. A small old-fashioned brass lamp with an art deco green glass lampshade gave off the only light on top of the white wooden radiator cover.

'What did you want to *explain*?' he asked caustically. 'How your boyfriend isn't really a drug dealer? Or did you want me to keep the secret that you and Carl are having an affair behind his back?' Blown away by his impressive credentials in the Nosy Neighbour league, I was temporarily at a loss for words, once a rarity, but that seemed to be happening more frequently since I'd moved here.

'Nick is *not* my boyfriend and neither am I having an affair with Carl, not that I have to explain any of it to you.'

'Whatever you say. Walls have eyes and ears round here you know.' I was overpowered by a huge wave of dislike. Now I understood why Nick didn't want him to know anything, but I'd backed myself into a corner. What should I do? Silence from the usually verbose Mini Amanda.

'Nick is growing the cannabis in his greenhouse because his mum has multiple sclerosis and eating it is the only real relief she can get at the moment because she's feeling terribly poorly.'

36

Live TV

'We have a possible new member for Clothes My Daughter Steals,' Samantha announced in the cab on the way to Channel Five a few days after the mad party weekend. 'You just need to meet them, Lila, see if you like them.'

'When?' Lila asked as we wound through traffic, my tummy clamped shut, nerves firing on all cylinders.

'Whenever you're free to meet, they're ready and available at your convenience.'

'I'm free this afternoon.'

'I'll ring them when you're on air and see if they're around.'

The green room at *Good Morning with David and Mina* resembled a doctor's waiting room, but instead of faded posters warning about prostate cancer and the first signs of dementia, there were pictures of celebrities in tired black frames dotted all over the walls. Large official photographs of both David and Mina hung boldly in the centre like holy deities surrounded by satellite minions. The wonky coffee table in the middle displayed today's papers as well as current magazines fanned across its surface. Behind the square of sofas a table leaned up against the cool grey wall, loaded with the obligatory fruit platters and pastries, teas and coffees. A TV mounted on the wall rumbled along in the background showing *Good Morning with David and Mina* in real time as it was broadcast live on Channel Five.

My heart nervously hammered like a xylophone on my ribs and I was clenching every part of my body so tightly that I could have crapped out a diamond. I loathed live TV all because Jim had once put me forward for a charity makeover on local news as part of Children in Need when I'd begged him not to. 'Think of the exposure!' he'd bellowed, pound signs dancing before his eyes. I'd forgotten everything I was supposed to say, sweated all my make-up off, dropped the clothes down the back of the raised stage and vommed in my mouth, having to swallow it back down. I was so traumatised afterwards I couldn't speak. Jim said no one noticed, that I was great, but I knew I never wanted to do it again. I hated having to remember things on demand, with no time for retakes. I preferred to wing it. (Take that as an allegory for my entire life!)

Samantha had been sympathetic about my stage fright, but at the same time, there was everything riding on this for Lila and me. It was an unspoken test to see how we fared before they offered us a regular slot for a proper wage. No pressure at all...

'Guys, you're on in five. You all clear with what you're doing?' One of the runners popped in to check on us. 'You've all been dusted with make-up, yeah?' We nodded.

'Are you OK, Debbie?' Samantha asked, concerned. 'You're a bit quiet.' It had only been a week since Debbie's second blast of chemo, and this time her experience had been a bit different. Her eyebrows had started falling out, as well as her eyelashes. 'The most bizarre and gross thing is my pubes coming off in the shower, in my knickers, down the loo,' she'd said after her chemo-enforced bed rest ended. 'I knew I would puke; it goes without saying, but my mouth's burning, things taste wrong, and it's only going to get worse. Apparently I won't be able to taste a lot of things after the third or fourth round. But I can't focus on that, I have to focus on getting better.'

'I'm OK,' Debbie now replied to Samantha. 'Looking forward to meeting David and Mina. Honestly, this day out is such a treat when I was feeling so crappy last week.'

'You're not worried about live TV?' Samantha pressed her, giving me a cursory glance as I tried to squash down my own nerves.

'Not really. The amount of lectures I have to give in packed halls at university and conferences is good practice. This is fine, honestly.'

Why wasn't *I* fine then? And Debbie had cancer and wasn't feeling a hundred per cent. I needed to woman the fuck up.

'You know your dad used to throw up before wrestling matches,' Mum had said this morning as I fumbled about the kitchen attempting to make coffee while Grace was still asleep. Mum had come up to look after her while I zoomed off to Channel Five. She was going to stay a few days because I had four days' work. It was the summer holidays and magical free childcare had disappeared for six weeks... 'He used to get so nervous about a match that he would be in the toilet before going in the ring with his head down the bowl. His competitors always used to think he would be a pushover because they heard all the retching. And then this six-foot-four ginger man would wobble into the ring on shaky sea legs, and Bob's your uncle, Fanny's your aunt, he would have them in a half-nelson before you could say sick bag.'

'But he was probably scared about getting killed or breaking something.'

'It wasn't the fear of losing and getting hurt, it was the fear of winning and what that meant.'

'I don't understand.'

'Think about it. Winning creates expectations. You're expected to handle bigger and tougher opponents, to overthrow them. Things get harder. And if you can't do it, then you're considered a useless one-hit wonder, which felt worse to your dad than never winning at all. At least if he lost admirably, no one wanted anything more from him and he could just enjoy the sport.'

'So that was why he quit after only winning a few titles?' I asked.

'Yes.'

'Clothes My Daughter Steals, come and get mics fitted,' the other runner called through the door. Cunty McFuckflaps. This was it and I was no way near womaned up enough. My whole body was resisting standing up.

'I knew I'd seen you guys before,' a woman said excitedly, waiting by the coffee machine. 'I love your vlog. That David O'Donnell makeover was inspirational. And you're the woman who shaved her head?' Debbie nodded. 'Good on you. Good luck with chemo!'

'Wow, now I know what it's like to be you, Lila!' Debbie laughed as we hurried to keep up down the corridor, my legs moving of their own accord, my thighs gradually turning numb, pins and needles spreading up my back.

'Wait until they start going through your rubbish bins to see what dirty snacks you eat, then you'll know you've made it.'

My hearing dipped in and out of range. I attempted humming *Black Beauty* in time with the yoga breathing that Jacqui had said would help – the Golden Thread one used in labour – but to no avail. The chunder bus had left the garage and was on its way. A potted palm tree stood innocently just before the partition screen where the monitors were tucked away from the actual studio. Debbie and Lila rushed ahead, eager to get their mics fitted before joining David and Mina on the sofa during the advert break. I slowed down, swallowing like a dog trying to counter the force of nature that is vomiting in public.

I suddenly had a picture of Dad in my mind, his kind face and gentle manner belying the fact that he could disable an opponent in less than a minute with timed agility and brute force. 'Let it out,' he said. So I did. Into the palm tree. Curdled milk stung the inside of my nose and strings of puke hung from my chin. I didn't have a tissue. *Are you even a mum if you don't have at least one tissue squirrelled away in a pocket somewhere?* Mini Amanda castigated me. Debbie turned round when she heard the splatter and rushed over with a tissue like a hero. Lila was already round in the waiting area.

'Are you OK?'

I nodded. Then shook my head. I could feel more coming. I dry heaved into the pot plant until I was sure it was over. Debbie handed me another tissue.

'Oh, no!' the runner cried, returning to see where we were. 'Are you OK to go on?'

'Yes. Just nerves,' I said. 'Sorry about the plant.'

'Hey, no worries, you're not the only one to puke in there,' he said, smiling. 'I could tell you dozens of actors and performers who've puked with nerves before coming on the sofa. We should just get a sick bucket and do away with the plant.' That made me feel marginally better, but I still had to face the music.

'Come on,' Debbie said. 'Imagine everyone naked. It's what I do when I have to speak to a thousand people.'

'A thousand people is a lot of people to imagine naked!'

'It is, but normally by the time I've finished imagining them all, I've finished the lecture!'

Twenty minutes later, the interview a total blur behind me, I breathed a huge sigh of relief as I walked back to the green room on unsteady legs, Debbie and Lila chatting animatedly ahead of me. I had no idea what I'd even said or how the others had fared. If this was going to be a regular occurrence I had to find a way of beating my stage fright that didn't involve beta blockers or vodka shots.

'So I can't believe Norman accused Linda's son of growing drugs,' Lila said incredulously as we wound our way back down the corridors, this time without a runner to guide us. Samantha must have been gossiping.

'Yes! Samantha told me she even went into Norman's house to see if she could smell the drugs coming in through the walls.'

'What? That's crazy!'

I still felt guilty when I thought about my conversation with Norman the other night. I'd had no idea what he'd really been hiding...

Norman had remained momentarily silent once I'd confessed about Linda's medicinal cannabis in his hallway.

'I'll just go. I probably shouldn't have said anything, but I was sick of knowing something that potentially might change your mind for Linda's sake. Or maybe not.'

I turned to open the front door when Norman spoke.

'My son died because of drug-induced psychosis.'

Bloody hell, words failed me.

'I'm so sorry, Norman,' I said eventually. 'I had no idea.'

'No one here knows I had a son or was married. Everyone assumes I have always lived purely as a gay man.' I honestly wasn't sure if people even knew that much. 'I love your vlog you do with that little Chinese girl,' he said brightly, swerving subjects. 'The woman on the vlog with MS, is *she* Nick's mother? She looked completely different from the woman I see arriving next door.'

I was even more speechless, if that was actually possible. *Norman watched the vlog.*

'Yes – Linda. Why did you never say anything about watching it?'

'I don't know. After you came in here and pretended you couldn't smell the cannabis, I felt stupid talking to you properly about it.'

I felt bad now, poor Norman. 'You must think I'm a terrible person,' I said, my shoulders drooping.

'No, I just thought you were having a fling with Nick and taking his side.'

I laughed contemptuously.

'Oh, I got that completely wrong then?'

'You could say that. Look, I just need to text Carl – he's babysitting – and tell him I'll be a little bit longer.'

'Go back to Grace. She'll be missing you.'

'She's asleep!' I texted Carl. 'Carl said I could stay as long as I like.'

Norman looked at me, his crinkly eyes quite beautiful when you actually looked into them, like flickering sky lanterns. I bet he had been quite something when he was younger. I hazarded a guess he was pushing sixty-odd now, but it was hard to tell.

'Would you like to have a glass of something?'

The parquet wooden floors in the living room were covered in luxurious red Turkish rugs. A glass and brass bar stood against one wall rammed with all the drinks you could ever think of, some of the traditional spirits hanging on optics from a shelf above with discreetly hidden lighting. Framed theatrical posters lined the walls, and several flyers had been mounted in a neat row above the bar, all depicting a drag night at Madame Jojo's, Fiona Angel obviously star billing, her name splashed across the top.

I perched on the classic brown leather Chesterfield sofa and Norman handed me a gin and tonic with ice and a slice, then sat at the other end with his vodka and tonic.

'How long ago did your son die?' I asked warily.

'Thirty-five years ago. He killed himself.' I felt like the air had been punched out of my lungs. 'He was sixteen.'

'Oh God, that's so young.' I instantly thought of Freya, only a year older, and my eyes prickled at the thought of anything like that happening to her.

'It was...' He braced himself and smiled at me, his eyes watery. 'Frankie had always been such a happy boy, but he got in with a bad crowd when he was twelve, smoked weed – they all did – and he just couldn't take it.' Norman's voice had slowed down, each word carefully considered, like they had been waiting in line for years to escape.

'Did he start taking other drugs?' I asked naively.

'No, just cannabis, but he was addicted to that. I won't bore you with it all. He nose-dived so quickly and was unable to do pretty much anything by the time he was fifteen. He had stopped smoking by then, but the after-effects were catastrophic; the psychosis was embedded. His childhood had been stolen from him.' He stopped and sipped his drink, his shoulders sagging. 'I didn't know about the full dangers of cannabis, but it's the same as any other drug. It's as deadly as some of the traditionally scarier ones like heroin and crack, if your body reacts the way Frankie's body reacted to it. The doctors said he could have had an underlying mental health issue inherited from his natural father and possibly the drugs exacerbated it.'

'So, you adopted him?' I tried ineffectively to grasp the facts.

'No, I brought him up as my own with his mother. Another long and boring story you won't want to hear.'

'Oh, I do!' I settled back against the black and red velvet cushions and tried my drink.

'His mother, Marie, was a friend of mine in the sixties, we worked together in the theatre. She was a seamstress, costumier. She fell pregnant from a married actor who insisted she get an abortion. It was still illegal then, so Marie was terrified. I offered to marry her, insisting she was doing *me* a favour. My parents were constantly asking when I was getting married, would I meet a nice girl at church. They didn't like me working in the theatre: theatres were full of sin, apparently,' Norman laughed disdainfully. 'So it killed two birds with one stone. Marie is black, like me, but Frankie's biological father was white. We didn't know if people would suspect.' He sipped his drink, his eyes glistening in the lamplight from the bar.

'Did Frankie know you weren't his real father?'

'No. His skin was lighter, but not drastically so, and because we didn't say otherwise, no one said a word. People see what they want to see. Marie and I lived like man and wife, even sleeping in the same bed, but that was where it ended; she knew I was gay. We were very fond of each other and loved Frankie, but it became increasingly difficult over time to keep up the charade because she had met someone significant and I had tentatively begun to explore the fact I was homosexual rather than getting caught up in the religious guilt surrounding it.

'We were so young when we got married and didn't think past the initial crisis, but Marie was desperate for another child, and her lovely young man knew about our unconventional arrangement. Lots of men had beards – wives or girlfriends as a cover because homosexuality was illegal until 1967 – so our arrangement wasn't frowned upon. Also, this was London, very different if we'd been living somewhere else.'

I nodded in agreement.

'We decided to divorce, horrifying my parents, so Marie could get remarried. Neither of us wanted to admit it, but that probably prompted Frankie to experiment with drugs and to get in with the wrong crowd.'

'Oh shit, Norman. That's dreadful. But you can't blame yourself. As you say, there was every chance he had an inherited underlying predilection to addiction.'

He nodded sadly.

'Do you keep in touch with Marie?'

'Christmas cards only now. She has two boys in their thirties. She's still married, living in the Midlands, a nice conventional life. I can't actually see her: it brings back memories, flashbacks. I know she feels the same. We tried to do the right thing and it just didn't work out.'

I leaned over the sofa and grabbed his hand.

'Things were different then; what you did was admirable and right at the time. Frankie knew he was loved. You don't know that if you had stayed together the outcome would have been any different.'

'Thank you.'

'So the smell coming from Nick's house must have been another hideous trigger.'

'Yes. I kept seeing Frankie's face, the day before we found him. He'd given up, wasn't there. An empty carapace...'

'I can't even begin to imagine, Norman. I'm so sorry. The death of a child is something you never recover from.'

'I had tried to block it out, but this forced it to the surface. Maybe it's a good thing though... Why is Nick so secretive about it?'

'Because his dad is anti-drugs and he's scared of losing his job if anyone reports him. The whole thing is like an undercover operation.' I explained about John's police background. 'So, in fact, your and John's views are actually quite similar on the topic.'

'However, I think if it *can* help Linda, surely that's a good thing. I don't think it's going to turn her into an addict! I was more terrified Nick was a dealer, like the ones who supplied Frankie. But I actually found that scenario quite hard to believe as Nick doesn't seem to fit that stereotype. In the end, it became about the fact he was lying and messing with my old head.'

I sat there quietly absorbing everything he'd said. No one ever really knew what went on behind closed doors, even in the Mews where life was much more open than in a regular neighbourhood.

'What do you do, Norman? Or rather, what did you do, when you worked in the theatre?'

'I started off set-building but ended up in hair and make-up, my true love.'

37

New Beginnings

'Norman, meet Lila,' Samantha said as we trooped into his house straight from the cab.

'Hello, dear,' he said, holding out his hand. 'Pleased to meet you. You and Ali were especially eloquent on the sofa this morning. Loved dressing to impress a serious illness and fake it till you make it, wonderful. And wasn't Debbie great too, talking about the different wigs and her cancer journey? She's good in front of the camera, such an accomplished communicator.'

'I can't believe it,' Lila cried in the hallway, suddenly registering who Norman was. 'This place is like some secret showbiz village. Who else is hiding here, Beyoncé's mum and dad and the cast of *EastEnders*?'

'Don't even ask,' he laughed. 'You don't want to know.' It was so bizarre seeing Norman in his element, without a permanent scowl or pained look behind his eyes. I was sure that other version of himself still existed but I guessed this version had just come out of an extended hibernation.

'What do you want to drink? Tea, coffee? I've made some shortbread biscuits if you'd like one.'

'Now you're talking, Norman,' Lila said. 'I love shortbread and tea!'

He ushered us into his lounge where he'd set up the biscuits on a pretty china plate on his glass coffee table.

'I'll just make the tea. Back in a mo.'

'How did this come about?' Lila hissed under her breath. We'd kept her in the dark because we didn't want any preconceived judgements before she met him, knowing what she already knew from the Mews gossip.

'Ali fell upon the idea the night of the drug bust, as it were…'

'Why should we work together?' Lila asked Norman in her flagrantly direct manner as he poured tea into our china cups. 'What are you going to bring to the table, apart from initially doing this for free?'

I checked out Norman to see if he was offended by her youthful inexperience and ballsy attitude. Instead, it appeared he was enjoying himself.

'Oh, young lady,' he laughed, sitting down, taking up his teacup and drinking while we all waited for him to finish his sentence. 'I can bring whatever you want – what are your wildest dreams?'

Lila burst out laughing, hailing shortbread crumbs onto her lap.

'We need someone who can work alongside the girls, helping to create a wonderful experience for the women. Sometimes it may be frivolous, but sometimes a degree of sensitivity will be required,' Samantha explained.

Norman stood up. We all looked at each other in alarm.

'Come on. I'll show you something.'

We trailed after him into the hallway and up the stairs, past the main bedroom and to the very top floor and a door on the left. He pushed it open. The thick curtains were drawn and he strode across the cream carpet to pull them apart. Sunlight revealed a roomy studio lined with built-in wardrobes on two walls and a tailor's dummy in one corner dressed in the most flamboyant fish-tailed sequined dress like a bird of paradise. By the door stood an old-fashioned white lacquered dressing table with a movable mirror housing cut-glass beakers rammed with make-up brushes and hair brushes, bottles of expensive perfume, trays of lipsticks all laid down flat and a giant powder-puff box topped with a white froufrou pompom.

A wooden streamlined desk was stashed under the windowsill with three picture frames curved round the right top corner. I walked over to inspect them. One, in black and white, was of an excruciatingly young Norman holding a baby who looked about one, then another frame with Frankie looking maybe ten, waving at the camera from a merry-go-round. The biggest frame displayed a collection of pictures, some overlapping, all of Norman and another man. He had an ethereal quality about him, like an actor working out who he was supposed to play next, not revealing his true self. He reminded me of Jeremy Irons.

'That's Lucas,' Norman said, as if I was supposed to know who he was.

'Ah,' Samantha said behind me. 'I've heard you talk about him before. He was an actor, wasn't he?'

'Yes, mostly theatre and rep. But he also specialised in drag.'

'What was his drag name?' Samantha asked. 'I bet David knew of him.'

'Fiona Angel. He was a regular compere at Madame Jojo's all through the eighties and early nineties until he got really sick.'

'Oh, I love Madame Jojo's,' I said. 'I've been there a few times – the one in Soho?' He nodded. 'I wonder if I ever saw him too.'

There were more framed posters of theatre productions hanging up on the walls and some stunning photos of women having their make-up done in front of professionally lit mirrors. I assumed Norman had been the make-up artist. He caught me looking at them.

'I did the make-up for the West End shows. Worked my way round them all. Plus, I always did Lucas's, then ended up doing everyone's at Jojo's.'

'Wow, so you know everything there is to know about dramatic stage make-up. How about subtler make-up, all the smoky eye trends and pared-down styles?' Lila asked. 'The older ladies shy away from lots of slap.'

'Oh, please, I invented the smoky eye!' Norman said as he tossed his head in a camp way. We couldn't help but laugh. 'Do you want to see some of Lucas's outfits?'

'Yes, please!' we all cried.

He opened all the cupboards to reveal rails of glitter, marabou, sequins, chiffon in all the colours of the rainbow, shoe racks, wigs presented on polystyrene wig stands on shelves. It was like a one-stop shop that probably wiped the floor with David O'Donnell's walk-in wardrobe. My inner magpie couldn't help itself as I gravitated towards all the glittery stilettos, picking up a silver pair and marvelling at their beauty.

'Did you carry on working in the theatre?' Lila asked, fingering one of the sequined gowns.

'No. Once Lucas died, that part of me died along with him. I used to love the theatrical elements, the transformation of someone's face into a new character, painting a different story, but I felt so dead inside and it killed the drive. I let it all go. Looking back, it was probably the one thing that would have helped the most, but I found the memories too hard to live with. Until now.'

'So, you're free next Friday?' Lila asked Norman. 'We're doing Isabelle and Debbie.'

'I might be washing my hair.' He smiled broadly, revealing the most perfectly straight teeth, and tapped his closely cut salt-and-pepper Afro hair.

'How did you suggest it?' Lila asked after we'd left Norman's for a quick powwow at Samantha's.

'I just asked him. I could tell he would say yes. I talked to him for ages about all sorts and gathered he's very lonely. He did hesitate a bit, maybe because he's hidden a huge part of his life for so long, but perhaps it was time for a change.'

'Did you see the little boy and the baby?' Lila asked. 'Do you think he has kids?'

'No idea,' Samantha said. 'They could have been relatives. I have a feeling they're not on the scene now.'

I kept quiet; it wasn't my story to tell.

'Well, we'll have to see how this works out,' Samantha added. 'I'm sure Norman isn't suddenly going to become the super-chilled professional we need. He's still Norman and Norman has always been a spikey bugger.'

'Keep an open mind,' I said. 'You never know, he might surprise us!'

38

Chakra Cleanse

'You may feel dizzy, hot, cold or sick, or all of the above!' Francesca warned after an unexpected initiation that involved her requesting the animals and spirits from all four corners of the world to assist in opening the sacred space for us in her spare room upstairs. She doused me in citrusy shamanic Florida Water, used for cleansing heavy vibes, then she sat me on the edge of the bed that she'd pulled away from the wall.

Francesca had texted earlier when I'd told her about puking in the pot plant.

Let's see if we can get to the bottom of your nerves and knock them on the head.

'How are you feeling? What are we here to do?' Francesca, my mad friend, who stashed secret wedding dresses under this very bed had vanished. In her place was a professional shaman with a fitting bedside manner and commanding aura surrounded by a throng of invisible spirit animals.

'I want to be able to go on TV without having a panic attack.'

'So you feel panicky?'

I nodded.

'Panicky...' And she made me blow into a polished pink stone I had chosen from her collection of crystals. 'What's under the panic?'

'Fear.'

She repeated and I blew that into the stone too.

I trawled through a few more scenarios, including anger at Alice for putting me in such a difficult situation, bewilderment at why I constantly chose the wrong men, anger at my inability to hold on to money, rage at Jim for EVERYTHING, then at the bottom, the bedrock that underpinned it all: 'Not good enough,' I squeaked, tears burning inside the bridge of my nose.

'So, that's it,' Francesca said calmly. 'Not good enough.' And I puffed into the stone like I was blowing away my words. 'Lie down.'

I leaned backwards onto the bed and she covered me with the quilt. Francesca placed the stone on my heart. I closed my eyes, and before you could say Beardy Weirdy,

I'd fallen down a rabbit hole. Francesca's hands cradled the back of my head, preventing me from slipping away into a topsy-turvy unending void. Sometime later she blew in my ear and snapped me back to my body where images flickered across my murky mind's eye: Dad standing on a podium similar to an old photo from his wrestling days. Me stepping forward and placing a gold medal round his neck. Mum next to him with her arm snaked round his waist, looking up to him, full of love. It made my eyes sting and a sob dragged itself up from my belly as tears coursed down the sides of my face, pooling in my ears. My heart brimmed with a love it couldn't contain, making me want to reach out and bring him back.

The rattle jolted me away from a jungle scene with a hummingbird flying high above it. More blowing in my ear. An eagle arced overhead and Francesca slipped her hands under my back, moving away from my head, and I sank further into a deeper state, calm now, no pictures or people. Just before she spoke, a jaguar slunk across the back of my mind.

'When you feel ready, open your eyes. No rush.'

I lay there for a moment, fizzing, not sure what had happened.

'You OK?'

'Very dizzy. That was fucking weird.'

'Yes, I sensed you found it difficult. There was a man here, very tall, grey receding hair, freckles.'

'Dad! I saw him on a podium with Mum. I was putting a medal round his neck. They were so in love.'

'How did it make you feel?'

'Inadequate.' More tears sprung from nowhere. 'I want that, but I never get it.'

'I think you need to take them off that pedestal. It probably wasn't perfect if you look back without those rose-tinted glasses on. Maybe by unconsciously choosing rubbish men, you will never be disappointed that they're not like your dad, and now he's dead, he's almost canonised in your mind.'

I nodded in agreement.

'The child in you needs to be at peace with it. Be kind to yourself while you let these things come up, as they will. Acknowledge anything that surfaces and wrap it in love.'

'I will,' I sniffed.

'Remember, facing success can sometimes be as daunting as facing failure – they are intrinsically linked, polar opposites. You're programming yourself to fail with men and money, but what if you programmed yourself to succeed? You may still fail every now and then, but so what? Failure is part of success's journey.'

I laughed thinly. 'Well, I have certainly tried very hard at failure so far.'

'I cleared the chakras that were blocked. Obviously your heart chakra was choked with heavy energy, as was your throat chakra. You need to communicate freely if

THE SINGLE MUMS MOVE ON

you have to think on your feet in front of a camera. I also released the eagle in your chest – the fight-or-flight mode you seem to be permanently tapping into. You will hopefully stop catastrophising about TV appearances now. See – that's another example of you self-sabotaging success – this job is important and you *are* good enough to do it. You deserve it, Ali.'

'Can I pay you?' I asked in the hallway, just as Ian wandered out of the kitchen with a mug of tea.

'Hello, Ali!' he said, abnormally pleased to see me. 'Ready to face the world?'

'Er, yes, thanks. Francesca has hopefully worked a miracle.'

'I'm sure she has. Good luck with all the TV stuff.' He gave me a genuine smile, not the usual stretching of his sealed lips across his teeth into a measly half-moon.

'Thanks,' I mumbled.

'I made you one of your Yogi teas; it's on the side,' he said to Francesca, and he subtly grazed her arm with his fingertips as he walked past to the living room.

'You don't have to pay me!' Francesca said, ignoring the fact Ian had just crossed the barricades. 'It's good for the soul to do freebies every now and then.'

'I got us some wine,' Mum said once Grace was in my bed so Mum could sleep in hers. 'And I also found all these when I was clearing out some of the boxes from

Penge I'd still not unpacked.' She placed two photo albums and a shoe box full of loose photos on the coffee table.

'Oh, all the old pics!' I cried, settling on the sofa next to her.

She poured us each a glass of Rioja. 'There's some good ones in the second album.'

I'd already picked up the shoe box and the first picture I pulled out of the photo lucky dip was one of Dad straight after a wrestling match, the referee holding his arm up in the air to show he'd won.

'Oh my God, that's so freaky!' I cried. 'Coincidence!' Mum looked at me nonplussed, so I explained what had happened at Francesca's.

'Oh, Ali, your dad wasn't faultless. Far from it! He was just a normal man who could be as annoying as the next person. Remember how he wouldn't learn to drive because he was so scared of failing the test, or crashing – just like he was scared of winning in the wrestling ring?' I nodded. 'I had to drive him everywhere, and when the business was booming and he was travelling all over the place giving lectures on how to create intricate plaster moulds for restoration work, he still refused to learn. He was a stubborn so and so. We used to fight about things all the time in the early years.'

'But we never heard you. I just remember it being cosy and happy, and Dan, Alex and me having fun. It was always busy and full of laughter!'

'Of course you didn't hear us – we went out to the garage and tore strips off each other. He used to drive me mental sometimes and I had to suck it up because ultimately we loved each other. I'm sure, well, I *know* I annoyed the crap out of him too. It's finding that middle ground. All romance, chiselled jaws and racing hearts don't last. Eventually what you're left with is friendship and respect, and an understanding of each other's bad habits, and you have to try not to rise to them. No one is perfect.'

'He was perfect to me,' I said in a small voice, my heart fluttering in my chest. She put her arms around me as a single tear slid down my face. 'I miss him. I wish I could go back for a day and take Grace, show her what Dad was like, what we were *all* like. Alex in his judo outfit thinking he was Bruce Lee, jumping out from behind the front door to karate-chop me. Dan mooning round the whole time thinking he was bloody William Wordsworth with his notebook of long words. All my friends round the kitchen table after school gossiping about boys. You making spaghetti pie, always there when we needed you.'

'Oh, the spaghetti pie – I'd forgotten about that. Grace would turn her nose up at it!'

'It felt like nothing could go wrong then. I wanted that for Grace, but from the start it's been a fight to keep my head above water: money, childcare, where to live.'

'I didn't work, love. You do. I wasn't a single mum. You juggle so many things. I don't know how you do, but I'm so proud of you, Alison, and I know your dad would be too. Grace is a credit to you. She doesn't know any different. She'll just grow up seeing a strong mummy who worked for a better life for her.'

I nodded, tears streaming now. The chakra cleanse had certainly unleashed a barrel-load of memories and feelings about my childhood that I longed to smell and savour. I took Francesca's advice to heart and just let the memories hit me full force while I cried, sometimes laughing through my tears, Mum holding me, occasionally offering another tissue, letting me ask questions when I needed to, until I was spent.

'Can I have some wine now?' I asked in a tired voice.

'Of course! I need some too.' Mum hugged me. 'I feel like your dad was here just now. You know what he would say about the whole perfect-man syndrome?'

I shook my head.

'He would say look for someone to whom you will never run out of things to talk about. Yes, you have to fancy them at some point, but don't be deceived by first impressions; you can grow to fancy someone too. I thought your dad was a gangly ginger streak of piss when I met him at fourteen. He kept asking me out and I kept saying no. It was when he invited me to one of his wrestling matches that I realised he was something else. A gentle giant with a will of iron. The unconscious part of me that maybe wanted one day to get married must have finally woken up and spotted the partnership potential.'

I knew the well-worn tale of their famous courtship, but I never knew she had thought he was a gangly ginger streak of piss first! I could hear Dad laughing in my head.

'Do you think you'll ever meet anyone else?' I asked, picking up my wine.

'I would have said no a few years ago, but the hole in my chest has eased off, life fills in around it and grandchildren help enormously. Maybe one day. God knows how, though. I was fourteen, Ali, and the world's a different place now. You order a partner the same way you order a takeaway now. I can't see me doing that.'

'Well, I know a lady who might be able to guide you,' I laughed, blowing my nose on a soggy tissue. 'I'm going to knock on Elinor's door and see if she's in!'

39

Full Circle

'How are things with Carl now? You don't still fancy him?' Jacqui asked. It was the night before she had to return to Australia and, as usual, we were dealing with the denial about her leaving by sinking a bottle or two of cheap fizz. We'd congregated in the Bishop on our favourite leather banquette seat back from the door, but close enough to it so we could inspect everyone who walked in and judge the fuck out of them.

'Have you asked if he went to the doctor or anything?' Amanda said.

'Yes, he's been to the doctor! I weirdly don't fancy him any more, though – the spark just died for me, which makes it easier now he's the official photographer for

Clothes My Daughter Steals. Neither of us wants it to be uncomfortable.'

'What did he say about the doctor?' Amanda insisted. 'Did he *really* go? Men can be funny about their willies.'

'They put his name down for psychosexual therapy, but the waiting list is ridiculous. I don't think he can afford to go private.'

'What a shame about all of it,' Jacqui sighed, sipping her commiserative glass of fizz. 'I could see you with him, he's so pretty.'

'But in such a complicated mess, and so recently sober,' Amanda surmised. 'He really does need to be on his own. Starting a new relationship is as tricky as it is exciting. I'm not sure I could begin a new relationship with someone who was freshly sober. It's such a glaringly huge chasm that wine normally fills. I would be so self-conscious about my own drinking.'

'Maybe you wouldn't drink?' I said.

Jacqui and Amanda looked at each other and burst out laughing.

'As if!' Amanda cried.

'So what about Francesca and the toy boy Qi Gong twat?' Jacqui laughed. 'God, he was a squirt, wasn't he?'

'She shagged Ian.' I just let that settle on the table.

'What?' Amanda and Jacqui screeched in unison so piercingly that people on other tables turned to see what the fuss was about.

'Shh,' I said, flapping my hands at them. 'We can't mention names too loudly in case anyone hears.'

'What the fuck happened there?' Jacqui hissed. 'She hasn't had sex for a million years.'

'I knew something was up when I went for my chakra cleanse, but I also think I saw them up to something at the party when they were pissed, but dismissed it. They were acting like they had a secret.'

'So they're back together? Happy? After all that time?' Amanda asked cynically. 'What about wanting to leave and start again and shag Teyo?'

'Turns out Teyo's performance at the party and Ariel's drunken reaction to him even being there snapped her back to reality.'

'Why shag Ian, then?' Amanda wanted to know. 'Why not jump on Tinder if you just wanted a secret shag? It is possible not to get found out.'

I'd asked the same thing when we were taking Jo's dogs for a walk over the weekend...

'Because he was there, and I was drunk and pissed off,' Francesca let slip.

'But you want to leave!' Jo snapped as she bent over and picked up a stick for Bert, hurling it so far across Dulwich Park that the dogs would need to get a bus to find it, their stumpy legs not bred for covering long distances.

'I knew you would be like that about it!' Francesca had said touchily. 'I shouldn't have admitted it.'

'It was obvious earlier,' Jo countered back. 'He was all over you and you let him in the no-fly zone.'

'He wasn't all over me! He touched my back.'

'Same difference.'

'Anyway, yes, we have done it a few times,' Francesca revealed further as we passed the duck pond where kids screamed with laughter on the pedalos, other kids whizzing past like bullets on the recumbent bikes, weaving between people, chasing each other along the paths. I missed Grace and she'd only been gone a day.

'Are you back together?' I asked.

'No, I don't know what I want long term. At the moment I just want sex when I want it.'

'You *did* want to get married,' Jo said, prompting her. 'And living in the same house is confusing, surely.'

'I don't want to marry Ian any more. And I haven't moved back into our bedroom.'

'What if you want to meet someone else?' I asked, totally perplexed about what was going on here. 'Shagging Ian isn't going to be conducive to that, is it?'

She shrugged. 'The sex was good. I'd forgotten how it could be, but it's also like an out-of-body experience because I'm not associating it with him. It's like I'm having sex with myself, I'm turning myself on like I have been doing for fuck knows how many years, but he just happens to be there.'

'So he's like a sex robot or a giant man-sized dildo?' Jo barked out in her sergeant major voice across the duck pond. 'He could be anyone then?'

'That's a bit below the belt!' Francesca cried, and Jo burst out laughing. I couldn't help a snigger escaping. Francesca playfully hit Jo on her arm.

'Do you not have any feelings for him?' I asked. 'He doesn't bring anything to the bedroom?'

'Well, yes, of course he does. I haven't been touched by him for so long I'm having to get used to it again. I do have feelings but not like he wants me to. I'm fond of him. And that's an enormous improvement on wanting to sleep in a separate bed for the last two years and puking in my mouth at the thought of him touching me. I think I took myself to that place as self-protection and my walls are still up pretty high.'

I had no idea how you came back from wanting to puke in your mouth at the thought of sex with a partner. Desperation was a powerful aphrodisiac.

'How does *he* feel?' Jo asked. 'Does he want to go the whole hog?'

'Yes, he wants to get married, says he loves me. But every time he says that it makes me want to run away. I'm happy with how things are right now. Maybe I will want to be on my own eventually. But the truth is, I would have to live miles away from London if I could even find a property with my small share of the house.'

'So if I offered you a flat rent-free for six months in Forest Hill with three bedrooms so the girls could live with you, you'd take it? One of my tenants has just moved out and it needs doing up, but I can work round you,' Jo continued to push.

'You don't like Ian, do you?' Francesca shot back instead of accepting.

'Neither do you!'

'Why do you care?' Francesca protested. 'I'm not complaining about it; I'm telling you what's going on.'

'Because you've been going on about leaving him for two years. I've offered to get you on your feet several times, but you've always referred back to the girls turning against you, which I understand completely.'

'Yes, and I still stand by that! Especially after Ariel's reaction,' Francesca said snappishly.

I kept my head down. Years of friendship were being rocked to the foundations here, though I was sure they could weather it.

'You're scared of leaving him and the Mews, of being on your own. Teyo is finally off the scene, Ian doesn't seem too bad now he's paying you attention again after the ridiculously long drought. You also can't live your life and be miserable just because the children might not like it. What will happen when they leave home? You'll still be there, even more unhappy and older, making it harder to find someone else.'

I winced.

'Jo, I love you, but take a look at your own garden before you go pulling out the weeds in everybody else's. I'm going back to the Mews. I have a client coming at four and I need to align my chakras or they won't have a good experience.' Francesca kissed my cheek and stalked back the way we'd come, her green silk scarf flapping out behind her in her haste to escape.

'You know she has wedding dresses hidden under her bed?' Jo asked as the dogs waddled towards us; they never did find the stick.

'Yes, I know. We tried them on months ago when Teyo was still in favour.'

'What do you think?'

'Oh, no, don't drag me in to this. I have no idea. If she's happy, just let her be.'

'But she could leave if she really wanted to.'

'Of course. Anyone can leave anyone if they're willing to pay the price. There's always going to be collateral damage. Maybe that's what she's weighing up.'

'I wouldn't stay with someone who ignored me for years, no matter if they had had a breakdown or whatever and I had tried and tried to help. Move on, pastures new.'

'It's never that simple when kids are involved. And also you only know what her experience is. What about Ian's?' Spoken like a true resident of Switzerland.

★

'Jo's reaction said so much more about her than it did about Francesca,' Amanda said when I'd told them about the set-to in the park.

'Yeah. Who are we to judge how Francesca conducts her life? If she can manage a friends-with-benefits relationship with her baby father, good for her. I think most people would like that!' Jacqui agreed.

'And as I said before,' Amanda harped on, 'we don't know about Ian and how he felt. Maybe he felt rejected? Sometimes you're against the current for years in a long-term relationship, especially if one of you has depression, or cancer, or another major trauma, a sick child or the fucking menopause. What then? Relationships aren't a quadratic equation, there are too many variables – we all know that. If someone manages to be in one that is, God forbid, against the norm, so what?'

'Well said, my friend,' Jacqui chimed. 'Let's drink to relationships outside the boring box!'

We clinked glasses.

'I hope she's happy,' I said.

'At least she's getting laid!' Jacqui cheered.

'Yes, lucky her,' I moaned, hoping my fanny hadn't knitted itself together in protest over *my* longest drought ever.

'Now, I'll be back in exactly four months. Can you please have had sex by then or I am buying *you* a sex robot for Christmas.'

'Rampant Rabbit will get jealous...'

As the evening drew to a close, we gossiped about the lack of like-minded women in the Sydney suburb where Jacqui lived.

'You know, I've been there a year now, and I still haven't found my Australian equivalent of you two. I can't call anyone a slag or a twat as a term of endearment. They're all grown-ups, with zipped-up senses of humour. I love the women I teach yoga to, but they're all a bit earnest.'

'I think it will happen, but remember people like Ali and I don't just grow on trees – we're special!'

'Of course you are!'

'Even when we're old and smelling of wee in the old people's home I'll still be saying you're a slag and no one will want to visit you because you smell like a ten-day-old Tena lady,' Amanda said with a straight face.

'Oh, I love you girls! You get me!' Jacqui said, leaning in to hug us. 'See you at Christmas.'

As we got up to leave, I glanced at the bar and caught Nick's eye. I hadn't seen him sneak in; he was waiting for last orders, standing next to a tall blonde woman. *Was he with her?* He nodded his head in that blokey way, when blokes spot other blokes they know on a train platform or in a shop but don't know what to say. So instead they ram their hands in their pockets and touch their balls for reassurance, then nod with raised eyebrows, signalling: I've seen you, mate, and I greet you, now I'm moving on. I copied him and followed the girls outside. We still hadn't actually spoken since I'd got shirty with him about Norman.

I walked all the way home up two hills to get some much-needed exercise. It was depressing because as soon as we hit August, the light evenings began their slide towards dusk earlier and earlier. 'All downhill till Christmas,' my dad always used to say after the summer solstice. He wasn't wrong. I turned up the secret alleyway down the side of Terry's Tool Hire, and out of nowhere someone had inched behind me, forcing the hairs to stand up on the back of my neck. I turned round, praying it was one of the Mews lot, just got off a bus back from a night out.

40

Bride of Chucky

'It was you who stole my bike.' Ifan was looming over me, stinking of beer. Instead of the eyes that used to flicker between adorable and sexy, his were now just disturbingly similar to those on 'Most Wanted' posters. *Have you seen this man suspected of killing three people and two gerbils...?*

'I don't know what you're talking about. I haven't seen your bike.' I turned away from him and apprehensively strode on jelly legs towards the gate less than ten metres ahead. He roughly grabbed my arm and I pulled away, but he had a vice-like grip and dug his fingertips into my elbow, making me wince.

'It *was* you. You knew the combination on the lock – it hadn't been broken with bolt cutters.'

I shook my head, trying to worm out of his grasp.

'And thanks to you, shouting about the infection we got, my name is mud on the strip. I bet I caught the fucking thing from you, anyway.'

'Get off. You're hurting me.'

'Good. You ruined the start of something with a girl I really liked. We were going to move in together.'

'Really? She had her own flat too, did she? You can't stand on your own two feet, always looking for a meal ticket. I can't believe I fell for it too.' I couldn't help myself. My fight-or-flight mechanism had obviously malfunctioned and instead of wriggling out of my denim jacket and flying up to the gate, I decided to stay and fight.

'You weren't complaining. You can't be on your own either, always out shagging random blokes. How else do you think it was so easy for me to move in with you? You were desperate for it.' I hit him with my free left hand, not my hand of choice, so he got off lightly with a bit of a limp effort. I managed to catch him by surprise, though, and the slap echoed satisfyingly, stinging my palm.

'You fucking bitch.' He jerked my arm so it felt like it popped out of its socket.

'I would step away from her if I were you,' a stern voice said from the bottom of the alleyway.

Ifan jumped.

'None of your business, mate. Just me and the missus having a little barney.' He dropped my arm and I started rubbing it.

'I'm not your anything,' I spat at him. 'Don't ever come near me again.'

Jo stepped out of the shadows and Ifan exploded into boisterous laughter. I wondered if he found her yellow shorts and black leather jacket teamed with red Adidas trainers amusing. She was carrying a ubiquitous blue plastic bag from the zombie apocalypse shop.

'What's so funny, you Welsh twat?' she said in a deep growl.

'You're a fucking female midget. I can't believe I thought you were a bloke.'

'I don't see how that makes any difference. I may be small, but there's no cure for being a cunt. Now hop it.'

'Or what?' Ifan said, starting to get lairy. 'You gonna head butt me in the knee?'

'No, but I could grab your pathetic bollocks right now and rip them through your jeans and ram them in your mouth before you could scream "midget".' She stepped towards him intimidatingly and he fleetingly glanced at me in alarm. Jo did look crazy right then. Her face set in a snarl mimicking her ankle-snapping dogs, her hands bunched into neat little fists just like Bride of Chucky.

'She means it,' I said darkly. 'I can kick your head in while she sits on you. She may be small, but she's all muscle.'

'You two are fucking mental!' He turned on his heels and ran straight into Nick, sending him flying. Jo offered her hand and pulled him up.

'What was going on here? You both mugging people?'

'No, some arsehole threatened Ali. What a tool!' Jo shook her head.

'You OK?' Nick asked, concerned. 'I saw him earlier. He was at the back of the pub and followed you guys out; I didn't think anything of it, to be honest. Do you know him?'

'An ex-boyfriend.'

'Come on, let's get in the compound away from all the nutters,' Jo said. 'Fancy a nightcap?'

'I will,' I said.

'I'll leave you ladies to it. Glad you're OK, Ali.'

'I've got some things for your mum. Is she round next week?'

'Oh, er, yeah, that would be great. She'd love to see you. Night.'

'So, that was Ifan the cunt?' Jo asked as she poured me a glass of port from her insane bottle collection stacked up on two curved open shelves underneath the end of one of the kitchen work surfaces. Blue Bols, crème de cassis, sherry, golden tequila, cherry liqueur, Amaretto, Calvados – all battled for space amongst innumerable other shelf mates with equally exotic labels.

'Yes.'

'Good riddance, I say. You're way too good for him.' She sipped her Calvados and eyed me knowingly over the top of her glass. 'Whatever happened with you and Carl? You make such a nice couple.'

'Nothing ever happened, we're just mates.'

'I saw how you looked at each other: there was chemistry there. Something happened, I know it. You're good for him – you could both be very happy together.'

'We're not compatible. He's also got an awful lot on his plate and his sobriety must come first.'

She looked like she was going to persuade me, but thought better of it.

'And it's too close to home.'

'Yes, and don't I know all about that!' she sighed instead. 'Bloody hell, Debbie hates me. I don't know what I did wrong.'

'She doesn't hate you at all.'

'Well, she made it clear she didn't need my help. I keep fucking up. The last few ladies have all ended up being nightmares. It's made me think, am I going for the wrong ones?' She looked at me like I might have an answer.

'I think it would be the blind leading the blind, me giving you advice,' I laughed, still thinking it was a shame about her and Debs. 'Maybe pick ones that don't need fixing.'

'Jesus, you're sounding just like Francesca now. She's always saying that, offering to cleanse my chakras, reset my head. I don't mind reflexology and massage, and all the nice gentle things she does, but fuck me, I'm not sure I could cope with out-of-body journeying to the rainforest to find my spirit animal and then bringing it home to guide me in making choices for the rest of my life. What if my spirit animal is a poisonous blue frog? I can't see a frog picking me a nice lady to settle down with.'

'It isn't like that! You deal with your past, so you can make better choices.'

She blew through her lips like she didn't believe me.

'Try it, you might find it helps.'

She shook her head. 'No, my past can stay where it is: in the past. Move forward. Anyway, I can't do anything about Debbie. I guess things will eventually improve but it doesn't help living in each other's pockets here. The advantages usually outweigh the disadvantages in the Mews, but the only way I can see this being less awkward is if I go away for a while.'

'That's a bit drastic, isn't it?' I sipped my syrupy port.

'No, I could kip in the flat in Forest Hill and do it up, rent my room out here for six months to cover the cost.

One of the dog-walking ladies I know told me about a colleague who needs somewhere for six months, a doctor, nice woman. I've met her, we had an informal chat about the possibility of her moving into my house here. But if Francesca wanted to have the flat she still could.' She knocked back the remains of her Calvados in one hit and poured another measure. 'I don't know, I just think I need to get away from here for a while, get out of Debbie's way. I keep saying the wrong things and upsetting her. How is she? I know she's had her third dose of chemo today. I texted her to see if she needed anything, obviously got no reply. I still care about her; she's going through something horrendous and I want to help.'

'Elinor's with her today. She's poorly, apparently, very sick. I doubt she'll text anyone back.'

'She wouldn't text me anyway,' Jo said, shrugging. 'Yeah, it's probably better I get away. I've more chance of finding a nice lady without ghosts of girlfriends past hanging over me.'

'Or maybe you should just be on your own?' I suggested controversially. 'I've realised that it's probably what *I* need. I always thought I would feel better with a boyfriend, but I don't think I will. Seeing Ifan tonight proved he still makes me feel mental, and I need to get over that. I'm going to try to consciously be on my own.' I could almost hear Mini Amanda start an elaborate

Roy Castle tap dance routine in celebration that I was finally taking some advice on board. I wasn't convinced *I* believed it, though. I was honestly not like her. She loved being on her own, which is why she never had any trouble getting boyfriends and had managed to bag a second husband. That kind of natural indifference is like a man magnet, a reworking of an uncontrived 'treat them mean, keep them keen'. I, on the other hand, would flirt with Siri just to have someone to interact with.

'Maybe,' Jo said, sounding as unconvinced as I felt. 'Though I have met this lovely lady recently. She's trying to rent the shop underneath my flat – I own the freehold – but she's just come out of a tricky relationship with a bloke who fleeced her. I've asked her for a drink to talk about it.'

'Does she know you're a lesbian?'

'I think even the Queen knows I'm a lesbian. It's just a drink!' She winked at me. Nothing was ever just a drink with Jo. Another 'project' on the horizon, another drama triangle...

Debbie was laid low after the chemo and I popped in on Tuesday night once she'd stopped puking. Isabelle let me in and kindly made me a coffee to take through. She looked tired, her youthful face glazed with worry, dark smudges beneath her eyes.

'Charlie gets so upset seeing Mum like this,' Isabelle said in a small voice as she made my drink in the kitchen. 'He's had to go to Dad's for a few days.'

'It must be hard for both of you. I'm sure your mum loves having you here as a support, though. She will understand about Charlie. I would if it was Grace.'

'Hello!' I said as I walked through to the living room, almost spilling my coffee at the sight of Debbie. She was smaller and even paler than previously, and her bald head was protected by a cosy blue woollen beanie. I wanted to cancel this Friday's vlog right then; she didn't look well enough to stand up, let alone be fussed over and asked to try on clothes. A gust of wind might blow her over.

'How are things today?' I asked uneasily.

'Better than yesterday. I've managed to eat a banana, though I can't tell if it tastes like a banana. My throat and mouth are a bit raw.' I sat on the chair opposite the sofa.

'Look, do you think we should postpone to another week?'

'No!' she cried hoarsely. 'I have to do it. It's what kept me going yesterday when I couldn't stop puking. I imagined myself at Samantha's having my make-up done, Isabelle trying on clothes, having fun like a normal teenage girl. Please don't cancel. I know I will feel a lot better by Friday.'

'I'm not thinking of cancelling it. Just moving to another time.' Though if I was honest, I had no idea when that would be as I was busy next week and Grace was back and then Lila went on holiday.

'There's never a good time when you have cancer. You have to just do things. I could so easily just sit here and give up because I feel so fucking awful, but I can't; I want to live.' I got up and hugged her.

'Oh, Debbie, you're wonderful! OK, Friday it is. You're going to love the make-up artist!'

41

Norman's Wisdom

'Norman!' Debbie cried as he opened the door to her at Samantha's. She was wearing her lovely strawberry-blond wig this morning. 'What are you doing here?' We'd kept him a secret. 'You're not the amazing make-up artist, are you?' she asked doubtfully.

'I am the very same. I've come out of retirement. How are you feeling? Round three of chemo can start to feel brutal.' He stepped aside so Debbie and Isabelle could come in. If Debbie had eyebrows, they would have been raised in surprise. We all knew Norman as a buttoned-up Oscar the Grouch.

'Oh, I'm feeling more human today, though I'm not sure I look it – that's your job to perform a miracle!' Debbie looked marginally better than she had on

Tuesday. There was a definite touch of colour in her cheeks.

'Debbie, I can rejuvenate a corpse, so we'll be grand.'

I held my breath, not sure how she would react.

'Oh my God, that's music to my ears,' she laughed, and I sighed in relief.

Debbie stoically let us film her without her wig or any make-up, and Carl asked her to pose for some before and after photos for social media. The internet seemed to have a boundless appetite for emotional makeover stories. I wasn't going to plug Spanx today – it wasn't the right vibe – but Norman had come up top trumps.

'I just emailed their PR department. All I had to do was mention Lila, Clothes My Daughter Steals, David O'Donnell and they couldn't send them quickly enough. I got them the same day from a nice leather-clad young man on a motorbike.' He winked playfully.

Debbie giggled, and as I watched Isabelle, the mantle of ceaseless worry seemed to slip temporarily from her shoulders. Having some light relief and remembering to be a normal teenager again was just what she needed.

'Do you want to try them? Lucas used to wear them when he lost all his hair. Though they have improved massively in the last fifteen years.' He opened the pink cardboard box, emblazoned with the gold Magic Brows logo, and pulled out Cellophane-wrapped packets of eyebrows, all different colours and sizes. There were eyelash kits too, extensions, whole sets of different lengths and colours, natural and the outlandish.

'Oh, fabulous!' Debbie cried, clapping her hands together. 'Can I try different ones? I always wanted big bushy Madonna eyebrows like she had in the "Like a Prayer" video.'

'Oh, yes!' Norman laughed. 'Lucas used to do a "Like a Prayer" homage with the crucifixes and dancing Jesus. It used to go down a storm.'

'Can I have some eyelash extensions, please?' Isabelle asked politely. 'I've always wanted to try them but they're so hard to do on your own.'

'Yes, darling. I'll show you some tricks so you can have a go at home too.'

We piled through all the clothes I'd had sent over. Debbie's arms were aching from her veins collapsing and she wanted to cover up the bruises. I dug out some lovely pieces from Debenhams, M&S, H&M and Zara for the Christmas season, so long sleeves were in. As I hung the clothes up and steamed them on my rack in the kitchen, Lila sat with Norman as he prepped Debbie, and Carl snapped away as unobtrusively as possible.

'Did Jo tell you about moving out?' he hissed under his breath as I walked back in while Debbie was busy perusing the eyebrows with Isabelle.

'Yes. I wonder if she'll tell Debbie. I gather she's made up her mind. It's all happened rather quickly.'

'The new woman, Christa, is coming over this week to go over a rental agreement. Should we tell Debbie?'

I stopped what I was doing and grimaced, usually a sign I needed Mini Amanda to step in, which she did from her office in Switzerland: *Jo owes Debbie nothing. They're not in a relationship. Debbie ended it, so can't really complain if Jo is moving on with her life. Don't get sucked into another drama triangle.*

'Stay out of it, Carl. It's not our shit. Remember how you hate Jo meddling in your crap.'

'True. Smile!' I pulled a thickie no-brain face as he clicked, relieved we could be us again without our own excruciating soap opera.

'So, Debbie, how many rounds of chemo have you now had?' Lila asked sensitively while the camera rolled.

'Three, and three to go.'

'How have you been coping?' Norman dabbed at her face with his brushes, a master craftsman at work, deftly zipping between paint pots of trickery, camouflaging shadows with concealer, disguising tiredness with highlighter, adding a healthy glow with cheek stain.

'This week has been tough. All the hair from my body has now completely fallen out, so that's unpleasant. At least my hairy toes are nice and clean!' Lila laughed and Norman smiled. 'And my lady moustache hasn't needed plucking – so there's an upside somewhere. The thought of this has been like a shining beacon at the end of the tunnel. And Isabelle is looking forward to trying on some clothes. We need to be us again. Charlie, my son, is going to pop in when it's all finished to give us his verdict.'

'Try these slug eyebrows, see if you can pull them off. I have some of Lucas's more dramatic wigs in the kitchen – we can team them with different brows. I've stuck on regular lashes that should stay put for a few days.'

Debbie's eyes lit up. 'You've never said much about Lucas,' she said. 'What happened to him? I know he died a while ago.'

Norman hesitated and glanced at Lila, who was sitting next to Debbie in front of the white screen.

'Do you want me to switch the camera off, Norman?'

'No, it's fine. I don't mind sharing.' He steadied his hand and dipped a tiny brush into a pot of gold eye shadow, tapped it so it rained a fine haze of ochre glitter, and swept it over Debbie's eyelid. 'Lucas eventually died of lung cancer. He'd never smoked in his entire life. It unfortunately appeared many years after he got the all-clear from an initial kidney cancer. The doctors weren't sure they were related or if it was caused by years of passive smoking, performing in clubs and theatres before the smoking ban.'

'Oh God, how awful,' Debbie empathised.

'Yes, I'm so sorry,' Lila offered.

'Don't be – he had a great life. He wouldn't want anyone to be sad or feel bad, me especially. He wanted me to go out and meet someone else, have another great romance. But I couldn't.'

'How long has it been?' Debbie probed gently. I silenced my immediate to-do list; I noticed Carl had stopped clicking, Samantha had put down her omnipresent phone and Isabelle had stopped flicking through the lashes.

'Fourteen years. He died just after I moved in next door. We'd been together twenty years.'

'That must have been very hard,' Lila said quietly. 'Moving house is one of life's biggest stresses, and then to top it off with a partner dying.'

'He was more than my partner,' Norman said wistfully, applying more glitter to Debbie's other eye now. 'He was my life, which I know isn't healthy, but I chose him over my family, my history, my everything. He was first diagnosed with cancer six years after I met him in the theatre. I was still so far in the closet to my family, the wood panelling was imprinted on my back, and I had divorced my wife because we both knew I was gay. She'd met someone else and I needed to free her. My family were cross; they are very religious so divorce was frowned upon. So when I eventually got together with Lucas, I knew they could never meet him, even if I introduced him as a friend. He was way too camp, way too flamboyant. They would have guessed straight away and then they would have known about me.'

'Do you not think they knew deep down anyway?' Lila asked, transfixed.

'No, it would never have crossed their minds that I might be gay – it was considered against God's law. I would be cast out into hell forever when I died. Fire and brimstone.' He chuckled to himself. 'So I said to Lucas we would have to be together in secret, until my parents died. But they were showing no sign of dropping off the planet!' He chortled louder this time. 'So I compromised, kept my little flat and then lived with Lucas the rest of the time. When my family visited, I just entertained them there where there was no trace of who I really was and I always visited them alone. This was before social media, so snooping was harder.'

'Didn't Lucas mind being a secret? Did he ever feel that you were ashamed of him?' Debbie asked.

'No, he was amazing. He said if I wanted him to meet them, he would tone down who he was, be less, be conventional, but I didn't want that. I think that was one of the only rows we ever had. That and the fact ketchup does *not* go in the fridge! I told him he was never to make himself less for someone else, that he was his authentic self and should remain that way. He told me I was making myself less for my family, allowing them to deny who I was. He was right, but my parents would never have accepted who I really was. This was all such a long time ago, when it wasn't as easy to be who you are.'

'Norman, it's still hard to be who you are, even now,' Lila said lightly. 'Look at David O'Donnell, outed by a newspaper because he's living his real life cross-dressing. He had to make himself less so society didn't ridicule him. But look at the reaction he got. The people supporting him outweighed all the trolls.'

'True. I think the crux of it was *I* didn't accept myself. So when Lucas was diagnosed the first time, I tried to juggle his illness and my family and I couldn't. I wanted to be with him, help him through the hospital visits, the chemo, the fear, and something eventually snapped. I told my family.'

We all collectively held our breath. Norman changed brushes and searched through his silver flight case for the next mercurial pot in his transformational arsenal.

'They disowned me.' He artfully traced the top lash-line where the fake lashes curled up from the lid edge. 'Even my brother.'

'Oh, Norman,' Debbie said, patting his knee. 'You poor wee thing.'

'Even your mum?' Lila asked in a hushed tone, clearly astonished that people could be so cruel.

'Yes. She was very much a woman who did what her husband told her. But one day, she turned up at Lucas's flat – I had let my one go by then. I don't know how she found me. Lucas was lying down recovering from a round of chemo. She said: "Norman, I love you, but your father will never allow this." I asked her if she wanted to come in, she refused, but she gave me a long hug on the front step. She was crying. That was the last time I ever saw her as my mother. I tried so many times to see them, turned up unannounced, but it was horrendous. The insults... the bigotry, the anger about who I was and what I represented: shame on our family. In the end I had to stop trying for my own mental health. They just shut me out...' Norman reached into his make-up box for a different brush. 'Anyway, I'm assuming my parents are dead now. They must be – I'm seventy.'

A gaggle of cries echoed around the room.

'How are you seventy?' I shrieked, walking over and peering at his perfect skin.

'Good genes!' he laughed loudly. 'Always moisturise!'

'Norman, I don't think I've ever seen you in a pair of jeans,' Debbie joked.

'Now, Miss Sassy Pants, we need to choose eyebrows... these or these?' I didn't understand how Norman could laugh after that confession. I thought back to my own 'story', Jim leaving me when Grace was newborn, making me homeless. Other friends, people I since told after the event, all asked the same thing: how did you carry on, knowing you were about to be made homeless with a newborn baby? And the answer was the same every time: you just do, because what is the alternative? There are only so many hours in the day you can sit and cry.

'Are you ready to see yourself?' I asked Debbie a bit later on after we had tried on about four outfits, the clear favourite being a navy jumpsuit with three-quarter-length sleeves, wide legs, cinched waist and a galaxy of teensy gold stars.

'I can't believe it's from Marks and Spencer,' Isabelle laughed. 'I would never go in there in a million years.'

'I get your knickers from there,' Debbie said indignantly.

'Mum!'

Norman had persuaded Debbie to try on a very long blond wig that he set in a piled-on up do with a gazillion pins. Her eyebrows matched her hair – they looked freakily real and framed her dolled-up eyes perfectly. Isabelle had been given a pared-down look by Norman but with accentuated eyes and lash extensions that she was pleased with. He waved her hair with tongs, and I got her to wear giant gold hoop earrings and gold high tops.

'Please can I wear trainers with it too?' Debbie begged. 'I don't like heels, especially at the moment. I like being comfortable.'

'I don't have any. Sorry, I didn't think.' I felt bad because I should have known that.

'Let me nip back home, I might have some things,' Norman said. He wandered back in ten minutes later with a bin bag full of booty.

'Oh, you're like Shoe Santa!' Debbie cried.

We all crowded round to see what Norman had grabbed.

'Jesus, Norman, where did you get these Nike Jordan's?' Carl was impressed 'They're from the eighties! They're mint.'

'Lucas collected all kinds of shoes. We bought them when we went to New York once. He found them in a thrift store.'

'They're my size,' I commented, eyeing them hopefully.

'I like these,' Debbie said, pulling out a pair of rainbow Nike high tops.

'Mum! You look better!' Charlie said, clearly relieved when he arrived towards the end while Carl was taking the final few pictures. 'You look like you again, maybe a bit prettier!'

'How about me?' Isabelle asked.

'Yeah, you look OK.' She hit her brother lightly on the arm.

'What have you got from the makeover?' Lila asked to camera. 'What advice can you share with others on a cancer journey?'

'Never lose sight of who you are. You are still you, even with cancer. You are allowed to be OK, even when you're *not* OK. And this vlog has helped see me through the chemo haze. It has helped my kids glimpse their mum again. And we had fun. That is so important! When you feel dreadful – and I have done this week – adding a bit of glamour can lift your spirits. And fake eyebrows – what a revelation – thank you Magic Brows!'

42

Blood Ties

I knocked on Norman's door at the end of the following week with Grace and Samantha. The latest vlog episode had beaten all previous records for engagement. David O'Donnell, Trisha and Mina had shared it on all social media platforms across what felt like the entire world. They even talked about Debbie's journey on the sofa, wishing her well the following morning. We now had over sixty thousand subscribers and the numbers continued to steadily rise. Magic Brows expressed their 'sincerely hopeful wishes' to advertise with us, which was further reason to celebrate. And we had appeared in several newspapers as more than a makeover vlog. 'Clothes My Daughter Steals is a therapy session with a real heart and some serious glitter,' Samantha had read out loud from the *Metro*.

Samantha had received a windfall of emails from people requesting to come on the vlog, something she was now having to consider if we wanted to keep people engaged. 'It starts getting messy with the liability insurance policies – who's covered and who isn't, all that jazz. People could sign waivers absolving us of blame should, God forbid, anything happen they don't like during a makeover. I'll have to think about it, get Amit, my lawyer, to have a look at everything,' she'd said before we popped into Norman's. But the biggest surprise had been an email request about something completely different.

'Hello, boss lady,' Norman said, opening the door. 'What can I do for you two, and the lovely Grace?'

'Can we come in?' Samantha asked in her professional agent voice tinged with trepidation.

'Oh God, what is it? You're sacking me already because my highlighter wasn't visible from the moon?'

'No! We're coming in, make way!' I said jokingly. 'I promised Grace you had some amazing shoes upstairs. Can we show her?'

'Of course, follow me.' Norman led us up to the studio and opened all the cupboards so Grace could browse the shelves, a magpie like me.

'Now she's busy, we need to talk to you,' I said, feeling nervous, and we stepped onto the landing.

'I've received an email from a member of your family,' Samantha said softly.

'What? How?'

'They must have found my details at the end of the video. I have my website address on there as a point of contact. That's how we get sent freebies, all that sort of thing.'

'Who contacted you? My parents must be dead.'

'They are, I'm sorry,' Samantha said.

Norman nodded slowly, biting his lip.

'One of your brother's children got in touch. They'd seen the footage shared somewhere, and the penny dropped.'

Norman opened his mouth and then closed it.

'Shall we go downstairs so you can sit down?' I asked.

He nodded again.

'Grace, don't move anything. We'll be downstairs, OK?' She didn't even hear me; she was hypnotised by all the glitter.

'Do you want to read the email?'

'Yes please.'

Samantha whipped out her phone and showed him.

'I can't read that, it's too small.'

'Yeah, I know. Ali, can you make it out?'

I squinted. 'Just about. "To whom it may concern,"' I read out loud.

I was wondering if you can help me. I came across a video on YouTube that has been going viral, and think my uncle may be the make-up artist on there. His name is Norman Francis and I have found out that my father, Ambrose, was discouraged from keeping in touch with him years ago because he was gay. This all came about a few years ago when Nanny Elizabeth finally died. I had known about him but they all talked like he was dead. Anyway, life got in the way, I had a baby, and then a friend shared this video with me, because I'm a make-up artist too, and said how sweet it was with the old gentleman and the poor woman suffering from cancer. I then put two and two together when I heard his story. Is this my uncle Norman?

With kindest regards, Rochelle Hughes

'Ambrose, wow, he had a daughter...' Norman sighed broodingly. We sat in silence for a moment. I handed Sam her phone back and picked my nails.

'Do you want me to forward you the email?' Samantha asked eventually. 'Then you can deal with it yourself?'

'Yeah, sure, thanks,' Norman said vaguely, staring into the distance.

'I need to shoot off to a lunch meeting. Are you going to be OK?'

'I'll be fine. I always am,' he said pragmatically.

'I can stay for a bit,' I offered. 'Make us some tea, or something stronger?'

'It's ten in the morning!' Norman protested.

'So? You've had a shock!'

'Are you going to reply?' I asked after Samantha had left. Grace had returned downstairs and Norman had put on *The Wizard of Oz* for her to watch. She was standing in front of the TV wearing a pair of enormous ruby stilettos, like glittery canoes on her feet.

'I think I should, but what if this gets Rochelle into trouble? Ambrose won't be impressed she contacted me.' He looked doubtful.

'Norman, she's a woman with a baby and probably can't fathom why anyone would want to deliberately cut themselves off from a member of their family. She's a grown-up and allowed to do what she wants, just like you were when you chose Lucas over them.'

'I know. I guess I'm just apprehensive. I've often wondered about them over the years, thought of trying to track them down, but couldn't face rejection again. It was bad enough the first time round when I had someone worthwhile in my life to alleviate the sting.'

'You have a worthwhile life now. You're putting yourself out there and engaging again after so long. We need you at Clothes My Daughter Steals – you were a mega hit online – did you read some of the comments? People saying how much your story touched them, how you've helped them with things in their own lives. Your story is important.'

He laughed quietly.

'This could be a second chance at family, help you feel less alone.'

'Yeah, I know. It's just overwhelming when you've made peace with the fact you have no family.'

'I don't think family means what it used to any more. My friends are also my family. I would have died of a broken heart if Amanda hadn't let me stay in her attic after Grace's dad left us. She supported me, we supported each other. Just because someone is related to you by blood doesn't mean they get to call themselves your family. They have to earn it, that's what I think. Anyway, the Mews is like a madhouse family!'

'How about you?' Norman asked, deflecting from his own dilemma. 'You have anyone special?'

'Nope. I'm single.'

'Him next door thinks you're pretty special,' Norman said, looking right at me with raised eyebrows and pursed lips. He nodded his head for added emphasis.

'Norman! He does not.'

'Really? I see a different story. He likes you so much he can't look at you.'

'When have you even noticed this?'

'The walls have eyes and ears, remember,' he laughed softly.

'Oh, Norman, you're making things up.'

'You scared him.' He laughed loudly now. 'When you told him off about the cannabis, because he could tell you have no idea how he feels.'

'Norman, I couldn't scare anyone!'

'You scare me!'

'Oh, no, I'm sorry.'

'I'm messing with you. You remind me of Lucas. He was always the life and soul of the party. We were friends for a long time before we became partners. He was always dancing so close to the sun, always getting his wings burned with the wrong men. He was actually very sensitive underneath all the brash exterior. The drag act, Fiona Angel, was really a projection of who he wanted to be but without props and make-up he felt he couldn't pull it off.'

'What made you get together in the end?'

'The fact that I could be myself with him. Other men – and there weren't many for me – wanted a piece of flesh or didn't understand my roots, but Lucas did. He was from an Irish Catholic background and was in a similar trap to me. He was happy to be friends, like I was with Marie. He knew all about Frankie. One day we were talking about a date he'd been on; the guy had wanted him to dress as Judy Garland and whip him, then asked if he had any feta cheese.'

'Feta cheese?'

'Yes, and Lucas asked him, what do you want feta cheese for, to make a salad? The man took great offence. It was his accent – he was Spanish – and he had been asking if Lucas had any fetishes.'

I burst out laughing.

'I know! It's funny and when he told me I reacted the same as you. That was when I knew I would rather spend my days laughing at the same things than not. Turns out he had always felt that way and was just waiting for me to catch up. But he knew if he had pushed me, I would probably have run a mile.'

'Oh, I love that story. You must miss him dreadfully.' I felt a pang in my chest.

'I do, but I think it's time I moved on. I can hear Lucas telling me off for being a recluse. He lived to wring every last drop out of each day.' He slipped away somewhere else for a moment, smiling reflectively. 'So what shall I say in this email...?'

My phone burst into life as soon as I set foot in my house.

'I've met someone!' Mum said, her barely concealed excitement audible.

'Mum! A man?'

'Yes!' she giggled like a teenager.

'Was this after Elinor set you up on Guardian Soulmates?'

'Kind of. It didn't quite go to plan, though.'

'Did he have to carry his beard in a shopping trolley?'

'What?'

'Nothing, sorry, carry on.'

'I had met one man for coffee like Elinor had suggested, just in Herne Bay, far enough away that I wouldn't bump into him afterwards if I didn't like him.

Anyway, that was two weeks ago when I got home from yours. He took my Soulmate cherry.'

'I gather that didn't work out?'

'No! He was dreary. Elinor is so right, many of those boring buggers want someone to look after them. No one is interested in doing exciting stuff.'

'So what happened after that?'

'Oh, I got inundated with men. Honestly, it's like I'm twenty-five and look like Jean Shrimpton. I think they're all desperate. Anyway, I was on my date, and yes, you guessed it, dull, so I said I had to leave, made my excuses and in my haste to escape I dropped my umbrella on the floor of the café. I didn't notice and this other man caught me up outside further down the street.'

'Don't tell me, he was a sex god.'

'No! He was funny, though. Keith was in there having lunch with his daughter. He's from Manchester originally. We got talking and he's just moved here. His wife died a few years ago and he decided on a fresh start to be near his kids. Anyway, we've been on four dates.'

'Mum! In old people land that's practically marriage! Have you done the deed?'

'Alison!' I didn't want to think of my mum having sex, like normal people. I was sure everything died after the menopause anyway, if you believed articles online. That's why all nanas took up knitting, wasn't it – to compensate?

'If you must know, I have had sex for the first time in over four years.'

'MUM! That's gross! I think I'm actually going to be sick in my mouth.'

Instead of instilling me with renewed hope, Mum's story veiled me in a grey fug that clung stringently round my throat. I honestly had no idea how I was ever going to meet anyone by 'being on my own', because if I was brutally honest (sorry, Amanda, we can't be robots like you), I wanted to be in a relationship. I felt like I was denying who I really was. I wasn't built to live on my own; I liked having someone to care for, to buy things for, to daydream about, to make plans with. It wasn't just about having sex on tap, though that would be most welcome at the moment; even Rampant Rabbit was in hibernation. I needed a real live man.

I was glad Mum had met someone, but it would be typical if my sixty-nine-year-old mother beat me to the altar. Obviously it wasn't a race, and I didn't expect every relationship to end with a ring. However, I did want to get married one day, even if it was outdated and one in four marriages dissolved into bitter squabbles about who got to keep the four-door hatchback and the contents of the freezer. Being honest about how I felt somehow loosened the fug's grip. The difference from previous times when I had really wanted a boyfriend was that I didn't feel desperate. I didn't want a relationship to take away my Single Mum badge, or my

Crap with Money certificate, or my Sole Breadwinner hat – these were all part of me whether I liked it or not. Fuck me, maybe I had graduated to actually, well, *almost* becoming a grown-up?

Don't get cocky, Mini Amanda said in my ear. *One step at a time.*

43

Double Dumping

His name was Jack, he was thirty-five years old, he was super-cute, he worked in insurance and he was meeting me in the East Dulwich Tavern for a drink that Wednesday night. Once I had stepped into my power (as Amanda had explained it to me in Beardy Weirdy terms), and I had realised I could date for the hell of it with no expectations, it felt a bit like shooting fish in a barrel. I had been on several dates via Bumble, an app Ursula had told me about.

'Bumble is where you have to go if you want something more real. The women are in charge, you choose, the men can't choose. They can only say yes or no if they have been selected. A girl from work's sister's friend met her fiancé on there,' she'd explained reverently.

'That tenuous link makes it sound like one of those urban myths!'

I sat waiting at a small round table near the bar and stared dreamily out of the window. This was technically our second date, the first one having been a swift coffee to scope each other out, like dogs sniffing anal glands, only more hygienic. I had declined all second dates so far, leaving Jack out in front for the race to claim my heart. He was a bit late, so I decided to go through my work diary for the coming weeks. After half an hour, I checked the app – no text to say he wasn't coming. I sidled up to the bar to order a glass of red to pass the time.

'Hello, Ali,' Nick surprised me as I unsuccessfully tried to catch the barmaid's eye. 'You here on your own?'

'No, I'm waiting for someone. What are you doing here? On a hot date?'

He laughed gawkily. 'Yeah, kind of.' I looked over his shoulder and spotted the blonde girl from last time sitting at a table for four.

'Oh, you are! How's it going? Sorry, you don't have to say.'

'Do you want a drink?' he asked, ignoring the question while managing to attract the barmaid over towards us.

'Yes, why not? Thank you.' I sat back down with my Merlot after more small talk and thought I would virtually twiddle my thumbs on Instagram, which inevitably led to being sucked into a cyber rabbit hole of fashion pages, stylist feeds and foodiegrams. I flicked up my gaze from my phone like a light-shy miner, eyes blinking, and realised I had been in the pub forty-five minutes. Nick caught my eye and beckoned me over.

'Do you want to sit with us while you wait for your date to turn up?' he asked when I wandered over.

'No, I don't want to intrude.'

'You wouldn't be, would she, Emily?'

'No, sit down, it's fine.' She smiled at me, but I couldn't tell if she meant it or not.

'You'll have to sit here now,' Nick said. 'Look!' I glanced back at my seat and saw that some cackling girls had claimed it, stealing stools from all the other tables.

'I won't be long; I'm sure he'll be here in a minute. I'll just check the app. I'm Ali, by the way.' No message. *Where was he?*

'So how did you two meet?' I asked to fill the space.

'On Bumble,' Emily answered.

'Oh, like me! It's so much better than Tinder, isn't it?'

'God, yes. Some of my friends have had horror stories on there,' Emily agreed, laughing.

'Did you have some disasters then?' Nick asked me interestedly.

'Oh, yes.' And I described my squirrel date in minute detail, making Nick and Emily laugh.

'Do you want anything from the bar?' Emily asked when I'd finished. 'It's my turn.'

'No, I'm fine, thank you.'

Nick ordered a beer.

'Have you seen the mad vet in East Dulwich since?' he asked, draining the dregs of his pint.

'No. This is my first foray onto the scene since then. My mum's new relationship inspired me, really.'

'Your mum has started dating on apps?' He laughed sceptically.

'Noooo, but *your* mum would love the story.' And I explained how Mum had met Keith, embellished with a few artistic details of my own for dramatic effect. Emily placed Nick's beer in front of him and sat down with her white wine while I continued the tale.

'You should come round and see Mum and tell her that. She keeps talking about her fifteen minutes of fame on the vlog.'

I laughed. This was a different experience from sitting in his kitchen. I always felt like he was carefully selecting each word before he spoke, he was so guarded. With all the underhand cannabis-growing, you would be permanently cautious about who you let in to your inner circle.

'So you two are neighbours?' Emily concluded.

'Yes. I moved in at Easter and it's been an eye-opener ever since!'

We talked about the Mews and my initiation with the shisha pipe, Nick mentioned Jo's previous attempts to conscript him into the fold, then told me about the time they'd had a street Christmas Party with carols and a hot dog stall and Jo had asked everyone to contribute. He gladly gave money to get her off his doorstep, but wondered how he was going to avoid the party so made plans, thinking it would all be over by the time he got back at eleven.

'As you can guess, it was still going strong, kids all roaming feral on scooters, an actual bonfire on the street in an old-fashioned metal bin. So I climbed over the mansion's fence, round the side, over another fence until I found my back garden and attempted to climb over that, falling at the final hurdle and knocking myself out on a fence post. I came round on the grass next to the greenhouse looking at the stars, completely forgetting how I'd got there until later.'

'All that just to avoid a party!' I couldn't stop sniggering at his puzzled face, like that was normal behaviour.

'I was shit-faced, there was no logic.'

'Where's Emily?' I asked suddenly, looking round. 'She went to the loo about ten minutes ago.'

'Maybe she got locked in.'

'Shall I go and see if she's OK?'

He nodded.

The stalls were empty when I pushed open the door. I returned from my recce to find Nick scrunching his eyes up, reading a text.

'She wasn't there.'

'I know, she texted me,' he said flatly.

'Is everything OK?' I sat back down. 'Fuck, I just realised I haven't checked to see where Jack is.' I clicked on the app again, no texts. 'Little fucker has just ditched me without letting me know.'

'It happens, apparently,' Nick said. 'I've been ditched too.'

'What? During an actual date? That's a bit shit. What reason did she give?'

He shrugged.

'You don't want to say?'

He shrugged again and sucked his lips inwards, reverting to the awkward bugger he usually was.

'Are you OK?' Even though I had been unceremoniously dumped, I found I was fine about it.

'Yep, do you want another drink?' he asked, suddenly galvanised.

'Why the fuck not? I'll get them, same again?'

My head was pounding like a second heart, a teeny hammer chiselling away emphatically behind my left eye. This wasn't my ceiling. What had happened to my 'stepping into my power'? My unattached inquisitive exploration of my new self without bowing to the patriarchy? And how the fuck did I even know what any of those words meant? I must have been subjugated by Radio Four...

'Do you want a tea?' Nick said, poking his head round the door.

I lifted the duvet to scan my body to make sure I was clothed. I noticed I was wearing a Clash T-shirt: classy. And that my period had started. Not so classy.

'I'm really sorry, but I think I have bled all over your bed.' Nick didn't bat an eyelid.

'Do you want me to go to the shop and get you something before work?'

I goggled. *Was he for real?*

'No, I mean yeah, but don't bother. That's too much trouble, I can run home in a sec.'

'Ali, it isn't. I don't mind. The shop's just there. Did you know they sell everything? I was in there the other night and found disposable knickers. I can get you some of those.' He played it straight so I wasn't entirely sure if he meant it.

'Why were you looking in there for disposable knickers?'

'I wasn't, I just said I found them, next to the deodorant.'

'They obviously know their market round here!'

'So shall I get them?'

'The knickers?'

'No! Tampons, pads? What's your poison?'

'Tampons, please.'

He nodded. 'Back in a mo.'

I ventured to the loo and blotted away the worst of the Rorschach stain, then jammed my pants full of bog roll so it felt like I had the *Weekend Guardian* down there, before stripping the bed. Thankfully it was just a *Snow White* splattering rather than *The Texas Chainsaw Massacre* and the mattress protector was pristine underneath.

As I bunched the sheet up in my hands something felt fundamentally wrong. Had we snogged? No. Did I fancy him and wish we had snogged? I didn't think so. Was it awkward like it usually was when Linda was here? No. Did it feel normal? Yes! I didn't have the visceral urge to run out of the house, climb in my bed and pull the covers over my head like usual after an embarrassing incident. We had just talked and talked in the pub, he'd apologised for being a dick about Norman and we laughed, then ordered a pizza back here before I passed out in front of the TV. He'd woken me and asked if I wanted to lie down in the spare room. I had drunk a lot but blacking out wasn't my party trick, neither was executing a messy vomcano. However, wine and periods were like oil and water.

I stood fully dressed in the kitchen, aimlessly opening the clinical cupboard doors, playing hide and seek with the washing machine, when Nick returned.

'It's the one on the end,' he pointed. 'But don't bother. I can do it when I get home.'

'Actually, I can do it at mine. Sorry again.' He handed me the blue plastic bag synonymous with the zombie apocalypse shop.

'Ah, my disposable knickers. Thanks. How much do I owe you?'

'Nothing! I got you a collection. I wasn't sure what, er… you needed.'

'Thank you for last night. I had a real laugh – those two losers don't know what they're missing!'

He smiled and treated me to the blokey head nod.

'When is your mum here?'

'Tonight. But don't feel you have to come round. I know you have Grace.'

'I can bring her; we'll pop in about eight? I have an amazing dress for Linda.'

'Ooooh, the walk of shame!' Norman called out from his front door, as I stumbled back to my house with the sheet. I turned round to find him smiling, wrapped in his red silk dressing gown.

'It isn't what it looks like,' I shouted over my shoulder.

'It never is. The walls have eyes and ears!' He started laughing and I waved goodbye.

I checked my phone when I got in and there was a message from Jack in Bumble.

I am so sorry I was a no-show last night. My dog got run over and I got carried away with the vets. He's OK, just a broken back leg. Poor thing in a cast. Would you forgive me and be free another time?

Your poor dog. I hope he's OK. Of course I will forgive you. I met with a friend and we ended up having a good night, so it's all good. I'm free Saturday afternoon after four.

44

Nick

Nick smiled politely when Ali squeezed in the story about Jack and the injured dog while Grace had nipped to the loo. He didn't want to admit that he thought it was a ruse because maybe Jack's other date had fallen through, or hadn't put out, or he was actually married and his wife had come home unexpectedly just as he was leaving to meet Ali on Wednesday night. He kept his thoughts to himself. He'd heard all the outlandish stories about dating apps, about ghosting, about husbands and wives having secret profiles to test if they still had 'it'. A self-indulgent ego massage after familiarity had bred contempt. Hell, he had been Kelly's test. A long test, six and a half months until he'd ended it. He'd had to because he'd started to question his moral compass, something he hadn't faced before. He didn't want to be part of someone's family imploding and he also realised he liked Ali more than he cared to say.

She had started creeping distractingly into his head during boring meetings; he'd dreamed about her a few times – not sentimental romcom scenarios or smutty sex dreams, just ordinary stuff. In one of them they were at Sainsbury's buying a chicken for dinner. He caught himself hoping he would see her outside of the Mews in 'real' life. He watched her on the vlog more than once. There was something about her that loosened the strangulating barrel straps around his rusty heart. It wasn't just what she looked like; she was kind, and for some reason that was a huge draw – a new experience for him. Yes, she had a child, but normally where that would have been a no tick on his Tinder profile preferences, with Ali, it wasn't an issue. Grace was part of her and he wanted to show her his skateboard and see if she could stand up on it. He could buy her a small helmet...

He'd felt tied up inside when he suspected Ali was having an affair with Carl. When he caught them kissing after the party, he was staggered with how much it had unplanted him. He didn't know what to do about it, though. What usually worked didn't. He'd broken it off with Kelly, so that distraction wasn't available any more. So he fired up Tinder and Bumble and scouted for someone to ameliorate his temporary dip into what felt like teenage madness. The alternative of manning up and flying solo was just too harsh right now.

He was usually content to be alone. Work, Mum, his friends up north and down here were enough, and if life or work was melting his brain, dating apps were his fall guys. Pre Ali, Emily would easily have poured oil on troubled waters, and she was lovely. But she *wasn't* Ali, something that she had kindly pointed out on the date that Ali had three-wheeled on.

> I'm not upset, I can just tell when I need to leave. Your eyes said it all. I have better offers so I hope you'll both be very happy. Emily x

The text hadn't even garnered giving a mini fuck, and then what followed had been the most magical, easy, fun evening he had spent for as long as he could remember, since Shelley all those years before. He couldn't imagine ever running out of things to say to Ali. The air of innocence that she spun out from her laughter and amusing stories was refreshing. She also scared him in equal measure because he could tell she didn't feel the same way.

'Oh, son, you have it bad,' his mum had said when Ali took Grace home.

'What are you talking about?' he'd protested.

'Alison.' She didn't need to elaborate.

'You're barmy!' He'd been fortifying his emotions with indifference and quiet observation while his mum had cooed over the elegant party dress, and got caught up in Ali's excitement at suggesting she host a Christmas party so Mum could wear it.

'Not as barmy as you if you let this one slip through your fingers. She's a jewel. Don't let pride get in the way.'

'Mum, I don't have any feelings for Ali.' As he said the words they cut like a deep betrayal so that he almost winced.

'Just tell her how you feel or ask her out. This Jack is a bounder; we both know that. She's not the best judge of character, by the sounds of things. It could be your chance to shine. He'll let her down at some point...'

Nick stared at his mum. He hated it when she was right. But acknowledging it meant it was real, and if it was real, it meant he could fail.

'What do I do?' he asked in a weary voice.

45

The Penny Drops

'Hiya,' Nick said, his voice sounding like he'd swallowed a pack of razor blades. 'You got a minute?'

'Yeah, do you want to come in? I'm meeting Amanda in a bit, but it's fine. Is everything OK?'

'Yes.' He followed me into the living room and I sat down on the sofa while he balanced on the edge of the chair like he was ready to take flight at the first sign of trouble. The room inexplicably felt charged and I noticed his hands were trembling.

'Look, I was wondering if you wanted to go out for a drink sometime,' he blurted out, looking like he'd surprised himself as well as me.

'Oh. As in a *date*?'

'Yes, I suppose so.' He looked like the prospect of it was in the same league as root canal without an anaesthetic.

'Wow. I mean, that's really sweet of you, but I don't see you that way.'

'I know, but I thought I would ask, see how you feel. I'll go.'

'No, you don't have to go. I'm obviously dating people on Bumble, but I... it feels weird going on a date with you, because of, well, because we're neighbours.'

'But you and Carl?' *Touché.*

'I know. But nothing happened, and I'm glad it didn't. This is where I live and I can't shit on my own doorstep. Look at Jo and Debbie. It's so uncomfortable for them, so bad that Jo is moving out for a while.'

'But Jo and Debbie are different.'

'How so?'

'You're all part of the Mews clique. I'm not. I can go for weeks without seeing anyone. Anyway, there's no point. I just thought because we had a great time the other night when we got dumped, you might want to give it a spin. But no worries.' He stood up and rubbed his hands together like he was trying to warm up. 'Have a nice evening with Amanda.' He looked right at me, his sharp blue eyes unexpectedly unnerving me. He walked towards the door and opened it.

'Thanks. Have a good weekend. And I'm sorry. I'm happy to have a drink as friends.'

'Sure. Well, don't let my embarrassing declaration stop you from visiting Mum.'

'Don't be silly. She'll never forgive me. She's helping me plan the Christmas party!'

'It's still not the end of the summer!' he groaned, stepping into the corridor. 'Bye!'

I sagged against the back of the sofa; my stomach tied into a slipknot that only I had the key to release.

'So you turned down the chance to go on an old-fashioned date with someone you like as a person. Who went out and got you tampons after you bled all over his bed, whose mum adores you, and instead you'd rather take your chances with Bumble psychos? I need reinforcements. Why the fuck is Jacqui in Australia? She needs to help me here.'

Amanda knocked back the dregs of her red wine in one fell swoop and promptly poured another glass as we sat in our usual banquette in the Bishop. It was busy, for once, people having migrated back to the city after spending the summer abroad or in their holiday homes on the coast. Fuckers. This was the beginning of the August Bank Holiday weekend and the official slide of summer into autumn. The leaves had already started crisping up round the edges on the horse chestnut trees lining Lordship Lane, and the low-slung sun burned in the sky, barely managing to break over the roofs at the

Mews, casting shadows where once it had toasted the corner of the garden. School started in a week.

'Help you with what? Persuading me to date someone I don't really fancy?'

'No, making you see he was doing a Julia Roberts. He seems like the kind of guy that won't keep trying; I don't get the impression he responds well to the Palaeolithic "treat them mean, keep them keen" rule of dating, or any kind of game. He'll cut his losses and let you go.'

'Julia Roberts?'

'Yes, you know, from *Notting Hill* – "I'm just a girl, standing in front of a boy, asking him to love her."'

'Oh God, I love that scene. I can't help how I feel, though, *and* he lives over the road.'

'He said he never sees anyone for weeks, and I believe him – his nickname is the Spy, after all! And you *can* help how you feel, open your eyes and look from a different perspective. It isn't always lightning bolts, wet knickers and shagging up against a wall. It can be a slow burn, a long game, a choice, or an old-fashioned courtship that makes you feel like you've found your way home.'

'You shagged Chris on the first date!'

'I know, but I didn't let him in my heart for months. I even binned him. I didn't believe I actually *liked* him liked him. That took time. We even had this conversation in reverse, remember?'

'Yes, I remember.' I recalled telling Amanda she was irrational for dumping someone as lovely as Chris, who seemed to be crazy about her. But all she had needed was the space to catch him up...

'You have nothing to lose by going on a date, just one date. And if it feels forced, if you feel icky inside, don't go on another one. You've technically already been on one with him.'

'As friends! Well, I have my date with Jack tomorrow; I'll see how I feel after that.'

Jack was handsome, for sure, and he churned out the animated chat that I usually found entertaining, but I felt I was overlooking something. He was talking about the dog, an amusing anecdote about him trying to cock his leg and falling over from the weight of the plaster, wee cascading like the peeing statue in Brussels I'd sniggered at on a school trip. But all I could think about was I wanted to be at home. That it was a Saturday afternoon, that I could be sorting stuff for work next week, making cakes for Grace. *That he wasn't a gangly ginger streak of piss.* Jack had just bought me a second drink and I found I didn't want it. I felt displaced. His eyes weren't the right eyes. I couldn't dredge up the words to join in the banter, someone else occupied my head.

Are you at home?

No reply.

Suddenly it mattered. Why did it matter now? Why hadn't it mattered yesterday? Cunty McFuckflaps.

It's Ali BTW.

No reply.

It was five by the time I speed-walked back to the Mews from the Plough pub. Poor Jack – I'd garbled some shite about period pains and high-tailed it out of there, deleting my Bumble profile as I steamed up the road with *Black Beauty* for company whistling under my breath.

Nick's car still wasn't parked in front of his house. Should I knock in case he had left it somewhere else? What if he was on a date? What if I didn't really like him and this was just some Beardy Weirdy shit that Amanda had planted in my head to fuck me over, in the nicest possible way, of course. I'll knock. No I won't. Yes, just do it. But what if he tries to kiss you and it makes you want to vom? What if he doesn't? I knocked. I shouted through the letterbox. Now who was being a stalker?

'Hello, decided he's the one for you after all?' Norman said through his kitchen window. He'd opened it specially to enjoy the show.

'Do you know where he is?' I asked calmly

'He went away this morning, with a rucksack. I'm assuming he's away; it's the bank holiday, after all.'

'Oh.' I felt crushed.

'Do you want to come in, darling? I have a G and T with your name on it.

'What made you change your mind?' he asked once I'd slumped on the sofa.

'I don't know whether I have. I just need to see. I don't know how I feel, Norman.'

'Not many of us do at the beginning.' He smiled at me, his eyes twinkling. 'Rochelle replied.'

'Oh, Norman. You must think I'm so rubbish! What did she say?'

'That she'd love to meet me. That Ambrose doesn't know she's in contact.'

'And?'

'I'm meeting her and her baby on Monday in a café near where she lives in Sidcup.'

'Oh, you must be so excited.'

'I am, but also weirdly feel very similar to you. What if we don't get on? What if that whole "blood is thicker than water" stuff is a myth? What if I don't want to carry on a relationship with my family who let me down?'

'Rochelle didn't let you down. That was your parents. She's different. I think you'll get on like a house on fire.'

'Well, I think you and the Spy might find the same.'

I walked back home at nine after a fair few drinks on an empty stomach, my head whooshing. Ransacking the bread bin was the last thing I vaguely remember before going to bed...

I hadn't set an alarm, but it was going off in my dream where dogs in miniature red plaster casts were weeing on my leg and toppling backwards, spraying in the air like Lilliputian yellow fountains. It wasn't an alarm; my phone was ringing. I reached for it on the bedside table, worried in case it was an emergency: Mum or Grace always at the forefront of my mind.

'Yes? Is everything OK? What's happened?' I mumbled, the dogs still barking, the dream hanging on by its sharp claws.

'I'm outside your house.'

My eyes focused on the back wall, working out the level of daylight seeping over the top of the curtains. 'What time is it?'

'Seven in the morning.'

I shuffled up to sitting, suddenly wide awake, my heart hammering in my chest.

'Can I come in?'

'Give me a minute.' I finished the call and sat there racking my brain. *Why was Nick here?* Toe-curling mortification suddenly slammed me in the guts as

I recalled ringing him when I was shit-faced eating Marmite toast. Please God NO! What had I said? I couldn't remember! He hadn't answered, that much I'd fathomed, so I'd left some cringe-worthy rambling message. Cunty McFucksticks AND flaps! I then fearfully checked my phone and had five missed calls from him ranging from 10 p.m. to 1 a.m. this morning, and two texts.

I know you're drunk so I'm going to take what you said with a pinch of salt. I'll ring you in the morning.

That had been at ten fifteen last night.

Fuck it. I'm driving back.

That one was at two this morning.

I pushed back the duvet, staggering to the loo to do some serious first impression investigation. Hungover and bleary of face, smudgy of eye and hair overtaken by shagger's clump matted together from restless sleep and too much product, I reached for the toothbrush and flash-cleaned my mouth. He would have to take me as I was but skanky death breath was a bridge too far.

Wearing only my Oasis T-shirt and yesterday's knickers, I walked down the stairs, absolute dread overriding any other emotions. *What had I said?* What if I didn't really fancy him and he'd driven all this way on the false promise of whatever I'd blathered last night? I unlocked the front door, creeping quietly into the hallway in case I alerted Elinor. My hand shook as I unbolted the shared front door and turned the handle.

'Hello.' Instead of Hugh Grant, Nick was standing on the step with his anorak hood up against the light drizzle, rain drops splattered on his glasses. He thrust a tired bunch of pink and red garage carnations at me. 'I got you these delightful flowers. Sorry they're a bit crap. The selection was pretty poor at Watford Gap services.' He smiled hopefully.

'Thank you. That's very sweet. Come in.' I took the flowers and pulled my T-shirt further down over my bum as I stepped aside so he could get out of the rain. I followed him through the open door into my house.

'Can I take my coat off?'

'Of course.' I felt awkward and exposed and wished I was wearing something else. As he hung his coat on the banisters I walked into the kitchen to find a vase, glad of something to do. He followed me.

'Would you like—'

'Where did you—'

'No, you first,' I insisted, putting the flowers down on the breakfast bar. 'I'm assuming you've driven a long way.'

'Where did you want to get married?'

'What?'

'You asked me to marry you last night, when you were drunk. I drove all the way from Derby to say yes.'

I tried to speak but nothing happened. I swallowed profusely, then found my voice.

'Shit.'

'Not the response I was expecting.' His expression was deadly serious. Then he burst out laughing. 'Your face!'

'Oh my God, you fucker!' I picked the flowers up and hit him with them.

'You don't know what you said, do you?' He smiled at me.

'No. Please enlighten me.'

'I will if you come out for breakfast with me. The French Café opens at nine.'

'Do you want a cup of tea in the meantime? Nine is a while off.'

He stared at me then, his eyes searching out mine. My heart began throbbing in the base of my throat.

'I'd love a cup of tea,' he said gruffly, his voice catching. 'You look cute in your Oasis T-shirt. They're my favourite band.'

'Mine too,' I croaked, rooted to the spot. 'Thank you for driving to see me. I bet you haven't slept.'

'It was worth it.'

'Oh.' I now didn't know how I felt or what else to say. I turned away from him, grabbed some mugs from the cupboard and then picked up the kettle to start filling it from the tap.

'I don't think I've ever witnessed you lost for words,' Nick said quietly.

I put the kettle down and turned round. He grabbed my hand and gently drew me towards him. He brushed my hair out of my eyes, then kissed me on the lips, softly at first, igniting desire that I'd previously doubted. He pulled away, leaving me swaying slightly, my head spinning.

'So, my tea?' he asked innocently. I gaped at him. *Was he joking?*

'Sod your tea. I think it can wait.' So this was what Amanda had meant when she said something about finally coming home. I kissed him with more urgency this time and he wrapped his arms round me, making me wonder if we would actually make it out for breakfast at all...

46

Norman

Norman finished elaborately wrapping his Secret Santa present. He'd wangled it so he had ended up with Ali, performed some insider trading and sneaky swaps. He'd found the perfect gift for her. Well, he hadn't had to look far: they were displayed in Lucas's mausoleum upstairs. He appreciated they upended the ten-pound limit, but technically he had spent no money.

Norman was looking forward to Ali's party; his first Mews do where he would be bringing guests. Ambrose was going to come with his daughter, Rochelle, her husband, Mike, and their daughter, Mya. Ambrose's wife had died three years ago and, according to Rochelle, he'd recently begun to talk about the past after shutting down completely and becoming a bit of a hermit, a family trait, it would appear. Norman had tentatively met up with Ambrose a few times though they didn't mention how he had ignored Norman for the best part of thirty-five years. Norman knew it would come up eventually, like a niggling splinter trapped deep in his skin. It wouldn't be able to help itself but rise slowly to the surface and work its way into the world. But for now, it remained consciously embedded, and already forgiven. Lucas had made sure of that.

'It's not their fault,' he'd wisely suggested to Norman at the time. 'We can rage against the world all we want. I could look at the unfairness of cancer, but the truth is, the more you complain and hold on to that anger, the more you just ruin the time you have. Anger takes up so much energy, forgiveness doesn't. Make a choice. You don't have to forget, just remember without the anger. You forgive and you let in light.'

Norman tied the red ribbon in a bow and curled the ends with scissors. He wondered why he'd only just remembered this now; he'd wasted so much time living in the dark. He heard Lucas whisper in his ear, the last thing he'd ever said: 'No journey is ever wasted.'

Mya was making friends with all the children. Grace was in charge of her, along with one of Ali's friend's children, a sweet girl called Meg, who Mya had attached herself to, holding her hands out to be walked round and round the room. Norman was introduced to Freya, Grace's older sister, who was responsible for topping up people's drinks. He had noticed how Ali hugged her when she'd squeezed past her in the kitchen to find more sausage rolls.

The gathering swelled in numbers as Jo's lodgers piled in, bringing Christa the doctor, the most recent addition to the Mews, along with several of Ali's friends (Norman especially liked the sarcastic blonde one from Australia). All the Mews regulars were in attendance as well as Lila and Hayden, Ali's mum and new partner, Keith, which meant by five in the evening the house was densely crammed like a tin of sardines and people spilled out into Elinor's house next door. The rest crowded into Ali's small back garden, lit with candles and outdoor fairy lights, creating a frosty Mews Santa's grotto, the temperature only fit for the brave.

'Norman, your grand-niece is adorable,' Linda said, sipping a glass of sherry, holding on to her husband, John's, arm. 'I think Christmas is better with children, don't you?'

'I do, Linda. They make the world go round.'

'Hello, Norman,' John said. 'I believe you're taking madam here shopping next week for her Christmas day outfit.'

'Yes, we're looking forward to it. Ali's given us her stylist discount card for Debenhams so we're going to splash some cash in Bromley!'

'She's a lovely girl, isn't she? Ever since Nick's met her he's a changed man. I've never been to so many dinner parties,' John smiled at Norman, still completely clueless about Nick's contraband growing in the greenhouse. Norman had taken to hiding the cannabis plants and dried flower heads in his bathroom so Nick could have his parents over at weekends. Earlier, Norman had caught Nick stealing a kiss from Ali as she poured more red wine into the giant stockpot on the hob.

'She is. They make a smashing couple.'

'Well, yes, I'm hoping for a ring on a finger soon,' Linda stage-whispered conspiratorially. 'He needs to get a move on. She's the best thing that's ever happened to him.'

'Linda!' John half laughed. 'Let him decide for himself. She's not going anywhere. Don't rush the poor boy.'

Norman spotted Ambrose out in the garden wearing a Santa hat Ali had plonked on his head. He was chatting to Francesca and Elinor, whose face had lit up like a sparkler, laughing at something he'd whispered in her ear.

'Have you seen that?' Rochelle sighed, edging up to Norman. 'Dad's turning on the charm. I've not seen him like this for years. Who's that woman?'

'One of the Mews ladies, lovely Elinor.'

'She's single?' Rochelle asked, surprised.

'I believe so. Not had much luck on the dating front. Apparently all the men are needy.'

Rochelle snorted. 'They probably are, though! They all want looking after. Apart from you, Uncle Norman. You don't want to meet anyone else?'

'Oh, you know what? No. Life has just been rebooted for me, and now with the vlog going stellar and the odd guest TV appearances with the girls on *Good Morning* makeovers, it's all a bit crazy. I'm seventy! Life has a way of surprising you sometimes. And of course, meeting you is the cherry on top.'

Rochelle squeezed his hand, flooding Norman's heart. Blood was thicker than water after all.

'Your hair is looking mighty fine, Debs,' Norman commented as she walked into the living room from Elinor's. 'Growing back nicely.'

'Aye, thanks. I can't believe it's a different colour! I think I like it.'

Norman thought Debbie had blossomed in the past month as her radiotherapy had drawn to a close. Lucas had been the same the first time: it was like his body and his mind had shaken off the dried chrysalis, revealing the next incarnation. Norman hoped with all his heart that this was it for Debbie, that there would be no secondary rearing of the monster's head. Her poor children didn't need that.

He wondered if the other reason why Debbie's recovery was in full bloom might be because Jo had temporarily moved out. The change in dynamics could also explain why Francesca was bumbling along with

Ian now they were being left undisturbed by daily judgement. Norman knew all about marriages of convenience. They served a purpose until they were outgrown. Francesca looked happy enough, happier than she had for a few years. Maybe bumbling along was what suited her. Not everyone gets the Big Love Affair. Norman was aware he was very lucky on that front. He'd experienced his and the memories were enough to last a lifetime. He felt he was on a fresh path now, and who knew what was in store…

'Hello, hello!' Jo's voice bellowed through the doorway like a diminutive town crier. Norman couldn't work out if she was supposed to be one of Santa's elves in her green tights, red short dungarees and hiking boots or if this was coincidentally her chosen attire. 'Look who I bumped into.'

Samantha swayed into the room wearing a Mrs Christmas rich red velvet dress and hat, her runaway bosoms hidden under all the white fake-fur trim. Norman chuckled. Samantha was a secret show-off who probably could have been anything she wanted to be, which was why she brokered such a range of talent. Norman stood back and leaned against the wall adjacent to the sofa. He was going to enjoy the showstopper finale…

'Ladies and gentlemen, boys and girls, please let me introduce Santa Claus and his helpers,' Samantha announced imperiously, bowing and sweeping her hand to welcome in the man himself. Everyone from Elinor's side of the building had rushed in, urged on by the gaggle of children shouting that Santa had arrived.

'Ho, ho, ho,' Santa boomed in a contrived deep timbre, his face completely hidden by his overreaching hat and theatrical beard-and-tach combo. 'How are we all today?'

A few apathetic mumbles of 'good' rippled through the assembled crowd, reaching Santa, who had now arrived centre stage flanked by two grown-up elves that Norman knew were Samantha's sons, Billy and Scott. The coffee table acted as a natural proscenium with the over-decorated tree a perfect glittering backdrop.

'I can't hear you. I said how are we all today?' Santa put his hand up to his ear.

A wall of screech hit him face first and he pretended to topple backwards into the tree, the elves just catching him in time. The children all started laughing, while the adults were asking in hushed tones who this joker was.

'I'm here to hand out presents. First of all, I have sweeties for all the children.'

Scott handed him a black bin bag stored behind the tree and Santa rummaged inside, distributing Cellophane bags filled with chocolates to all the enchanted children, even the cynical older ones, who looked like they wanted to still believe.

'Now, there is a Mews Secret Santa this year. If I call your name, come up and collect your gift.' Norman received a mug with the Neighbourhood Watch logo printed on one side and BIN DAY! in black letters on the other. He started laughing and looked around the room, trying to weed out which one of them was responsible. Norman lifted the mug up to Nick, trying to catch his eye across the room where he was standing at the breakfast bar opening his present of a spy kit.

'Norman!' Ali squealed when she opened hers. 'Nike Jordans!'

'I don't know what you're talking about,' he said, keeping a straight face, but smiling in his heart. They'd gone to a good home.

'Oh, you lucky lady!' Carl exclaimed, examining his *Yoga for Hipsters* book. 'They're pure class.'

Ali leaped over the piles of discarded wrapping paper by the sofa and enveloped Norman in a hug.

'Are you sure? I know how precious they are to you.'

'Lucas would approve. Life is for living, and those trainers need to be out in the world. I can't think of a better person to wear them for him.'

'Ladies and gentlemen, boys and girls, it's time for Santa to go, but first here is my glamorous assistant, Trisha, to help me sing a goodbye song.'

A frantic wave of whispering broke out round the room when a statuesque Trisha Templeton, clothed as an elegant Christmas tree, appeared in the doorway. Her green silk maxi dress was adorned with tiny gold stars and asymmetric gold threads zigzagged the entire length. Topping her mane of celebrated golden locks, a red glittering star headband shone. Only Trisha Templeton could pull off a Christmas tree with such *élan*.

'Oh my God, I love her!' Ali's mum cried, and started clapping, and everyone else joined in, even the children, who had no idea who she was. Meanwhile the elves had moved aside, and Santa had acquired a microphone.

'Who wants to hear a song?' Santa called down the microphone. The room bellowed back a resounding yes. 'Great, well, let me get into something a bit more comfortable then. Trisha?' He handed her the microphone and started peeling off his hat and beard. Everyone cried in appreciation – underneath all the fuzz, Viola awaited fully made up, expectant hairnet in place. She shimmied out of her Santa costume, letting the baggy trousers fall to the floor and pulled down the secretly fitted full-length red sequined torch-song dress, resplendent with white marabou trim.

'Boys, my hair!' Scott handed her a blond wavy wig and Trisha skilfully fitted it. 'I'm ready to go!'

A backing track started up from a small PA system stowed away underneath the windowsill.

'*I saw Mommy kissing Santa Claus...*'

Norman smiled; Lucas would be over the moon his Christmas outfits were having another airing...

Epilogue

The East Dulwich Forum

13 December 2014
Re: Annoying Christmas Party Terry's Tool Hire
Posted by: Fiwith2dogs 10.03 a.m.
I can't believe it, well I can, those fuckers in the Mews behind Terry's Tool Hire are at it again. All I could hear was some dreadful person singing Christmas songs all evening, then it all kicked off again at midnight with a shitting disco. They really do think they're above the law. Did anyone else have their evening ruined by it?

Re: Annoying Christmas Party Terry's Tool Hire
Posted by: 67_Alfie 10.27 a.m.
Yes, it went on till one in the morning. Our dog kept barking all night because of it and then puked all over the

bedroom rug. I feel like billing them for a clean-up. Selfish wankers.

Re: Annoying Christmas Party Terry's Tool Hire
Posted by: Linzicatlady64 10.35 a.m.

I called the noise police but I don't think they did anything. One day those people will get their comeuppance.

Re: Annoying Christmas Party Terry's Tool Hire
Posted by Neighbour12 11.05 a.m.

I believe you all have no Christmas spirit. Perhaps you should go out and find it, or instead, enjoy life. This time of year is for celebrating surviving another twelve months no matter who your God is. The people in the Mews know how to live life to the full. Take a leaf out of their book and embrace it all. You never know when it may be gone. Happy Christmas!

Re: Annoying Christmas Party Terry's Tool Hire
Posted by: Oldskoolraver 11.26 a.m.

Well said, Neighbour12. Remember bin day is Monday! Happy Christmas.

Acknowledgements

I would like to thank Vicki Hillman and Daisy Hillman-Derry for moving to the Mews just so I could write a sequel to *The Single Mums' Mansion*! There would be no sequel without all the amazing people who live there and shared stories with me. Thank you to Jane Compton (for nudging me forward), Julia Whittington, Alex Sargent, Carolyn Trendall, Nick Baker and Virginia Calder.

Thanks to my agent, Charlie Viney, for always being a gangster and watching my back. Thanks also to Sarah Ritherdon, the best editor in the bookiverse, to Yvonne Holland and Sue Lamprell for your eagle-eyed detection and fine tuning, and to all the brilliant people at Head of Zeus and Aria. Thank you for all your dedication and hard work.

Thanks to Fiona Angel for letting me steal her name, and to Andrew Watson for his infamous feta cheese story. Special recognition to Joanna Hoggarth for being my dating app expert and donating the squirrel dating disaster! Thank you, Neil Sheppard, for the character chapter idea (and curing my writer's block), and for always listening to me driving myself insane when the process takes over my life. Big thanks to Remziye Kounelaki for her expert advice about sexual health and answering all my text enquiries so quickly!

I'm also very grateful to Susie Hoggarth and Anne Hillman for racing through the first draft for me and bolstering me up. Thank you to additional readers: Katie and Joanna Hoggarth, and Vicki Hillman and Nick Baker for their valuable fashion and plotting advice. Thank you also to my dear friend, H, for all information regarding Alcoholics Anonymous.

Well done, Ele Clark, Susie and Charlie for suggesting I draw a map at the front of the book. I loved doing it!

As usual writing wouldn't be possible without the unwavering support of Neil and my children, Lilla, Teya and Danny. Sorry for disappearing into a void for months at a time and not showering or getting out of my pyjamas.

Finally, a MASSIVE thank you to everyone who bought *The Single Mums' Mansion*, and to those of you who wrote to me about your own journeys. It really does mean the world to me. We're all on the same path and we just need to keep going forward!

About the Author

JANET HOGGARTH has worked on a chicken farm, as a bookseller, children's book editor and as a DJ with her best friend (under the name of Whitney and Britney). She has published several children's books, the most recent ones written under the pseudonym of Jess Bright. Her first adult novel, *The Single Mums' Mansion*, which was a huge bestseller, was based on her experiences of living communally as a single parent.